ELYSIAN
Dreams

Volume Two of CRESCENT CITY

JACK CALDWELL

White
SOUP
PRESS

White Soup Press, c/o Jack Caldwell, 3140 Sunset Beach Drive, Venice, FL, 34293.

info@cajuncheesehead.com

https://cajuncheesehead.com/
http://whitesouppress.com/
http://austenvariations.com/

ISBN: 978-0-9891080-4-1

Back cover beads: copyright © 2013 Arina Habich
Layout & design by Ellen Pickels

Dedication

For Barbara

For those who are gone and for those who remain.
May America never forget.

Author's Note

Elysian Dreams is Volume Two of the *Crescent City* series. The story resumes five years after the end of Volume One, *Bourbon Street Nights*. The author suggests that story be read before this one.

Crescent City

Prologue

New Orleans is one of the most well-known and misunderstood cities in the United States. Millions of people have visited it, and millions more wish to. Because of television, movies, books, and music, most Americans think they know what the City That Care Forgot is all about. Mardi Gras. Bourbon Street. Jazz Music. Cajun food. Political corruption. The Big Easy. A place that's under water.

All true—and completely incorrect.

The Crescent City is a unique place in America. European in flavor, Catholic in culture, it has one foot solidly in the past while it tentatively reaches for the future. The city is extremely tribal, a patchwork of neighborhoods and suburbs. French Quarter. Garden District. Mid-City. West Bank. Metaire. Arbi. Gentilly. Algiers. Northshore. Chalmette. Lakeshore. Kenner. Gretna. Lower Ninth. It is a kaleidoscope of class, race, and heritage.

It is rich and poor. It is black, white, other, and mixed. It is French, Irish, Cajun, English, Spanish, Italian, Haitian, Cuban, Vietnamese, Salvadoran, and a dozen more. Like most large cities, it can be a violent place, yet tourists are rarely preyed upon by anyone except street hustlers. It is both sacred and profane: voodoo existing cheek-by-jowl with Roman Catholicism. Sport is the other religion. Residents prefer their own neighborhoods, the Yats having little to do with the Uptowners or the Blacks with the Hispanics.

But everyone subscribes to the peculiar rhythms of the city. The people live, eat, worship, and party by a distinctive calendar. One can tell the seasons of the year by the food. King Cake during Carnival. Crawfish for Lent. Shrimp and tomatoes in summer, crabs and oranges in fall, and Réveillon dinners during Advent. The relatively mild winters mean festivals all year long.

Louisianans work hard so they can party hard. The state has the country's largest bulk port. It is among the nation's top petroleum producers. Two of the world's biggest oil refineries are there. Its people make sugar and harvest seafood. They build ships, oil rigs, and spacecraft.

New Orleans is a series of contrasts. Friendly to strangers but devoted to family. Beautiful and dirty. Corrupt and faithful. Fragrant and smelly. Homey and extravagant. Avant-garde and uptight. Bizarre and formal. Loved and hated.

One cannot grasp the totality of the Crescent City from a guidebook. To truly understand New Orleans, one must live there.

Volume Two

Elysian Dreams

Dramatis Personae

Leon Anderson VP at Delta Global Shipping, lives in Algiers.

David Baugham Special Agent with the FBI New Orleans office.

Annie Betancourt Exotic dancer known as "Spice," resides in St. Rose.

Catherine Bingley Wealthy widow, lives in Baton Rouge.

Charles "Chuck" Bingley Senior lender for Gallic National Bank of New Orleans, lives in Covington.

Jane Boudreaux Bingley Wife of Chuck Bingley, daughter of T.B. Boudreaux, part-time nurse in Mandeville.

Elizabeth Boudreaux Communication Manager at Economic Development/New Orleans, lives in Metairie.

Thomas "T.B." Boudreaux Owner of a small oil field service firm, lives in Chackbay.

Frances "Fanny" Boudreaux Wife of T.B. Boudreaux.

Mary Boudreaux Third daughter of T.B. Boudreaux. English teacher at E.D. White Catholic High School in Thibodaux.

Catherine "Kit" Boudreaux Fourth Daughter of T.B. Boudreaux, attends community college in Houma.

Lydia Boudreaux Youngest daughter of T.B. Boudreaux.

Dr. Chris Breaux Psychiatrist, LSU Medical Center, New Orleans, lives in Uptown.

Carrie Bingley Buford Wife of John Buford, daughter of Catherine Bingley, works for the Louisiana Department of Administration and lives in Baton Rouge.

John Buford Lawyer in Baton Rouge and captain in the Louisiana National Guard.

John "Trey" Buford, III Son of John and Carrie Buford.

Frank Church Salesman and community theater actor.

Marianne "Mari" Dashwood Insurance company clerk and part-time jazz singer, lives in the Faubourg Marigny.

William Darcy President/CEO and majority stockholder of Delta Global Shipping Inc. (DGS) of New Orleans. Lives at Dansereau Plantation in St. Charles Parish and a condo in the Warehouse District.

Gina Darcy Sister of William Darcy, student at Auburn University, Auburn, AL.

Edward Denham General Manager of Jean Laffite Resort & Casino, Gulfport, MS.

Anna Elliot Assistant to the mayor of New Orleans.

F. Edward Fitzwilliam Chairman of Delta Global Shipping. Uncle to both Richard Fitzwilliam and William Darcy. Lives in Fort Lauderdale, FL.

Richard Fitzwilliam Captain in the New Orleans Police Department assigned to the Third District, cousin of William Darcy, lives in Mid-City.

Olivia Fitzwilliam Wife of Richard Fitzwilliam.

Jan Hill Administrative assistant at Economic Development/New Orleans.

Kaywanda Johnson Secretary at Economic Development/New Orleans, lives with her mother in Gentilly.

Emma Weinberg Katz Wife of George Katz, daughter of Abe Weinberg, lives in Lakeview.

Dr. George Katz Surgeon and instructor at Tulane University Medical Center and Medical School.

PO3 Donald Lauck Petty officer, third class and Aviation Survival Technician (AST) in the US Coast Guard.

Charlotte Lucas Economic developer at Economic Development/New Orleans.

Eddie Masters Vice president at Economic Development/New Orleans.

LTJG Jeremy Price Lieutenant (junior grade) in the US Coast Guard, helicopter pilot, lives in New Orleans East.

Betsy Reynolds Long-time housekeeper at Dansereau Plantation.

Lucy Steele Entertainment coordinator at Jean Laffite Resort & Casino.

Adam "Bubba" Teresina Biology teacher and assistant football coach at ED White Catholic, fiancé of Mary Boudreaux.

John Waguespack Assistant manager, responsible for entertainment at Jean Laffite Resort & Casino.

Abe Weinberg Retired architect, lives with his daughter and son-in-law in Lakeview.

LCDR Fred Wentworth Lt. Commander in the US Coast Guard, helicopter pilot, and squadron leader, lives in Belle Chasse.

Gregory "G-Daddy" Wickham Unemployed small-time drug dealer in New Orleans.

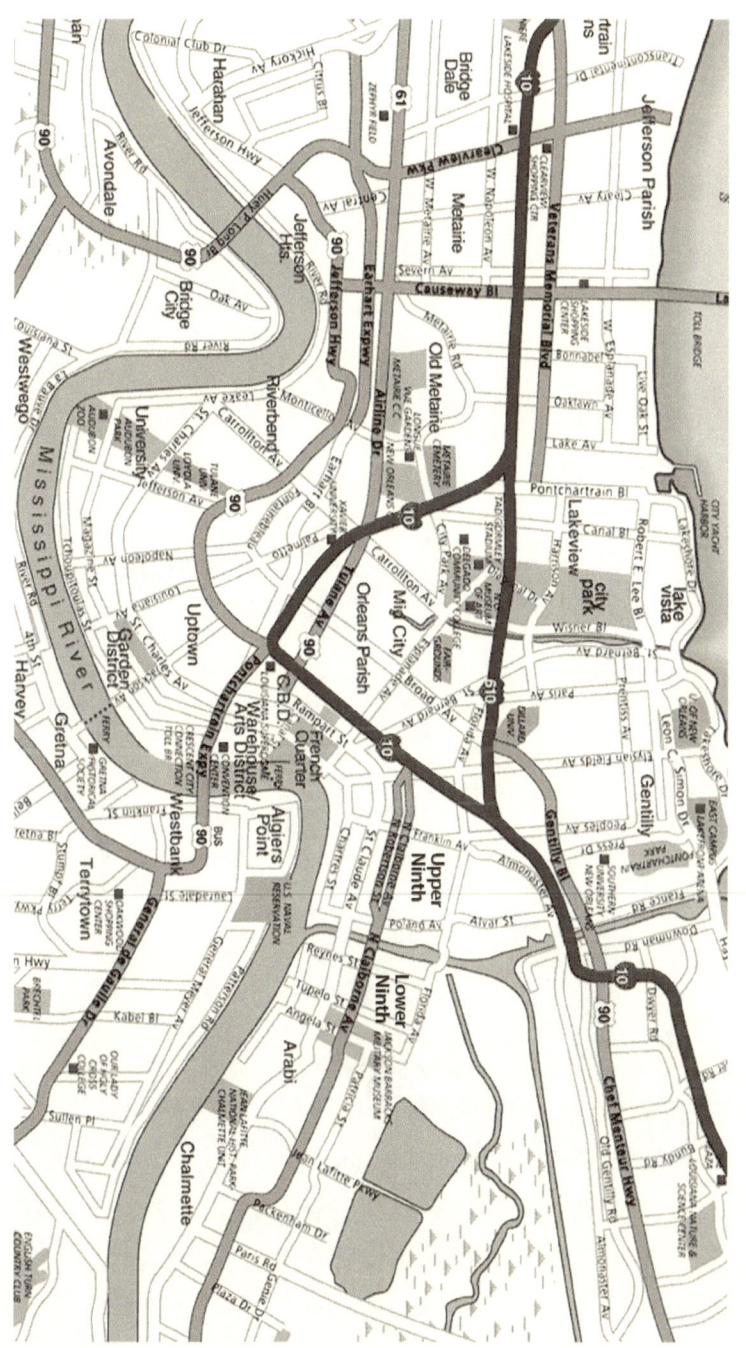

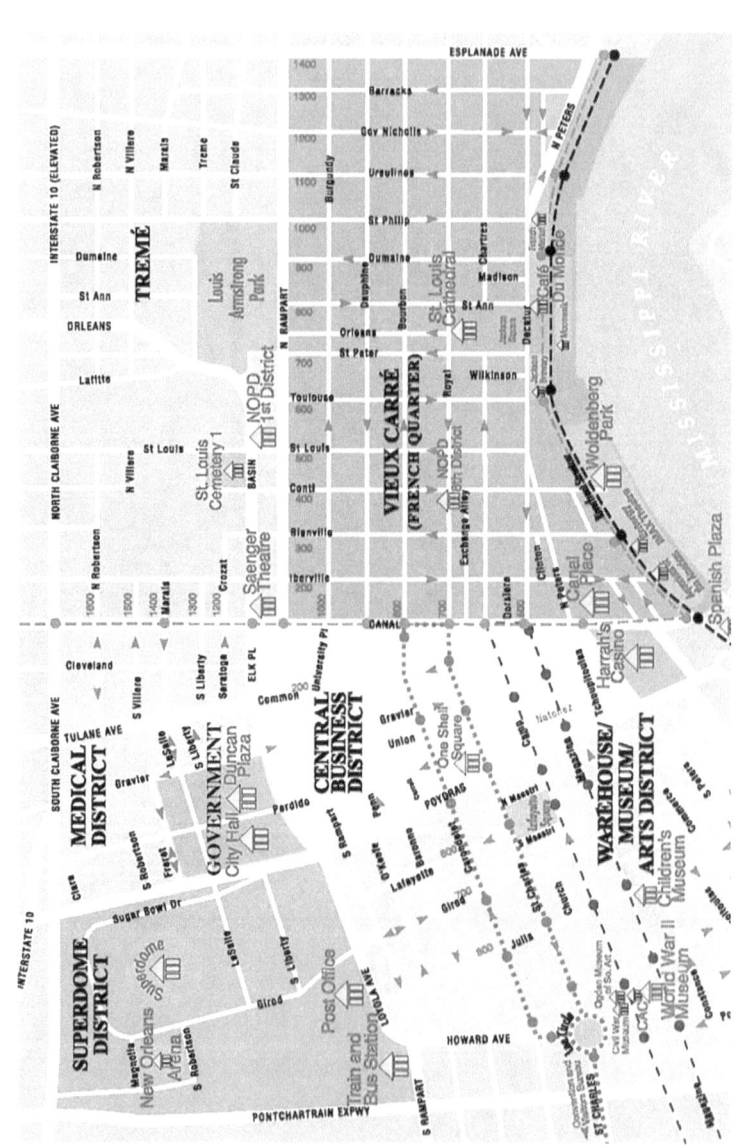

Part One

New Orleans is the only place I know of where you ask a little kid what he wants to be, and instead of saying, "I want to be a policeman" or "I want to be a fireman," he says, "I want to be a musician."
— Alan Jaffe

If you have to ask what jazz is, you'll never know.
— Louis Armstrong

New Orleans ladies
A flair for life, love and laughter
And they hold you like the night
Holds a chill when this cold wind's blowing.

Them Creole babies
They strut and sway from dusk till dawn
And they roll just like a river
A little wave will last forever.

All the way
From Bourbon Street to Esplanade
They sashay by
They sashay by.

"New Orleans Ladies"
by Hoyt Garrick and Leon Medica
1978 © Break Of Dawn Music Inc.
used by permission

Chapter 1

Friday, July 23, 2004: Gulfport, Mississippi

From the back of the darkened cabaret, Lucy Steele, entertainment coordinator for the Jean Laffite Resort & Casino, looked up from her notes at the combo on the stage. "All right, Miss Dashwood, let's hear something."

Marianne Dashwood held a brief conversation with her band, a quartet comprised of piano, drums, string bass, and guitar. "We're going to do 'My Old Flame,'" she said into the microphone in her hand.

As she was singing the lovely jazz standard, a tall man walked into the back of the cabaret. The stage lights prevented anyone on stage from seeing him approach Miss Steele.

"How are the auditions going?" the assistant manager asked in a low voice.

"Not bad," Lucy answered in the same manner. "We might have a winner here."

The man looked at the stage, listening closely. "What's the name?" he asked.

Lucy looked down at her sheet. "Marianne Dashwood and her combo."

The man's hands clenched into fists as he stared at the stage. "I know her. Great voice, but she's trouble."

Lucy glanced up. "Really?"

"Yeah. Diva with a capital 'D.' Thinks she's Mariah Carey or something. Real pain-in-the-ass. Get rid of her."

"Damn, she's good, but we don't need one of those. Don't worry. I'll take care of it."

As the man turned to leave, Lucy grasped his hand. "John, you wanna party tonight?"

He hesitated a moment. "Sure. Your place?"

"Nine o'clock. Bring the stuff."

"You got it, Miss Steele." John Waguespack caressed her chin before leaving the room.

The song over, Marianne shaded her eyes with her hand. "We're going to do 'Stormy Weather' now," she called out.

"Go ahead," answered Lucy Steele, knowing it wouldn't make any difference how well Miss Dashwood did with the song. As far as the Jean Laffite Resort & Casino was concerned, Marianne Dashwood had been blacklisted.

A SHAKEN JOHN WAGUESPACK CLOSED THE DOOR TO HIS OFFICE AND sat heavily in his chair. After a moment, he opened a desk drawer and retrieved a bottle of Johnny Walker Black. He poured himself a shot into a water glass and tossed the drink back in one gulp. He poured another scotch and sipped it this time, thinking of his narrow escape.

Since finishing up at Southern Miss, Waguespack had worked hard to move up in the casino world. Six months after coming to work at the Jean Laffite, a major Las Vegas player had bought the joint. The company liked what it saw in John Waguespack, and he was now an assistant manager in charge of entertainment, answerable directly to the general manager. Another year or two, and Waguespack could earn a promotion and transfer to Vegas. There, the sky was the limit. The last thing he needed was a ghost from his past.

Waguespack took another sip. It had been close—too close. If Marianne had seen him, would she have recognized him after five years? Would she make trouble for him if she had? Could he take that chance? Well, it was done. She would never work at the Jean Laffite while he was there.

He thought some more. Maybe it would be a good idea to call his colleagues at the other casinos—warn them off her. It wouldn't hurt.

As he dialed his office phone, Waguespack thought about another subject. Lucy was a damn good fuck buddy as long as she got to party with cocaine. While he didn't use the nose candy much, it was handy to have some on hand for just this sort of occasion. He played it cool at work and treated Lucy like any other co-worker—he didn't want a sexual harassment suit—but off the clock was a different story. He had learned his lesson from his time in New Orleans. There was plenty of pussy out there. He just had to have the cash and the flash to land it. Waguespack thought about his supplies. He had enough, he judged.

"Hey, Tony, it's John," he said into the receiver. "How're things over there? … Good, good. Look, I just wanna give you a heads-up about something. … Nah, this one's on the house. There's this diva-wannabe out there I want to warn you about. Her name's Marianne Dashwood."

OVER TWENTY THOUSAND FEET ABOVE THE MISSISSIPPI GULF coast, a Cessna Citation XLS+ in the corporate colors of Delta Global Shipping cruised westward through the early afternoon sky. Aboard were two of the company's top officials. Leon Anderson, Vice President of Marketing, was catching a nap after the morning meeting in New York. His companion and boss gazed out of the window, considering his life.

William George Darcy had almost finished his first year as President and CEO of DGS. During the previous four years, he had worked in every department in the firm: finance, operations, marketing/sales, logistics, even maintenance. Meanwhile, his uncle F. Edward Fitzwilliam had served as the chief of the company. William worked hard, learning the ropes from the inside out. Twenty years of training and experience were crammed into four, one of them at the London offices of the company's European subsidiary. When Uncle Ed ascended to take the ceremonial role of Chairman of the Board, William took the reins of the corporation.

Immediately, the sharks began circling. How was a twenty-seven-year-old going to manage a worldwide multi-million dollar shipping concern? The stockholders and institutional investors were concerned. William wasn't fazed. Hard work and a ton of face-to-face meetings had turned the tide. His position was secure.

But at what cost? William rubbed his weary face with his hand. A personal life had been out of the question. If he wasn't in the office, he was on a business trip. In addition, he was trying to be a father to a teenaged sister.

And I screwed that up royally, didn't I? Almost as well as I did at Tulane.

William sighed. At least Gina didn't show any lasting effects. "Didn't show" didn't mean there weren't any, though. *Maybe she's as good at hiding her feelings as I am.*

Well, she's going back to Auburn in the fall. Out of state will be good for her. And she'll have her debut in January. Damn, I wish Dad could be here to see it.

He isn't, Will. Get over it.

William was satisfied the need to prove himself to the corporate world was over. Now he could commit himself to local things. For example, Economic Development/New Orleans had been on him to join their board of directors as his father had done before him. Now, he had the time.

But Elizabeth Boudreaux worked there.

So what? I've moved on. She's moved on. The past is the past. Just because I've ruined the best thing I could've had is no reason to hide from life. The worst that could happen is she would refuse to talk to me. How would that be different? I haven't talked to Elizabeth for five years.

Ha! Chris would be proud of me. He's been on my ass for ages about this. Just took me five years to listen to him. I'll think about the EDNO request. Meanwhile, it's time I rejoined the human race. I'll start tonight.

The co-pilot came on the intercom. "Gentlemen, please fasten your seat belts. We've been cleared for initial approach to New Orleans Lakefront Airport."

The sleek corporate jet began its descent over the expanse of Lake Pontchartrain.

Lakeview, New Orleans

EMMA KATZ SAT ON HER MAT ON THE FLOOR OF THE YOGA STUDIO

in the *Kapotasana*, the Pigeon pose, preparing to assume the *Eka Pada Rajakapotasana*, the One-Legged King Pigeon pose.

She was in a modified split with her right leg bent inwards and on its side before her and the left stretched out behind her. Reaching back, she took hold of her left toes with her left hand and raised her elbow up toward the ceiling. She then reached back with her right hand as well, bringing the right elbow up. Bending backwards, she let her head come back until the sole of her foot was touching the top of the head. She held it for a minute before slowly releasing it.

Back in the Pigeon pose, she placed her hands on the floor, carefully sliding the left knee forward, then exhaled and lifted up and back into *Adho Mukha Svanasana*, the Downward Facing Dog pose, her hands and feet on the floor with her pelvis high the air, looking like an inverted V. She relaxed and slid down onto her knees, then forward into the *Balasana*, the Child's pose.

She finished with the *Savasana*, the Corpse pose, lying flat on her back, allowing her body to feel heavy and breathe normally. After a few breaths, she deepened her breathing, relaxing and letting her mind empty.

Emma was not a vain woman, but she took pride in the fact that her figure was exceptionally toned and trim in her dark purple tights. She found her daily regimen of light eating and yoga kept weight off, improved her strength and flexibility, and allowed her to deal with the stresses in her life.

After five minutes, she slowly moved her fingers and toes, awakening her body. She brought her knees into her chest and rolled over to one side, keeping her eyes closed. She then slowly brought herself into a seated position.

Emma got to her feet, gathered up her belongings, and moved to the showers. Quickly stripping off her tights, she rinsed off in warm water, preparing for the evening. And Abe.

Fifteen minutes later, Emma was in her Volvo S60, rolling down Robert E. Lee Boulevard toward her home in Lakeview. Try as she might, she felt her tension rising. As she pulled into the driveway of her ranch house, she had to go back into her deep breathing exercises just to open the car door.

Emma let herself in the house. "Papa, I'm home!" She heard his answering grunt from the den.

"Anything on the news?"

"No, the world's still here, Bennifer or no Bennifer."

Emma nodded and returned to the kitchen to start her *Shabbat* meal while waiting on her father. Since his heart attack and retirement, Abe spent most of his days in his La-Z-Boy in the Katz's den.

Emma quickly assembled the ingredients for the evening meal. Since her marriage, she had become a fairly good cook, thanks to lessons from Mrs. Taylor, *The Kosher Cajun Cookbook,* and watching a lot of Food Network. Tonight's entrée was pomegranate chicken.

Emma was almost finished placing the food onto serving platters when the phone rang. She hesitated before picking up. "Hello?"

"Hi, sweetheart," her husband said. "I'm sorry, but it looks like I'm going to be late again."

"But—" Emma bit her lip and took a breath. "All right, George. When do you think you'll be home?"

"I don't know. I'm sitting in on an emergency quadruple bypass. Don't wait up."

Emma sighed. "I'll put a plate for you in the fridge."

"Don't bother. I'll grab a sandwich here. Love ya."

"I love you too. Drive safe." Emma hung up the phone while she desperately held on to the frayed end of her emotions. It was the fifth time that month George had worked late. The fifth time he had ruined dinner. But she was not going to cry over it—not again.

Emma had slipped into her practiced facade of control by the time she brought the platters to the table. Abe was waiting for her.

"Looks good, princess. Where's George?"

"He just called. An emergency came up. He'll be late."

"Again?"

Emma busied herself with setting out two plates. "It happens."

"Yeah, comes with the territory, being married to a surgeon."

Plates served and *challah* covered, Emma pulled a long scarf over her head and lit two candles. "Papa, would you recite the *kiddush*?"

Downtown

THE LIGHTS WERE ON LATE IN THE NINETEENTH FLOOR POYDRAS Street offices of Economic Development/New Orleans. Communication Manager, Elizabeth Boudreaux, finished a column for the monthly newsletter and munched on a chicken Caesar salad. She was catching Marianne's performance at a French Quarter jazz club that evening, and rather than drive all the way to her Metairie apartment to grab dinner before driving back to the Quarter, Elizabeth decided to get a jump on this assignment.

Her phone rang. "Hey, can I convince you to come back?" a voice said from the receiver.

Elizabeth laughed. Peter Kimmel, her old boss at the ad agency, started every phone call to her that way. "Nope, I'm chained to the wall here. What's up?"

"We have the proofs for your new ad campaign ready."

Elizabeth glanced at her clock. "And you're calling me at seven thirty to tell me that? How'd you know I was here?"

"I didn't. I was going to leave a message on your voice mail. But since you asked—why are you still at work?"

"Why are you?"

"Because since my best worker abandoned me for EDNO, I've got to do all this stuff myself. Now, answer the question."

"Because I have no life."

"What about Anthony Riviere? I though y'all were dating."

"*Were*, darling, *were*. We broke up over a month ago."

"Is it because he's working for Senator Landrieu in Washington now?"

Elizabeth sighed. "Partly. Long-distance romances are hard, but it just pushed up the inevitable. Tony's a nice guy—for somebody else."

"You always were picky, Lizzy. What are you waiting for?"

Elizabeth dodged the comment. "You, Peter darling."

"Right. I'd just have to divorce my wife of thirty years. Lizzy, do yourself a favor and get out of that office. It's Friday night, for God's sake."

"It just so happens I'm meeting some friends in the Quarter."

She glanced at her clock on the office wall. "Oops…I've got to get going or I'll be late."

"Good. Go have fun. I'll talk to you next week."

Elizabeth hung up the phone, saved her work, grabbed her purse, and dashed for the elevator, waving at the cleaning crew as she ran by. She walked out of the lobby onto the street, knowing she could retrieve her car from the parking garage later. Her heels clicked as she walked down St. Charles Avenue towards Canal Street. Across Canal, St. Charles became Royal Street as Elizabeth entered the French Quarter. She made her way up one block towards the Lake to get to Bourbon Street, and then continued along through the warm summer evening as darkness fell and the streetlights came on until she reached a small jazz club.

As expected, there was a table in the back reserved for her party. She was the first to arrive, so she sat down and ordered a chocolate martini from the waitress. Her drink delivered, Elizabeth looked around the club as she sipped the decadent concoction. The place was about three-quarters full, tourists making up half the crowd—based on clothing and fanny packs.

At eight precisely, the lights dimmed slightly as the band came on the stage. *"Ladies and gentlemen,"* an announcer intoned, *"Marianne Dashwood!"*

A spotlight illuminated one wing of the stage, and Marianne walked on in a black-on-black sequined pantsuit. The spaghetti straps of the top showed off her shoulders. She smiled at the light applause and started into the first song of the set, the Gershwin standard "'S Wonderful."

Elizabeth swayed with the music, lightly keeping time by tapping on the table. Suddenly, she was aware of a presence near her. She glanced up behind her and was startled to see a tall, dark-haired man standing next to the table.

"Hello, Elizabeth. Long time no see."

A FEW BLOCKS AWAY, WILLIAM DARCY EXITED THE CANAL PLACE Cinema with his sister, Gina. They stood outside the theatre on the third floor of the Canal Place shopping mall, next to the food court.

"Want to get a beignet?" William asked.

Gina thought for a moment. "No, that's okay. Let's go home."

They moved towards the escalator. "So you can IM your friends?"

"Of course. Chat awaits!"

They walked out the front door, next to Saks Fifth Avenue, onto Canal Street. The warm summer night air enveloped the pair.

"Pretty night," William offered as they strolled past Harrah's Casino towards the Warehouse District.

"Yeah. Too bad you're spending it with me."

"What do you mean? There's nobody more important in my life than you!"

"Sad, ain't it?"

"Gina!"

"Will, you know I, like, totally love you, but you shouldn't be spending a lovely Friday night with your sister. How lame is that? You should be out walking hand-in-hand with some babe."

"I *am* with a babe."

"Eww—gross! You know what I mean!"

William squeezed her hand. "Yeah, I know what you mean."

French Quarter

AFTER THE FIRST SET WAS DONE AND THE BAND RETREATED BACK-stage, Marianne reentered the cabaret from a side door and made her way to the back of the room. As she approached the table, Elizabeth waved.

"Mari! Look what I found"—she grinned as she pointed to the man sitting beside her—"acting like I hadn't seen him in years instead of last week!"

Marianne greeted Elizabeth first before turning her attention to the gentleman. "Do I know you, sir?" she asked as she gave him a kiss on the cheek.

"I would hope so." Dr. Chris Breaux gave her hand a squeeze as he helped her to a chair.

Elizabeth gave him a mock-severe look. "Don't be too nice to him, Mari. He was late."

"What can I say? Work, work, work." Chris held up his hands as he grinned. "At least I heard your first song."

"The fruits and nuts in the psych ward giving you trouble, Chris?" teased Marianne.

"Mari!" Elizabeth laughed.

"Nah, she's right," Chris said as he leaned over to kiss Marianne's cheek again. "I could open a store."

Elizabeth shook her head. "You two really deserve each other."

Marianne laughed as she hugged her boyfriend's arm. "I know. Isn't it great?"

Lakeview

IT WAS WELL AFTER ELEVEN WHEN A WEARY DR. GEORGE KATZ finally pulled his Lexus into his driveway. Quietly letting himself in, he saw Abe had fallen asleep in his recliner again. George used the remote to turn off the TV before making his way to his bedroom.

He found the lamp on his side of the bed still on, but his wife was sound asleep, a book by her side. Gently he placed the book on her nightstand before undressing in the bathroom. As he again approached the bed, he took a moment to gaze at Emma. Her dark hair was splayed over her pillow as she lay on her side, facing the nightstand. The room was warm, despite the air conditioning and ceiling fan, and she had pulled the covers down to her waist. Her lovely face was relaxed, her breathing deep, and her glorious breasts were barely contained by her nightgown.

George sighed. Emma was so beautiful it hurt. Such a precious gift he had been given. It was his responsibility to care for it. Yet, he was a man, and he ached for her. Perhaps, if Abe was sound asleep and Emma was willing …

George's musings were interrupted by the blare of the TV. Abe had awakened.

Muttering a soft curse, George walked over to his side of the bed. Extinguishing the light, George got in and went to sleep.

Faubourg Marigny

Elizabeth went home immediately after the second set, so only Chris was waiting for Marianne after she finished backstage—which was all right with the two of them.

Holding hands, they chatted about work as they walked to Marianne's house off Esplanade. It was a run-down, four-room shotgun a few blocks outside the Quarter that she had bought and renovated just as the gentrification boom took off. Formerly housing poor working-class black families, her street was now filling up with Yuppies, gays, and artistic types.

"So, it doesn't look too good for Jean Lafitte?"

"No," Marianne said sadly. "The woman holding the audition told us how great we were and hoped they could find a spot for us on the schedule. You know, the classic 'don't-call-us' line. I took a day off from work for that?"

"I'm sorry, babe."

She leaned into him. "I know, thanks. I'm more upset for the guys in the band. They really wanted the gig. Oh, well, we'll just have to try harder at the other casinos."

The pair reached Chris's GMC Envoy parked in front of Marianne's house, and she turned to embrace her boyfriend. "Thank you for coming by tonight," she said after they kissed.

Chris groaned. "I wish I could come tomorrow, but I gotta fly out to a conference."

Marianne hugged him. "I'm gonna miss you."

"I'll be back Tuesday."

"Weekend conferences suck."

"You said it. I'll call, and I'll see you at the rehearsal studio on Wednesday." He kissed her again before releasing her.

Her happiness was tinged with a taste of disappointment as Chris climbed into his SUV. He had a look of longing as he closed the door softly. For not the first time, Mari wondered why Chris didn't seem to want to take their relationship further than sharing hot kisses. She stood before her front door as he pulled away to drive home.

Chapter 2

H i, Dr. Katz!"

George gave the nurse working the floor of the surgery unit at Tulane University Medical Center a tired smile as he continued to his office. He picked up his phone messages at the secretary's desk before entering his office and closing the door. He plopped down in his chair and rubbed his eyes, the messages still in his hand. Most were from pharmaceutical salespeople, and he didn't want to deal with them right now. He had less than a half-hour before his next procedure and four hours before he could go home.

Home. The word did not bring him the pleasure he anticipated when he married Emma. But he had no comprehension how his life would turn out when he kissed her oh so many Mardi Gras before.

George and Emma dated throughout the summer of 1999. As the strength of their relationship grew, so did their passion. Both were eager for a more intimate relationship than just dating, but Emma living at home put a crimp in that. Abe always seemed to be around and took a great deal of pleasure in George's company. It wasn't as though the older man had set out to frustrate the young couple, but he accomplished it. Emma would not spend the night at George's condo with her father at home.

Finally, opportunity presented itself when Abe left town for an AIA convention. George immediately arranged for a quiet dinner for two at his place. Emma wore the sexiest dress she owned and brought an overnight case.

The two tortured themselves by pretending to enjoy the light dinner. They never got to the cheesecake dessert as they attacked each other on the living room couch. George damned near lost it when he quickly discovered Emma had seen no reason to wear a bra that night. Within minutes, they were undressed and entwined upon George's bed, losing themselves in delight.

George had every intention of making that night an unforgettable one, and he accomplished it. But his resolve to be slow and gentle with Emma flew out the window with the unveiling of her gorgeous body. He barely remembered to don protection. Only after his mind-freezing orgasm did he realize Emma's whimpers were from pain, not pleasure. He had forgotten Emma was a virgin, and he had acted like an animal.

George sat on the edge of his bed in complete mortification, facing away from her, his head in his hands, berating himself, until he felt Emma's hand on his shoulder and her gentle voice speaking his name. The next moment he had her in his arms, holding her tightly and apologizing again and again into her hair. She reassured him of her love, and in that instant, George knew he was going to marry Emma and spend the rest of his life loving, cherishing, and protecting her.

And he did. Emma set their wedding for the summer of 2000, after her third and final year at Tulane. When George protested her dropping out of school, she declared her career would be that of a doctor's wife, and therefore, further college education was a waste of both time and money. She could not be talked out of it, and her decision fueled George's determination to take care of his precious girl. He wanted the best for her, and only a ten-day honeymoon to Paris would do. For three days, they delighted in the sights of the City of Light, enjoying the museums and sipping wine in a sidewalk café on the *Champs-Élysées*.

Their nights were full of love and care; George gently worshiped her body as she deserved. Her pleasure came first, and he handled her like a fragile treasure. George learned his sweet Emma had a strange quirk: she grew loud and profane when she reached her pleasure. Emma was mortified, but George was amused.

It was late on the fifth afternoon that the phone call came, the one that informed them of Abe's heart attack. Their first response was to fly back immediately, but they were advised by Emma's sister, Irene, it wasn't necessary. Abe was out of danger, the attack being a mild one, and while he needed by-pass surgery, it could wait a couple of weeks. He would remain under observation at Ochsner Medical Center.

Emma and George tried to recapture the magic of their first halcyon days, but it was a lost cause. Emma still worried about her beloved Papa, and George was on the cell phone three times a day getting updates.

It was a subdued Dr. and Mrs. Katz who returned to New Orleans as scheduled. George monitored the successful triple by-pass at Ochsner while Emma packed—not her things to move into George's condo but her husband's belongings to move to the Garden District. The pair had decided in Paris that the Katzes would live with Abe and care for him.

After Abe was released, it quickly became apparent that the house, so loved by Emma's mother, was now impractical. The bedrooms were all on the second floor, and climbing stairs was out of the question for Abe. Emma set out and found a ranch-style house near their old Lakeview neighborhood. It cost more than George felt they could afford, given the renovations it needed, but the in-law suite near the garage, on the opposite side of the house from the master bedroom, was a big attraction. Abe sealed the deal by pledging the profits from selling his house to finance the renovations.

Nothing went smoothly. Abe retired from his firm, so the group health carrier tried to deny coverage. While Emma fought that, Abe listed the Garden District house for a hundred thousand dollars more than the market could bear. The house sat unsold for months. Without the promised cash infusion from Emma's father, George had to bear the entire cost of buying the house and renovating the kitchen.

Once they moved in, it was discovered there was virtually no interior insulation. A telephone conversation in the kitchen could be heard clearly in the bedroom. Abe's habit of staying up late to watch television put an effective damper on the Katzes' love life. Struggling to keep quiet while making love destroyed romance.

Unfortunately, there was never enough money to solve this problem. It would take over a year before the insurance company settled and paid for Abe's medical expenses. Abe finally sold his house, but only after Emma talked him into lowering the price. Then, the ranch house's foundation needed repair, Emma's car broke down, and the air conditioning went kaput one hot July day. It seemed fate was doing everything it could to thwart George Katz.

Emma and he had decided to put off having children. They never knew when the next disaster would take place, and there was Abe to consider. Abe liked children, but he had not reacted well to his medical condition. Abe became depressed and cranky. Emma and George wanted to give him the peace of mind he needed to recover his spirits as well as his health before turning his life inside out by starting a family. So, the sacrifice was made.

It seemed to George they had been sacrificing for Abe for years. Emma had borne the brunt of work at home, seeing to Abe's every request. Thank goodness, Mrs. Taylor came by twice a week to give Emma the chance to get out of the house to do shopping or go to yoga, her newest activity. Otherwise, he was sure his wife would have gone insane.

Still, George wondered what it would be like if, instead of driving back to Lakeview, he was walking to a downtown condo where only Emma was waiting for him, their nights to do whatever they wanted without worrying about anybody else.

If only Abe had…

George clamped his mind shut before he could finish the thought. He would *not* wish Abe dead. He would not. Abe was his friend and he was family. He would not betray him, not even in his mind.

Sighing, George began returning his phone calls before his next procedure.

Friday, August 6: Pontchartrain Causeway

Chuck Bingley was behind the wheel of his Camry, traffic on the Causeway was zipping along, SportsTalk on the radio, and he was heading home on a Friday afternoon. Life was very good.

After college, Chuck landed a job at Gallic National Bank in the commercial lending department. He had been made one of the senior lenders in the downtown office. He knew he could make vice-president in another five years, with a substantial raise. The future was bright.

The only potential worry was that a national credit card company was looking to get into banking and had eyed Gallic as their entrée. The top management swore up and down they would never sell the bank if it meant moving their headquarters out of New Orleans. So Chuck did his job and took a wait-and-see attitude.

He glanced at the mile marker flying past, showing the distance he had travelled on the Causeway. He turned on the hands-free device and dialed home.

"Hey, honey, I've just passed the nine-mile marker. Just fifteen miles to go before I hit the North Shore."

"Wonderful, Chuck," answered his wife, Jane. "Dinner will be ready. We've having pizza."

"Again?"

"I know. I'm sorry. But work went overtime, and I couldn't get to the store today to make groceries."

"Aw, that's okay. Pizza's great. How're the kids?"

"Just fine and waiting to see Daddy. And so is Rufus."

"Does my big baby miss his daddy?" Rufus was their Great Dane puppy.

"He sure does. He hasn't left me alone since I got home."

"I'll be there soon. Do we need anything at the store?"

"No, we can wait until tomorrow."

"Okay, I'll be home as soon as I can. Love you."

"Love you too. Bye."

Chuck Bingley sat back to enjoy the rest of his favorite part of his forty-five mile commute. He lived in Covington, across Lake

Pontchartrain from New Orleans, so a major part of his trip to and from work was the twin-span, twenty-four mile long Lake Pontchartrain Causeway, the longest bridge in the world. First time drivers on the span would think he was insane; each two-lane span had no shoulder and the speed limit was sixty-five miles per hour. Everywhere you looked there was water, and the bridge was only sixteen feet above the lake.

However, the toll-financed bridge had a few innovations that made it one of the safest roadways in the United States. There were numerous call boxes along the bridge. Seven crossovers were situated four miles apart, and motorists were encouraged to use them. The Causeway police stationed a cruiser or a truck at each crossover to respond to emergencies. They even helped to change tires.

The police also enforced the speed limit. They looked the other way during rush hour, but that was it. You go anywhere near eighty any other time, and you'll owe the court two hundred fifty dollars.

Yes, the Causeway was a great break in Chuck's commuting routine as long as there was no fog. When that happened, then escorted convoys turned the trip from twenty-five minutes to an hour and a half.

The joy stopped when Chuck hit the North Shore. Once a sleepy place filled with fishermen, lumberjacks, and the occasional vacation cabin, St. Tammany Parish was now the fastest growing place in the state. The population was north of 200,000 and continued to increase. The traffic was awful. It would take another half-hour before Chuck pulled into his garage just outside of Covington.

Jane and Rufus were there to greet him at the garage door. Chuck's weekend had officially begun.

Tuesday, August 10: Downtown

AT LEAST ONCE A WEEK, DR. CHRISTOPHER BREAUX, LSU MEDI-cal Center's newest psychiatrist, shared lunch with his friend and mentor, Dr. Segura, chewing the fat or discussing issues with patients and coworkers. The two sat in easy camaraderie in Dr. Segura's office. Chris munched on a turkey and Swiss with potato chips. The older man, eating a garden salad with low-fat ranch dressing, eyed his young colleague's meal with undisguised envy.

"Wanna bite?" offered Chris.

"No, I better not. Joy has been after me to lose another ten pounds. Gah, I feel like a rabbit sometimes." At Chris's laughter, Segura added, "Your time is coming. You'll be eating grass for meals too. Just wait."

"Maybe, if I had a wife who was as intent on keeping me around as Joy is."

"I guess so. Either that or she just likes torturing me. So, how are things? No, not work—we talk enough about that. Are you working on getting yourself somebody to worry about your weight?"

Chris put down his sandwich and took a sip of water before answering. "Funny you should bring that up. I need some advice. I think I told you about the lady I'm dating, Marianne Dashwood."

"The singer, yeah."

"Well, we have a history." For the next fifteen minutes, Chris talked about Marianne's time at Loyola and the events there, and how she had gone off to Shreveport to finish school and had spent a year entertaining people aboard one of Disney's cruise ships before returning to New Orleans. Chris and Marianne had corresponded during her three years away, and he was one of the first to greet her when she came back. He had helped her form her band while she got a daytime job in the claims department of a large insurance company. They were just friends at first. She spent much of her time practicing her music and working with her combo until a few months ago when Chris asked Marianne to dinner. One dinner turned into another and then another and then lunch regularly. One good night kiss became many, each one deeper and more promising. They had fallen in love so easily it took a while to realize it had happened.

Dr. Segura nodded as he listened. At the end of Chris's mono-logue, he smiled. "Sounds like a firm foundation for the future, Chris. You became friends first. That's important; it will help you over the rough times."

"You think there will be rough times?"

"There are *always* rough times, my boy." Dr. Segura sobered. "Unless there is more to this."

"Well, yes."

"Mmm-hmm. May I be frank? Are the two of you intimate?"

Chris shook his head. "No. That's what I want to talk to you about. It's normal that I want to take our relationship to the next level. I believe Marianne wants that as much as I do, but I'm worried. Marianne says she remembers nothing about what happened five years ago."

"The assault in the fraternity house?"

"Yes. What if the assault has affected her subconsciously?"

"Has she shown any behaviors that would lead you to think that she has been damaged emotionally?"

"No, but that doesn't mean she hasn't. I'm afraid of triggering something."

Dr. Segura nodded. "Very wise of you. It is not unusual for a victim of an assault to compartmentalize and submerge their deep distress over the event for years. On the other hand, some people recover almost completely from the trauma. It's impossible to predict. You said before that Marianne had received counseling?"

"Yes. Both here and in Shreveport. So, what do I do?"

"Chris, you care for Marianne very much, don't you?"

"Yes, I do. I'm in love with her."

"Does she know this?"

"I haven't actually said the words, but I think she knows how I feel."

"Don't bet on it. Saying the words and really meaning them, carries great power. If you truly want a deeper relationship with her, you should be open about your feelings and intentions. Trust is very important. Many victims of sexual abuse suffer from trust issues for some time. You must be open with her and encourage her to be open with you. You cannot rush her, though. Show she can trust you by example."

"So, you're saying that I should lay all my cards on the table before we become intimate?"

"*Everyone* should, Chris, but in your situation, I believe it's vital."

"Thanks. You've given me a great deal to think about."

"If more people would take the time to consider the consequences of their actions before acting as you have, we would have a lot less heartache in this world."

The 2004 Hurricane season began in earnest as two storms emerged in the Gulf of Mexico. Tropical Storm Bonnie made landfall on August 12 in the Florida panhandle, causing minimal damage.

But all eyes were on the other storm. Hurricane Charley, a monstrous Category 4 storm with winds peaking at 150 miles per hour, was making a beeline toward the metropolis of Tampa/St. Petersburg before veering slightly south at the last moment to slam into Charlotte County on August 13, wiping out the sleepy little city of Punta Gorda and causing devastation inland. Eighty percent of the county's buildings were damaged. Charley's gusts were still in excess of 100 mph as it passed through Orlando before entering the Atlantic Ocean near Daytona Beach. Downgraded to tropical storm, Charley wreaked havoc along the Atlantic seaboard from the Carolinas to Rhode Island. Ten deaths and fifteen billion dollars in damages were laid at the storm's door.

No one knew Florida's agonies were just beginning.

Monday, August 23: Third District Headquarters

Richard Fitzwilliam walked through the halls of the NOPD Third District, stopping before an office. He looked at the nameplate adorning the door: *Captain Richard Fitzwilliam.*

The room was sparsely furnished with a 1970s-era desk and a metal swivel chair that might have been new during the Vietnam War. But he smiled anyway. It was *his* office. After fifteen years, Richard had made it to captain.

Fitzwilliam moved the box of personal items off the desk and sat down. The office was small, maybe ten-by-ten. But it had a door and a window. Nothing to sneeze at when you didn't work downtown.

Fitzwilliam began to empty the box. On the top was a photo

of his old narcotics team from his Second District days. He froze. How did that get there? He must have packed it without thinking. There was no way he would have kept the thing intentionally, as Jones's smiling face was right there in the front.

Unwillingly, his thoughts flowed back to his last encounter with her, three years earlier.

July, 2001: Second District Headquarters

IT HAD TAKEN PID ALMOST TWO YEARS TO COMPLETE THEIR IN-vestigation into the mole in the Second District. A sting had been set up, and Fitzwilliam was neck-deep in it. Officer Jones had fallen for it hook, line, and sinker, and to save her own skin, she ratted on the drug gang that had moved in from Treme. Antoine "Junior" Jarvis and his crew were a vicious bunch that had been implicated in a dozen murders. The destruction of the gang was a big win for the NOPD. It almost offset the shame of a traitor in blue.

Jones and her attorney were doing what they could to make the best of a bad situation. The NOPD had tapes, both audio and video. It came as a rude shock that they could trace cell phone calls. Jones was caught red-handed with over ten pounds of cocaine under her garage, her fingerprints all over it. She deposited marked money in her bank account. She was hooked, gaffed, and in the boat. The only thing left to do was to cooperate and try to work a deal for her to spend a short term in the Orleans Parish Prison rather than be a guest for twenty years or more in the Louisiana Correctional Institute for Women in St. Gabriel. The inmates *really* didn't like incarcerated cops in St. Gabriel any more than the males liked them at Angola.

Fitzwilliam had watched the last thirty minutes of Jones's de-briefing through the one-way mirror with a mixture of sadness and disgust. As the ADA was wrapping up, Fitzwilliam tapped on the glass. A hand signal told him that he could enter.

Jones was clearly surprised by her boss's entrance. The lawyer started to protest, but a reminder that the plea deal hadn't been formally approved shut him up. Fitzwilliam sat down across from his former partner and stared at her. She could not meet his eyes.

"The only reason you're here, Jones," Fitzwilliam growled, "and not at central lockup, is your cooperation. You've told the DA everything you know about Jarvis?"

Jones glanced at her attorney who nodded. "Yeah."

"You know Jarvis was killed in a gun battle with the Special Operations unit."

She shrugged. "Didn't think Junior would be taken alive."

"Convenient for you." She shrugged again. "Still, we got enough to send you away for a long time unless you're straight with us."

"Is there a reason for this?" demanded the lawyer.

"Oh, yes. One last case to close." Fitzwilliam opened a manila envelope and extracted some eight-by-ten photos. He spread two of them on the table before Jones. "Thomas Bertram," he said as he pointed to the male, "and Sarah Smith. Talk to me about them."

"I don't know them," Jones claimed.

Fitzwilliam's mouth twitched. He was watching Jones very carefully, and he saw the shock of recognition in her eyes before she could get control of her expression again. He knew all the sacrifice he had made to trap Jones was worth it. He pulled a third photo. "Gregory Anthony Wickham. Goes by the name G-Daddy. Know him?"

Jones said nothing.

"You're risking your deal, Jonesy." He pulled a plastic bag out next and laid it next to Bertram's photo. "Recognize this?"

"It's one of my business cards. So what?"

"We found this in Bertram's wallet. Bertram's wallet was in the back pocket of his jeans when we found him in the Manchac swamp, dead of a gunshot wound to the back of his head. How do you think your card got there?"

"No idea." Her eyes were void of emotion.

"Now, see, I've got this idea about that. I think Bertram here came by the precinct in early March of 1999 to see me and, instead, saw you. That's how he got your card."

"I don't remember that."

"Ah, the problems of getting old. The desk sergeant remembers, though. He also remembers you walking Bertram out of the precinct and you not coming back for a while." He stared at her.

She became intently interested in her clenched hands. "Sometimes I go get a snack or something like that. On my break, ya know."

Fitzwilliam glared at Jones for a moment longer before pulling out two other photos. "You called Wickham, didn't you? You sold these two out for cocaine, didn't you?"

"My client's not involved in any murder," claimed the lawyer.

Fitzwilliam abruptly stood up and slammed the photos down on the desk. Jones gasped. It was the crime scene shots of the bodies, ravaged by over three months' exposure to the elements. "You had these two kids killed for dope, didn't you?" he shouted. "*Didn't you?*"

"I-I didn't kill anybody," Jones whimpered.

"All right, this interview's over!" cried the red-faced lawyer.

Fitzwilliam was incensed. "Go ahead and walk outta here! I'm gonna tie you to this, and I'll see you get the needle. You're on a one-way trip to Death Row unless you talk!"

"I ain't takin' the rap for no murder!" cried Jones.

"Talk, damn you!"

The ADA placed a hand on Fitzwilliam's shoulder. "Enough of this."

Jones shook her head. "No, no, I ain't got nothin' to say. Nothin' against Wickham." She looked at Fitzwilliam. "If you had more than this, you would've hit me with it at the beginning. You can't tie me to this. You've got nothing."

Fitzwilliam became desperate, watching his chance of connecting the crime to Wickham fading. "What about these kids? What about justice for them? Jonesy, I know you're eaten up about this. Tell me what you know. Help me put Wickham away. You were a cop. Do something good."

She looked everywhere in the room, except at him or the photos. "No. Not against Wickham." She got to her feet.

"Why? Why are you so scared of him and not Jarvis?"

"'Cause Jarvis is dead, an' Wickham ain't." With that, former Officer Jones left the interrogation room in handcuffs.

August, 2004: Third District Headquarters

FITZWILLIAM LOOKED AT THE PHOTO ONE LAST TIME BEFORE TOSS-
ing it into the trash can. Jones had gotten her plea deal and was
serving ten years in Parish Prison. Her earliest parole hearing would
come up in 2008. Three members of the Jarvis gang were in Angola,
but Wickham still walked free.

Fitzwilliam's involvement in the sting against Jones had cost
him the trust of the Second District. Sure, Jones was a bad cop and
needed to be taken down, but Fitzwilliam had turned on his own
people, and so a seed of doubt had been planted as to his loyalty
to the rest of the precinct. Nobody liked a whistle-blower, and it
didn't help that the NOPD had decorated him for his involvement
in the investigation. Fitzwilliam was no fool. He had seen what
had happened and, while not surprised, he was still disappointed.
Within six months, he had requested and received a transfer. His
precinct captain had taken early retirement.

The sprawling Third District covered a large part of the city from
Carrolton to the Lake, from the 17th Street Canal to the Industrial
Canal, including Lakeview and Gentilly. Fitzwilliam was able to start
anew. He served in both the Street Crimes Unit and Community
Policing. He was able to earn the trust of his fellow officers. They
would write off, in time, Fitzwilliam's service in the Second District
as an unfortunate experience, dealing with an inferior precinct. The
competition between the districts had always been fierce.

Fitzwilliam's promotion was met with almost universal approval,
except at home. In the aftermath of the mole investigation, Richard's
wife, Olivia, had hoped he would take the opportunity to leave the
NOPD with his head held high and go to work with either the state
police or the FBI. She could not understand why her husband would
continue to work inside a police department so rife with politics,
corruption, and backbiting. Now that Richard was a captain, there
was no way he would leave before his twentieth year, if then.

Fitzwilliam gave Olivia multiple explanations for staying on the
force, but she knew he avoided telling her the mysterious truth. He
couldn't; even to his own mind, it sounded insane. There was no

way Richard Fitzwilliam could leave the NOPD while Gregory Anthony "G-Daddy" Wickham was on the loose.

Fitzwilliam could not explain why Wickham had become such an obsession. He remained a small-time drug dealer, and except for the Bertram/Smith murders, he was not implicated in any other killings.

Still, the man bedeviled him. Wickham had turned up again in late 2001, turning his cousins' lives upside down. God knows what that monster would have done to Gina Darcy.

To date, Fitzwilliam considered his war against Wickham had been a failure. He couldn't get him for the incident at the AI house five years ago, there was no evidence linking G-Daddy to the Jarvis gang, and without Jones's testimony, there was no solid link to the murders. Wickham had disappeared after the situation with Gina. Right now, Fitzwilliam was 0-and-4 against the bastard.

Still, Richard Fitzwilliam wasn't going to give up. He was a Saints fan, after all, and if there was anything the city's woeful NFL franchise had taught its fans, it was the comfort of faith. *Believe*, a recent Saints ad campaign had asked the city. Fitzwilliam did believe—in his team and in himself. He would get Greg Wickham.

Whatever it cost.

Chapter 3

Nature was not done with the Sunshine State. Hurricane Francis was a Category 4 storm with 140 mph winds as it tore through the Caribbean. But by the time it came ashore near Sewall's Point on Florida's Atlantic coast on September 5, the winds topped out at 105 mph. Strangely, it crossed the state from east-to-west, its track, combined with that of August's Charley, making a huge X over Orlando. Some jokers quipped that the universe was marking the famous vacation spot as some cosmic target.

On the same day, east of Grenada, the ninth storm of the year was born. The storm was named Ivan.

Monday, September 6: Downtown

WILLIAM DARCY STABBED THE BUTTON FOR THE NINETEENTH floor as he adjusted his tie. He couldn't believe he was this nervous. He had been at meetings with the titans of industry in New York, London, and Shanghai. Why would seeing one woman turn him into a bowl of mush?

He knew why. She was the best woman he never had.

William made his way from the elevator to the double glass doors of the offices for Economic Development/New Orleans. Seated at the reception desk was a young, attractive African-American woman, a telephone to her ear. She waggled her French-manicured fingers at William.

"That's right, that's the number to the Convention and Visitors

Bureau. They can handle— Say again? ... Yes, they can locate a hotel close to the Quarter. Hmm? ... Oh! Sir, I'm afraid New Orleans doesn't provide *that* kind of service. You may want to try Las Vegas. Good bye." She hung up the receiver with a bit more force than necessary.

"Mr. Darcy?" she asked brightly as she walked from around the desk, holding out her hand. Her flowery dress floated around her knees. "Hi. I'm Kaywanda Johnson. Welcome to EDNO. Congratulations on joining the board, sir."

"Glad to be here, Kaywanda." He shook her hand. "Interesting phone call?"

"Oh, that? We get a lot of calls for visitors' information because of the website. Folks tend call the first site they get. That guy was looking for *company* while he was here." She waggled her head. "Do I look like an escort service?"

William chuckled. He figured Kaywanda could handle herself pretty well.

"Your meeting will be in the boardroom. If you'll follow me?" Kaywanda led William into a room just off the lobby. The boardroom had a wall of windows overlooking Poydras Street. The large table in the middle had two dozen chairs around it. At least thirty more lined the walls. On the wall opposite the windows was a screen. A projector hung from the center of the ceiling.

"Can I get you coffee or water or anything? No? Well, please make yourself comfortable. I'll let everybody know you're here," Kaywanda said with a smile as she closed the door.

William walked about the room, hands in his pockets, looking at the portraits of the past board chairmen. He glanced at his father's photo before turning to the bank of windows. Directly opposite was a large office building. He idly wondered if someone at that moment was looking out *their* window at him.

The sound of the door opening caused him to turn around— and freeze.

ELIZABETH BOUDREAUX POUNDED FURIOUSLY ON HER KEYBOARD,

finishing her portion of the presentation. As usual, Eddie had changed something. Eddie Masters might be the most gifted economic developer in the state of Louisiana, but he had an annoying habit of "polishing" a presentation right up to the last moment. This meant everyone else had to alter their portion too.

She did *not* need this, today of all days.

A middle-aged black woman stuck her head in. "Your nine o'clock is here, Lizzy." Economic development organizations ran lean and mean. That meant Jan Hill was the administrative assistant for just about everybody in EDNO.

Elizabeth glanced at her clock. Five minutes early. Of course, William Darcy would be five minutes early. *He was probably early for his own birth*, she thought crossly.

"Thanks, Jan. Let me finish this." Another fifteen seconds passed and Elizabeth was able to save the PowerPoint presentation to the shared drive on the server. *Do I have time to go to the rest room and freshen up? No. Rats.*

She pulled out her compact. She wore her hair up in a carelessly professional way. A gold necklace danced about her collarbone. She could use some powder, but there was no time. She fixed her lipstick, grabbed a folder of information for their guest, and left her office. With every step she took, her anxiety grew.

What does he look like now? Is he involved with somebody? He could be married, for all I know. No, Chuck would've told me. Why has he avoided us all for years? He sees Chuck, Chris, and George, but except for Emma, he's had little contact with the rest of the old gang. Mari and Jane hardly see him at all. He missed both Chuck and Jane's and George and Emma's weddings. Why? Does he still resent the past? Has he forgiven me for what I've done? I wish he wasn't here!

Before the doors of the boardroom, she took a deep breath, smiled at Kaywanda at the receptionist's desk, and turned the doorknob.

William was over by the windows, back to the door, hands in the pockets of his navy suit. Elizabeth fought to remember her prepared greeting.

"So, William Darcy, we meet again."

William started and then turned fully towards her. His expression changed from surprised to bemused. "It looks that way, Elizabeth. How are you?"

Elizabeth relaxed at his grin. Her gambit to break the ice worked. "Good, William, I'm real good. And you?"

"Good. Not as good as you, though. You look great."

"Thanks." She wished she could say the same about him, but she couldn't. She was a little shocked at his appearance. She expected William would be dressed in his Hart, Schaffner and Marx best, and he was—a navy suit, snow-white shirt with French cuffs, and a bright blue tie. He tried to pull off being relaxed with his hands in his pockets, but she could see he had lost weight since the last time she had seen him, and there were rings around his eyes. He looked tired. And most upsetting of all, flecks of grey were in his hair.

As Communication Director, part of Elizabeth's job was to keep current with news and rumors in the business community. The battles waged by the new wonder boy of the shipping industry were fodder for business journals and cocktail parties alike. William had fought hard to earn respect and protect DGS. She now saw the price he had paid.

Oh my God, William! How bad has it been for you?

"Thank you for coming in for this orientation session. We'll get started in a minute," she managed. "Do you want some coffee?"

"Sure, that would be great."

"Come on, I'll show you where we keep the stuff." She led him back through the lobby into the heart of the office. Most of the space was a huge room with cubicles set in the middle. There were some private offices set along one wall, while the far wall remained open to the windows.

"This is our bull pen," Elizabeth explained. "Most of the team works out here. The vice presidents and the CEO, Carl Eden, have the offices."

"Where are you?"

Elizabeth blushed. "I have an office. I need the room for my stuff and a door to close when I'm handling a reporter." She walked up to a middle-aged black woman. "And this is Jan Hill, our administrative assistant, with whom I'm sure you've already spoken on the phone."

"I sure have." William extended his hand. "Glad to finally meet you in person, Jan."

Jan smiled. "Thanks, Mr. Darcy. Welcome on board. Lizzy will take good care of you."

Elizabeth laughed. "Don't let her fool you. Jan really runs things around here."

"Most good secretaries do. I'd be lost without mine."

"You just remember that, Mr. Darcy, when it comes to bonus time."

"I do, Jan. By the way, where's the boss?"

"He's in Washington with our lobbyist, trying to save the National Finance Center."

"We'll talk more about that during our briefing," explained Elizabeth. "Let's get that coffee."

Elizabeth took William into the break room. On one counter was a bank of coffee makers and three airpot dispensers, marked regular, decaf, and voodoo.

"Name your poison," Elizabeth offered.

He pointed at the voodoo pot. "Is that dark roast? I'll have some of that."

"Brave man. How do you take it?" she asked as she fixed two cups.

"Black is fine."

She handed him his coffee and then fixed her own with sugar and cream. As they returned to the boardroom, William noted the bullpen was empty.

"They're in a meeting with Eddie Masters, preparing for our meeting," she explained.

William took a sip. "I appreciate it, but I hate to take them from their work."

Elizabeth didn't have to mention that caring for the board members and the investors was part of the job. William knew that as well as she. "Eddie likes to have everything prepared. Ah, they're breaking up now." She waved at the group of people leaving an office. "Let me introduce you."

Moments later, they were assaulted by the intelligent and irrepressible Eddie Masters, Vice President of Economic Development, and number two person in the organization. "Mister Darcy, I'm glad to meet you," he cried. "Our CEO, Carl Eden, couldn't be here today and sends his best regards. Let me introduce everybody on the team." He then ran through the names of his coworkers. "All set to learn some stuff?" Masters asked as he rubbed his hands together.

William nodded, and the group made its way to the boardroom, Masters delivering the history of EDNO on the way. Elizabeth was proud she resisted an impulse to roll her eyes. After William took his seat, she handed him a portfolio of information and sat at the other side of the table with her coworkers.

Masters launched into a ninety-minute soliloquy on the various projects the organization was pushing. The biggest was the reuse of a soon-to-be closed naval facility on the Mississippi River called Government Quarter. After the Navy pulled out, various military and federal law-enforcement regional agencies, such as the Coast Guard, DHS, ICE, ATF, and FBI would be relocated on the grounds in improved buildings.

From her position, Elizabeth could observe William's reaction to Masters' monologue. Eddie had the habit of interrupting his subordinates during their portion of the presentation, effectively talking over. He was immersed in the minutia of EDNO, and while he was a supportive boss, the staff soon learned Eddie Masters would always take over a meeting.

The staff got used to it, but Eddie could be overpowering to the uninitiated. Elizabeth nervously looked at William, concerned about his response. He showed little emotion, paying attention and taking notes. When he noticed Elizabeth's gaze, he flashed a grin. She flashed a quick smile in return. Masters, of course, seemed oblivious.

"Well, we've covered a lot of ground. Are there any last questions, Mr. Darcy?" Masters declared after an hour and a half.

"Not today, but I know I'll be working with your transportation people in the future." He turned to them. "My administrative assistant, Barbara, will be happy to arrange an appointment. I'd like to thank all of you for taking time out of your busy day to show me the ropes. I know I'm the new kid on the block when it comes to the board, but I plan to dedicate as much time as I can to it. My father served on the board and always spoke highly of your efforts. It's an honor to follow in his footsteps."

Elizabeth stood up, impressed that William spoke to her coworkers as colleagues rather than employees of Masters. "I just have a few more housekeeping items to go over with Mr. Darcy."

William spent the next few minutes taking his leave of each of the participants, most of his time spent with Masters. Finally, he and Elizabeth were left to themselves. They looked at each other and grinned.

"Alone at last," they said in unison before cracking up.

"I'm sorry about Eddie. He does go on a bit."

"I'll say, but he seems to know his stuff." William paused and smiled. "And doesn't mind letting the whole world know it in minute detail." They laughed again. "Well, what else do you need?"

"Just some personal stuff for the board. We can do it now or later if you need to go." Now they were alone, Elizabeth's nerves returned.

"No, I've got time. Let's get it done."

A few minutes later, William sat before Elizabeth's desk as she dug out a form. "Thanks for your cooperation, Will. We would like some information about you. It's all optional, but we like to really know our board. Your title with DGS. You're president?"

"President/CEO, yes."

"All right." She made the correction on the form. "Communications to your business address and email account?"

"Sure." He verified his home address and birth date. Then Elizabeth hesitated. "Marital status?"

"Single."

It took all her self-control not to look up at William at that moment. She was embarrassed at the relief she felt. "All right, we can skip the next few questions."

"What are they?"

"Spouse's name, birth date and anniversary, children's names and ages." Elizabeth was turning red. "Well, that's everything. Just have to add it to the database."

"You know, Elizabeth, it's good to see you again," His eyes bore into hers.

Elizabeth turned to him, surprise evident on her face. "It's good to see you again too, William."

"You've done well with yourself, I see." William was no longer an up-and-coming titan of industry. He was the boy she knew from school.

For an instant, Elizabeth was transported to a place in her past. She was back on a fraternity house porch on a warm, late summer evening, enjoying a good conversation with a tall, handsome graduate student, the sounds of the street in her ears. She had seen the same look before, but she didn't know what it meant. Too late, she learned in a most terrible way. Now, she wondered if it meant the same.

For years, Elizabeth wondered whether William had ever read her letter of apology. She still didn't know, or whether he had forgiven her, but it seemed he could at least tolerate her presence now. When she heard William was to join the board, she vowed, if given half a chance, to apologize in person. Before she committed herself, though, she wanted to make sure William would hear her out first. Now seated before her desk, his earnest gaze gave Elizabeth courage. The time was now.

"William, I've wanted to tell you—"

Kaywanda stuck her head in the door, shattering the moment. "Excuse me, Mr. Darcy. Lizzy, your lunch date is here."

Elizabeth hid her irritation. "Thanks, Kay."

"I guess I ought to leave." William got to his feet, his expression inscrutable.

Elizabeth's heart sank, knowing she missed her chance. "I'll walk you out." Wondering what was going through William's mind, she decided to tease. "I think you know my date."

"I do?"

Elizabeth led a confused William to the small lobby.

"*William!*" cried Marianne as she flew into his arms.

"Hey, Marianne! How's my favorite singer?"

"How would you know?" she pouted. "You never come to my performances."

"Sorry, gal. Life is running me ragged."

"Then get you a woman and slow down." Marianne winked at Elizabeth, who turned beet red. "Hey!" Marianne said as they broke the clutch. "We're gonna grab some lunch. Wanna come along?"

"I wish I could, but I've got a business lunch I can't get out of." William seemed sincerely sorry.

"Oh, pooh! You sure you can't make it? Lizzy, can you talk him into it?"

Elizabeth wondered what the hell had gotten into her friend to make the woman want to embarrass her to death. "Mari, I'm sure if William was free, he would come."

Marianne didn't giving up. "Then give us a rain check, huh?"

William smiled. "You got it—next time, and I'm all yours. Ladies, I've got to go. Kaywanda, thank you for your help."

"No prob, Mr. Darcy," said the receptionist as she returned to her office chair.

"Mari, be sure to tell Chris I said hello. Elizabeth," William stopped and smiled, "it was great seeing you again. Enjoy your lunch, and I'll see y'all soon." He waved as he left though the doors.

Marianne turned to Elizabeth. "Soo…William's back, hmm?"

"Mari—" Elizabeth said dangerously.

Kaywanda piped up. "Oooh, sounds like history there."

Elizabeth turned to the receptionist. "I knew Will Darcy in my college days. An old friend." She turned back to Marianne. "Let's get something to eat." *Before you say anything else.*

Working in the same building, it was routine for Elizabeth and Marianne to have lunch together at least once a week. Sometimes they ate in the building's cafeteria, but this summer's day they walked down the block to Commerce Restaurant. Patrons in dresses and suits stood in line with blue-collar workers and students to place their orders.

"Wha'cha want, hawt?" asked an elderly black woman behind the counter when it was Elizabeth's turn.

"Po'boy, large—half shrimp, half oyster—dressed."

"Right. An' you, hon?" Marianne ordered the lunch special of red beans and rice. After paying for their meals and receiving their Diet Cokes, they stood at the head of the line for a couple of minutes waiting on the food. They then made their way to an open table. Elizabeth unwrapped half of the twelve-inch monster, saving the rest for dinner.

Elizabeth noticed the expression on Marianne's face. "All right, Mari, what is it?"

"Nothing. It was nice seeing Will Darcy again, wasn't it?" Her grin grew wider.

Elizabeth put her po'boy down. "Now, what's that supposed to mean?"

"What is what?"

"Your comment."

"I didn't make any comment."

Elizabeth rolled her eyes. "Don't play innocent with me! You know what I'm talking about." She paused. "I'm glad everything went well today. I was nervous about seeing Will again, but now I have, and it seems we're able to get along. I'm very happy. Satisfied?"

"No." Marianne sat still, her hands in her lap, and gave Elizabeth an aggravated look. "Elizabeth Boudreaux, maybe you can fool yourself, but you can't fool me. Don't try to sit there and pretend you weren't affected by Will's visit today. You know, and I know: you've judged every man you've dated in the last five years against the standard set by William Darcy and found all of them lacking. You dumped Tony Riviere because of that."

"Tony and I dumped each other. Besides, I thought you didn't like him."

"I didn't. Don't try to change the subject. You're still in love with William. And I won't be satisfied until you either let him go and move on, or do something about it now that he is back in your life."

Elizabeth sat in stunned silence.

"Well, I'm sorry, but you asked." Marianne returned to her lunch.

Elizabeth said nothing and reached for her sandwich before changing her mind. "You're right, Mari, I have been kidding myself." She held her face in her hands. "I was *so* nervous before he got there, and yet when I saw him, it was like old times. I don't think I breathed easy until he admitted he was still single. I'm hopeless."

"I could've told you Will wasn't married."

Elizabeth shook her head. "I thought he may have kept it quiet. You know how he likes to keep personal stuff to himself."

"Lizzy, he wouldn't have been able to keep something like *that* from Chris or Chuck. Besides, he's a public figure in New Orleans. He wouldn't be able to keep it quiet. You're not being sensible."

"I've never been sensible when it comes to William." She sighed and lifted her head. "All right, I admit it. I still love him—a little. I'm glad we can be friends again. I can be happy with that."

Marianne reached out. "Don't you want more?"

Elizabeth smiled sadly. "Mari, what about William? Does *he* want more? No, I'm not going to get my hopes up. As far as I know, nothing has changed. I have his friendship again, maybe, and that's good enough for me."

William walked down Poydras Street with a decided bounce to his step. It was foolish to have been apprehensive over the meeting with Elizabeth. In fact, it could hardly have gone better. She seemed to have no ill feeling over what happened five years ago. She seemed genuinely happy to see him, and he thought the invitation to lunch was sincere.

He surreptitiously studied the photos displayed in Elizabeth's office while being interviewed. There were several of her and Jane, a couple with Marianne, and some vacation shots. No guys. It looked like she was as unattached as he was. Maybe there was a chance.

Hold it, cowboy, just one second! Your track record reading Elizabeth Boudreaux sucks. Don't make that mistake again. Just take it easy and be open—and see what happens. At the very least, you'll have to explain your behavior at Tulane.

Still, a wide grin broke out on his face, echoing the sunny September day, as he stepped to the doors of the WTC. *But I've got a second chance!*

New Orleans had its own World Trade Center, a four-hundred-foot architectural landmark towering over the intersection of Canal and Poydras. The WTC had magnificent views of the grand, meandering Mississippi River and its bustling port, as well as New Orleans's distinctive skyline. The Plimsoll Club, a private dining club for businesspeople, occupied the thirtieth floor of the building. The membership was dominated by the shipping, fabrication, petroleum, and finance industries.

William, like his father before him, was a member in good standing. He ate there often enough to be recognized by the maître d' and was shown to his table immediately. Within a few minutes, Ben Leahy, the president of a refrigerated warehouse firm on the Industrial Canal joined him. They decided to take advantage of the lunch buffet and were soon eating and talking business.

"Do you think you've ironed out your problems with the state over your incentives?" William asked.

"Yeah, we think so. EDNO has been helping us." Leahy ran his hand through his thinning hair. "The state's great at making promises, but they don't seem to wanna pay up in the end. We fronted the refurbishment of state's facilities, and we want our reimbursement. The administration keeps poor-mouthing us, saying priorities have changed. They ask us to be patient, and they will pay up someday. Hell, I need my money now! I ain't gonna wait for Big Momma to set up another committee."

William chuckled. The current governor of Louisiana had made history as the state's first female governor. Unfortunately, she had proven a better candidate than a governor. Her first legislative session was clumsy and disorganized. Major appointment to boards and administration posts went unfilled. Her first foreign trade mission was to Cuba, even though there was little Louisiana could sell to the island nation. The trip accomplished nothing but to offend the small but vocal anti-Castro Cuban population in New Orleans.

Worst of all, the governor had a tendency to set up a commission or committee rather than take a stand on almost any issue.

"Speaking of EDNO, I'm joining their board," William said offhandedly.

"Yeah, I thought I heard that. Taking your daddy's place?" For a region of over one and a half million people, New Orleans was really a small town.

"It wasn't exactly reserved, Ben."

"EDNO let me know about those state incentives in the first place. Their communications gal…what's her name? Boudreaux! Elizabeth Boudreaux. Tony Riviere's girlfriend. She's sharp."

William looked up. "What's that?" His stomach dropped to his knees. "Tony Riviere, the lawyer? I thought he moved to Washington. He's working for the senator, isn't he?"

"Yeah, but he flies back every other weekend from what I heard." Leahy dug into his lunch.

The two men began talking of more mundane issues, but only one was enjoying his meal. William Darcy's had the distinct taste of ashes.

Wednesday, September 8: Lakeview
Emma walked into the unlocked Lakeview Players Community Theatre. Wandering into the theater from the lobby, she saw a man with a ponytail working on a set on the stage, wood, power tools, and sawdust all around.

"Hello!" Emma cried.

"What?" screeched the man. "What do you want? Auditions are closed! We cast the play last week!"

"No, no, I'm not here to try out."

He puffed himself up. "Oh! And why not? Who wouldn't want to be in *my* play?"

Emma looked around to see if there was anyone else to deal with other than this lunatic. "I'm Emma Katz. I was referred to you by Susan Vernon to help with the set."

He clapped his meaty little hands. "Ah, a volunteer! Wonderful! I am Reginald de Courcy, the director of the play *Guest in the House*."

That couldn't be his real name. "Oh. Did you write it?"

"Err…no, it was written by Hagar Wilde and Dale Eunson. But the staging is all original! My own creation!"

"I've had some experience in set design with Tulane Summer Lyric."

"Excellent! As you see, we've begun on my set. Would you like to see the sketches?"

"Certainly." Emma made her way to the stage. Meanwhile, de Courcy flounced his way to his notebook. He had a page opened by the time she got there and spent the next few minutes going over his elaborate plans.

Emma took it all in with good grace. She had dealt with amateur director wannabes in community theater before and learned to let their egos roll off her back. She needed a reason to get out of the house. Getting back in set design ought to do it.

At least here, people will appreciate what I do.

Just then, the front door opened again. "Ah, Frank!" cried de Courcy. "You're late, as usual!"

A good-looking man in a shirt and tie walked down the aisle. "Sorry, Reggie, but I do have a job. I see we got a visitor."

"Yes! This is our new set designer, Emma Katz."

Set designer? How did that happen? thought Emma.

The director pointed at the newcomer. "This naughty fellow plays Dan Proctor in the play and has volunteered to help with the construction of the set."

"That's me, an all-around fellow." He stepped on the stage and crossed to Emma. "Since our director has neglected to do it, let me introduce myself. I'm Frank Church."

HURRICANE IVAN PASSED OVER GRENADA ON SEPTEMBER 7, battering several of the Windward Islands as it entered the Caribbean Sea. It rapidly intensified and became a Category 5 hurricane north of Aruba on September 9. The monstrous storm weakened slightly as it moved west-northwest towards Jamaica.

Chapter 4

The last major hurricane to strike the city of New Orleans was a slow-moving killer named Betsy. The Category 3 storm ran up the east coast of Florida in September of 1965 where it executed a perfect 270-degree loop, crossed over the Florida Keys, reenergized in the Gulf of Mexico, and crawled up Bayou Lafourche during the night of September 9.

The wet, powerful monster took eight hours to crawl inland, spawning countless tornados and dumping torrents of rain. While Betsy's forty-mile-wide eye passed west of New Orleans, the city was in the powerful northeast quadrant, the worst sector of any storm. The Mississippi River rose ten feet. The storm surge overpowered the levees of Lake Pontchartrain, the Mississippi River Gulf Outlet, and the Industrial Canal. Gentilly, the Upper and the Lower Ninth Wards, and the communities of Arabi and Chalmette in neighboring St. Bernard Parish went underwater. Some people drowned in their attics trying to escape.

In all, 164,000 homes were flooded and seventy-six people lost their lives. Adjusted for inflation, the economic cost was between ten and twelve billion dollars.

It was ten days or more before the water level in New Orleans dropped sufficiently for people to return to their homes. Weeks would pass before power and running water could be restored in the neighboring parishes of Lafourche, St. Mary, and Terrebonne. It took even longer than that to repair flooded houses in Orleans,

St. Bernard, and Plaquemines.

The federal government was concerned, and President Lyndon B. Johnson took time away from running the Vietnam War to fly down to see the damage. LBJ and the Congress pledged it would never happen again. The US Army Corps of Engineers would not only repair the levees, but build newer, better ones, guaranteed to withstand a Category 3 storm.

It was easy for the Congress to make promises. Funding those promises was another matter. Priorities always changed, elections had to be won, and the Corps never received enough appropriations to do the job in the next four decades, from either Democrats or Republicans. By 2004, a major part of the project, the levees of southern Jefferson Parish, the soft underbelly of the metro region, had not been constructed.

In the thirty-nine years since Betsy, there were near misses, notably 1969's Camille and 1992's Andrew. Much weaker storms would occasionally roll in. The citizens of the Crescent City, like most in the Gulf region, accepted the storms as a part of life, the price one paid for living in paradise. The people weren't stupid or foolhardy. They all knew, just like the citizens of San Francisco knew, the "Big One" would hit. It was only a matter of time.

But neither earthquakes nor hurricanes would dispel the human spirit. The Louisianans went on with their lives with one eye always on the Gulf.

Sunday, September 12: Metairie

Elizabeth Boudreaux turned off the six o'clock news and called her boss. "Carl, I really don't like that Ivan out there. If it's okay with you, I'd like to take off tomorrow."

"Where're you going?"

"Chackbay with my family. It's high ground there. Is that okay?"

"Tell you what. You go on. If the mayor calls for an evacuation tomorrow, I'll send everybody home. Otherwise, we'll count it as a vacation day. How's that?"

"Carl, you're the best!"

"Drive safe, Lizzy."

An hour later, her bag packed and her refrigerator empty, Elizabeth pulled out of her Metairie apartment to make the ninety-minute drive to Chackbay.

Monday, September 13: Downtown

IT COULD NOT BE SAID MONDAYS WERE CHUCK BINGLEY'S FAVORITE day of the week. He much preferred Fridays, for that meant he would be spending the next two full days with wife, Jane, two-year-old daughter, Hailey, baby son, Brett, and dog, Rufus. He knew his contemporaries considered him a homebody. He only smiled and nodded. He had an angel at home.

But this Monday was worse than most. There was a big storm in the Gulf, the forecasters were going nuts warning everybody "Ivan the Terrible" could be there in two days, and Chuck's ass of a manager insisted on the regular 9:30 a.m. meeting with his lenders.

At least traffic on the Causeway was light. Other people's bosses weren't insane.

In record time, Chuck pulled into his reserved space in the Gallic National Bank's parking garage. The number of cars was low for a Monday, which only further aggravated him. The garage elevator took him to the bank's lobby, and Chuck was surprised to see all the tellers were in place. Sure, evacuees would need cash, but GNB spent a fortune on ATM machines. Why risk people's lives? It didn't make sense.

Minutes later, Chuck was behind his desk, coffee on the credenza, polishing his weekly report. After killing twenty minutes, he wandered back to the break room and discussed Ivan with a couple of the other lenders. At 9:20, they began to congregate in one of the bank's meeting rooms.

The bottom of the hour came and went. Most of the chairs were filled as the commercial lending team awaited their leader. Ten minutes later, the manager's secretary walked in.

"Hey, where's Manwaring?"

The embarrassed secretary looked at her papers. "He called. He won't be coming in today."

The room exploded.

"But," she continued, trying to restore order, "he wanted the quarter-to-date figures to be reviewed, and I have them right here."

More protests ensued. "The mayor's supposed to have a press conference at ten to talk about evacuation, and we're sitting around here talking numbers?" one lender cried.

"This is bullshit!"

Chuck spoke up. "Hey, everybody, it isn't her fault. Let's just get this over with so we can hear the press conference."

There was grumbling, but the work was quickly done.

IT WAS ESTIMATED THAT IN 2004 THERE WERE ONE MILLION PEOPLE living in the four-parish area of Orleans, Jefferson, St. Bernard, and Plaquemines. The question always was how to evacuate that many people with only four ways out.

In 1998, the near miss of Hurricane Fredrick showed the evacuation routes were inadequate. The solution was to re-direct traffic onto the opposite lanes of the Interstate. That way, the arteries could handle twice the traffic. The plan was called Contraflow.

Contraflow was not easy to implement. One problem was how to re-direct traffic. Having cars go the wrong-way up the exit ramps was impractical. Instead, millions were spent making special crossover lanes on the interstates, blocking them with removable barricades. This took time.

There was also the problem of clearing traffic from the incoming lanes. State police and other law enforcement personnel would have to physically block all entrances to the interstates and clear the traffic before the barricades at the cross-over lanes were removed.

The Louisiana State Police hated Contraflow. Not only did it consume an enormous amount of manpower, they pointed out the difficulty in responding to an emergency on the interstates, especially on the elevated portions. Their concerns were noted, but the engineers observed that the shoulders were available, and Contraflow would only remain in effect for a limited period during the height of the evacuation. Risks would have to be taken.

The concept of Contraflow was very popular with the citizens, so the politicians placed the highest priority on the project. The last part was completed just before the 2004 hurricane season.

Contraflow had never been used. Everyone expected some bugs, but the idea was so simple, what could go wrong?

Ivan was the first test.

Downtown

At the EDNO offices, every eye was on the TV set in the boardroom. The mayor's press conference got going at 10:30, delayed by the governor. He announced a voluntary evacuation of the city at 6:00 p.m., in accordance with the existing regional evacuation plan. Coastal areas such as Grand Isle, Lafitte, and lower Plaquemines would get a head start; those communities were closer to the Gulf and more prone to high water cutting off escape routes. St. Bernard and the rest of Plaquemines would be next, as well as low-lying areas in New Orleans East. Finally, Orleans and Jefferson would evacuate.

Carl Eden turned to his troops. "Get home," he told them, "and those of you that are getting out, get packing. Make sure we've got your cell numbers in case we need to get in touch with you."

Everyone dashed back to their desks except Kaywanda Johnson, who went to talk to Jan Hill.

"What's up, Kay?"

"You know how my momma is. She won't wanna leave. What'll I do? I can't leave her." The unmarried Kaywanda lived in Gentilly with her divorced mother.

"Oh, babygirl, you sure you can't talk her into it?" Jan had taken the younger woman under her wing as if they were related.

"Oh, no. She lived through Betsy, an' she thinks nothin' could be worse than that."

Jan thought. "The mayor said the Dome will be available."

"But he said it was for special needs. Momma ain't no cripple." When she got stressed, Kaywanda's speech and vocabulary reverted back to the neighborhood slang she worked so hard to suppress in the office.

"Look, Kay, if that storm hits and there's no power, they won't turn you away. They'll have AC, food, and water. You take her there if you lose your lights."

"You leaving?"

"My husband's got people in Donaldsonville."

"Okay. I better get home to Momma."

"You take care, babygirl."

Lafayette

MARIANNE'S FIRM HAD SENT RECORDED PHONE MESSAGES TO STAFF, advising them not to report for work, and Chris was not needed at the hospital, so the two left town at six to drive to Lafayette in Chris's Envoy. Chris crossed the Mississippi River on the Huey P. Long Bridge and made good time on US-90 until he got to Lafourche Parish. The evacuation from Grand Isle and lower Lafourche was in full force and only got heaver as they crawled into Terrebonne Parish. There was nothing they could do about it because they had to cross the Atchafalaya River at Morgan City, so the two relaxed in the SUV and sang show tunes to while away the time.

Once they crossed the state's second largest river, Chris escaped the mind-numbing traffic by jumping off US-90. He made up time going cross-country, using his knowledge of local roads to work his way to the Breaux homestead south of Lafayette. They got there a little after eleven.

Mrs. Breaux greeted the two refugees with hugs and kisses. "Oh, bless me! I've been so worried about you two! Did you have anything to eat? You must be hungry. Now, Mari, you just sit yourself down right there while I fix you both a nice sandwich. Ham and cheese all right?"

Chris grinned as he kissed his mother's cheek. "I'll just get our bags out of the truck, Mom."

"May I help, Mrs. Breaux?" asked Marianne.

"Why, certainly, dear. The bread's in the pantry right over there."

"No mayo on mine, Mom," came a voice from the den.

Chris stopped on his way out of the room. "Mike isn't working today?" he asked in a low voice.

Mrs. Breaux's face colored. "He was laid off."

"Again?" Chris whispered.

She shrugged her shoulders resignedly before she turned her attention to the refrigerator.

Marianne placed a loaf of bread on the counter and sat at the kitchen table. Mike Breaux, Chris's younger brother, wandered in barefoot, a dirty ZZ Top T-shirt worn un-tucked over his jeans.

"Hey, Mom, grab me a beer outta the icebox while you're there, will ya? Woo-hoo, Mari, you're lookin' goo–ood!" It was obvious Mike hadn't been awake long.

Marianne was in a T-shirt and shorts, she wore no make-up, and her hair was pulled into a ponytail. "Thank you."

Chris returned with their suitcases as Mike opened the Bud his mother had placed on the counter. "Hey ya, Chris. I see ya got away from the city okay."

"Yeah, it took us a while, but we made it." Chris left the luggage in a corner and joined Marianne. She took his hand in hers.

Mike grinned at Marianne. "Why you wastin' your time with a stick in th' mud like my brother, huh?"

She smiled sweetly. "Just lucky, I guess."

"I see y'all both got it bad. I only hope it lasts. It don't, ya know. I oughta know." He took a long pull on his beer.

Chris had a neutral expression. "Where's Jimmy?"

Mike belched lightly. "With his momma."

"And where are they?"

"Margie's got herself a boyfriend. She said they were gonna stay with his people up in Opelousas."

"They're safe, then."

"I guess so. Hell, the judge gave her custody—that's her job. That an' spendin' my money." He took another drink of beer. "Ya think if she marries again, the judge'll reduce my child support?"

"Here's your sandwich, Mike," his mother said in a clipped tone.

"Thanks," he mumbled as he took a bite and wandered back into the den with his lunch and drink. Meanwhile the couple shared their meal in the kitchen, talking about the evacuation with Mrs. Breaux.

After lunch, Chris moved the luggage into his old bedroom. "There should be some empty drawers for you to use," he told Marianne.

She closed the door. "What's up with your brother?"

Chris sat on the bed. "Since Margie divorced Mike two years ago, he fell apart. I don't blame Margie at all. I love my brother, but he was a lousy husband. He's only gotten worse. He's drinking more, lost the job he had when he was married, and two more besides. He can't afford to live anywhere else, so he moved back home. My parents know he's a mess, but they just can't throw him out on the street."

"Can't you talk to him?"

"I can't, sweetheart. I'm too close. I've suggested counseling, but he rejects it."

"What's that about your nephew, Jimmy? Mike was awful!"

Chris rubbed his head. "Yeah. To be honest, we were relived Margie won full custody. She and Momma love each other, despite the divorce, and she brings Jimmy around every chance she gets as long as Mike isn't in the house."

"I can't imagine what that does to your parents."

"They're conflicted, to say the least, but they've made up their minds to love all the people involved, no matter what. That's the price they're paying to keep a relationship with their only grandchild. They're not stupid, though. Mike buys his own beer."

He sighed. "I'm the one who's lost touch with Jimmy. It was hard enough to play uncle from New Orleans. With a divorce thrown in, it's nearly impossible."

She joined him on the bed and gave him a hug. "My poor baby." They shared a kiss. "Chris, I feel bad about kicking you out of your room."

"It's okay. I'll manage on the couch."

She toyed with his shirt. "I was thinking...you don't have to."

"What, have *you* sleep on the couch? No way!"

Marianne did not like his joke. "You know what I mean!"

"In my incredibly Catholic parents' house?"

Mortified, Marianne responded, "We don't have to do it. We could just share the bed, or you could sleep on the floor. I just want to be close to you."

Chris gave his love a long, sweet kiss. "Oh, my Marianne. The sweetest, loveliest girl in the world."

"Chris, don't you want to—you know, *be* with me?"

"Don't tempt me, babe," he whispered as he looked deep into her eyes. "If you knew how very much I want to be with you—my good God! Believe me, I want you *very* much. Marianne, I love you, but I want our first time to be as special as you are. And it won't be if we're trying to be quiet in my mamma's house."

Marianne almost demanded to know just when he figured the time would be right, but she demurred. "All right, Chris. But I'll hold you to that." She kissed him lightly. "Now, let me put my things away, okay?"

"All right," he grinned as he left for the den.

But Marianne did not start to unpack. She was tired of waiting, but she had to admit Chris was right: the Breauxs' house was not the right place or the right time. But she had plenty of opportunities back in New Orleans. A seduction needed to be planned. If a Cajun man wasn't going to get off the stick, it was time to see what a Mississippi girl could do.

It has to be something good. I'm not letting him get away.

Downtown

AFTER THE MEETING AND PRESS CONFERENCE, THERE WAS NO AN-nouncement from the Gallic management until a terse email came in at 11:30.

```
All non-essential personnel are dismissed. Tellers
and operations personnel shall leave after their
shift is over.

                                  — GNB Management
```

It took Chuck ten minutes to shut down his computer and gather his papers. As he was walking to the elevators, he came across the VP of Operations, Ted Bennett.

"Hey, Chuck. Getting out of here?"

"Yeah. It took the guys upstairs long enough to dismiss us."

Bennett looked around. "Just between you and me, the CEO's really pissed with Manwaring calling you guys in and then not showing up himself. I don't think he knew y'all were here until a half-hour ago."

"When are you leaving?"

The older man rubbed his neck. "Not until my people go home and everything on the computers is backed up to the reserve servers in Dallas. Maybe nine tonight if I'm lucky."

"You getting out?"

"My wife is packing right now."

The elevator doors opened. "All right, take it easy, Ted."

"You too."

Chuck dodged the vehicles leaving the structure as he hurried to his car. He switched on the local all-news station and pulled out. Knowing most people would use I-10 to get out of the city, he made for Tulane Avenue.

Sure enough, the radio station verified the Interstate was gridlocked. Chuck made great time, and he estimated he would hit traffic around the Causeway Boulevard interchange.

Just after Tulane Avenue became Airline Drive around the Jefferson Parish line, Chuck realized his easy ride was over. All four lanes of Airline were at a standstill. Before he knew it, his Camry was trapped as other cars sandwiched him in.

Chuck looked around in confusion. Hundreds of taillights stretched before him, but there was nothing on the radio about Airline. The announcers were talking about the horrible conditions on the Interstate and the Westbank Expressway.

The station has airborne traffic spotters. Are they blind? Can't they see this? What the hell's going on?

Just then the news broke. "We're getting reports that the situation on the surface roads—Airline, Jefferson, and River Road—is just as congested as on the Interstate. All we can say, folks, is to keep your cool, stay in your lanes, and let this work itself out. Contraflow is scheduled to go into effect at six p.m. Our producer is trying to get through to the state police to see if there are any plans to move the schedule up."

Chuck flipped open his cell phone and tried to call Jane. Nothing. *No signal? What the hell?*

He noticed the driver in the car next to him had a cell phone to her ear. Everyone else was trying to make calls, and that overloaded the network. He steeled himself to wait a minute and try again. This time he got through.

"Hey, honey, it's me."

"Where are you?"

"Stuck on Airline about two miles from Causeway Boulevard."

"I've been watching the coverage. The traffic is awful."

"Tell me about it. Where are you?"

"Home. The clinic let us out early. I got the kids from day care."

"Is the traffic bad up there?"

"Terrible. How long do you think you'll be?"

Chuck considered. Traffic was crawling at a stop-and-go pace of about five miles an hour. He thought it ought to clear up on the bridge. "A long time—maybe four hours. Let's see, it's noon now. Look for me about four."

"Okay, honey, drive safe. You got anything to eat?"

"No, but I'll be okay. Love you." Chuck switched off his phone and tried to settle in for the battle ahead.

Lakeview

"George," Emma barked on the cordless phone, "I need you at home!"

"I can't. We're in the middle of preparations here at the hospital. They need me."

"But I need you too!"

"What's wrong?"

"It's Papa. He won't evacuate."

"What? I thought we settled that at breakfast. You and Abe are supposed to pull out of here. I've got the reservation in Lafayette all set—"

"Here! You talk to him!" Emma shoved the phone at her father. "Umm…Abe?"

"You might as well save your breath, George. I'm not going."

"Look, this storm's a bad one. It's a Cat 4, at least."

"Don't matter. I'm an architect. I *know* we've got nothing to worry about. Have you *really* looked at the levees on the lakefront and river? Fifteen feet high! Thousands of tons of earth and materials. Nothing this side of an atom bomb is getting through there!"

"Abe, you're not a structural engineer."

"Look, you're a doctor. Would I second-guess a diagnosis from you? I know what I'm talking about. Besides, that isn't all. There hasn't been a major strike against a big US city since forever. I'm telling you, the heat sink around big cities push those damn things away. Remember Andrew? Missed Miami. This year, Charley was headin' right at Tampa when it turned at the last minute. I'm safer here in my La-Z-Boy than in some motel in the country."

"What about losing power? Let's say you're right, and Ivan goes into Mississippi. We could still have the lights go out."

"What about it? It'll be back in three days or so. Be like camping out."

There was a pause. "Abe, please put Emma back on."

Emma took the phone and walked back to the kitchen. "Well?"

"Has he been like this all day?"

"Since the mayor's press conference. He's been watching the coverage, and all the reports of the traffic jams got him stirred up. I think the thought of sitting in traffic is the real problem. What are we going to do?"

"Emma, I can't leave right now—"

"George!"

"Wait! I might be able to get away for a little while later—say around seven. Let him calm down, and we'll talk some more on what's to be done, after the next storm advisory."

"All right."

"Hang in there, babe. I know it's hard."

"It never ends. Please hurry home."

"I will. Oops, they're calling for me. I've got to go! Love ya."

"I love you too," Emma said to the dial tone.

Meanwhile, Abe was still holding court from his recliner. "I'm telling you, princess, that storm's not coming here. Bet you a thousand dollars—right now."

Emma, tired from arguing, just walked to her bedroom.

Chackbay

ELIZABETH LET HERSELF OUT OF THE BACK DOOR OF HER PARENTS' house and watched as her father, dressed in stained oil field coveralls, finished preparing the place for a storm. All the loose things about the house—anything that could become a missile in hurricane-force winds: water hoses, lawn furniture, tomato cages, and garden gnomes—had been put away in the garage. Everything else too heavy to carry was placed on its side. The only thing left to do was secure the swing set in the backyard, the very one her father had built out of used oil field pipe for her and her sisters so many years ago.

She'd help, but her father would only shoo her back into the house. This was man's work, he'd say. Twenty-one years of living with him taught Elizabeth there was no arguing with T.B. Boudreaux.

Elizabeth looked up at the sky as she walked the yard. The house was just off Highway 20, and the traffic was steady. It was such a normal, warm September day. There was very little wind and hardly a cloud in the sky. Only a few cirrus clouds competed with the odd jet contrail. Nothing that hinted that Death was churning in the Gulf.

It was always that way before a storm. Lovely, sunny days that gave no clue what was coming. Eventually, the wind would freshen, and low clouds would dash across the sky in an unusual manner. Was that how her ancestors knew a storm was approaching? Was that very few hours the only warning they would get in the days before radio and television and satellites?

Elizabeth's musings were interrupted by a large pick-up truck turning off the highway into the drive to the house. She waved as she moved towards the dual-wheeled behemoth and saw two people get out: a slim girl with glasses and a giant with a ball cap over his shaved head.

Elizabeth called to her sister and her sister's boyfriend.

"Is Kit inside?" Mary asked as she hugged her.

"Yeah, she's online last time I saw her."

"Figures. She wanted to show me a website—some fan fiction place. I'll go get that over with, and we'll talk later."

Elizabeth turned to the massive man next to her sister. That the six-foot six-inch, two hundred fifty-pound Adam "Bubba" Teresina was a high school football coach surprised no one. What turned people's heads was that he was also the biology teacher at E.D. White Catholic High, where both he and Mary taught. The massive Bubba was really a teddy bear firmly wrapped around Mary Boudreaux's finger.

"Just in time to help Daddy lower the swing set, Bubba," Elizabeth grinned.

Bubba eyed the contraption. "Oo-wee, that looks heavy. He made it himself?"

"Mmm-hmm. Everything all set at your folks' place?"

"Yeah, we just came from there. They canceled school this morning. Well"—he rubbed his hands together—"might as well get it over with. Hey, T.B.! You ready to tackle that thing?" Elizabeth's father, waved his agreement, and the two men moved towards the massive apparatus.

I think Momma's more anxious for a proposal than Mary, Elizabeth recalled, knowing the two were waiting until their paychecks were large enough to think of marrying and getting a house. *I hope it happens soon. Momma will get off my back for a while.*

She stopped. She wasn't being fair to Fanny Boudreaux. Her mother hadn't bugged her about being unmarried for a while. Not since Lydia.

Oh, Lydia—where are you?

Chapter 5

In 1969, the Swiss-born psychiatrist Elisabeth Kübler-Ross identified the five stages of receiving catastrophic news: denial, anger, bargaining, depression, and acceptance.

Many incorrectly assumed the stages only referred to how people dealt with the approach of their own demise. A reasonable error as the book in which they first appeared was entitled *On Death and Dying*. Dr. Kübler-Ross stated that those stages could be felt for grief of any kind.

The good doctor died in August of 2004 at her home in Scottsdale, Arizona. One wonders whether, if she had been alive in September, she would have extended her theory to hurricane evacuations because, by three o'clock in the afternoon, Chuck Bingley was going insane.

In a little over three hours, he had not driven four miles. In the worst stop-and-go traffic he had ever seen, he had made the two miles to Causeway Boulevard. Now he wasn't even at the intersection with I-10, and there was still over a mile to go before the bridge. He had no illusions as to what awaited him there. Assuming five miles per hour, it would take him almost five hours to cross the 24-mile long Causeway. Surely, traffic would be worse on the North Shore.

There were only two good pieces of news. He had filled up his gas tank the night before, so he had plenty of fuel. And his bladder wasn't giving him any trouble yet.

What he could not understand was why the traffic was so bad. He could just make out the Interstate. Three lanes of traffic going west were at a near-standstill while almost no cars at all headed east. He just knew some of the traffic heading for the Causeway was trying to avoid the I-10.

What the hell are they waiting for? Start the Contraflow!

Baton Rouge

A KEY PART OF THE CONTRAFLOW PLAN WAS THAT IT COULD ONLY be initiated by the governor. That was not seen as an obstacle; what governor wouldn't use Contraflow as soon as possible?

No one counted on Louisiana having a governor as indecisive as Big Momma.

Above all things, the governor hated making a wrong decision, especially one that could be placed solely on her doorstep. Her personality demanded she receive nauseating amounts of advice and counsel until she achieved a consensus. Only then would she move forward. If successful, she could take credit for leading the process. If the plan failed, she could point to bad advice.

The governor's main advisor for traffic issues was the head of the state police, who personally and instinctively hated Contraflow. He wanted to hold firm on the 6:00 p.m. commencement. With him as back up, the governor was able to withstand for hours the demands from the elected officials to speed up activation. Contraflow would become effective at six as planned.

The governor might be able to ignore the telephone calls she wasn't taking, but she and her political advisors couldn't ignore the pounding she was receiving in the media. Talk radio was having a field day. The bad publicity proved too much.

Finally, at 3:00 p.m., the state police commander announced Contraflow would commence in an hour. The orders went out and law enforcement officials across the region began closing ramps and clearing traffic off eastbound I-10 and I-12 and southbound I-55.

At just before 4:00 p.m., the crossover lanes were opened to traffic for the first time.

Metairie

By then, Chuck Bingley was working his way from depression to acceptance as he waited at the intersection of Causeway Boulevard and West Esplanade. For the last thirty minutes, Chuck idly wondered how many of the cars would still be evacuating across the Causeway when Ivan hit the area in two days. How would a car react to 100-plus mile-per-hour winds, anyway? Could a Camry hold up, or would he be blown into the lake?

A lone Jefferson Parish deputy was handling traffic control, allowing cars from the major cross street to turn onto Causeway, to either go north across the lake or to enter I-10 to head west. Chuck had been there at the head of the line for about a half-hour, watching the harassed deputy do his job. Of course, just because a lane of traffic had the right-of-way didn't mean it could move. The traffic was still crawling at a snail's pace, if at all.

You know, things could be worse. I could have his job.

By 4:30, the wheels of Chuck Bingley's car finally made contact with the concrete roadbed of the Lake Pontchartrain Causeway.

Eight miles down—thirty miles to go.

Warehouse District

William Darcy sat at his desk in the practically deserted offices of DGS. All operational controls had been handed off to the company's branch office in Houston. Except for William and a handful of computer operators, everyone had been sent home. Data from the DGS computers was being backed-up and transmitted to two locations: the European office in London and a contracted facility in Utah. The DGS jet was on its way to Dallas to ride out the storm. William was waiting for traffic to lighten up so he and the two ice chests of stuff from his refrigerator could make the run to Dansereau Plantation in something under four hours.

Dansereau Plantation House was a great place to ride out a hurricane. Not only was it on some of the highest ground in St. Charles Parish and built like a bunker, it had a natural gas electric generator attached to the main electrical circuit, set to kick on at the first interruption of power. It would run the whole house, AC and satellite TV included. As long as there was natural gas, he would live quite normally. Only a direct strike by a tornado would ruin his day.

William had a sense of *déjà vu* as he scanned the latest meteorological data from the company's contracted weather forecasters on his computer screen. The last time he had done this was back in 1998 as he looked over his father's shoulder at Hurricane Mitch.

The models were grim. Hurricane Ivan was a strong Category 4 and was expected to intensify as it got away from the mountains of Cuba and entered the warm waters of the Gulf. The cone of probability had New Orleans on the western side of its projected track.

The weird thing was Ivan wasn't behaving as forecasted. The weather gurus kept saying it was going to run due north, or even north-northwest, and make landfall somewhere between New Orleans and Mobile. But the damn thing wouldn't turn left. If anything, it kept cheating to the right—eastward. *Might it go into Florida? Could those poor bastards get hit yet again?*

William rubbed his eyes. Conjecture was a waste of time. His duty was to prepare his company for the potential of a strike from a major hurricane. Had he done everything he could? Had he protected his people?

William had to do *something*. He got up and left his office to check on the progress of the computer guys.

Covington

Chuck made better time on the Causeway. His Camry was rolling above the placid waters of Lake Pontchartrain at the breathtaking rate of ten miles an hour. Things slowed considerably once he reached the North Shore, but progress was made. He pulled into his driveway just as his watch hands moved towards seven o'clock. The family rushed out to greet him with kisses, baby Brett in Jane's arms.

Chuck wearily picked up his daughter, Hailey, who immediately put her father's neck in a death grip. "Jesus H. Christ—that was the worst seven hours of my life!"

"Chuck, the children."

"Sorry, babe. I am *so* glad to be home." The little family walked into the house, where the master was set upon by the remaining member.

"Rufus! Rufus, how's my big boy?" Chuck said in a singsong voice to the six-month-old grey Great Dane in his den. The puppy was all legs and tail, his big cheerful face at Chuck's waist level.

"No, no! No jump!"

It was a lost cause. To Hailey's screaming delight, Rufus placed his front paws on Chuck's shoulders and gave his face a thorough tongue bath. Jane admonished the dog while unsuccessfully suppressing her laughter. Soon the entire party was on the couch, except for Rufus, who took his station at Chuck's feet.

Chuck took Jane's hand. "Have I told you I'm glad to be home?"

Lakeview

Abe Weinberg was very satisfied with himself. "I told you it wasn't coming here. I told you."

George tried to reason with him. "Abe, the weatherman didn't say that. We're still under a Hurricane Warning." He was not a happy camper. His head was pounding, and his stomach was in knots.

"It could still hit us, Papa," Emma chimed in.

He shook his head stubbornly. "Ivan hasn't changed direction all day. Look at the track. It's heading right for Pensacola. We're perfectly safe here."

George lost his temper. "That damn thing's almost a Cat 5! Remember Hurricane Camille? That thing will kill us if it hits here!"

"I damn well remember Camille, and *it* didn't hit us, either! I'm not leaving!" Abe scowled. "I told you. You want to leave, go on. Nothing's stopping you. But I'm staying here. You just go without me."

"We can't just leave you!" Emma pleaded.

"Why not? I can take care of myself! I've been doing that for almost seventy years! I don't need a daughter of mine to baby-sit me!"

"Papa, your heart!"

"Nothing's wrong with my heart."

"Bullshit! You've had a triple by-pass!" George barked.

Abe crossed his arms, resembling a stubborn child. "I'm not leaving, and that's final!"

George threw up his arms. "Oh, screw it! Go on and stay here! Go ahead and die! But you're not going to kill my wife too! Emma, you're leaving!"

Emma was shocked speechless. It was the first time her soft-spoken husband had raised his voice. George's wide-eyed anger faded, and covering his face with his hands, he mumbled, "Emma, I'm sorry. I'm sorry for yelling."

"I can't leave Papa—you know that."

"Okay, this is what we'll do. We'll monitor the storm tonight, and if it looks like it's moving this way, you BOTH leave at sunup, all right?"

Emma sighed. "All right. Papa?"

Abe was still pouting. "You're going to stop yelling at me?"

"Papa—"

"All right, all right!"

"Good," George breathed. "I've got to get back to the hospital. Em, please keep your bags packed. And Abe, I'm going to monitor the reports from the break room. If that thing's coming here, and we say go, and you keep giving Emma shit, I will come back here and…" He took a breath. "I'll throw you into the car myself. We clear on that?"

After Abe nodded, George gave Emma a peck on the cheek and stormed out of the house. Emma dashed after him and caught up as he was getting to his car. George looked past his wife at the house. "That son-of-a-bitch! He absolutely drives me crazy sometimes!"

Emma's intention was to thank George for his help and the compromise, but her husband's tone offended her. "Well, now you know what I have to put up with all day."

"Emma, he's your father! Can't you do *something* with him?"

"What do you think I've been trying to do?"

"I don't know. Can't you get Irene to take him?"

"Are you saying you want to throw my father out of the house?"

George struggled with his voice. "No," he managed, "but it would be nice to have my own house with my own wife without somebody else telling me how to run it!"

"George!"

"I better go before I say something I'll regret." He climbed into the car and shut the door. Just as he put the car in reverse, he slammed it back into park and lowered the window. "Em! Em, I'm sorry."

She leaned in, and they shared a quick kiss.

"I'll be on the cell," he said. "Call me, okay?"

"Okay." Her eyes started to water. "I'll talk to you in the morning. Love you."

"Yeah. We'll see what happens tonight. Bye." He backed out of the driveway and drove down the street.

Emma slowly walked back into the house. Abe was still in his recliner, but his eyes were on her, rather than the TV. "George left?"

Emma nodded woodenly.

"Princess, it'll be all right. You'll see. That storm won't come anywhere around here."

Emma just nodded again and walked to her bedroom.

Ivan weakened by battering the Jamaican coast for hours. The tempest resumed a more northerly track, and regained Category 5 strength as it passed through the Yucatán Channel late on September 13. Twelve thousand residents and tourists were evacuated from Isla Mujeres off Mexico's Yucatan. Once over the Gulf of Mexico, it weakened slightly to Category 4 strength and approached the Gulf Coast.

Chapter 6

Hurricane Ivan made no change in its track overnight, and when Tuesday dawned, it was still moving relentlessly north. While Louisiana and Mississippi sighed in relief, the exodus out of the Florida panhandle and southern Alabama continued throughout the day.

The storm remained a powerful Cat 4, and the computer forecasts still showed it could turn west, so the forecasters maintained the warnings all the way to New Orleans. As the hours passed, however, there was no change in the track. The frustrated experts could not explain why the models showed a westward bias.

Wednesday, September 15:
I-10 outside of Baton Rouge

BY WEDNESDAY, WITH THE CERTAINTY THAT THE MONSTER WAS targeting the Alabama/Florida line, the warning for the Crescent City was lifted, Contraflow was discontinued, and the people who had fled began to return. Thousands from the expected strike zone were still evacuating, so the New Orleanians were driving against traffic. Chris found Marianne to be unusually quiet on the trip back, and he wondered why.

"Hey," she broke the silence as they left the snarl of traffic in Baton Rouge behind them, "are you busy on Saturday night?"

"No. Aren't you singing at Le Chat Noir?"

"Yeah, we got a gig there. Are you coming?"

"Sure, I'm coming. Don't I come to most of your gigs?"

"Yes, you do. And I want to thank you."

Chris smiled. "You're welcome, *chere*, but you know I wouldn't miss it."

Marianne was quiet for a time. "Chris, would you do me a favor? Dress up nice on Saturday night. Your black suit—you know, the one I like."

He glanced over at her. "Is this a special occasion?"

She smiled sweetly at him. "Do you need a special occasion to dress up for me, sugar?"

He narrowed his eyes. "You're up to something."

She turned away. "Okay, fine. Don't dress up."

"All right, all right, I'll do it. Don't get mad."

She turned to him again, her smile as sunny as the day outside. "Thank you, Chris. You're so sweet."

Chris still thought he was being played, but he saw no profit in challenging her. Instead, he watched the low clouds streaming by. "Those clouds are really booking it."

"Yeah," she agreed. "Seeing that always scares me. To think the storm is throwing off those clouds from hundreds of miles away."

He watched closely. "Moving in from the north—that's good. As long as it doesn't shift to the east, we'll be fine."

"Unlike those poor people in Florida. Is God mad at them or something?"

He glanced at the stream of cars in the westbound lanes, most of them with Florida plates. "Don't know. Guess it's their turn this year."

JUST BEFORE IT MADE LANDFALL EARLY IN THE MORNING ON THE sixteenth, Ivan the Terrible had yet another surprise for the meteorologists. Its eye wall weakened considerably, and the southwestern portion of the storm fell apart. Now a strong Category 3 storm, it rumbled ashore near Gulf Shores, Alabama, at about 3:00 a.m. with top winds of 130 miles an hour and a storm surge of ten to fifteen feet. But the brunt of the storm surge hit Florida's Panhandle, east of the eye. In Pensacola, Ivan toppled giant oaks that had weathered hurricanes for decades and took a bite out of the famous beaches. More than a million residents from Florida to Louisiana lost power.

The people of New Orleans breathed a sigh of relief, knowing they had dodged yet another disaster, as only Plaquemines and St. Bernard Parishes suffered a moderate amount of wind damage. They had no idea how great a calamity missed them until the sun rose that morning.

Thursday, September 16: Pensacola, Florida

IT WAS MID-DAY BEFORE LT. COMMANDER FREDRICK WENTWORTH could launch his US Coast Guard helicopter. Call-sign Cajun 101's mission: Hurricane Ivan damage assessment. The winds were still dicey, but Wentworth was one of the best. He didn't join the USCG to fly a desk.

Freddy Wentworth was New Orleans born and bred, a star on the Warren Easton High football team. His grades earned him an appointment to the Coast Guard Academy. Accepted for flight training, Wentworth was determined to finish at the top of his class. Thanks to hard work, smarts, and dedication, he rocketed up the ranks. He was one of the youngest men to command a squadron, and it wasn't because of his skin color.

Wentworth expertly piloted the orange HH-65C Aerospatiale Dolphin through the low, gray skies. Other Coast Guard pilots preferred the much larger HH-60J JayHawk version of the Sikorsky BlackHawk, but Wentworth thought the bigger chopper felt like a bus. The Dolphin was faster and had more range, especially with the new engine. He could drive rings around those JayHawks and still get the job done. The interdiction boys were flying the armed MH-68A Stingray, but Wentworth didn't need guns to do search-and-rescue.

The rain had ceased, but the winds were still gusty. Turbulent was hardly an adequate word for this flight; they were trussed up in a sack with rocks and run through a clothes dryer. His right-seater, LTJG Jeremy Price, called out the damage. "Man, Orange Beach looks bad. A Cat 3 did all this?"

This wasn't Wentworth's first rodeo. "It's worse at Perdido Key according to the navy. Call it in."

"You think the Flora-Bama made it through?" Price asked as he keyed the microphone.

"Be nice if it did," Wentworth allowed though he didn't hold out much hope for the famous watering hole at the Florida/Alabama line.

In the back, PO3 Donald Lauck had his binoculars trained on the other side of the aircraft. His was the most uncomfortable ride. While the two pilots were strapped tight in their seats, the only thing holding Lauck in the rocking aircraft was a safety line and his own experience. He was one of the best aviation survival technicians in the unit, and Wentworth always asked for him.

The men cataloged damage for the recovery teams and looked for the survivors of anyone who had been foolish enough to challenge the might of a hurricane. Their flight path took them northeast towards the interstate and Pensacola. The mangrove swamps had been beaten up badly by Ivan's winds. Other helos were working the beachfront—what was left of it.

"Tally-ho on I-10," Wentworth called out.

Price raised his binoculars and cried out, "Holy shit!"

"Report, damn it!" growled Wentworth.

Price looked at him with round eyes. "I don't believe it! I think the I-10 Bridge is gone!"

"Are you sure?"

"Get closer, Skipper."

"Working on it." Wentworth was fighting his aircraft; they were just on the good side of acceptable flight conditions. It was like riding a rocking chair going down a flight of stairs. Another couple of knots or so and he would have to abort.

"Cajun 101, Pensacola," the radio broke in. "Do you have a 4-1-1 on the Escambia Bay Bridge?"

Price keyed his radio, "Pensacola, this is Cajun 101. En route—wait five." The minutes crept by, and Price's attention was on the instruments, more concerned over his skipper's battle with the elements than with the mission. They flew over scores of damaged roofs and countless downed trees.

It was Lauck who cried out first. "Mother of God! Look at that! What the fuck happened?"

Wentworth worked the stick and the collective to put his Dolphin into a lazy orbit over the bay. What he and his crew saw shocked them.

"Price! Call it in! Do it!" yelled Wentworth.

Price fought to keep his voice level. "Pensacola, this is Cajun 101. We are now in orbit over the I-10 Bridge over Escambia Bay. Confirm heavy damage. I repeat—confirm heavy damage."

"Affirmative, 101. Are there any vehicles in the water?"

Price turned back to Lauck. The AST leaned out as far as he could, one hand holding his binoculars to his eyes, the other in a death grip on the door frame. He triggered his voice-actuated mike. "Scanning the area now, Pensacola. Negative, I repeat, negative evidence of vehicles in the bay."

"Understood, 101. Damage report."

"Many sections of the bridge are missing. Sections missing on both spans. The eastbound span is in worse shape. I would estimate a quarter-mile of the bridge has been destroyed."

There was a pause. "Can you make an evaluation as to the condition of the pilings?"

"There are a few that seem to be leaning, but most are upright. It seems the bridge sections were lifted off the pilings before sinking to the bottom of the bay."

"Understood, 101."

Price took over the conversation. "We will continue to orbit, photographing the damage, until we receive a vector to our next assignment."

"Understood, 101—continue to orbit until reassigned. Query—are conditions conducive to flight operations, or do you wish to abort?"

Price turned to Wentworth. His answer was a terse nod of the head. "Pensacola, we're up here as long as you need us."

"Affirmative, Cajun 101. You're the man. Wait one for your new vector."

The Dolphin continued its slow, bumpy circle around the devastation. Wentworth could see patrol cars with their lights on blocking all entrances to the bridge. The people on the ground knew it had been hurt, but only eyes in the sky could make a proper evaluation.

"Ain't nobody gonna use that bridge anytime soon," Price said to Wentworth as Lauck snapped photo after photo.

"Yeah, the western door to the Redneck Riviera is gone."

Baton Rouge

CAPTAIN JOHN BUFORD OF THE LOUISIANA ARMY NATIONAL Guard made one last walk-around, assuring himself his people were all stowed in the trucks. Crossing over the asphalt of the parking lot of the Baton Rouge armory in his desert camouflage uniform, he paused before his command vehicle, a Humvee, still in the desert camo colors used in Afghanistan. Pretending to straighten his beret, he scanned the crowd until he found his target.

Tall and red-haired, Carrie Buford was easy to spot. She stood near the Guard offices, their two-year-old son, Trey, in her arms.

Buford nodded to the two special people in his life, and his wife waved in return. He climbed in the Humvee and barked, "Let's get this show on the road, Mack."

His sergeant put the Humvee in gear. "Yes, sir. Next stop—Alabama."

Chapter 7

Friday, September 17: Third District Headquarters

Two days after Ivan hit, Richard Fitzwilliam tossed his copy of the morning's *Times-Picayune* onto his office desk. He had devoured the reports of the Escambia Bay Bridge disaster. The cause was still inconclusive. Theories being bantered around varied between shifting pilings, poor design, rogue waves, and storm surge.

Fitzwilliam walked around his desk to stand before a map of the region, spanning the Mississippi line to Lake Maurepas. He stared hard at the six-lane I-10 Twin Span connecting the city with Slidell. The bridge failure in Florida was a regional calamity. Commercial trade along one of the country's vital east-west highways would be disrupted for years. What was far more disturbing for the rest of the Gulf Coast was the fact that the Escambia Bay Bridge was not unique. There were many spans of similar design and construction from Florida to Texas, and two of them were right in Fitzwilliam's backyard.

He passed a hand over the map, running from the five-mile Twin Span to the twenty-four-mile Causeway. Both were almost identical to the Pensacola bridge. What would a similar storm do to New Orleans? There weren't many ways into the city. If a storm cut off half of them, how could the city recover?

Pensacola has been hit by hurricanes before, he thought, *bad ones, and has never suffered this kind of damage. What was different this time? The experts said the surge was between ten and fifteen feet, about the height of the bridge. Could that be enough? But how? Concrete doesn't float.*

Fitzwilliam shuddered. *God, I hope it was shifting pilings. I pray the Florida engineers screwed up somehow. Because if that wasn't the reason, we're in big trouble here.*

Lakeview

EMMA WAS BACK AT THE LAKEVIEW PLAYERS THEATER ON FRIDAY afternoon, painting the set. She was doing the trim work while Reggie de Courcy and Frank Church did the walls.

"You know, you're awfully good at that," Frank observed.

"Thanks, Frank. Practice makes perfect."

"It's amazing you don't get any paint on your pretty clothes"—he held up his hands—"unlike me." His work shirt and jeans were spotted with paint.

Emma snorted. "Pretty clothes? This old stuff? You need some glasses."

He shrugged. "Looks good on you."

Emma colored. It had been some time since anyone had complimented her on her appearance.

"Wonderful, wonderful!" de Courcy cried. "We should be finished tonight."

"You'll have to do it without me. I have to be home in an hour," Emma reminded him.

"We'll get it done, don't worry," Frank assured her.

"Well, I can do some touch-up on Sunday," Emma offered.

"I will be here," de Courcy assured her.

A few minutes later, Frank put down his brush and walked over to de Courcy. Emma was on the far side of the set. "Reggie, you still looking for a stage manager?"

"Yes," he admitted sadly. "I've found no one since Juan abandoned me, the bitch!"

"How about Emma?"

The director brightened. "You think she'd do it?"

"You can ask."

He frowned. "We have two Friday evening performances."

"You and I can cover for her Sabbaths. She can work after sunset on Saturday, you know."

"Yes, yes. All right, I'll ask her right now. Good thinking, Frank!" De Courcy padded over to the lady, who was just starting to clean up. Frank could tell by the conversation that Emma was hesitant, but when he saw the smile on de Courcy's face, he knew she had agreed.

Good, that worked, Frank thought as he surreptitiously ran his hungry gaze over Emma's Barbie Doll figure.

Saturday, September 18: LSU Medical Center

Dr. Chris Breaux worked his rounds in the psychiatric ward at the LSU Medical Center at Charity Hospital. It wasn't too bad a day. Only one new admission to the ward—some guy who thought he was John Lennon's brother. At least he wasn't suicidal. Chris hated those because he couldn't save them all. Chris hated to lose.

He checked his watch. Six more hours on his shift, then Marianne.

Warehouse District

Chris walked into the lobby of Le Chat Noir nightclub on St. Charles Avenue just after eight thirty. The hostess knew him by sight and escorted him to his table. Chris thought the smile on her face was rather broad. The reason became apparent when he saw his table.

Normally, when he attended one of Marianne's gigs, he sat far in the back to take in her performance and make notes on her interaction with the audience. Tonight was a surprise. His table was dead center front, the stage right before it. The table had two chairs, a single red rose in a bud vase, and a RESERVED sign.

"Are you sure this is my table?" he asked the hostess. Her smile just got wider as she nodded and held out his chair. Chris took his seat and noticed a card on the table addressed to him.

"Enjoy the show." The hostess nodded at the card as she left.

Nonplussed, Chris picked it up. His eyes grew wide as he turned it over and saw the lipstick imprint on the back. *Sealed with a kiss.* With a shy smile, he carefully opened the envelope and read the card within.

My darling Chris, this is for you.

All my love,
Marianne

Chris replaced the note in the envelope and slipped it into an inside pocket of his suit jacket. Just as he began to look around to see if anyone was aware of the flush he was sure covered his face, a waitress approached.

"Dr. Breaux? I'm here for your drink order. Just to let you know, there's a bottle of champagne set aside for you. I can get you a glass or something else if you prefer. All on the house." She could barely keep a straight face.

First time I've ever been seduced. "A glass of the champagne is fine."

Within minutes, the flute of bubbly was produced. Chris sipped as he scanned the crowd. The room was filling with locals and conventioneers. The tourists were easy to pick out with their overly casual clothes. The fanny-packs were a dead giveaway.

Chris was happy for Marianne; this was a good crowd. But, he reflected, it was strange for the management to give up a prime table. He wondered what Mari had told them.

The lights went down, and Chris focused on the stage. The members of Marianne's combo took their places. The keyboardist grinned at Chris, nodded, and began the introduction to Marianne's first song. Her voice came from all around them in the dark, singing, "Dream a Little Dream of Me."

The lights grew bright as Marianne took the stage, acknowledging the applause with a wave. Chris was knocked out. Marianne was a lovely woman, but tonight she was gorgeous. Her thick, dark hair was swept back, and her eyes, heavily outlined, were glowing. She was poured into a bright red halter dress, cut low in the front and back, the hem dancing an inch above her knees. Her slim legs were encased in sheer black stockings with four-inch red pumps. She was a classic torch singer. She stared at Chris, her blue eyes bright, as she finished the song.

Chris almost forgot to clap as the crowd exploded in approval. Marianne smiled at him before turning to the audience.

"Good evening, everyone. I'm so happy you all could come tonight. We've a great show planned for you."

Chris gulped his wine as Marianne continued her set. And quite a set it was. Marianne, always an emotional singer, sang with more feeling, more passion, than ever before. Her bandmates fed off her, playing with great style and enthusiasm. All that was missing was a grand piano for Marianne to crawl over, *a la* Michele Pfeiffer. About an hour into the set, Marianne, sitting on a stool after finishing "One for My Baby," nodded to her combo.

"Ladies and gentlemen, tonight we've got something special for you. As you know, New Orleans is a city of music. But what you may not know is we have a heritage of musicians from all walks of life. You know Harry Connick, Jr., right? Well, his daddy, the former District Attorney, is a pretty fine musician too."

"Is he as cute?" shouted out a secretary from Phoenix.

"No comment, dearie," replied Marianne without missing a beat, which brought a great laugh. "Anyway, our coroner—yeah, that's right, our *coroner*—plays a real mean trumpet. But tonight I want to introduce a very special and talented guest sitting right here."

Chris's ears pricked up.

"Ladies and gentleman, please welcome a fabulous member of the LSU Medical Center's staff, Dr. Christopher Breaux! Chris, come up here!"

He mouthed, *Are you kidding?* Her answer was to reach out her hand. Reluctantly, Chris rose to general approval and climbed on the stage.

"Chris is not only a brilliant psychiatrist—yes, he's a shrink, but he isn't *mine*, though you may think I need one right now! Chris is not only a brilliant psychiatrist but a wonderful piano player. And I'm going to ask him to play something for us."

The crowd roared as Marianne's eyes pleaded with him. To renewed cheers, Chris gave in and walked over to the keyboard. The keyboardist gave way to him with a grin on his face.

What? Chris mouthed to Marianne.

"How about Gershwin? 'Someone to Watch Over Me.'"

"Really?"

Her eyes blazed. "Yes."

Chris nodded and began the introduction, concentrating so he wouldn't screw up. That look Marianne gave him had nothing to do with singing. They did the song nice and slow, Marianne slinking around him, pouring her heart out through her voice. Chris couldn't help getting lost in the performance. The only way he knew he didn't totally screw up the song was by the audience's thunderous applause.

Marianne took Chris by the hand and made him take a bow. Just as he was leaving the stage, Marianne kissed him on the cheek. The crowd hooted and hollered.

"Yes," Marianne admitted after Chris reclaimed his seat, "he's my boyfriend. So, he's off-limit, girls!" She resumed the set, singing melancholy songs with joy on her face. She finished the set with her usual finale, "Do You Know What It Means to Miss New Orleans."

A few minutes later, Marianne, now in a short black dress, made her way to the table in the now-dimmed cabaret, recorded music filling the air.

"You were fantastic," Chris declared after greeting her with a quick kiss.

"Thanks, sugar. You ready to go?"

"But you just sat down."

"Baby, we're going home. Now."

Faubourg Marigny

CHRIS FOLLOWED MARIANNE TO HER HOUSE OFF ESPLANADE. Parking was limited, so Chris had to park around the corner.

Marianne had already unlocked the front door by the time he joined her. Once they were inside, she gave him a scorching kiss, full of desire and promise.

"Give me a few minutes, Chris," she requested before she broke away and walked seductively to her bedroom. Chris began pacing in the living room, conflicted. He suspected what was going to happen, and as much as he wanted it, he had made a promise to himself. Was she ready to hear that? Was he ready to say it?

"Chris," came her voice, "you can come in now."

Chris's mouth went dry. A dozen candles offered the only light in the bedroom. The ivory silk sheets were turned down. And Marianne knelt on the bed, dressed in only a red and black demi-bra, thong, and garter belt holding up her sheer stockings, her arms wide in welcome. She still had on her heavy stage make-up. The pearls Chris had given her on her last birthday were around her neck.

"I wore this under my dress," she teased. "All the time I was singing, I was thinking about this moment. Do you like it?"

"Yes." He moved towards her.

He stood by the bed as Marianne embraced him, kissing his lips as she ran her hands along his shoulders. "This coat's got to go, baby."

He complied as she loosened his tie. Soon he joined her kneeling on the bed. He stoked her back as she unbuttoned his shirt. Suddenly Chris broke the embrace and took her hands in his.

"Marianne, wait."

At her quizzical look he continued. "I love you totally and desperately. I want you more than any other woman in my entire life! But I can't—I swore, Marianne."

Marianne looked horrified and tried to pull away, but Chris's grip was too firm.

"Marianne, I want to marry you."

She froze. "Say again?"

He looked deep into her eyes. "Please, please say you will marry me, be my wife, make me the happiest man on earth."

"You're serious? You're asking me to marry you?" Marianne's confused expression changed to one of surprise. "You won't make love to me unless I agree to marry you?"

"I'm saying you're the most important person in the world to me, and I want to spend the rest of my life with you. I love you. Please, Marianne."

"Oh—God, yes! Yes, I'll marry you!"

She embraced him, hugging him tightly, covering his face with kisses—kisses he returned with equal fervor—kisses of joy and delight which soon became those of wanton desire.

She took his face in her hands. *"Now* will you make love to me?"

"Well, you don't have a ring, yet. Are you officially my fiancée without a ring?"

"Chris Breaux, hush!" She kissed him firmly, passionately. "You're wearing too many clothes. Love me, Chris. I need you."

"My God, you are beyond beautiful," Chris murmured as he caressed Marianne's breasts in the afterglow of their lovemaking. The room was strewn with their clothes and undergarments.

She watched his hand caress her nipple. "You're blind, lover. I'm too small."

"You're perfect. I love your breasts. They fit so well in my hands." He leaned down to place a kiss on each tip. He then sweetly kissed her lips.

Marianne's expression turned serious. "Chris, why did you ask me to marry you? I mean, before we made love."

"Because it would have been the height of bad manners to ask you afterwards."

She laughed and rolled her eyes. "Yeah, right! Chris, I'm serious!"

"Two reasons, Mari. One, I promised myself I would prove to you the depth of the love and respect I have for you. I wanted this night to be a celebration of that love."

"Are you talking about what happened back at school?"

He nodded. "Yeah. I wanted there to be no mistaking—"

"Chris, no. I know you only want the best for me, but I've put all that behind me. Really, I'm over it. What happened then, that's done. When I'm with you, I think of only what's going on between us. I love you so."

He kissed her. "Which brings up my second reason: What we're going to tell our children?"

She stared at him for a moment. "Oh, God!" she laughed.

"They're going to ask," he responded in a reasonable voice. "At least, when you tell them Daddy proposed after one of your concerts, you don't have to leave in that he also screwed you senseless first."

"No," she replied with a bawdy grin, "only afterwards. Chris, that's so silly!"

"So, what would you do?"

"Lie to them, like everybody else."

They both cracked up over that. Marianne was the first to recover. "When do we get married?"

"I thought I would leave that to you. How big a wedding do you want?"

"Oh, baby, I don't want anything big and fancy! Something nice. Our families and close friends—the guys in the band too."

"So, where shall we do the deed? Jackson?"

Marianne thought it over. "I don't know. Mom's not a regular churchgoer, and we don't have that many friends up there anymore. I really like your folks. Can we get married in Lafayette at your family's church?"

"Sure. You know they're Catholic, right?"

"Yeah. Is that a problem?"

"No. it actually solves a couple. I'm not the world's greatest Catholic, but my folks are pretty devout. It's no big deal to marry non-Catholics as long as we agree to raise the kids in the Church."

Marianne thought some more. "To be honest, I'm no better a Methodist than you are a Catholic. I believe, but does it matter what path we travel as long as we arrive at the same place?"

"That's one way of looking at it."

She lay back and looked at the ceiling with a smile. "I remember the services we sang at when I was at Loyola. The candles and the flowers. The music echoing in the church. It still gives me goose bumps." She turned over. "Let's do it in Cajun country if you think they'll let in a heathen like me."

"Okay. We'll get in touch with the parish priest next week and make an appointment."

"So soon?"

"Yeah. Catholics book their weddings as much as a year in advance if not longer. There's also some pre-marriage stuff we have to do."

"A year? Yikes! Can't we speed it up?"

"Up to the priest. But let's take a look at our schedules." Chris sat up and counted on his fingers. "It's almost October now. Six months is late March. That's Lent. Who wants to get married during Lent?"

"You're right. And April is Jazz Fest."

"April, June and October are the busiest months for weddings."

"We're trying to get some gigs in May." Marianne groaned. "Oh, Chris, that pushes us into the summer!"

"Is that too long?"

She lay in his arms, her hands gliding over his body. "Hmm, as long as you can keep me *distracted*, I should be able to make it."

"You're the one doing the distracting!"

"Okay, I'll behave myself for now. So, July or August is our best bet?"

"Yeah, or the weekend after Labor Day." Chris then took Marianne in his arms and pressed her against his body. "Now, all this talk about distraction has had an interesting effect on me."

"I've noticed."

Sunday, September 19

MARIANNE BURNED UP THE TELEPHONE LINES THE NEXT MORNING, sharing the news. Her happy mother raised no objection to a summer wedding in Lafayette. Emma's congratulations were sincere if a bit muted. Marianne would worry about that later.

Elizabeth's reaction could not be called muted at all. "He did? It's about time!" Elizabeth's voice could be heard halfway across Marianne's den.

"Calm down there, Lizzy. I've only got two ears. Don't blow

away one of them."

"Sorry, I'm just so excited for you! So, how did he do it? I want details!"

"He proposed here after my concert. It was very lovely. Umm, hang on. Chris is trying to get my attention."

"I've got Will on my cell phone," Chris reported. "He said yes."

"Wonderful! I'll talk to him later." Marianne returned to her call. "Lizzy, I want you to stand in my wedding."

"I'd be happy to. Who else is in the party?"

"Well, my sister, Margaret, will be Maid of Honor. Then, there's you and Emma at least. Chris has already asked Will to be Best Man."

There was a pause. "Will's going to be in the wedding? Wow, that's a first."

"What do you mean?"

"Well, I'm just surprised. He missed both Jane's and Emma's."

"Lizzy, do you have a problem with Will? I thought y'all were friends."

"We are! You know, it's really none of my business."

Chris walked over, seeing the frown on Marianne's face. "Something wrong?"

"It's Lizzy, asking about why Will missed the Bingley and Katz weddings."

"No! It's all right!" Elizabeth cried.

"I'll take it," Chris offered. "Lizzy, you have a question about Will?"

"No! I was just being nosey. I'm sorry."

"Lizzy, I can't speak for Jane's wedding, but didn't you know he was out of the country for Emma's? He was living in London that year."

"I didn't know that. Chris, please let's drop it. I'm really embarrassed I opened my big mouth. I would be honored to be in your wedding, and having Will in it just makes me happier."

"Having you involved makes Mari and me very happy too. Here's the pretty girl, again." Chris handed the phone back to his fiancée, who spoke to Elizabeth for a few more minutes before hanging up. She turned to Chris before calling the next person on her list.

"Was Will really in London when Emma and George got married?"

"Yeah. He was working in the European offices of DGS."

"Well, that makes sense, but what about Jane and Chuck's?"

Chris gave her a knowing look. "I think you know the answer to that."

Marianne nodded. "He was avoiding us, particularly Lizzy. Then a couple of years ago, he changed and came back in our lives. Do you know why?"

"I think he came to grips with everything that happened: the scandal, his dad's death, running the company, blaming himself—"

"Blaming himself?"

Chris shrugged. "It's the way Will is. He took responsibility for how things turned out five years ago." As Marianne began to protest, he held up his hand. "I don't agree with that, either, but it's water under the bridge. I think it's best we let it go."

Marianne sat, quietly thinking. *Lizzy still loves him. Does Will realize that? Should we clue him in? Does he still care for Lizzy? Should we help? Do we dare?*

"Marianne, no," Chris said.

She was startled out of her contemplations. "What?"

"We are not setting up Lizzy and Will."

Her jaw dropped. "How do you know I was thinking that?"

"Because, my love, you can't stand having your friends one bit less happy than you are."

"So, you think I'm happy, huh?"

"Yes." He leaned down to kiss her.

"Well, you're right."

It was some time before Marianne got back to her telephone calls.

Chapter 8

Nature wasn't through causing consternation. Hurricane Ivan had lost cohesiveness over Georgia, and the remnants drifted into the Atlantic. Then, to everyone's surprise, a portion of it completed an anti-cyclonic loop and moved across the Florida peninsula. Over the warm Gulf waters, it became a tropical storm again and tracked westward. On the evening of September 23, the revived Ivan made landfall near Camaron, Louisiana as a weak tropical storm. Ivan finally dissipated for good on the twenty-fourth as it moved overland into Texas.

Two days later, on September 26, Category 3 Hurricane Jeanne followed the path laid by Hurricane Francis three weeks earlier, slamming into the Atlantic coast city of Port St. Lucie.

In this so-called Summer of Storms, Florida had been hit by a record five tropical storms, three of them major hurricanes, killing over one hundred people and causing thirty billion dollars in damages.

The year 2004 would have a total of fifteen named storms, including a rare tropical storm in late November, nine of them hurricanes. Forecasters warned the nation was entering a period where more storms and more intense ones could be expected.

Monday, October 11: Baton Rouge
CARRIE BUFORD, A PERMANENT EMPLOYEE IN THE STATE'S OFFICE of Administration, marched down the halls of the State Capital Annex building, a large binder under one arm. Her dancer's legs were

still taut, and the click of her heels rang through the building. She was dressed in her usual power suit: jacket and pencil skirt in a navy pin stripe, a cream blouse, and stiletto heels. Her state ID badge swung from a lanyard around her neck. Her makeup understated and red hair pulled into a tight bun, she appeared no-nonsense and professional. A woman going places.

She would have pulled it off if she could only stop yawning. But it was hard to impress the eagles in the morning when your night owl kept you up all night.

Just wait, she vowed, *just wait 'til the next time you have an early tee time, Johnny-boy. I'm going to rock your world so hard you'll have trouble breaking ninety.*

She entered the small conference room to find her appointment already waiting for her. "Anna, it's so good to see you!" she cried, tossing the binder on the table and enveloping the African-American woman in an affectionate hug.

Anna Elliot, a fellow former member of the LSU Golden Girls and current assistant to the mayor of New Orleans, returned her friend's hug. "Girl, you are looking *good*. That soldier-boy taking care of you?" Carrie's bawdy grin was her only answer, and Anna cracked up. "Ooo, I'm *so* jealous!"

"No luck on the boyfriend front?"

Anna sat down, crossing her long, shapely legs. "There's only *one* thing on their minds, and since I'm no hottie from the 'hood, they can just take their act somewhere else." Her blouse had red, white, and blue vertical stripes, the colors of the City of New Orleans, and her blue suit jacket had a silver *fleur-de-lis* on the lapel. "And how's that baby of yours?"

The two spent another couple of minutes catching up, but they had work to do, and time was slipping by. The purpose of the get-together was to compare notes prior to the meeting of a committee the governor had created to review the response to Hurricane Ivan. Carrie was representing the state, Anna the city.

Carrie checked her notes. "It seems the state police have become a believer in Contraflow. They report no problems."

"No problems, you mean, once they started it," Anna shot back mildly. "The governor should have been listening to the local officials."

"That's the purpose of this committee—to fine-tune the response and improve communication and coordination. As for the local reaction, it didn't help that they didn't follow the plan. Jefferson Parish ordered an immediate evacuation at 10:30 a.m., right after the governor's speech. They were supposed to be last, not first. What good is a plan if the officials who helped draft it panic at the first opportunity?"

"Carrie, there was nothing the city could do about Jefferson Parish jumping the gun."

"True, but what about the city? Why didn't the mayor use the school buses as outlined in the plan?"

"Those buses belong to the Orleans Parish School Board. We'd have to get their cooperation."

"Then get it or force it. He *is* the mayor."

"The mayor's legal counsel disagrees. We're not sure the mayor has the authority."

Carrie sputtered. "Not sure he has the *authority*? Anna, he's the mayor! Believe me: he has the authority. Check your state law."

"We're more worried about local ordinances. Another issue is the school board is very territorial. They're already concerned about the possibility of the city taking over the schools like Chicago has. We take those buses and anything happens to them, they could sue the city. We're self-insured, so it could cost us hundreds of thousands of dollars."

"Is that why he didn't order a mandatory evacuation?"

Anna nodded. "Our lawyers aren't sure he has the legal authority, and without it, we're left hanging naked to lawsuits."

Carrie's mind wrestled with the fact that the mayor of the state's largest city was more concerned with liability issues than public safety. Her years in state government had taught her to hide her feelings; otherwise, Anna would have beheld one disgusted woman.

"Okay, enough on that. At least the refugees didn't tear up the

Superdome like they did in 1998 during Hurricane Georges."

"Amen to that."

"Next item. Did you have enough satellite phones?"

Tuesday, October 12: On the Mississippi River

IT WAS A CHAMBER OF COMMERCE DAY IN THE CRESCENT CITY. Clear, sunny blue skies, temperature around seventy, and no humidity. A mild October day Louisianans live for. Elizabeth leaned against the railing, soaking in the weather, the breeze fingering through her hair, the aroma of the river filling her senses.

She should have been working. After all, this outing was her idea. Instead of the usual "dog and pony show"—a guided bus tour of places, industries, and infrastructure New Orleans was trying to promote to the national media sandwiched with lectures and PowerPoint presentations—they were on a tugboat on the Mississippi, touring the port.

This was a two-day press junket promoting the Ports of New Orleans, South Louisiana, and St. Bernard. Their guests were ten reporters from national news publications, industry magazines, and *USA Today*. Normally, Elizabeth would be chatting them up, answering questions, and offering targeted information. The goal was to have positive stories in publications like *Newsweek, Fortune, The Economist*, the *Washington Post*, or the *New York Times*: stuff read by the decision makers for corporations. New Orleans' reputation wasn't the best, and EDNO's mission was to turn that around.

But with Eddie Masters on board, she wasn't going to get a word in edgewise. He was in pure Eddie mode, filling the reporters' heads with facts and figures. No one could rattle off statistics like Eddie. Elizabeth sat back and let her co-worker do his thing.

She took a deep breath. Elizabeth was already stressed out by this event, the biggest she had planned in her short tenure at EDNO. But there was another reason. They were on a DGS tugboat, and to Elizabeth's surprise, William Darcy had invited himself on the jaunt.

It wasn't unusual for a volunteer to join the organization for these events. Nonprofits like EDNO depended on help from their investors and partners. But the president of a large shipping company playing tour guide on a tugboat was rare, to say the least.

Behind her oversized sunglasses, Elizabeth couldn't keep her eyes off the cool and collected young tycoon standing next to the somewhat excitable economic developer. William radiated power and confidence in his navy suit, white shirt, and striped tie. Only his hair above his Oakley sunglasses was ruffled.

She hadn't seen him since his orientation, and she couldn't help wondering whether he was avoiding her. She was afraid their warm conversation several months ago was an anomaly, or even an act.

Eddie pointed out the facilities along the riverbanks, including the Naval Support Activity Center. "We're going downriver past the Audubon Institute's Species Survival Center, and we'll turn around near English Turn."

"English Turn? Isn't that the golf course where they play the PGA tournament?" one of the reporters asked.

"No, it's got something to do with the Battle of New Orleans," said another.

"Actually, the incident you're speaking of happened in 1699." Everyone turned to William Darcy. "It was right after the founding of the city by the Le Moyne brothers, Iberville and Bienville." His strong, clear voice carried easily over the roar of the tugboat's engines. "Bienville was heading down river when he came across a British warship coming up river to choose a site for a settlement. Bienville convinced the captain the territory was in the possession of the French, and they had a large force in New Orleans. It was a lie, of course. Except for a handful of men with Bienville, the place was completely open.

"But the British believed him, turned their ship around, and left the area. The bend of the river where this happened is called English Turn, and the golf course is named after it." He paused. "It changed the history of the world."

"How do you get that?" asked a reporter.

"New Orleans is the most strategic location in North America. Control New Orleans and you control the Mississippi River and, therefore, two thirds of the United States.

"This is why New Orleans is so important. This is the largest bulk port in the nation. Here, we ship the food and grains of America to the rest of the world. Here, we produce the oil and gas that fills our pipelines. Our refineries and plants make the plastics and chemicals we can't live without."

William was on fire. "The British knew this place was important. That's why they invaded Louisiana during the War of 1812. President Lincoln knew this place was important. It was the first major city seized by the Union in the Civil War. The Nazis knew this place was important. They had U-boats crawling off the mouth of the Mississippi River during World War II. The Soviets knew this place was important. We were a first-strike target for their ICBMs during the Cold War."

He spread his arms to the reporters assembled. "And that's why we have you here—to remind the rest of the country that this place is important. Maybe one of the most important places in the nation." He leaned back, his speech ended. "Sorry for the lecture. I hope I didn't bore anyone."

"No, no, don't apologize," cried Eddie. "I don't think anyone could have explained how important we are better than that, Mr. Darcy." He turned to the reporters. "Now, if I can call your attention to the side, I'll show you the Port of St. Bernard."

While the group was thus occupied, Elizabeth approached William. "That was quite the talk, Will. I didn't know you knew so much history."

William grinned. "It's a hobby of mine. I'm sorry. I guess I got carried away. I sounded a bit like Eddie Masters," he added *sotto voce*.

Elizabeth almost giggled. "I think they found what you said fascinating." She put her hand on his forearm. "Don't ever apologize for your passion, Will."

William glanced at her hand, still clutching his arm. A warm, funny feeling grew in the pit of Elizabeth's stomach. William opened his mouth to speak.

"Hey, Lizzy," Masters called, "we have a question for you."

She smiled weakly. "Back to work." She moved over to the other side of the boat, slightly disturbed and disappointed. She could have sworn William was going to say something.

William drew a sigh of relief. He had almost blown it big-time.

Since orientation, he had purposely avoided Elizabeth. His desire for her had reignited even though she already had a boyfriend. What good would it do to torture himself by spending time with the one woman he always wanted and could never have? A woman who was unavailable. He couldn't trust himself not to blurt out something stupid, something that would only pain them both.

Today's incident proved the wisdom of his choice. When she touched his arm, fire raged through his soul. He nearly declared himself. He almost begged her to give him another chance. He fought the impulse to confess his love for her.

What a disaster that would have been! William had no choice. He had to limit his interaction with Elizabeth for both their sakes.

Chapter 9

Thursday, October 14: Gulf of Mexico, off Grande Isle

A twenty-two-foot Bayliner cabin cruiser bobbed in the calm nighttime waters of the Gulf of Mexico five miles off the mouth of Bayou Lafourche. The motor off, the boat floated about one hundred yards from an automatic oil production well. Two men were in the boat, one standing in the stern, searching the horizon with binoculars. The harsh light from the rig gave an artificial garishness to the scene. Every thirty seconds, the silence was shattered by an ear-splitting foghorn.

"Do we have to be so close?" whined Greg Wickham.

"This is the rendezvous point. Just suck it up," advised his companion. Like Wickham, he was dressed in dark clothing.

"It hurts my ears, Pyke."

"Tough shit." Pyke continued his watch out to sea.

Wickham sat in the passenger seat in the cabin, enclosed on three sides and open to the cockpit and stern, feeling pissed-off. Once, he was the king drug-dealer of Uptown New Orleans. Now, he was barely making ends meet as an errand boy for Dr. Carter Naquin, a pain clinic owner in Houma and small-time drug importer.

Greg "G-Daddy" Wickham's downward spiral began five years earlier when he brought in Junior Jarvis to eliminate the snitch, Tommy Bertram. Wickham, for all his bravado, had never killed anyone, and he was scared the crime could be traced back to him. Unfortunately, Wickham proved a poor negotiator. He offered forty percent of his business to Jarvis for the contract, but Jarvis took seventy-five. The gangbanger assured his new partner that business would increase. But within two years, NOPD busted Detective Jones, G-Daddy's mole inside the police force, Junior Jarvis was dead, and the gang was broken up by arrests and desertions.

Wickham tried to pick up the pieces afterwards and failed. Other gangs moved in. The high roller customers were gone. He found himself scratching out a living selling to high school students again, an almost fatal mistake. He should have backed off when he learned the little girl's last name was Darcy. But her brother was out of the country, and the opportunity was too good to pass up. When Darcy returned early, Wickham's survival instincts took over. He knew Darcy would sic Fitzwilliam on him, and he didn't wait around for the damn cop to find and kill him. He took off for the swamps.

For the last two years, Wickham had kicked around the southeast part of the state, doing odd jobs and minor dealing with short returns to the city. He was also using product more than before. He met Pyke and, through him, Carter Naquin. Dr. Naquin was strictly small stuff but lucrative. Lucrative for Naquin, that is. Wickham was still looking for a route back to the Big Easy—to become G-Daddy again.

Pyke lowered the binoculars. "Somebody's coming."

Wickham looked out in the moonless night. After a moment, he saw the running lights of a boat approaching. There were two flashes from the craft.

"It's them," breathed Pyke. "Get the bag."

Wickham moved down into the forward cabin and retrieved a locked satchel containing a hundred thousand dollars in hundred-dollar bills. Usually, transactions were handled via electronic transfer between offshore banks, but this was the largest deal Naquin had ever scored. He didn't have the time to launder the last bit of cash, so an exchange was agreed upon.

Wickham's eye fell momentarily on Pyke's favorite toy lying on the U-shaped mattress: a black market, fully-automatic, M-16 assault rifle.

Pyke's voice came from above. "C'mon, Wickham, move your ass!"

Wickham returned to the cockpit while Pyke stood against the stern. The other boat's engines were a growing grumble. Pyke nervously fingered the Glock in his waistband.

"Keep your eyes open, but don't make any sudden moves, okay? Slow and easy."

Wickham nodded. The Columbians were known to shoot first and ask questions later if they felt threatened.

The long, sleek go-fast cigarette boat rumbled alongside. It carried three men: a driver, another man holding an AK-47, and a third with his hands on his hips. The leader, Wickham figured. Pyke waved once and said something in Spanish. The third Columbian answered back in the same language. Wickham had eyes only for the guy with the rifle.

Later, Wickham would never know why he had moved. Something just *felt* wrong. One moment, everything was cool as it had been many times before. The next, guns were drawn. Wickham didn't know who started it. He couldn't tell whether Pyke had gone nuts, the Columbians were trying to rip them off, or everybody simply jumped to the wrong conclusion at the same time. Whatever the reason, the nighttime quiet was suddenly filled with the crash of gunfire. Wickham didn't wait around to watch. He was already halfway into the forward cabin, bullets ricocheting around him.

Hitting the floor hard, he tossed the satchel away. He lay still, petrified, waiting for death to slam into his back. Nothing happened. Suddenly, the go-fast's engines revved up. Instead of leaving, Wickham realized with horror that it was coming around. The Columbians intended to board the Bayliner.

In one motion, he grabbed the M-16 and chambered a round. Keeping low, he crawled halfway out of the cabin. He saw Pyke lying face-up on the deck near the stern, his Glock a foot away from his outstretched hand. He couldn't tell if he was alive or dead.

Wickham heard shouts in Spanish as the Columbians grew close. He knew he had only one chance, so he stayed low, out of sight.

A hand grabbed the starboard gunwale.

Wickham jumped to his feet and held down the trigger. The M-16, on full auto, sprayed the air with bullets. There was something to be said for being lucky. His timing couldn't have been better. He caught one of the Columbians in mid-leap towards the Bayliner, and he fell dead into the Gulf. The rest of his rounds brought down both the boat's pilot and Mr. AK-47 as he tried to bring his weapon to bear. Wickham kept the trigger depressed until he had emptied the clip.

In a silence as sudden as the violence before, Wickham found himself alone in the middle of the Gulf. The only sounds were the rumble of the go-fast's engines and the bleating of the horn from the rig nearby.

"Wickham?" Wickham turned to see Pyke, gasping, still alive and struggling to move. "D-did you...get them all?"

"Yeah, yeah." He moved over to inspect his partner. Pyke's chest was soaked with his blood.

"G-get the package...from the other boat. Then...get in touch with...Naquin. He's a doctor."

Wickham nodded, turned to the helm, and fired up the engine. He was no sailor, but he was able to maneuver the Bayliner alongside the cigarette boat.

Meanwhile his mind was racing.

We gotta get outta here. The mother ship'll start gettin' suspicious when the go-fast don't report back in. Crap, they'll be after us, now! Can't use this connection again. Shit, a million street value in coke and a hundred grand in cash, and we could still end up dead. What I could do with—

And only two guys know I work with Naquin.

A plan started forming in his brain.

The Bayliner bumped hard against the cigarette boat. Wickham, after putting the engine in idle, leapt aboard, rope in hand, and made it fast to a cleat. He glanced at the carnage before returning to the Bayliner.

"Y-you got the stuff?" Pyke groaned as Wickham approached him.

Wickham said nothing as he reached down and picked up Pyke's

Glock. He hefted it a couple of times and glanced at his partner's prone body. Pyke's eyes grew wide as his intent became obvious. He opened his mouth to speak. Whether it was to curse, beg, or protest, Wickham would never know as he calmly shot Pyke through the head.

Wickham looked at the pistol again. *Fingerprints*, his mind screamed. He tossed the gun overboard; the M-16 joined it a moment later. Donning work gloves he found in the console, he retrieved the satchel and boarded the go-fast boat. To his relief, he found the drugs on board. Whatever caused the gunfight, the Columbians had not planned to cheat them. He also discovered a bonus: a case containing a dozen hand grenades.

Wickham knew there was no way of keeping this incident secret. Instead of trying to hide it, it would be better to sow confusion. The first step was to do something strange and unexpected.

He spent the next fifteen minutes manhandling the two dead Columbians from the cigarette boat into the cockpit of the Bayliner, laying them over's Pyke's corpse. The third body had drifted away in the darkness. Wickham's clothes had gotten bloody in the process, so he stripped them off. In just his underwear, he retrieved his duffle bag and the spare jerry can of gasoline from below.

He fished Pyke's car keys from the dead man's pocket before emptying the can over the bodies. As a final flourish, he draped the macabre assembly with his stained clothes and returned to the go-fast.

He was momentarily startled by a squawk from the boat's radio. It reminded him to hurry. The drug-runners' mother ship, several miles away, might have another go-fast boat to send when their people failed to check in. Wickham secured the money satchel and his duffle, took a grenade from the case, and engaged the engine. Coming around the Bayliner, he pointed the go-fast north, back towards shore, as he pulled the pin from a grenade. He tossed the tennis-ball sized bomb into the cockpit of the Bayliner and floored the throttles. The twin screws of the inboard engines bit hard into the waters of the Gulf, and the boat jumped forward.

He was almost a hundred yards away when the grenade detonated. It set off the gasoline, and a fireball lit the night. The Bayliner was engulfed in flames but still afloat until the internal gas tanks went off. The huge secondary explosion almost shattered the burning craft, bits and pieces of fiberglass and flesh blown in all directions. By then, Wickham was almost a mile away.

The explosions didn't go unnoticed by the manned oil platforms. However, they were miles away, and when the flames died down, it was impossible to pinpoint the location. The calls to the Coast Guard were not very helpful.

Friday, October 15: Port Fouchon

WICKHAM'S LUCK HELD THROUGHOUT THE NIGHT. HE HAD NO idea how to return to Port Fouchon where Pyke had launched the Bayliner, but he was able to follow a shrimp trawler to the ship channel. He cruised up the channel to the deserted public boat launch. During his voyage, Wickham had rinsed off much of the blood and gore in the go-fast and dressed, removing the plug in the well to drain the water as he ran towards shore. He replaced the plug and secured the boat to the dock. As calmly as he could, he walked to Pyke's truck, unfastened the Bayliner's trailer from the hitch, and drove to the dockside. He quickly transferred the drugs, money, duffle, and grenades to the truck, as well as the Columbians' AK-47, hidden in a blanket with a full clip. From the truck, Wickham retrieved the anti-theft device for the steering wheel. He parked the truck at the opposite end of the parking lot from the abandoned trailer and returned to the cigarette boat. In the darkness, his activities had gone unseen. He cast off and slowly piloted the go-fast past the vast commercial port into the Gulf.

Coming around as the sky began to lighten, he ran the go-fast up the coast for about fifteen minutes before pulling close to shore. Making sure the beach was deserted, he pointed the boat due south and fastened the anti-theft device to the steering wheel, locking it in place.

Wickham took a breath, stood by the helm and jammed the

throttles forward one last time. As the powerful engines roared to life again and the boat shot forward, Wickham leapt overboard. He swam inexpertly to shore as the smugglers' cigarette boat flew towards the distant oil platforms. As he waded onshore, he wondered whether the boat could actually hit one of the rigs. The chances of that happening were astronomical, but it would be one hell of a thing to see. He looked one last time at the go-fast boat, growing ever smaller in the pre-dawn grey, its engines fading in the sounds of the surf. Wickham, soaking wet, then began his two-mile walk back to the truck.

The sun was just coming up as he turned on the ignition, still wearing the work gloves. He pulled out just as an SUV hauling a Welcraft turned in. He drove the truck up the main road to Highway 1, and then up the highway for thirty minutes to the parking lot south of Golden Meadow where he had met up with Pyke the afternoon before. There was little activity that early in the morning, so he was alone as he moved the money, the duffle, and the drugs to his Camaro. He made sure his car was secure before he returned to Pyke's truck and began the drive to Houma and the second part of his plan.

Gulf of Mexico

It was difficult to sink the fiberglass boat, even shattered, and the Bayliner's smoldering hull was still afloat when it was spotted by a Coast Guard helicopter a couple of hours after dawn. A patrol boat reached it by mid-morning. With the number of human remains aboard, it was treated as a crime scene. Smuggling was definitely involved. Whether it was drugs or terrorists could not be determined. The patrol boat took the hull in tow and slowly made its way back to port where the forensic people with the FBI and US Customs awaited.

Houma

Carter Naquin had always wanted to be rich and live in a big house. He became a doctor solely because doctors made lots of money. What he didn't like to do was work. He quickly learned people would pay *anything* to have their pain alleviated, and thus he found his calling in life. Prescribe whatever painkillers the patient wanted, the more expensive the better, and he would be the richest man in town. He wasn't cheating anyone, he told himself. It was the insurance companies that paid. Political contributions to the right people gave him protection.

He built his pain clinics and made his money, but the arm candy he married proved to be more high maintenance than he anticipated, especially since Dr. Naquin still liked to date. That was all right with Mrs. Naquin as long as *her* extra-curricular activities were unimpeded.

The price of their expensive, open marriage was cocaine: coke to party with and coke to subsidize the lifestyle. His cousin, Louis Pyke, proved to be a good man to handle that part of the business. And business was good. Naquin built a six thousand square foot mansion in the highest style of south Louisiana. It was over-the-top: four-car garage, swimming pool, Italian marble everywhere, a sauna with a tanning booth for the little woman, and a separate guesthouse dedicated to their periodic orgies. For privacy, he chose a wooded lot north of Houma, halfway to Thibodaux.

The place cost so much that Naquin could only afford a massive entrance gate to his pleasure palace. He planned to replace the five-foot high chain-link fence that surrounded the rest of his four-acre lot later as his business grew. Unfortunately for him, Naquin failed to realize that, in his chosen line of work, security was most important.

At seven thirty in the evening, as was his routine after work and a visit to the gym, Dr. Naquin pulled his Cadillac into the driveway across the highway from a large sugarcane field and opened his remote controlled gate. As he drove in, he never saw a man step away from a tree near the gate. Carter Naquin's last sight on this earth was the muzzle blast of an AK-47.

Wickham shot up the windshield and driver's side windows. To his horror, the car continued to roll slowly forward. Only when the car failed to negotiate a turn in the driveway and ran into a tree did he realize the vehicle was moving on its own. Wickham knew he only had moments. Looking into the car to make sure Naquin was dead, he deposited the Columbians' assault rifle on the front seat, reached in to the remote on the car's visor, triggered the gate again with his still-gloved hands, and tossed a grenade in for good measure as he ran for the gate and across the highway. There was no traffic, and Wickham was almost into the cane field before the grenade went off.

He made his way through the stalks of sugarcane until he broke through to a farmer's dirt road where Pyke's truck was parked. He drove back to the highway about a quarter-mile from Naquin's estate and turned away, heading back towards Houma, the smoke from the burning Cadillac in his rearview mirror in the gathering dusk. Five miles down the road, just before he reached US-90 and the turn-off to Raceland, he saw two Terrebonne Parish sheriff deputies flying past him in the opposite direction, lights and sirens on.

The evening drive back to Golden Meadow was as nerve-racking as Wickham had ever experienced. His only chance to pull off this stunt was to get the truck away unseen. If he was successful, then he had eliminated any connection he had with Naquin, Pyke, or the incident in the Gulf. He would be safe.

Wickham was exhausted. He had been up the night before and had only caught catnaps during the day in a couple of rest stops between Golden Meadow and Houma. He had eaten nothing, not willing to take the chance some waitress or fast-food jockey would remember him. But as much as he wanted to eat and sleep, he knew he couldn't do either until he had completed his plan.

It was almost ten at night when he ditched the truck in the parking lot of a bar along the bayou side, south of Golden Meadow. Making sure he left nothing incriminating in the cab, he locked it and threw the truck keys into the bayou. He then walked the half-mile to the other parking lot and his Camaro. It was not unusual for people to walk along the highway, and he attracted no notice. Minutes later, he fired up his trusty red steed and turned onto Highway 1 heading back to US-90.

Wickham still had a duck-out spot in New Orleans. There, with his newfound cash and product, he would begin to rebuild his empire.

G-Daddy was back.

Chapter 10

Guest in the House wasn't a bad play, but it was very dated. Set in the late 1930s, the script involved the neurotic female cousin of a housewife happily married to a painter. This disturbed hypochondriac, suffering from ornithophobia, a fear of birds, wants to break up the marriage and have the painter for herself. After a great deal of angst, the neurotic cousin suffers a fatal heart attack when the couple's pet canary escapes.

What was a hit in 1942 was boring sixty years later. How could a community theater make this play interesting again?

Reginald de Courcy thought he had the answer. He changed the setting of the play to a time in the near future after "some enormous catastrophe" when sexual mores would be similar to the Victorian era. The bird became a robot parrot. Think *Wuthering Heights* with laser beams.

To say the least, de Courcy managed to ruin *Guest in the House*.

Emma Katz didn't care that the play was terrible. De Courcy thought it was genius, the actors were having fun, and she was able to get out of the house. There wasn't much for her to do as stage manager. De Courcy was a control freak, and he was running around everywhere backstage. The lighting technician had threatened to quit if the director stepped into his light booth again; it seemed he almost blew up the control board.

So Emma spent a great deal of time sitting backstage near the

Green Room with the actors. They were interesting people, especially Frank Church. His part, the impressionable brother of the housewife, only appeared at the beginning and end of the play. He usually found a place near Emma, and the two had fun laughing over de Courcy's latest foibles.

The show ran for two weekends. On the last Thursday night of the run, the two were sitting together as usual.

"Two more performances." Frank sighed.

"Last one for me," Emma remarked. "You're on your own tomorrow and Saturday."

"You *are* coming to the wrap party, right?"

Emma shook her head. "I wish I could, but my husband's family is coming in."

"Too bad." They sat in silence, listening to the dialog on stage. "How come you're not on stage?"

"I can't act." Her hands stroked her jeans, which, like her top, were black.

He leaned over. "You'd make a better model than Julia." The girl playing the nude model spent the entire play in a bathrobe.

"Frank!" She pretended to be affronted, but secretly Emma was flattered.

"Just kidding. But I am sorry we don't have a better play for your set. Maybe next time?"

"I don't know. I hate to leave my father alone so much."

"Aww, c'mon, Em, we can't lose you now!" He imitated de Courcy's high lisp. "The theater needs you!"

She giggled. "I'll think about it."

He leaned over. "I'm thinking about directing."

"Really? What play?"

"I'd like to do *Same Time Next Year*."

"Oh." It was a play about long-time lovers who got together once a year throughout their marriages to other people.

"I'd like you to design the set. Maybe even be in it."

"Frank, I said I don't act."

"I think you can—if you have the right director." He looked

deeply into her eyes.

"I-I don't know."

"Emma, I know I can do it. I know I can get the passion out of you…for the stage."

Emma looked at him.

Suddenly, they were interrupted. "Emma!" de Courcy hissed. "I need your help!"

She shrugged at Frank. "Duty calls. Later."

Frank forestalled her. "Let's have coffee soon. Talk about it."

Emma hesitated. "All right."

She got up to see what problem the director had gotten himself into, Frank's eyes following her as she walked away.

It would be an understatement to say Frank Church liked women. He *adored* women. Since reaching puberty, Frank had spent his life pursuing and bedding women. It was his goal in life to experience them all. Women came in so many agreeable shapes, sizes, colors, and textures. He had to sample as many as he could.

His only problem was that women refused to understand his avocation. They wanted *commitment*. Ugh, what an ugly term! The last thing Frank wanted was to settle into a life of boring monogamy.

As a salesman, he had the perfect occupation for his calling. Married women—bored, ignored, frustrated, lovelorn wives and mothers with workaholic husbands—were the ideal target. Usually, Frank chose mothers. They were the least likely to become romantically involved. Even if they did, when faced with the choice of latching onto Frank or keeping their children, the kids won every time. A bitter farewell and a tear-stained kiss, and he was free again.

The trouble was where to find them. He quickly learned secretaries were *not* good hunting. Oh, they were as amenable to seduction as the next girl, but when lust turned to love, it got damn sticky. Nothing could derail a sales career faster than a pissed-off secretary.

Dipping in the customers' pool was out. It was career suicide to go after co-workers. That left females not associated with his job.

Frank eliminated bars. Women who hung out in bars liked bars and liked drinking. Contrary to popular belief, a drunk woman is a lousy lay. And bars were *very* public. Someone was sure to see him. More often than not, husbands would be notified, and that was a bad scene all around.

Therefore, Frank's hunting grounds were places husbands tended to avoid: health clubs, grocery stores, and shopping malls. A couple of years ago, Frank found artistic places such as art classes and community theater were ideal. He could always find a ready supply of ladies who fit his criteria: lonely, unappreciated, and possessed of an adventurous spirit. His affairs would last the run of the class or production, his paramours enthralled until they parted, the ladies with a secret to hold in their hearts.

Frank didn't see himself as a predator. In his mind, he was providing a service to neglected ladies. He never wanted to break up a marriage. The last thing he desired was for some divorcée to hog-tie him into a committed relationship with her brats and baggage.

Emma Katz fit all his particulars except she had no children. But her dedication to her father made up for that as did her unbelievable body. Frank was a breast man.

That Daddy lived at home could be an obstacle. Frank preferred to have his assignations in the lady's house. The less they knew about him, the harder it would be for them to track him down in case everything went bad. But Frank was willing to make an exception in Emma's case if it meant he would have the enjoyment of her abundant charms.

Frank knew he was making progress. He would call her the next week for coffee and turn on the charm. Emma was ripe for the taking. As long as her stupid husband kept doing whatever stupid thing he was doing, it was only a matter of time before the lovely Mrs. Katz was sharing his bed.

Friday, October 29: Lakefront
"AND THIS GUY THOUGHT HE WAS CLEVER, USING GLOVES," reported New Orleans FBI office forensics investigator Kathy Taylor, "but we thought about it. What if it wasn't a Colombian smuggler who offed Naquin. What if Pyke wasn't alone. Did he meet Pyke

somewhere and ride down to Port Fouchon with the Bayliner in tow? He wouldn't be wearing gloves then. What would he touch? So, I had my people go over the passenger side of Pyke's truck thoroughly. Not too many clear prints, but we found a couple of partials."

Special Agent David Baugham thought the technician's grin was excessive for a couple of partials. "And…?"

The grin turned into a wide smile. "*And* a full set on a plastic Mountain Dew bottle on the passenger floorboard. We got a hit on IAFIS." She gave Baugham a form.

"Wickham, Gregory Allen. A/K/A G-Daddy. Drug dealer. That name…" Baugham searched through his file. "Yeah, here it is. Greg Wickham is on the list of known associates of Louis Pyke." He looked at the investigator. "Anything else?"

"Not yet. No other usable prints in the truck. Nothing on the trailer left at Fouchon or on the murder weapon found in Naquin's car. The only thing we could get off what was left of the Bayliner cabin cruiser were the dental impressions from the victims."

"What about the cigarette boat?"

"Lots of unknown prints—the Colombians, we think. We're waiting for a report from Interpol. *But* the prints on the wheel and the anti-thief device were smeared like in the truck."

"Gloves again?"

"I'd say so. Wouldn't hold up in court."

Baugham sat back, considering. "I like Wickham for this. It makes sense." He leaned forward and ticked off the points with his fingers. "Naquin's blown away execution-style. It's made to look like the Colombians got mad at him and killed him. But why were they mad at him? How did they know his schedule? Why use Pyke's truck, and why abandon it ten miles from the nearest port? And how do they get out of the country if they sent their boat into the Gulf without them?

"No, it looks more and more like a set-up by a Mr. Unknown, and that brings us back to Wickham."

"What if they were picked up by another boat?" asked Taylor.

"Still doesn't explain the cigarette boat." Baugham sat back. "Our boy might have gotten away with it if he had sunk the cigarette boat instead of sending it unmanned into the Gulf. That little bit of theater is going to hang him."

"How do you think it went down?"

"Pyke and Mr. Unknown—I'm thinking it's Wickham—go to meet their connection offshore of Port Fouchon. Something happens and everybody's dead except Unknown. He gets the bright idea to go into business for himself maybe. Whatever it is, he knows the Colombians don't take kindly to having their people killed. So he tries to confuse everybody and make it look as though one of the Colombians ripped everybody off."

"That's why he killed Naquin," said Taylor. "He would have known if Pyke had an accomplice."

"Yeah. I'll bet you Unknown had a car parked somewhere near the bar in Golden Meadow where he abandoned Pyke's truck." Baugham looked at Wickham's rap sheet. "One problem, though. Wickham's record is strictly nonviolent."

"That's only his arrest and conviction record. Maybe there're some things the police know that's not in there."

Baugham looked at the investigator with affection. "Who do you think you are, a special agent? Of course, there's more stuff. There's *always* more stuff. I'm going to have to make an appointment with"—he scanned the report—"Lt. Richard Fitzwilliam of the NOPD."

Chapter 11

The presidential election came and went in the Bayou State, and while the nation's eyes were turned towards Ohio, in Louisiana the attention was on the local congressional elections. Two long-term members of the state's delegation to Washington were retiring, the Democrats and Republicans exchanged seats, and the state's delegation remained split seven-to-three in favor of the GOP.

But there was more to it than that. Seniority was the coin of the realm in Washington, DC. No matter how hardworking or talented the newcomers were, they would not get the plum committee assignments and the power that went with them.

Louisiana was politically a weaker state on November 3 than it was the day before.

Thursday, November 4: Downtown

CHRIS COULD HARDLY TASTE HIS CAFETERIA LASAGNA BECAUSE HIS attention was focused solely on the beautiful woman sharing lunch with him, talking a mile a minute.

"And so Mom was looking at this magazine at the hairdressers and saw these bridesmaid dresses. So she calls me right up—while she's having her hair colored—telling me to go find this magazine. Hello! It's like six months old! So you know what she tells me to do? Go to the library! Can you believe that?"

Chris grinned stupidly. "Believe what?"

Marianne frowned. "Have you heard a single thing I've said?"

"No."

Her eyes narrowed. "I would get mad at you, but since you look so adorable, I'll let it go this time." She took a bite of her salad. "So, what's up with the rest of your day?"

"Just my rounds. Friday's gonna be a real ballbuster, though."

Marianne looked up. "Are we still going to Lafayette to meet with the priest?"

He reached over for his fiancée's left hand and gave the engagement ring a kiss. "Right after my last appointment. Mom's already making the shrimp étouffée."

"Mmm...thanks for telling me, Cajun-man. Now I'm *really* gonna enjoy my salad." She stuck out her tongue.

"Keep it up, and I won't tell you about our sleeping arrangements."

Marianne raised her eyebrows. "Chris, I *am* sharing a room with you on this trip, aren't I?"

"What, and shock my parents?" Chris knew his mother had already redecorated his old room to add a more feminine flair, but he decided to keep it a surprise. He laughed. "Don't worry, baby, you'll be bunking with me." She smiled. "But that's it. We *are* meeting with the priest, after all."

"Oh, pooh!"

A half-hour later, the two shared a kiss by the bank of elevators and went in opposite directions. It was a glorious November day, rare for Louisiana—temperatures in the sixties with almost no humidity. Chris decided on a cup of coffee before he hiked the dozen blocks back to the LSU Medical Center, so he crossed Poydras Street to a little French coffee shop on St. Charles near the Federal Court Building. He walked in, intending to grab a coffee to go, when his eyes fell on a familiar figure.

"Emma?"

Emma Katz whirled around at the sound of his voice, her expertly made-up face flushed. She was in a dark green, low-cut cashmere blouse with matching sweater and stonewashed jeans. It was only then that Chris noticed the man in a suit sitting across the small table from her. Chris moved over to them, curious about the horrified expression on Emma's face.

She leapt to her feet. "Chris! How wonderful to see you! You're downtown today?" Her voice was hurried and nervous.

Chris nodded. "Just had lunch with Mari." He kissed Emma's cheek, his eyes on the stranger. The man's face had gone pale when he greeted them, but now was flushed red.

What the hell is going on?

"Umm, let me introduce my friend. This is Frank Church. He's a salesman from…ah…"

Frank stuck out his hand. "Arc Tools."

"Yes," Emma said weakly. "Frank, this is Dr. Chris Breaux."

"Nice to meet you, Frank." Chris started to get a clue.

"Frank and I do community theater together," Emma explained.

Frank jumped in. "Yes! We were meeting about our next production to see if she'll design the sets. Maybe even act."

Chris nodded. "I heard you were doing that again, Emma. First time since college?"

"Yes." Her smile was brittle, and she wrung her hands.

Frank glanced at his watch. "I've got to go. Got an appointment in a few minutes. Nice to meet you, Chris. Emma, I'll get back to you on the design."

"Right." She pointedly shook his hand. "Goodbye, Frank."

Frank gave a rather fake smile, in Chris's opinion, and practically ran out of the café.

Emma looked around. "Well, Chris, it was good to see—"

"Emma." She was held in Chris's deep stare. "C'mon, I've got a couple of minutes. Let's sit down and catch up."

"I-I've got to go," she said as she picked up her purse.

"Just a couple of minutes."

Emma reluctantly joined him at the table. "Just a few."

Chris looked at her, considering. "How's George?" Her flush of guilt told him everything he needed to know.

"He's good. We're all good."

"And Abe? How's that working out for you?"

"I-I don't know what you mean. Abe's fine. He's got a clean bill of health."

"It's hard having him share your home, though."

She shook her head. "Chris, no, everything's fine."

"You know and I know it's not."

Emma refused to look at him. "I don't want to have this conversation."

He leaned back. "That's your prerogative. I can walk right out of here like I never saw anything. But if anybody asks me any questions, I'm going to have to tell them the truth."

He paused as Emma blanched. Chris hated to manipulate Emma that way, but he suspected his friend was in serious trouble. He had to try to help, and the only way he could was to get Emma to talk.

"I saw you having coffee in a downtown café with a male friend from the theater. Anything secret about that?"

Emma looked down. "Nothing. It's perfectly innocent."

"Right." His eyes bored into her.

"Stop that," she whispered.

"Stop what?"

"Stop staring at me!"

"You think I'm staring at you, Em?" His expression softened as his heart broke. "You won't even look at me."

"Please, just leave me alone."

"Is that what you really want?" He took her hand. "I'm your friend. I'm trying to help. Just hear me out." He lowered his voice. "Emma, you can blow me off or tell me to get lost, but I think you're in trouble here. I can help, but you have to be honest with me."

Emma tried to look up, to answer him, but her voice broke. She covered her face with her hands as she cried.

Chris patted her hand. "I'm here for you. Stay right here. I'll be back." He rose and walked over to the counter.

"What's wrong with the lady?" the barista asked.

"She got some bad news. Give me a large dark roast and a glass of water, please?"

A minute later, he returned to the table. By then, Emma had

gotten her tears under control. She gratefully drank the water as Chris sipped his coffee. "Better?" he asked.

She nodded.

"Look, do you want to talk about it?"

Emma bit her lip. "I'm so ashamed."

Chris's gut twisted, but he didn't change his open expression. "I'll listen. As a professional. No judgment. Just between us."

She looked at the table. "What about George?"

"It's different now. Doctor-patient confidentially."

She closed her eyes. "All right." Her voice was very small.

Chris looked around. "It's a nice day. What say we grab a bench in the park and talk?"

She nodded. Chris tossed a dollar tip on the table and walked his friend out of the café and across the street to Lafayette Square. Sitting her down on a shady park bench, he called his office, canceling his rounds.

"You won't get into trouble staying here with me?" Emma asked.

"It's cool. They'll get somebody to cover. Told 'em it was an emergency." He leaned back. "So. How are things? Really?"

Emma drew a deep breath and told him.

Chris, his elbows on his knees, watched the birds dance about the grass of Lafayette Square with envy. *Look at them—no worries, no cares. Just looking for the next worm or crumb. There's something to be said for that.*

The lady beside him dried her eyes. "You haven't said anything."

He glanced at her. "I didn't want to interrupt you. How do you feel?"

"Lousy."

"Anything else?"

Emma sighed. "Relieved, actually."

"Mmm-hmm."

"You knew that, didn't you?"

"It can be a great release, talking about things." He leaned back. "I went to school and paid thousands of dollars to learn that. Oh, and the ability to prescribe drugs."

She gave a snort. "Got any for me? I could use something right now."

Chris laughed. "No, nothing pharmaceutical. But, I do have some advice." He sobered up. "Want to hear it?"

She nodded.

"You need to talk to somebody. Somebody who can help you through all this."

"I thought you—"

"No, Em, not me. I'm too close." He smiled. "I told you, I'm your friend."

"Who, then?"

"I can give you a couple of names of some good therapists, or you could go see your rabbi."

She nodded. "Let me think about it."

"Okay. But I've got to tell you: no matter how strong you are, you need help. This thing is breaking your back. Look, it's like your car. When it's running right, all you need to do is to fill the tank and check the oil. But, eventually, something's gonna break, and it's got to go to a mechanic."

She thought about that. "Not everybody's head breaks, though."

"Not everybody's transmission goes, either. Wishing it was your tires won't fix it, will it? Besides, it's not your head, Emma. It's your soul. You've had a lot thrown on you. You just need somebody to help you."

"Help me learn how to cope?"

"Yes, and learn how to get rid of some of the burden you're carrying."

She looked at him, for the first time hope showing on her face.

"You've been doing too much, Emma. It's time you let go of some of that."

"But Papa, George—"

He patted her shoulder. "Talking to someone is only a first step. There are going to be more steps and by other people: Abe if he's willing. Definitely George."

She shook her head. "Papa won't do anything. George...I don't know."

"You may have to help him."

She turned to him. "How can I help George? I can't talk to him about this!"

"Do you love him? Do you want to stay married to him?"

"Of course!" she said with passion.

"Then you'll have to help him. But you can't do that right now. You have to help yourself first."

"I understand." She thought it over. "I'll go talk to the rabbi."

Chris released a breath. "Good. If you have any questions, call me. Anytime, day or night."

"Day or night?" Her dull eyes showed a ghost of a twinkle. "You sure Mari would approve of that?"

He laughed. "*Well*, maybe not *too* late. C'mon, it's time you got home, and I've got to get back to work."

The couple rose, and Chris walked Emma to her car. She gave him a kiss on the cheek before she got into the Volvo.

"Thank you, Chris, for everything. For...for not judging me. For understanding." She closed her door and drove off.

Chris began his journey back to the LSU Medical Center, the bounce in his step noticeably missing. There was a good reason for a therapist not to treat his friends. Sometimes they learn stuff they wish they hadn't. And then they have to get it out of their head somehow.

Talking things out with a therapist can be an alleviating experience for a patient. It can lift crushing burdens from their shoulders. The only trouble was that sometimes it got transferred to the therapist. An occupational hazard of Chris's profession was the difficulty practitioners experienced handling their portion of the grief, delusions, and anger pulled or poured out of their subjects. Some turned to alcohol and drugs in an effort to drown the burden of *knowing*. Others wrote, painted, or exercised extensively.

As Dr. Chris Breaux walked his abbreviated rounds in the psych ward of LSU's Charity Hospital, he was already planning his own treatment for management of too much information.

Lakeview

WHEN EMMA RETURNED HOME, THE HOUSE WAS QUIET. APPARently, Abe was taking a nap. She took advantage of the situation and sought the sanctuary of her bedroom.

Emma lay on the bed, a pillow clutched to her midsection, fighting the shame that threatened to overwhelm her. She tried to tell herself that her meeting with Frank was innocent—just some harmless flirtation. But deep inside, she knew she was fooling herself. She had picked the location for their meeting because the chances of anyone she knew seeing her downtown was low compared to Lakeview. She realized today's meeting wouldn't have led anywhere good.

If Chris hadn't come across us, would I have...? She couldn't finish the thought.

Glancing at her bedside table, her eyes fell on a photo from her wedding day. She and George looked so happy. She wanted to stay married to George. She wanted that very much. What had happened? Could she ever feel the way she felt on that day again?

She sat up and reached inside a drawer in her nightstand for a telephone book. A minute later, she was dialing.

"Hello. May I speak to Rabbi Tuckmann? ... Thank you, I'll hold."

A PLEASED GEORGE KATZ PULLED HIS CAR INTO THE DRIVEWAY. Two procedures had been postponed, so he took the opportunity to come home early and surprise Emma. Walking through the house, though, he saw no sign of her.

"Abe, where's Emma?" he asked his father-in-law.

The older man peered at him. "Don't know. Haven't seen her all day."

George was confused. "She leave?" Emma's Volvo was in the garage.

"Yeah, around lunch. I didn't see her come back, but I took a nap earlier. Maybe she's in her bedroom." As George walked that way, Abe added, "Ask her about dinner, huh?"

George found his wife asleep on the bed, the comforter pulled about her. He silently closed the door and quietly moved to her side. He sat down and stroked her cheek. Emma awoke with a start, her eyes wide in surprise.

"Hey," George said gently. "I got off early."

"Oh," was all she could manage.

"I thought we could go out to dinner somewhere." George grew apprehensive. "Em, honey, are you all right?"

To George's surprise, she sat up quickly and embraced him. "I will be. I will be."

Faubourg Marigny

MARIANNE HAD JUST TURNED ON THE OVEN IN HER KITCHEN when the doorbell rang. She quickly walked to the door and, before unlocking the dead bolt, peered through the peephole.

"Chris!" She hastily opened the door. "Come in, sweetie. I didn't know you were coming by."

"Hi. I'm not bothering you, am I?" His voice was distant and distracted.

"Of course not! I was just getting dinner ready."

"Oh. I'm sorry."

"Chris, get your butt in here!" She escorted her fiancé to the sofa in the living room and sat down next to him. "I'm glad to see you, sugar, but why didn't you call?"

"Sorry, I guess my brain's not working."

She scooted over. "Honey, what's wrong?"

"Work. It was bad today."

Marianne took her lover in her arms. "Oh, baby, I'm sorry. What can I do to make it better?"

Chris closed his eyes and relaxed in her embrace. "You're doing it."

She kissed his temple. "Then you stay right here."

"What about your dinner?"

"I was just getting ready to heat up a pizza. Want some?"

"Maybe later."

The two sat in silence, Marianne slowly caressing Chris's arm.

Finally, Chris spoke again. "Marianne, promise me something. If I ever do something stupid like working too long or ignoring you or taking you for granted, would you take a two-by-four to my thick skull?"

Marianne knew Chris was being serious. "Absolutely."

"Thank you."

Chapter 12

Tuesday, November 9: Third District Headquarters

Special Agent Baugham made himself comfortable in Fitzwilliam's office. "Congratulations on your promotion, Captain. Nice office."

"Thanks," Fitzwilliam said in a non-committal fashion. "What can the NOPD do for the FBI?" The FBI wasn't the most popular law enforcement agency among its peers, due to its habit of taking over investigations.

Baugham reached into his attaché case. "Tell us what you know about this man." He slid the file over the desk.

Fitzwilliam's heart almost skipped a beat after he opened it. "You're after Wickham?"

"We're looking for him. He's a person of interest in a case we're working. We understand you know this guy better than anybody on the force."

"Unfortunately." Fitzwilliam looked up at the FBI agent with a wolf's grin. "Special Agent Baugham, I'm now your new best friend."

Wednesday, November 17: Gretna

A WEEK LATER, ON A WET WEDNESDAY MORNING, A COMBINED force of federal agents, Louisiana state police, and Jefferson Parish sheriff deputies descended upon a small house in Gretna, executing a federal search warrant. In attendance were observers from the sheriff departments of Lafourche and Terrebonne parishes and

Captain Fitzwilliam of the NOPD. Guns drawn, agents of the FBI, DEA, and Customs Service secured the premises and began to search for evidence. They quickly found a floor safe and $75,000 in cash within. There was nothing else as it seemed the house had not been inhabited for some time.

"Looks like our friend was using the place to stash cash," Baugham reported to Fitzwilliam.

"Anything else?"

"No drugs or weapons. We'll see what the forensics team comes up with."

Fitzwilliam nodded, his hopes sinking. Wickham wasn't the brightest bulb in the package, but he had the Devil's own luck. Somehow, the bastard's animal instincts had told him to keep his assets in separate locations. The cops had his money but not his product. And unless the forensics people got real lucky, they had no idea where Wickham was holed up. In a metro area of 1.5 million people, he could be anywhere.

He looked down the street, blocked off by JPSO. A deputy was redirecting traffic from the crime scene, a black sports car being the latest vehicle turned away. The rain dripped off the brim of Fitzwilliam's hat as despair began to grow.

Will I ever catch that bastard?

GREG WICKHAM, TO HIS SURPRISE, FOUND OUT IT WAS HARD TO spend a hundred thousand dollars in cash. You couldn't deposit it in a bank without filling out federal forms, stating the source of the money. You couldn't buy any big-ticket items legally with cash without providing the same information. One could only use the cash in the black market where everything went at a premium.

Wickham wanted a new car, thinking his red Camaro was getting well known as his signature. But he had to settle for painting his trusty two-door black. He was investigating buying a stolen car that had the VIN numbers removed, but he had spent some time checking out the seller. He was on his way to his "bank" when he saw the red lights. His worst nightmare had come true—the cops had found his hidey-hole.

As the deputy turned him away, a terrified Wickham thanked his lucky stars that he had the car painted. Surely, the cops were looking for a red Camaro. But his black one would only protect him for a short time. He knew he had to go to ground.

As he made his way back to the Crescent City Connection, he beat the steering wheel in frustration. Seventy-five big ones were gone. All he had left was about fifteen G's and the cocaine. Lots of product, but with no organization to distribute it, he had only two options. One, he could sell the stuff at a steep discount to another dealer and get out of town. It was the smart play, but it meant Wickham was giving up the chance to make a million. He had never had that opportunity before, and he wasn't going to blow it.

The second option was to build his own organization. That was dangerous as the other gangs wouldn't take kindly to an interloper. Without the cash, he couldn't hire people or buy cooperation. And now the cops were after him.

Still, he had earned his chance to be rich. Bought it with blood. He was *made* now. He was a killer, a *dangerous* motherfucker. G-Daddy wasn't backing down to anybody.

Wickham made his way to his second hidey-hole, deep in the Upper Ninth Ward.

Saturday, November 20: Abita Springs

ABITA SPRINGS' MONEY HILL GOLF AND COUNTRY CLUB IS A beautiful example of golf in Louisiana. Winding its way through the pine-covered hills of St. Tammany Parish, the demanding tract is an essential stop on the state's Audubon Golf Trail.

Taking the tee box of the difficult tenth hole on this unseasonably warm day was a foursome, all guests of Chuck Bingley. William, having the honors, stood on the tee box, gazing at the hole. A glorious 457-yard downhill par-4, there was a slight dogleg to the left to a well-bunkered green. The mature pine trees lining the fairway gave the golfer the impression this hole had been carved out of the woods of North Carolina rather than built from a tree farm an hour north of New Orleans.

"Well, are ya gonna look at it all day, or are ya gonna hit?" asked his playing partner and competitor.

William grinned at John Buford. "Want to go double or nothing on this hole?" Buford waved his agreement. William set up carefully and played an easy draw right to the bottom of the hill.

Buford was more aggressive, his drive going almost three hundred yards, but leaving him an uphill lie. Chuck kept his ball in play, but Chris found one of the fairway bunkers. Chuck flubbed his second shot, and he was left with a hundred-yard pitch after his third. Chris got out of the bunker but still had two hundred yards to get home.

William's approach shot from a level lie landed just short of the green between the bunkers and trickled on. Buford's shot bled to the right and ended in the middle of a sand trap. The sand shot ended up stiff, and William missed his birdie putt, so they halved the hole with a par. Chris and Chuck each carted double-bogeys.

Approaching the eleventh tee, Buford said, "How about a push?"

"You're on," replied William.

"You know," Chris remarked to Chuck in the other golf cart, "it's worth losing my money to these two just for the privilege of watching them beat each other's brains in."

Chuck grinned. "Why do you think I invited them?"

Covington

St. Tammany was the fastest growing parish in the state as people fled the chaos of the city and the cookie-cutter sameness of suburbia to flock to the piney woods of the North Shore. Throughout the parish, developers carved their subdivisions out of the former tree farms so the commuters could have their little quarter-acre of paradise, driving to their high paying jobs in New Orleans, along the river, or to the Stennis Space Center just east of Slidell. Most of the local jobs were in the relatively low-paying service or retail sectors.

Chuck and Jane Bingley's slice of heaven was located near the parish seat of Covington. Chuck had his beloved house built near the street to maximize the size of the chain-link fenced backyard. On that Saturday afternoon, Jane sat on her patio with Elizabeth, Carrie, and Marianne. They watched the kids scampering on the lawn, treetops swaying in the late afternoon breeze. It was amazing how much noise three children could make.

"Hmm," observed Jane, "I think Trey's going to be in sports." Her nephew, John Taylor Buford III, was running all over the place, head down making a spurting sound.

"What's that sound he's making?" asked Marianne.

Carrie waved her hand. "His latest obsession. He heard a motorcycle, and now he's imitating it. *Constantly.*"

"How long has this been going on?"

"Three weeks."

"Great," said Jane. "Is that what I've got to look forward to when Brett reaches that age?"

"At least with a sister, he'll be potty-trained sooner. We just got Trey over the hump, as it were." Carrie stood up. "Trey! No, no!"

The child, no longer pretending to be a Harley Davidson, had approached the Great Dane puppy, Rufus. "Max?"

"No, Trey, that's not Max." She walked over and picked up her son.

"Who's Max?" asked Elizabeth.

"Max is Carrie and John's Boxer," Jane replied.

"Max just loves Trey and lets him climb all over him," Carrie explained. "The trouble is Trey thinks every dog is Max."

"Rufus is very sweet," said Jane. "I'm sure he wouldn't have any problem with Trey."

"I'm certain you're right, but we're trying to teach Trey not to climb on every dog he sees."

"Max!" Trey pointed at Rufus.

"No, sweetie. That's not Max. That's Rufus. Say, 'Hi, Rufus.'"

Trey looked at the dog, his face scowling. "No! *Max!*" he said triumphantly.

By this time, Jane's daughter, Hailey, decided to have her share of the conversation. "No, Trey. My doggie's name is Rufus, not Max. Don't be such a little baby."

Trey considered his cousin's comment for a moment and then screwed up his face. "Brruurrrpppttt!"

"Well, that ends *that* conversation," laughed Carrie. "It's nap time, young man." Carrie went into the house, Jane following with Brett. They returned after a few minutes with a pitcher of margaritas. The girls were into their first drink when the boys returned.

Elizabeth remained seated as the men were greeted by their ladies. Chuck got a hug and kiss from Jane before he was assaulted by both Hailey and Rufus. Marianne latched onto Chris and gave him a long, slow kiss, knocking off his golf cap. Buford's welcome was much more sedate—a peck on the cheek—as Carrie was not into public displays of affection. They stood close together, her arm around her husband's waist, and no one saw Buford's free hand gently cup her ass. Carrie only smiled as she had no intention of moving. Why else would she have worn a thong under her loose-fitting Capri pants?

"How did you play?" Marianne asked her fiancé.

"Not too good. Lost all the money. Everybody else won, 'cept when they played with me. Guess I'm the bad luck charm today."

Marianne kissed Chris' cheek. "You'll play better next time, sugar."

"It was fun watching John and Will go after it toe-to-toe during the middle six, wasn't it?" injected Chuck.

"You take him, Johnny?" asked Carrie in a low voice.

Buford shook his head. "Nah, not this time. Played good, though. Just wasn't my day."

Elizabeth looked around. "Where's Will? Didn't he come?"

Chuck answered. "He left right after the round. Had some charity thing to go to."

"And we have to make our farewells too," added Chris. "Mari's got a gig tonight." The couple wished everybody goodbye, which gave time for Elizabeth to hide her disappointment. She had hoped to see William that evening.

Jane turned to her husband. "Now that you've had your fun, how about getting started on the grilling? The chickens are all ready."

Chuck pouted. "Janie, don't I get a beer first?"

"You light the grill, and I'll grab one for you. John, want something?"

Seconding the beer order, the two men returned to the patio where Chuck lit the gas grill. Everyone was soon in chairs around the patio, Hailey in her father's lap, while dinner roasted. The conversation was lively and open, and every effort was made to include Elizabeth, but she still felt somewhat like a third wheel. She was odd-woman out, without a date.

She volunteered to hold Brett when it came time to retrieve the boys from their naps. She enjoyed playing with her nephew, but still she couldn't get William Darcy's absence out of her mind.

Is he really at a charity event, or is he avoiding me?

Chapter 13

George Katz pulled into his garage and walked into the house. "Hello! Where is everybody?"

"Right here." Emma rose from the couch.

"Em? What's going on? Where's Abe?"

"He's out. Mrs. Taylor took him to a movie."

"You're kidding me."

Emma nervously held out her hand. "Why don't you sit down?"

George put down his briefcase and walked over to the sofa. "Sure." He sat and was surprised Emma didn't join him. "Em? Is something wrong?"

"No. I mean— George, we need to talk."

George rolled his eyes. "What did Abe do now?"

Emma sat on the far end of the couch, her eyes focused on the backyard through the windows. "It's not Abe I want to talk to you about."

"Oh? Then what?"

"You." She turned to her husband. "You and me. Us. Our marriage."

George was stunned. "What about our marriage?"

Emma tried to concentrate on the advice Rabbi Tuckmann had given her: *"Be clear about your feelings. Be as positive as you can. Do not blame. Do not say, 'You are bad.' Rather, say, 'This is how your behavior affects me.' Do not forget to praise him for positive actions."*

"George, the first thing I want to say is I love you very much. You've worked very hard to provide for both my father and me. You've seldom complained about Papa living here, a situation that has been difficult for me, and I'm his daughter. I can't imagine how it affects you."

"Emma, it's okay. I know we have to have Abe with—"

"George, please, let me finish. This is very hard for me." She took a deep breath. "I trust you. You've given me no reason to mistrust you. But George, I wish I could say I'm as happy in this marriage as I would wish to be—as much as I could be—but I'm not."

"You're unhappy? Why? I don't understand."

"I feel we've become strangers in our own house. I hardly see you anymore. I feel more like your roommate than your wife."

George looked stunned. "I had no idea. I'm sorry. I've been so tired after work. Half the time you're already in bed. I was just letting you sleep. Oh, Emma, honey, I'm sorry. I'll do better. I'll try to be more attentive when I come home." He reached out his hand, but Emma wouldn't take it.

"You're missing the point, George. I don't just want more of your attention *when* you are home. I want you home *more*."

George blinked for a second. "Home more? You mean, work less?"

"Yes."

"Emma, I can't do that!"

"Why not?"

"I've got work to do, important work! I've got classes to teach, patients to care for, paperwork to do. Being a surgeon in a teaching hospital isn't a nine-to-five job. Somebody comes in, I've got to take care of them."

Emma struggled to be patient. "Just listen to yourself. You're not an emergency room physician; you're a cardiac surgeon. Almost all of your operations are by appointment. You set your own schedule—"

"Not all the time," George interrupted her. "Why, just last week, this heart attack came in—"

"George, stop it. Can't you see you're a workaholic?"

"I am not! What is this, some sort of intervention?"

"Yes, it is."

George laughed without mirth. "Where did you get your medical training? You don't know what you're talking about! Working long hours comes with this job!"

Emma fought to control her temper. The rabbi had warned her George would be in denial, and he might get insulting.

"I don't recommend you do this yourself," he had told her. *"It can get very rough, breaking through the denial. Unkind things are often said. Still, if you are insistent, remember to stay calm and stay on task. Stick to your points, and let everything else roll off your back."*

It was easier said than done. She gritted her teeth. "I am fully aware that you are a dedicated doctor, George, and you have a lucrative practice."

"Damn right! It's paying for this crappy house!"

"We do have expenses, but Papa has offered to chip in."

"I know, but I don't know if I want to sink any more money into this place."

"You've paid off your student loans."

"Yeah, finally." He rose to his feet and began pacing. "But malpractice keeps going up, Medicare keeps cutting back—"

"So you keep going after extra work."

"We can use the money."

"I do the books. We're doing well, enough so we have money in our savings account."

"Yeah, but what if something happens? The roof goes bad or one of the cars breaks down? I'd like to have a bigger cushion."

Emma started to relax, as she realized George was making excuses instead of just denying. She decided to dig a little. "I know it's hard on you being the only breadwinner. If I had stayed in school—"

George dismissed that with a wave. "I make enough for both of us. We talked about that before we got married. Besides, you've got a full-time job watching Abe."

"Yes." She would hold that issue for later. "But not everything you do at the hospital is for pay, is it? How many procedures did you observe this month?"

George turned to her. "Several. But it's part of my job to observe interns and the newer surgeons."

"George, honestly, how many of them were students or newbies?"

"Umm...most of them." Emma stared at him, and he colored. "All right, so I watch my colleagues sometimes. That's not a crime, is it?"

"Is there a problem at Tulane? I'm serious. If the quality of the physicians is in question, then I understand your need to supervise them closely. Please be frank with me."

George began pacing again, running his hand though his thinning hair. "No, there's nothing wrong with the other surgeons. They're all top-notch."

"I see. Then the only answer is that you find it more enjoyable to interact with your colleagues than with your family. You're more comfortable at the hospital than here."

He froze, shock on his face. "Emma, no, you can't believe that!"

She shrugged. "I do believe it. It's understandable. It's your livelihood, your life."

George crossed to her, bent over, and took hold of her upper arms. "No! You're my life! Nothing is more important to me than you!"

She looked him full in the face, dry-eyed and somber. "Then prove it."

"How? What do you want me to do?"

"I want you at home more often."

"Emma, I'll try, but they need me."

She broke away and stood up, facing away from him. "See? You're already trying to wiggle your way out of this."

"Honey, be fair. It's not just up to me. My supervisors—"

She kept her back to him. "Were you sent home today?"

George was taken aback. "How'd you know that?"

She turned and looked at him, one eyebrow raised.

George gaped. "You don't mean—"

"You were sent home at my request."

"Emma! What did you say to them?"

"That I thought you had been working too hard. Dr. Griffith agreed."

George groaned. "Aw, crap! He's my boss!"

Emma was emotionless. "He thinks you're the most gifted surgeon on the staff, but he's been afraid you might burn out. Our conversation was very enlightening."

"What do you mean?" His voice was unsteady.

"He told me he had been considering calling you in about it. I just beat him to the punch."

George stared out the back window in despair, both hands on top of his head.

In a comforting voice, Emma said, "It's only because he's so worried about you. He really cares, as I do. Oh, George, please, can't you understand?"

"I've got no words," he managed. "I've got to think. By myself." He started to the back door.

"George!"

"Not now, Emma. Not now." He let himself out the back.

Emma stood in the middle of her den, wondering whether she had succeeded in saving her marriage or wrecking it.

A HALF-HOUR LATER—A LIFETIME TO EMMA—SHE HESITANTLY opened the patio door. George had been sitting on a lawn chair in the cool darkness, staring at the swimming pool.

"George, are you hungry?" She could only see the back of his head.

"No—yes, a little." His voice was unemotional.

She bit her lip. "Something light?"

"That would be nice."

She retreated to the kitchen. A couple of minutes later, she joined him with a tray of grilled chicken salads and two beers. She placed it on the patio table before taking a seat next to her husband. George glanced at the beer on the tray.

"I thought you could use one," Emma said hesitantly.

To her surprise, George put his head down. "I don't deserve you."

"Why do you say that?"

"I've been out here thinking, and you're right. I've been a crappy husband."

Emma closed her eyes. "I never said you were a crappy husband."

"You might as well have. It's true. I've been running away. I haven't done right by you."

"Neither one of us is blameless, honey." She wanted to take his hand, but resisted the impulse. She knew they had to talk this out first. "I should have told you how I felt a long time ago. That's something I have to work on. But you said something just now. What have you been running away from? From me?"

"Not you, but everything else. The stress, the pressure, the—Em, I'm sorry to say it, but the disappointment. The disappointment of not having our life the way I wanted it, the way I intended it. When we got married, all I wanted to do was to love you, care for you. But when Abe got sick, everything changed. It didn't go bad, please believe me, but it wasn't what I *planned*. Honey, I know we had to take care of Abe. I recognize that. It just changed everything."

He looked at the sky. "We were going to live in my downtown condo for a couple of years, just enjoying being married. Have a lifelong honeymoon. I wanted to travel the world—to treat you like the princess you are."

"I am not a princess, George," Emma interjected.

"To me, you are. Instead, we have to plan our whole life around a near invalid. We had to buy this lousy house because it had two master suites and a single floor because Abe couldn't handle steps anymore. All the money I wanted to use for vacations we poured into this piece of crap.

"And Abe. Honey, I know it's been hard on him. It's not his fault he has cardiac disease. But he hasn't really helped, you know? He sits around, bitches, and demands attention. All the work catering to him has fallen on you.

"I'm not totally blaming him. I should have been here for you, taken some of that stuff off you. But I didn't. Instead, I ran away and hid in my work. I can see that now." He paused. "I haven't been very much of a man."

Emma knew she couldn't let George wallow in self-recrimination any more than live in denial. "Yes, it's been very hard for me to carry the burden of caring for Papa by myself. But I share the responsibility for what happened. I allowed you to escape to the hospital when we should have been working through this problem together. Like I said, I'm not blameless. I should have talked to you about how I felt long ago. I should have asked for your help. I should have trusted you with my feelings. Instead, I let all the stress and resentment build up. That was wrong of me.

"George, I have something to confess to you. I've been talking to Rabbi Tuckmann almost every day for the last few weeks. He's been helping me see why I'm unhappy, and we've been exploring ways that will help me deal with all the stress of caring for Papa.

"I do need your help and support because I can't do this alone. But I need a partner to share my burdens, not a savior who's going to step in and make everything all right for me. And I want to help you by sharing *your* burdens, but I can't do that unless you let me in. So the question remains—what are we going to do?"

George looked at her. Emma steeled herself to look back with no emotion whatsoever. George broke first.

"I'll do better."

As kindly as she could, Emma asked, "What do you mean by that, George?"

"I'm going to be here more—not hide at work. Be here when you need to talk. Be here when I need to talk. Try to help you with Abe."

"I want more than your help. I want—" Emma's voice broke. George's expression turned to concern as she struggled to continue. "I want *you* back. I want *us* back."

"I want that too," he whispered.

Before either knew it, they were holding hands so tightly, Emma thought it might cut off the blood to George's fingers. Yet, nether relented.

"I love you."

"I love you too."

They said nothing for a while as they allowed their mutual love to begin to heal their hearts.

Finally, Emma said, "You ought to eat." She reached over and handed out the salads. They munched and sipped the beers in companionable silence.

"Can I ask one more thing of you, George?"

There was a pause. "All right."

"Can we get away somewhere soon? Just the two of us?"

"You mean a vacation?"

"Yes." Emma almost laughed at the relief in George's voice. She wondered what he was afraid she was going to ask and quickly dismissed the thought. It didn't matter. George loved her and wanted to fix their marriage.

"What about Abe?"

"I'll take care of that."

"Okay. When?"

"Soon. Chanukah's early this year; it's on the eighth. Maybe over Christmas?"

"I don't know. I'll have to get time off."

"Please—will you please try?" she made herself say. "This is important to me."

George looked at her and nodded. "You go ahead and book it. I'll make it happen."

"Thank you, George. I love you."

"I love you too." He paused. "When is Abe due back?"

"About a half-hour."

"Rats. Not enough time."

"Not enough time for what?"

"For really good make-up sex."

She chuckled. "We have all night, George."

He sighed softly. "Yeah, but we'll have to be quiet."

She looked him straight in the eyes. "Then, we'll be quiet." As she kissed him, she relaxed as the first and most difficult part of George's intervention was completed. Phase Two would be during the vacation.

We'll be quiet tonight, my love—this time. But we're going to fix that "putting me on a pedestal" tendency of yours—and soon.

Chapter 14

An afternoon telephone call of some importance occurred the next day.

"Hey, Mari, it's Emma."

"Hey girl, what's up?"

"Nothing much. Say, isn't your mother a travel agent?"

"Yeah, back in Jackson. You're going on a trip?"

"I'd like to book an island vacation around Christmas."

"Whoa, last minute! I guess you're talking about the Caribbean. You know winter's high season down there, don't you?"

"I know, so I thought a travel agent might know of some last-minute deals."

"You've come to the right place. I'll have Mom call you. So, what are you looking for?"

"Something romantic. It's a second honeymoon of sorts. Something to spice things up, you know? I thought maybe Aruba or the Grand Caymans."

"Spicy? Ever thought of Saint Martin?"

"No. Is it nice?"

"Oh, honey, if you want to put some starch in George's shorts, let me tell you!"

One of the most beautiful and least known festival seasons in Louisiana is the local celebration of Christmas. Towns across the state hold charming, understated events to mark the end of the year. The north Louisiana city of Natchitoches is renowned for lighting its downtown along the Cane River the whole month long. Along the lower Mississippi River, families and groups build huge, fanciful bonfires on the river levees to light the way for Papa Noel on Christmas Eve. Plantation homes all across the state put on their holiday best and hold Christmas caroling concerts.

In New Orleans, the celebration is unique. The great mansions along St. Charles Avenue are dressed in a charming Victorian style. Creole restaurants offer traditional Réveillon dinners—special three- and four-course dinners served only at Christmas. A subtle loveliness descends on the city as it prepares not only for the birth of the Savior, but the madness of New Year's and the Sugar Bowl crowds.

Thursday, December 2: Warehouse District
William Darcy stuck his head out of his office. "Barbara, would you come in, please?" A moment later, he and his assistant were sitting at the small table in one corner of his office.

"You're going be mad at me," he began.

"Probably. What do I have to do?" She pulled out a pen.

"Prepare a Christmas party here for fifty on December 23. It's for the EDNO staff. I volunteered, being the new guy on their board and all."

"Mmm-hmm. How nice do you want it?" Barbara acted as though organizing a party for fifty in three weeks was a walk in the park. William knew it wasn't, and he hoped Barbara knew that he knew it wasn't easy.

"Do it up real nice."

"Full bar?"

William twisted his face. "What do you think?"

"If it was up to me, I'd go with beer and wine."

"Okay. And charge everything to me. This is my treat."

"Yes, sir. I'll get on it right away."

"Sorry to drop this in your lap at the last minute."

"It's all right. We do so much business with our caterer, I ought to be able to use an IOU or two."

Barbara left, leaving William Darcy in a pensive state. It was a spur of the moment thing to volunteer at the last board meeting. He wondered whether he was a glutton for punishment. Sure, EDNO had done good work over the last year, and they certainly deserved the recognition, but the tradition at the non-profit was to invite spouses and guests to parties. That meant Elizabeth would be bringing Tony Riviere. It was hard enough seeing her every time he did something for EDNO. How was he going to get though an evening watching her with another man, even one as respectable as Riviere? William looked out his window at the river.

When am I going to get over this? It's over and has been for five years.

But I've got no choice. I can be a man or a coward. I've been running away for too long. If I really love Elizabeth, I ought to be happy for her. Maybe this will be a good thing. Maybe I can finally put Elizabeth Boudreaux behind me forever.

Monday, December 6: Downtown

```
To: All EDNO staff
From: Carl Eden
Re: Christmas Party

DGS has generously offered to host this year's
Christmas party. It will be held December 23 in the
DGS boardroom from 5:30 to 7:30 p.m. Spouses and
guests are invited. Please RSVP to Jan Hill by COB
Friday.
```

Elizabeth's eyes flew open at the unexpected email. This would be the first time she and William would be at a social function together since college.

Why was he doing this? Her heart whispered he was doing it for her, but it was quickly hushed. Since their reunion in September, William hadn't shown the least indication of being anything more than a friendly acquaintance.

Yes, they had gotten along, and it seemed he had forgiven her. Had he read the letter? It seemed so. Yet…

"I thought I liked you, maybe even loved you, but it's clear I really don't know you. I don't know who the hell you are. But whoever that is, I don't want anything to do with her!"

Yes, William might have forgiven her, but it was impossible he had forgotten.

She sighed. Yes, she still loved him, but Marianne was right. It was time to put William Darcy behind her forever.

City Park in New Orleans is one of the largest urban parks in the nation. At over thirteen hundred acres, it is home to the Museum of Art, three golf courses, two stadiums, the Storyland children's area, nine athletic fields, eleven miles of lagoons, lakes, and bayous, and the world's largest collection of mature live oak trees.

A grand tradition every year is Celebration in the Oaks, when New Orleans' City Park is turned into a wonderland of lights hanging from the famous live oaks.

Friday, December 17: City Park

Chris knew the charming display was best enjoyed by horse-drawn carriage, which was why he was bundled up with Marianne on a chilly winter's night.

She huddled close, her nose securely in his neck. "This is wonderful, sugar. Thank you for thinking of it."

He held her tighter. "We locals sometimes forget we have things like Celebration in the Oaks. You warm enough?"

Her hand began exploring. "If I get cold, I'll just heat up my ol' hot water bottle."

"Watch it, honey. We're not alone."

"Don't mind me, folks," chuckled the driver. "Y'all enjoy yourselves."

Chris still thought it would be a good idea to change the subject. "Your mom is okay with you staying in the city for the holidays?"

Marianne nodded. "She knows my singing career is important. We have a lot of gigs between Christmas and New Year's with the bowl game and all."

"We'll run up to Jackson in January," Chris promised.

"What about your folks?"

He kissed her nose. "They know *you're* important, *chère*. Besides, I've got a surprise."

She jerked her head up. "What is it? Tell me!"

"My mom and dad are coming to the city Monday and staying in my spare bedroom through Christmas. They want to see one of your shows."

"They are! Wonderful!" They kissed until they were both breathless.

"Chris, let's go home after the ride, okay?"

"Sure. Are you cold?"

She whispered in his ear. "With your folks coming over, there won't be any overnighters for a while. I need me some Cajun lovin' to see me through the holidays."

"Right," he whispered back. Louder, he requested, "Driver, you can speed it up."

The man laughed. "Happens every time."

Thursday, December 23: Warehouse District

AT 5:30 P.M., THE DOORS OF THE BOARDROOM OF DELTA GLOBAL

Shipping were thrown open to EDNO and their guests. The room was a large rectangle, taking up much of the top floor of the four-story DGS building located on the river side of the protection levee at the foot of Poydras Street. One side was lined with windows overlooking the Mississippi. A door led to a small balcony. The board table in the center of the room was covered with appetizers. A temporary bar serving wine, beer and soft drinks was set up close to the double doors leading to the hallway. A second door led to the personal offices of the President/CEO and the Chairman. The hosts for the evening were William Darcy and his VP of Marketing, Leon Anderson.

The men were dressed in their usual business attire—suits and sport coats—with only Christmas ties as a nod to the season. The women's outfits were more suitable for a night on the town than a day at the office. Elizabeth, after much indecision, had decided on a dark green cocktail dress and heels, a red belt showing off her trim figure.

Most everyone who was married or attached brought guests. Elizabeth hung out with Charlotte Lucas, her co-worker, as neither had a date.

As they were introduced to Kaywanda's new boyfriend, Scott Davis, Charlotte asked, "And where did you say you met him, Kay?"

Kaywanda, in a tight purple dress, giggled as she tightened her hold on Scott's arm. "I was down at Re-Uzz-It—you know, that recycled building supply non-profit off St. Claude? I was looking for a new door for my momma's house, and Scott here was *so* helpful, showing me all the doors that had come in, taking measurements, and all that construction stuff. We got to talking and found we had so much in common and…well, here we are!"

Scott was graduate-school casual in a grey hound's-tooth jacket over a black crew-neck shirt and tan cargo pants. His shoes had seen better days. "I'm just working there until next fall. I start my graduate studies in Sociology at UNO in September."

Kaywanda piped in. "He wants to get his Ph.D. or become a social worker. Isn't that wonderful?"

They shared a little more small talk before the couple drifted off. Once out of range, Charlotte leaned over to Elizabeth. "So, what do you think of Kay's friend?"

"He's nice, if awfully—"

"White?" injected Charlotte.

"I was going to say Goth with all those piercings and tattoos, Char."

"That too," Charlotte laughed. "I like him. Kay needs somebody good."

Elizabeth and Charlotte had talked for a while with Jan Hill and her husband, a contractor from Jefferson, when Elizabeth noticed William Darcy approaching. He was in a navy suit with a tie in a holly pattern. Her gut clenched. She had wondered whether William was going to talk to her ever since she learned of his offer to host the party. Apparently, he was.

"Hi, Will." She moved over to invite him into the circle of conversation.

"Merry Christmas, Lizzy," he smiled. "I hope all of you are enjoying yourselves. Hello, Charlotte, Jan. Mr. Hill, pleased to meet you."

"Same here, Mr. Darcy." Mr. Hill's voice sounded like a gravel pit. "Very nice place you got here. Who built it?"

"Haven't a clue. You may want to ask Leon." He turned to call to Anderson. "Hey, Leon, we got a question for you." After introducing Mr. Hill to Anderson, the two, with Jan, wandered off discussing the design of the building. William turned to Charlotte. "Are y'all having a good time?"

"Of course! What a spread you've put out! I just might sneak some of that shrimp home in my purse."

"Charlotte!" cried Elizabeth.

William kept a straight face. "Well, don't take them all. Leave some for me. Saves me from making groceries over Christmas." It took a second for the girls to get the joke, and all three had a good laugh.

Charlotte looked out the window. "That's a nice balcony, Mr. Darcy."

"Please, call me Will. Want to see it? The door's right this way." He escorted the two women through a door onto the balcony overlooking the wharf and the river. The sun was almost down, the last pink streams of sunlight painting the nearby skyscrapers. The day was mild with only a light breeze off the river.

"Beautiful!" exclaimed Charlotte. They moved to the railing, watching some of the river traffic.

"Yeah. Sometimes, when I brown-bag it, I eat lunch out here. My office is right over there." He pointed at another door.

Charlotte breathed in. "How can you get any work done with this view?"

"It's tough sometimes. My assistant, Barbara, keeps my feet to the fire, though." They turned and observed the crowd within. "Everybody seems to be enjoying themselves."

"It was nice of you to host this party, and to invite the spouses too."

"Yeah, well, it's a tradition at DGS, as well. We had about two hundred people at the office Christmas party last Friday. We had to hold it at the Hilton. You didn't bring a date, Char?"

She shook her head. "Lizzy's my date tonight."

"Tony couldn't make it tonight, Lizzy?" William asked.

Elizabeth blinked. "Pardon me?"

"Didn't Tony Riviere come in this weekend from Washington?"

"I don't know. How would I know that?"

William frowned. "What do you mean? I thought—hold on a second. Aren't y'all dating?"

"Tony Riviere? No."

"But I was— You aren't dating?" He was clearly confused.

Elizabeth shook her head. "Tony and I broke up back in May. I haven't seen him since."

Charlotte discreetly slipped back indoors. The pair never noticed.

William blinked. "You aren't dating Tony Riviere."

"No, I'm not." Elizabeth started to smile.

"Oh."

Now Elizabeth was confused. "You sound like you're disappointed."

William started. "No! I mean… I'm sorry." He looked over her shoulder. "Tony's a nice guy. I'm sorry it didn't work out."

"It happens."

"Right. Breakups can be painful. I hope…" He looked at her. "How are you doing?"

"I'm fine, Will." She realized William was uncomfortable, but for all the *right* reasons. Her heart lightened.

"Good, good. You look good. Well, I mean. Happy."

"I am happy. Alone, but happy."

"Good, good. No! I mean, It's not good you're alone. I mean—" He stopped and slapped his forehead. "Oh, hell, I better shut up. I sound like an idiot."

Elizabeth giggled. "And how are you?"

"Me? I'm fine, fine. I'm not dating anybody right now, either. Been busy, you know."

"Yes, I can imagine."

"Lots of out-of-town meetings."

"I know how it is. It's hard to have a relationship when you're busy."

He gave her an unreadable look before he leaned over the railing and gazed at the river in the twilight. "It's lonely too. Finally, you get to the point of wondering if it's all worth it. The work, without having someone to share it with. Without having meaning in your life."

Elizabeth joined him watching a freighter navigate the bend at Algiers Point. "I agree. We weren't made to go through life alone. Everyone's looking for that special someone, wondering if they'll ever meet, frightened they won't, and scared they've passed up the opportunity. Torn between the mystery of the future and the regrets of the past."

She stole a peek at her companion, afraid she had said too much or not enough. She felt a warm rush as he turned his attention to her, his deep, dark eyes searching, wondering. His lips started to move.

"Mr. Darcy?" The spell was broken by the interruption by William's assistant, Barbara. "I'm sorry to disturb you, but Miss Darcy's on line one."

"Oh!" William glanced at his watch. "Tell her I'll be at the condo in a little while. Thank you, Barbara." As the secretary walked away, he turned back to Elizabeth. "I'm sorry, Lizzy, but I've got to cut out a bit early. Gina got back in town today from Auburn, and we've got this dinner to go to. Family thing."

"I understand. How is your sister?"

"She's doing fine. She's studying marketing and graphic arts, and doing real well. Between school and her sorority, she's staying busy."

"Nice to have her home for the holidays."

"It is. And you? What are you doing this Christmas?"

"What I usually do. Spend some time back home in Chackbay."

"I'm sorry. I should have asked. How is your family? I know how Jane and Chuck are doing, but what about the rest of them?"

"Oh! They're fine. My parents are just the same. Mary's teaching now, and Kit's in college."

"There're five of you all together, right?"

"Yes, all girls. Jane, Mary, Kit, Lydia and me. The Boudreaux Babes." She didn't know if William had caught the slight hesitation before she mentioned her youngest sister.

William seemed torn for a moment. "I've *really* got to go. I'll make my excuses inside. But before I do, I want to personally wish you and your family a very Merry Christmas."

"Thank you, Will, that's very nice. I wish the same to you too."

"Please give my regards to Chuck and Jane."

"I will. See you next year!"

William stopped and turned, confused. "What? Oh, right, next year. January. Yep, I'll be seeing you. You bet!" He grinned, waved, and stepped back into the boardroom.

Elizabeth sagged back against the railing, replaying the encounter in her mind. She was still staring off into space when Charlotte found her a few minutes later.

"Mr. Darcy just left. What the heck was going on out here?"

Elizabeth had been contemplating William's dimples. "What's that, Char?"

"What's with you and Will Darcy?"

Elizabeth was glad the gathering darkness hid her blush. "We were just catching up on old times. We did go to college together."

"Is that all?"

"Since when did you get so nosy?"

"Since when do you have a private conversation with the most eligible bachelor in New Orleans?"

"Where did you get *that*?"

"*Pontchartrain Guardian*—two months ago."

Elizabeth tapped a finger on her friend's forehead. "You read trash, you'll turn *that* into trash. Now, let's go inside. All of a sudden, I'm famished!" She made her way towards the door, Charlotte following in her wake.

"Hey! Leave some shrimp for me!"

"Not a chance."

St. Charles Parish

IT WAS NOT OFTEN A DINNER AT COMMANDER'S PALACE WAS BORing, especially one featuring the jokes of his uncle Edward and his cousin Richard. But as much as he liked his family and as proud as he was of his sister, Gina, William couldn't wait for the meal to end and to journey to the sanctity of his study in Dansereau Plantation to think.

At about midnight, he finally sat ensconced in an oxblood leather chair in the study with a B&B in a snifter, staring at the gas fireplace. It wasn't cold enough to warrant a fire, but William thought the glow of the flames helped set the mood for contemplation.

"Will?"

He looked up to see his sister at the door. "I thought you went to bed, Gina."

"I thought you did too. Anything wrong?"

"Nope. Just thinking."

"Can I come in? I don't want to bother you. I just want to be with you."

"Sure."

"What'cha drinking?"

"Aren't you a little young?" he teased. His sister wasn't yet twenty.

"Will, I *am* in college. Besides, you ordered the wine tonight and refilled my glass, as I recall."

"B&B. Help yourself." Soon, she was in the armchair next to him, warming the liqueur with her palms. William noticed her actions. "Hmm…methinks you've had this before."

Gina gave him a knowing look. "My usual is Frangelico, if you must know."

"Great. What are they teaching you at Auburn—drinking?"

"Humph! Frangelico's better than a Jager Bomb."

"What's that?"

"Jagermeister and Red Bull."

He shuddered.

"Or a Sex on the Beach, or a Red-Headed Slut, or—"

William threw up one hand. "I give up! Enough already!"

"Cheers, big bro."

"Cheers, squirt."

They sat and sipped as images flowed though William's head. He turned to his sister.

"You're looking forward to the ball?"

"Yeah, I guess."

"Anybody you want to invite? Other than the list we drew up before."

Gina thought. "No, there's nobody else locally. Why, got somebody in mind?"

"Maybe."

Gina jumped up and down in her seat. "Who? Who is it? Some fabulous babe?"

"Somebody from work."

"Oh, pooh!"

William grinned in his glass. He hated to prevaricate, but unless he was sure, he didn't want to get Gina's hopes up. Or his.

Gina was quiet for a minute. "What did you get me for Christmas?"

William chuckled. "Now, you know I'm not going to tell you."

"I'll tell you if you tell me."

"Nice try, squirt."

"I'll find out, you know. Mrs. Reynolds will tell me. She can't keep anything from me."

"Nice plan. Glad to see they're teaching you to think over there in Auburn, besides coming up with new alcoholic drinks."

"Thank you."

"Too bad Mrs. Reynolds doesn't know," he said as he sipped his drink.

"What? You tell her *everything*!"

"Not this time."

"You rat!"

"I've known about your 'secret source' for years. You're sharp, little sister, but it will be a while before you catch up with your older brother."

Gina looked at him with affection. "I'm never going to catch up with you, Will."

He looked over at her. "Yes, you will, Gina. You're an outstanding young woman, and I'm very proud of you."

Gina bit her lip. "Thank you."

William reached out a hand. "Thank you for being you, Gina. Don't try to be me. Be yourself."

"But, I want to—"

"Be yourself. It's easier and better. Trust me."

She nodded. "All right. I'm going to bed now, okay?'

"Sure."

"Don't stay up too late."

"I won't. Love you."

"Love you too. Good night."

After Gina closed the door, William returned his attention to the fireplace before him.

If this is going to work, I can't trust my instincts. I can read most people, but I can't read Elizabeth. I can't pressure her. I've got to let her take the lead.

I'll send two invites, anonymously.

Chapter 15

"Lizzy!" cried Kit Boudreaux. "Lizzy! Come see! It's *snowing*!"

With a yelp of joy, Elizabeth bounded off her family's couch and flew to the window. Sure enough, the weatherman's forecast had been right. It was snowing on Christmas Day in Louisiana.

Minutes later, Elizabeth and Kit stood on the front lawn amidst the fat flakes floating down from the sky.

"This is *so* cool! Do you think we can make snowballs?"

Elizabeth noticed the snowflakes were melting quickly on the grass, but she didn't have the heart to point it out to her sister. "Let's try!"

The snowballs they created were pathetic, but they didn't mind. South Louisiana got snow about once every twenty years. For it to snow on Christmas Day, of all days, was a miracle. Laughing and playing with Kit, as she hadn't done since high school, brought joy to Elizabeth—and hope. Hope that this was a sign of better days to come.

Covington

"No, Mom," Chuck explained into his cell phone, "we just can't make it to Baton Rouge today. The roads are all slick and icy ... What makes you think the back roads are in any better shape? C'mon, Mom, I know you're disappointed not to see us on

Christmas Day. The kids are too. What's that? … Of course, we're not going to Chackbay!"

He looked at Jane, who was having a similar conversation with her mother on the landline. She rolled her eyes. Chuck returned to his conversation. "We're staying right here in Covington where it's nice and safe. We'll get together in the next couple of days, all right? … Good. Say hi to Carrie and John. Merry Christmas. Bye."

Jane plopped down on the couch next to her husband. Hailey and Brett were engrossed with their presents under the watchful gaze of Rufus. "Your call as bad as mine?" She sighed.

"Catherine Bingley was on the other end. What do you think?" He grinned as he slid his arm around his angel. "So, no *Great Circle Drive* this year."

Usually, the Bingleys drove the hour to Baton Rouge first thing Christmas morning to exchange presents and have lunch. Then it was a ninety-minute drive to Chackbay for dinner, before jumping on the road again for the two-hour journey back to the North Shore.

"Nope," said Jane, playing with his shirt. "Whatever shall we do with all the free time?"

"I'll think of something," he said as he kissed her.

Baton Rouge

CATHERINE BINGLEY CLICKED OFF THE CORDLESS TELEPHONE. "Well! It looks like it's just us today," she announced to the couple with the child seated on the sofa next to the Christmas tree, decorated in blue and cream, presents wrapped in coordinating paper tucked artistically below.

"Whoop-de-do," said John Buford.

Carrie dug an elbow into his side. "I'm sure we'll have a fine time, Mom, especially since we know Chuck, Jane, and the kids are safe at home rather than chancing the roads today." Trey struggled in her arms, trying to get at the presents.

"Humph." Catherine wasn't completely convinced the others weren't on their way to Chackbay that instant. Heaven only knew that Boudreaux woman didn't have a brain in her head, so she may have badgered Chuck and Jane into traveling. "I suppose I can heat up the cinnamon rolls before we unwrap presents. Carrie, would you lend a hand?"

"Sure, Mom." She handed Trey to her husband. "Behave yourself."

Buford was sure she was not just talking to their son. Trey continued to wiggle as Carrie followed her mother into the kitchen. Buford grinned and placed his boy on the floor. "Go get 'em, champ," he advised.

Trey Buford was a good boy and always followed his father's advice. The carefully wrapped presents never stood a chance.

Chackbay

FRANCES BOUDREAUX REPLACED THE TELEPHONE HANDSET ONTO the base. "Well! It looks like it's just us today," she announced to her family gathered around the Christmas tree, decorated with angels and bows, presents plied high beneath it.

"Okay," said her husband, "can we get somethin' to eat, then?"

"Yeah, Mom," said Elizabeth, "let's just have a great Christmas. I'm sure we will, especially since we know Chuck, Jane, and the kids are safe at home rather than chancing the roads today."

"Humph." Frances wasn't completely convinced the others weren't on their way to Baton Rouge that instant. Heaven only knew that Bingley woman had no heart, so she may have bullied Chuck and Jane into traveling. "Well, I'll just throw the breakfast casserole into the oven before we unwrap presents. Kit, would you lend a hand?"

St. Charles Parish

WILLIAM SAT ON THE SOFA IN THE LIVING ROOM OF DANSEREAU, sipping his coffee and watching Gina model her new ski wear. To protect the floor, the new ski boots and snowboard were left in their packages.

"What do you think?" she asked cheekily. "Do I look glamorous enough for Vail?" The major part of her gift was a weeklong trip to Vail over Mardi Gras.

"My sister, the ski bunny." He grinned. "The ski bums will be all over you."

"Fat chance of that happening with you coming along." She stuck out her lower lip.

"Damn straight," he said as he sipped his coffee.

Chapter 16

George gathered the beach gear. "Ready to go, Em?"

"Just a moment."

George walked through the sliding glass door to the patio of their rented suite overlooking St. Martin's Orient Bay Beach. The one-bedroom condo had a full kitchen and a spa. George leaned on the railing, breathed in the mid-morning salt air of the Caribbean, and felt all his stress fade away.

They had arrived late in the afternoon the day before—just enough time to settle in, have dinner, and go to bed. George slept late for the first time in over a year, rising to the smell of coffee. Over breakfast, Emma declared she wanted to sunbathe rather than explore the island their first day. He had no great desire to sit around and sweat in the sun, but they had reserved two umbrella-shaded beach chairs, and he figured he could read the medical treatises he had brought along on the trip.

He had to agree that Emma's idea of an island vacation was a good one. They did need to get away from work and Abe and reconnect as a couple. He didn't consider that catching up on his reading was cheating.

"All ready, George."

Hearing Emma's voice, George turned around as she emerged from the bedroom. Emma was wearing a bronze bikini with a matching sarong wrapped around her waist. She had a gold chain with the Star of David at her throat, and her long, curly hair was pulled into a ponytail with a black scrunchie. His young wife looked spectacular. The top barely contained her generous breasts.

George was torn between admiration for his wife's figure and concern that she was showing too much. But he was determined to please Emma. "You look great, honey."

George was rewarded with a bright, slightly nervous smile. "Thank you, baby. C'mon, the sun's a-wasting." She slipped on her sunglasses, picked up her big floppy hat and beach bag, and led the way out the door to the elevator. George followed with the rest of their things.

As they walked onto the beach, George's attention alternated between appreciating his seductive wife's walk and finding their reserved beach chairs.

His attention was broken by Emma's giggle. "George! Didn't you see her?"

"See who?"

She gestured to the right with her head. Turning, he saw a tall young woman walking away from them, wearing a thong.

Only a thong, his brain finally registered. *We're on a topless beach. Of course, it's topless. This is the French side of St. Martin. The Euros love to go sans tops. Be cool, George.*

"I didn't see her. I was trying not to fall on my ass in this sand."

Emma grinned. "Sure you were." She continued on, giving her hips a bit more wiggle.

Once they found their chairs, Emma laid out a beach towel in the sun while George claimed the chair deepest in the shade of the large umbrella. Looking around, George noticed that there were a few other women who had selected the mono-kini as their swimwear *de jour*, none particularly attractive. He also witnessed the appalling sight of heavy-set, middle-aged men in Speedos.

By the time he settled in his chair, Emma was kneeling on the beach towel facing him, applying suntan lotion to her upper arms, her wrap lying in a pile beside her. "You better put some of this on, baby," she advised. "You're whiter than Casper the Friendly Ghost."

"How does a kid like you know about Casper?" he chuckled.

George mentally kicked himself at that moment. The rabbi advised him to stop treating Emma like a child. Like an idiot, he reminded his sexy wife of their age difference. He could tell his stupid comment hurt Emma by the way she stopped rubbing in the lotion. Would he ever learn?

But before he could apologize, she smiled. "Cartoon Network. Now put this on, *old man*." She tossed the bottle of lotion to her husband, took off her hat, freed her hair, and turned to lay face down on the towel.

George absentmindedly spread the lotion on his legs, thankful for the reprieve, and thought about which report to read first.

"Honey, put some lotion on my back, please."

Looking up, his brain froze. He saw the broad, gorgeous expanse of her back, unencumbered by a bathing suit top strap, flow seductively to the twin tan globes of her ass, separated by a thin strip of bronze fabric.

Emma is face down on a towel wearing only a thong! George whipped his head around to see if anyone else had noticed.

"George? The lotion?"

"What are you doing?" he hissed as he knelt down beside her.

"I'm just sunbathing, George. You've seen me do this before."

"But not half naked."

She smiled. "When in Rome, baby. The lotion, please? I don't want to burn."

George got to work, head swiveling around the entire time, wondering whether anyone was ogling his wife as he worked her back and legs.

"Umm, George? You forgot a spot."

"You mean *everywhere*?"

"Don't be such a baby, baby," she teased.

Looking around one last time, he applied the lotion to her ass.

"Oooh, looks like somebody's enjoying himself," Emma observed.

"Yeah, right. How am I going get back to the chair without

frightening small children?"

"I don't see any *small* children around here, do you?"

George stared at the sexy creature before him. "I don't see any children around here, period."

Emma blew him a kiss and relaxed.

George scurried back to his chair and draped his towel over his lap. He picked up the first report and tried to concentrate.

It was not long before he abandoned reading as a futile exercise. He used the report as a prop and relished the tempting sight inches from his feet. He let his hungry gaze linger on her. Emma's suntan lotion-coated body glistened in the noonday sun. She was tight, taut, and sleek. He was proud of her and dazed by his good luck. That a magnificent creature like Emma put up with a balding workaholic was baffling, and he cherished her patience and love as the greatest gift he would ever receive.

For lunch, he ordered chicken salads and water from a passing waiter. The man's frank appraisal of Emma's body when he returned with their order stirred George's jealousy. Emma reached back, refastened her top, and took the chair beside her husband.

"You know, the waiter was checking you out," he whispered.

"Really?" Emma sounded genuinely surprised. "You're not jealous, are you?"

"No," he said unconvincingly.

"Silly man." Emma laughed. They ate their lunch and talked about the island and their fellow tourists, just enjoying each other's company. As the conversation died, Emma reached over to kiss George.

"I love you, darling. Thank you for this lovely trip."

George smiled. "I love you too. I'm the happiest guy on this beach because I'm with the prettiest girl. I'm sorry if I didn't tell you before, but you look fantastic. I'm proud of you."

"I'm going to get a little more sun, okay?" She got up and moved over to the towel. This time she knelt facing the water. Taking a deep breath, she reached back and unfastened her top.

George's jaw dropped.

She looked over her shoulder. "Can you pass me the lotion, baby?"

"Emma!"

"Grow up, George."

George sat petrified, unable to move. Emma continued to look at him patiently. Finally, he retrieved the lotion and brought it to her. "Turning into an exhibitionist, Emma?"

"You know better than that. I just want to even out the tan. It's no different than a tanning booth."

"A tanning both is not in public."

"No one here is going to notice me. The lotion, please?"

"Should I apply it too?" he asked with a hint of husky desire.

"Oooh, you'd like that, wouldn't you?" He handed her the bottle. "I'll take care of this myself. Go sit down and be a good boy."

George returned to his chair to watch Emma apply the lotion. If he thought he was excited before, it was nothing compared to what he experienced now. Emma wasn't trying to tease him—her actions were matter-of-fact—but his response was not.

Completing her task, Emma reclined on the towel, her heavy breasts settling in delightfully.

George noticed several young men walking by as slowly as they could, trying to nonchalantly observe the attractive American. At first, he wanted to scream at them for daring to look at his wife, but he didn't. He would have done the same at their age.

Primitive thoughts flooded his mind. *Look all you want, losers. She's going home with me. She's my wife—my woman!*

Relaxing, he candidly gazed at Emma. *Yes, she's a woman, a gorgeous woman, a woman in love with me.*

He felt the all-consuming lust he had for her well up inside, something he had kept under tight control. He didn't want to frighten her. A man had to be gentle and loving to such as her. George had done that once before to his everlasting shame.

He observed the sweat trickle down the soft slope of Emma's breasts, her Star of David nestled between them. It was the most erotic thing he had ever seen. His desire for her was immeasurable.

He now realized how wrong he had been. Emma was a woman—a

living, breathing, wanton symbol of sex and desire and love. It was time he stopped treating her like a child and respected her as the woman she was.

For almost thirty minutes, he contemplated this new, exciting, and, frankly, frightening change in his relationship with his wife. Emma suddenly sat up and turned to him.

"Baby, I'm going in for a dip. Do you want to join me?"

"Sure."

With a lazy smile, Emma rose to her feet, stretching her arms over her head. George thought he was going to die. Rising, he took her hand and trotted to the ocean's edge.

"Race you!" Emma shouted as she plunged into the surf, George right on her heels. They dove in and swam for all they were worth. George slowed down and watched his wife swim. A plan had formed in his mind. When she began to flag, he slipped underwater, headed for her legs, and grabbed her ankle. Instantly, Emma kicked to free herself. George surfaced next to his sputtering wife.

"Darn you! You scared the crap out of me!"

"What do you mean, like this?" He started to tickle her.

"No fair! Stop it! *George!*" Screeching like a schoolgirl, she splashed water at her tormentor.

"What's the matter, can't you take it?" He embraced her, his hand now caressing. "You can sure deal it out."

Emma wrapped her arms around his neck, pulling her body into full contact with his. "Aww, are you uncomfortable, baby?"

"Not anymore." Tossing aside his inhibitions, he pulled her into a torrent of kisses that lasted until they slipped underwater. A moment later, they both were spitting out water and wheezing for air.

George gasped. "We'd better get into shallower water before we try that again."

Once they reached a sand bar, Emma was in George's arms again. "Now where were we?" she purred as she kissed him.

George allowed the raw desire he had held back for five years to come spilling out. He hungrily devoured her lips. Emma's yoga practice came in handy as she wrapped her legs around his waist, her bottom resting on his erection. His hands gripped her ass, holding her tight against him.

"Oh God," she gasped, "I want you so bad. You want me too, don't you, baby?"

George could only groan.

Emma smiled. "Yeah, I can feel you." She wiggled a bit.

"Ah! You're driving me crazy, Emma!"

"You want me right now, don't you? You wanna do me right here—just pull this bit of fabric aside and take me right in front of everybody."

George allowed one of his hands to move forward and under, causing his wife to yelp. "You're a dirty girl, you know that?" he growled.

"Only for you, George," she whispered in his ear. "I'm wetter than this whole ocean for you. I'd do *anything* for you."

George silenced her with a kiss. "Damn, I'm so turned on I can't see straight. I should do like you want—take you right here! But, we can't. There are people on the beach. Shit, this is tough."

Emma turned around to look at the beach. "We'll have to take this back to our room."

"Uh, I can't get out of the water right now."

Emma grinned. "I know. I'm sorry. Does it hurt?"

"Not yet, but it will if you keep this up."

"We can't have that," she declared. She unwrapped her legs and released his neck. She turned around, facing away from him and leaned back into his strong chest. She guided his hands to the underside of her breasts as she floated, her head under his chin.

"This isn't helping," he said.

They were quiet, soaking up the sun and enjoying the warm embrace of the water. George knew Emma anticipated their love-making as much as he did.

He broke the silence. "What's gotten into you, anyway? Not that I'm complaining."

"I'm seducing you, you big oaf."

"You're doing a damn good job of it. Is it the water or the island?"

Emma did not answer right away. "It's something I've needed to do for a long time. I want you to treat me like a woman, not a child."

George complained: "I do not treat you like a child!"

She replied quietly, "Oh, baby, yes, you do. You love me, I know, but…George, haven't you ever wanted to just let go and attack me? Just throw me on the bed and have at me?"

"I didn't know you'd like that. I wanted to treat you with respect—to cherish you."

"I feel cherished, but sometimes you act as though I'll break. I won't. I'm strong—stronger than you think." She turned in his arms. "You ready for the public yet?"

"I'll manage."

As nonchalantly as they could manage, they gathered up their belongings and began the journey back to their room. Emma decided to keep the fun going, so while she replaced her top she did not replace her wrap and exaggerated her walk through the sand. They stopped briefly at the outdoor shower before entering the building.

One passion-filled elevator ride later, they were in their condo. Emma dropped her bag just inside the doorway and continued to the bedroom, undoing her top. By the time she reached the bedroom door, she had discarded the top and hooked her thumbs in the waistband of her thong. She stopped and, in a motion born of her yoga training, pulled the bit of fabric down her legs, bending at the waist.

"Hurry up, baby, I can't wait," Emma announced as she continued into the bedroom. George joined his wife, and in a flash, he was as naked as she was. What happened next was not sweet lovemaking; it was raw sex.

George knew the secret Emma hid from everyone else: She was loud when she was truly excited—loud and profane. She egged him on with dirty words and moans, and George was surprisingly inspired. If Emma had felt cherished before, now she felt *wanton, wanted, possessed.* When George penetrated her, she screamed in delight.

They were animals going at it—she demanding all he had and more. Emma's gasps signaled her coming climax, which crashed upon them like a force of nature. George was only moments behind her. Sweating, he collapsed upon her. She, in her turn, wrapped her legs about him again, keeping him embedded deep within her, electric shocks still running through her. Both lay sweaty and gasping for air.

"Well," Emma finally managed, "I think I've been truly ravaged now."

"Ravaged, hell," George panted, "you've been royally fucked."

"I know. It was wonderful." She began to kiss him gently.

What had passed before was all hormones and adrenaline. Now that the lust had receded, love and contentment remained. Hands and lips began pleasuring again, but it was all light, slow, and sweet.

"My God, Emma! I've *never* felt like that before." George took her face between his hands.

"It was just what I wanted. I love you so much."

"Em," he chuckled, "you were cursing like a sailor."

"You seemed to like it."

"Yeah, I did. I thought you'd peel paint off the walls as you screamed when you came."

"You were pretty loud yourself, baby. Oh, don't go," she said as George began to roll off her.

"But I don't want to hurt you."

"Wait." Carefully, she rolled them both onto their sides, keeping their connection. "How's that?"

"You're amazing." He gave her a long and slow kiss. "I'm sorry I haven't done better by you before this."

"Hush, George. I adore you."

"I'll love you till I die."

The two slipped off and slept the afternoon away.

DESPITE EMMA'S PROTESTS, GEORGE INSISTED THEY DRESS FOR dinner. Emma compromised by wearing nothing beneath her silk strapless jungle-print dress. George looked sharp in a silk sport coat with a crewneck shirt and linen trousers.

George refused the first table offered them, requesting a four-top so that he could sit next to his wife rather than across from her. Emma looked achingly lovely in the candlelight, her star gleaming and her nipples just apparent beneath her dress. More than once, he kissed Emma's hand, thankful for this day and this woman.

"This feels like a honeymoon, Emma."

"It is—our second one. Our new life together."

"The old one wasn't too bad, was it?"

"It wasn't what it could be. It's not *this*. You love me and want to take care of me, but you won't let *me* take care of *you*. Let me in, George. Let me be your partner and lover and wife. You own my heart, baby," she said to soothe him, "but you won't let me be your equal in this marriage. Let me show you how much better it can be."

"I'm trying, really I am."

"I know. It will take some time. That's what this is all about: to show you that I am your equal in passion for this marriage and in the desire to make our life together work." She looked down. "It meant a great deal to me when you let Papa move in. That was a lot to ask of you."

George made to protest, but Emma cut him off. "I know it's been difficult for you; don't deny it. It's been very hard on me. Papa hasn't reacted well to retirement. And I know that you've been… holding back because of him." A tear ran down her face. "So have I."

She wiped her face with her napkin. "I don't want to hold back any more. That's what this vacation's all about. I want to be free with you and for you to be free with me."

George leaned in and kissed her. "I want that too, now. But we'll have to make some changes."

"Changes?"

He grinned. "Soundproof walls, honey."

Emma blushed, but her reply was cut off by the arrival of their food. The conversation was put on hold as they enjoyed their meal. Their free hands moved to each other's thighs. Over coffee, Emma started again.

"George, I love you, but I want three things from you. Three things that will make our marriage stronger and our lives more meaningful. Will you give them to me?"

"Ask me, Emma."

"First, I want you to go to counseling, either with me or by yourself. You could go to Rabbi Tuckmann or someone else, like Chris."

"Aw, honey—why? I said I'd change."

"You're a workaholic. I need you to spend more time at home with me. That won't be easy for you. I know you've been trying. Why not let someone help you?"

"Okay, I'll go see the rabbi."

Emma smiled. "Thank you, George. Second, I want us to start attending synagogue regularly and try to observe the Sabbath as best we can. We need to be connected to something bigger than ourselves, and that's our faith. Please, can you do this with me?"

George thought about the scheduling he would have to move around. "It might mean I'll be on call on Sundays, but okay. I can make it happen as long as there are no emergencies. What else?"

She kissed his hand. "I know about emergencies. You're a surgeon. You do what you have to do." She took a breath. "Third, I want to start a family."

George looked at her stupidly. "You have a family—" He caught on.

"I want to have a baby. Your baby. Our baby."

George stared at her. "When?"

"Soon." She smiled. "Now. Today. I want to start tonight."

George just gazed at her.

"What are you thinking?" she asked.

"I'm thinking we're going to need *lots* of soundproofing. Emma, are you sure?"

"I'm very sure. I'm ready. But are you?"

George pondered for a moment. "Well, yeah. I knew we'd start sometime." The more he thought about it, the more he liked the idea. He looked up at her and smiled. "Now's as good a time as any to add some more Katzes to the world." He kissed her hand again.

"You're going to make some amazing mother."

Emma's smile was heartbreaking in its loveliness. "Good! Then I have a fourth request!"

"A fourth one?"

"Yes, I don't want dessert. Get the check, and let's get out of here."

Once back in their rooms, Emma insisted on a small ceremony. She undressed and then her husband. Completely nude, she took his hand and led him into the bathroom. She solemnly reached in the cabinet, retrieved her birth control pills, and handed them to George. Staring into Emma's eyes, he dropped the package into the trash can.

She also had a present for George. "*The Joy of Sex*?"

Emma took the book with a bawdy grin. "This is our road map, lover. By the time we leave this place, we'll put a good dent in this book, I promise."

George took her in his arms. "That's a good plan."

They then began the process of conceiving a child. Their chance of success was minuscule, but it did not deter them from trying. The sounds of their efforts could be heard in Marigot.

Friday, December 31

Emma and George fell into a routine for the remainder of their trip. They would awaken late and take in the sights of French St. Martin and Dutch St. Maarten before and during lunch. They saw Fort St. Louis, Marina Port la Royale and Grand-Case. Emma shopped like crazy on Front Street in Philipsburg.

But they stopped going to the beach. They reserved time each day to perform the ritual of topless sunbathing in the afternoon on their private deck. They would then retreat to the bedroom for an afternoon tryst—picking out a random page from Emma's gift—when their cries would disturb no one. They even used the spa for their amorous activities.

In the evening, they would go out for dinner and dancing before returning to their rooms for late night lovemaking and sleep.

On New Year's Eve, they stood on the patio, the broadcast of the ball drop from Times Square in New York City playing on the TV in the room. They danced, dressed only in robes, to music only they could hear. They stopped to kiss, George's desire very evident.

Emma broke away. "What time is it?"

George craned his neck to check the TV. "Almost midnight."

Emma's eyes grew wide. "Come on! Hurry!" She grasped his hand and dragged him to a chaise lounge. She had made a resolution, and she meant to keep it. There was only one way she wanted to end 2004.

They could hear the countdown: "*Ten! Nine! Eight!*"

She untied his robe. "Lie down!" she ordered.

"Seven! Six! Five!"

Emma threw off her own robe and quickly straddled her husband.

"Four! Three! Two! One! Happy New Year!"

As they moved, the resort's fireworks display started going off. Their bodies were lit by the flash of the exploding rockets. Emma had to bend down to whisper in her husband's ear.

"Happy New Year, darling."

It was 2005.

Part Two

New Orleans is not in the grip of a neurosis of a denied past; it passes out memories generously like a great lord; it doesn't have to pursue "the real thing."

—Umberto Eco, *Travels in Hyperreality*

New Orleans food is as delicious as the less criminal forms of sin.

—Mark Twain

She can sing, she can play on the piano,
She can jump, she can dance, she can run.
For she's a wonderful girlie;
She's all of them rolled into one.

I adore her beauty,
She's like an angel dropped from above;
May the fish get legs and the cows lay eggs,
If Ever I Cease To Love.
May all dogs wag their tails in front,
If Ever I Cease To Love.

If Ever I Cease To Love,
If Ever I Cease To Love,
May we all turn into cats and dogs,
If Ever I Cease To Love.

"If Ever I Cease To Love"
by George "Champagne Charlie" Leybourne, c. 1871

Chapter 17

Visitors to New Orleans often wonder why such a beautiful place was built in a bowl below sea level. What the tourists don't know is this: New Orleans did not start out that way. Bienville selected the site for the present city because it was the nearest high land to the Gulf along the Mississippi River. Many parts of modern New Orleans are well above sea level, including the French Quarter and the Garden District. What confuses tourists is that the river seems higher than the city with oceangoing ships towering over nearby houses. They are right. The Mississippi *has* to be higher than sea level or it wouldn't flow to the Gulf.

The river that gave the city its reason for existence has always been its greatest threat. It is part of the great floodplain of the central part of the North American continent. Streams and rivers feed into the Father of Waters from the Appalachians and Smokies in the east and the Rockies in the west. If it rains or snows anywhere in the middle part of the United States, some of that water will flow past Jackson Square on its way to the sea. The rains and snowmelt of springtime raise the river level to dangerous heights, endangering towns and cities all along the Ohio, Missouri, Red, and Mississippi rivers. Spring floods can be an annual event. To protect their property, the people built levees to hold back the water.

In the twentieth century, the US Army Corps of Engineers was tasked by Congress to protect the nation from flooding. The levee system constructed by the Corps remains one of the great engineering feats in the history of mankind. In New Orleans, huge fifteen-foot-high, hundred-foot-wide earthen levees were built on both sides of the river's channel to keep the Mississippi tamed. Later, large, emergency river-diversion projects were built to prevent the possibility of the river overtopping the levees in the city.

The next major project was to shore up the levees for Lake Pontchartrain. Eventually, both Orleans and Jefferson parishes were protected by similar earthen walls.

Everyone patted themselves on the back for a job well done. Unfortunately, relying on the effectiveness of the levees would have an unforeseen consequence.

Monday, January 3, 2005: Metairie
ELIZABETH SAT ON THE COUCH OF HER APARTMENT AFTER WORK, looking once again at the mysterious, beautifully engraved invitation she had received the week before, addressed to *Miss Elizabeth Boudreaux & Guest.*

His Royal Majesty,
King Epicurean XIX,
Lord Gourmand of the Mystic Krewe of Epicureans,
summons your presence to partake
in the misrule & merriment at his
Annual Bal Masque,
to be held on Saturday,
the eighth of January 2005
at eight o'clock in the evening
in the Mardi Gras Ball Room,
Marriott Hotel, Canal Street.

Included with the invitation were two call-out cards. Whoever sent it meant to dance with her and her companion (if a female) at the ball.

Elizabeth had no idea who had sent the invitations to her. She had heard of the Krewe of Epicureans: one of the newer, high-end, non-parading Mardi Gras organizations. Chuck Bingley had recently joined, but he claimed he had not sent invitations to anyone. George Katz, another member, expressed his innocence as well.

Could it be Will Darcy? If so, why do it anonymously?

Elizabeth almost picked up the phone to call him, but she decided against it. What would he say? Could she handle it if he said he hadn't sent it? She would feel like a fool. And if he said yes...

Obviously, this was meant to be a surprise and a challenge.

All right, then, I'll accept your challenge, Mr. Mysterious.

She stood up and gathered her purse and keys. She had shopping to do.

Superdome

Since the Bowl Championship Series (BCS) came into being, the four big football bowl games were no longer all played on New Year's Day. Since the Sugar Bowl was played inside the Superdome, and the SEC-versus-the-world format insured a big television audience, the game was moved to a following night. This year, the undefeated SEC champion Auburn Tigers would be facing the ACC champion Virginia Tech Hokies.

Dressed in her best blue and orange, Gina screamed "War Eagle!" every chance she got from the balcony of the DGS suite. It fell to William to explain to the out-of-town guests why someone who goes to school on the plains of Auburn and pulled for the Tigers would yell about a bird.

Once the game started, a defensive battle ensued. The Tigers got the best of it, scoring three field goals before halftime. Coming out of the break, Auburn reeled off a five-minute drive, culminating in a touchdown. Auburn was now up 16 to nothing. That was when things got interesting. The Hokies seemed to wake up at the same time the Tigers got overconfident. Virginia Tech scored two touchdowns off Auburn turnovers in the fourth quarter, missing a two-point conversion. It was too little too late, however, and Auburn ran out the clock to preserve a 16-13 win and to finish 13-and-0.

"Woo-hoo, what a game! We damn near gave it away, but we won!" cried Gina. "How come we can't be the national champion, huh?"

"Because the number one, undefeated USC Trojans are playing the number two, undefeated Oklahoma Sooners in the Orange Bowl tomorrow night," William explained as they left the stadium. "Auburn's number three right now. The best they can do is second."

"Somethin' ain't right with that."

William was flabbergasted. "Where did you learn to talk like that? You sound like a hillbilly."

Gina blushed. "Oops, sorry."

"You've been spending *way* too much time in Alabama. You're going to turn into a redneck."

"Am not, you rat!"

Wednesday, January 5: Lakeview

ABE WANDERED INTO THE KITCHEN AND SPIED EMMA SITTING AT the island, looking through the phone book. "What're you doing, princess?"

"Looking up a general contractor. George and I want to do some renovations around here."

"What kind of renovations?"

"Oh, just some minor stuff. We're not happy with our power bill, so we want to put in more insulation. And we thought of making your room nicer. New carpeting, add a cable outlet for a TV—"

"TV in my own room?"

"Yes, maybe one of those new flat-panel ones."

"I like that. But why are you wasting your time with the phone book? Why didn't you come to me? I know every decent contractor in town."

Emma looked up from the phone book. "I didn't want to bother you."

Abe grumbled as he sat next to her. "Thirty years in architecture and my own daughter doesn't want to bother with me."

"I'm sorry. Do you want to help?"

Abe reached over for the phone book. "You just leave this to me. I'll find you somebody good."

"At the brother-in-law price?"

"Of course. I'll draw up everything too."

"Now, Papa, George and I have some fairly solid ideas as to what we want done."

Abe held up his hand. "As of now, you're clients, not family. Whatever you want."

Emma smiled and kissed her father's cheek. "Thank you."

Abe turned to her. "Don't mention it. It's the least I can do." He looked closely at her. "You look very happy."

"I am."

"Good. It makes my heart sing."

Emma patted his hand and left to check on the laundry.

"That vacation did you a world of good," Abe added. "You're a new woman."

Emma was glad her back was turned; otherwise, her father could not help but notice her face had just turned bright red.

Chapter 18

Elizabeth, dressed in a strapless, royal blue sequined ball gown, handed the valet at the Marriott the keys to her Honda CR-V. "Well," she said to her companion as she pulled her wrap around her shoulders, "let's go in."

Charlotte grinned from ear to ear. "Oh, I've always wanted to go to one of these real Mardi Gras balls! Thanks for inviting me!" She wore a purple and gold gown with a purple wrap.

"Don't thank me. Thank whoever sent the invitation." They strolled across the lobby to the elevators.

"I'll bet it was Will Darcy," said Charlotte as Elizabeth pressed the button to summon the elevator. "The way he looked at you during the Christmas Party—"

"Now, Char, it could very well be a surprise from my brother-in-law. Besides, Will Darcy wasn't looking at me in any special way at the party."

"If you say so." As the doors of the elevator closed, Charlotte mumbled, "If only somebody would look at *me* that way."

In the Mardi Gras ballroom, a page in white tie and tails asked for their invitations. Glancing at a series of letters and numbers along the bottom, he escorted the two to their seats. Elizabeth's nerves, already heightened, began to twitch when she saw their seats were second row, center, behind Richard and Olivia Fitzwilliam. Almost the best seats in the house.

"Hey, Lizzy! Wow, you look great!" Jane Bingley was in a white gown with gold trim.

"Look at you!" The ladies discussed their outfits for a moment before Elizabeth turned her attention to Chuck. "Thanks for the tickets."

Chuck, dressed in a tux, grinned and held up his hands. "Don't thank me. I had nothing to do with it."

"Then who did?"

Chuck shrugged, but Elizabeth caught his knowing look. Just as a smiling Emma Katz showed up in a form-fitted red halter, the lights dimmed, warning those gathered that the tableau was about to start. They took their seats near the Fitzwilliams, Elizabeth between Emma and Charlotte.

"Where's George?" asked Elizabeth.

Emma pointed at the curtain closed at one end of the room. "Most of the krewe members are back there."

Chuck leaned over. "A newbie like me sits out here for the first year."

Elizabeth nodded and turned her attention to the room. A light projected the krewe's seal onto the curtain. Several other members were standing around, acting as ushers. The room was filled. Most of the attendees in the lower rows, the "call-out" section, were women. The lights dimmed, and spotlights danced upon the closed curtain. A small band began a short overture, and the curtain opened.

"Ladies and gentlemen," the voice of the Master of Ceremonies filled the hall. "The Mystic Krewe of Epicureans welcomes you to their annual tableau and ball!" There was a burst of applause. "Please welcome the Grande Chef!"

The spotlight pierced the darkness to settle on a point on the back curtain to one side of the dais. The curtains parted and a masked man trotted out to loud cheers. He was the Grande Chef, the captain of the krewe, the true leader of the organization. He wore an elaborately flamboyant gold lamé chef's costume, including an oversized toque, or chef's hat, at least four feet tall. Taking center stage, he bowed to those assembled before making a grand gesture, and the lights went up.

"Welcome to Ingredients of the Imagination!"

Masked members of the krewe, dressed in cook's jackets, pants, and aprons of many colors, began entering the stage from both sides as the band struck up a Dixieland tune. They ran all about the place, waving at the crowd.

Elizabeth leaned over. "Which one's George?" Emma pointed to a reveler in red, an oversized chili on his head. Elizabeth laughed. "You match!"

The MC began after the song was over. "And now, please stand for His Royal Majesty, King Epicurean the Nineteenth!"

The band played a stately version of "If Ever I Cease to Love" as the curtain opened again, and a portly figure in white sequins strode out. Unlike the Grande Chef or the other members of the krewe, his face was visible beneath the wig and fake beard. He had a crown upon his head, a fur-lined short cape about his shoulders, and held a scepter in one hand, which he waved at his adoring subjects, many of whom were cheering.

Emma leaned over. "That's F. Edward Fitzwilliam, Chairman of the Board of DGS. I'm not supposed to say because the Grande Chef's identity is supposed to be a secret, but he just retired as captain. He's been running the krewe since forever. His reward is being king this year."

A knot formed in Elizabeth's midsection. "Really?" She glanced down at the people seated in the first row.

"Yes. The Darcy and Fitzwilliam families were among the founders of Epicureans."

"Why did they start their own krewe instead of joining one of the established ones?" asked Charlotte.

Emma sniffed. "If they did, it's doubtful George and I would be here except as guests. The Fitzwilliams belonged to other krewes in the past, and the Darcys would have been allowed in because they were related by marriage, despite their upriver roots. However, many of George Darcy's friends and business associates would never be permitted to join. Mr. Darcy didn't like that, and so he talked his in-laws into starting a new krewe."

Elizabeth asked, "Is your father a member?"

"No, Papa isn't into all that stuff."

The king took his seat on the throne, and the MC began introducing the maids. One by one, as the band played, young women in white gowns were escorted by krewe members around the floor. The members were in costumes symbolizing ingredients one might find in a kitchen, such as flour, sugar, and pepper. The audience gave the girls a polite greeting.

"How is it the krewe members are wearing the theme costumes rather than the maids?" asked Elizabeth. "That's not how other krewes do it."

Emma nodded. "Yes. Well, the krewe took a page out of the old-line organizations and kept the elegance of the maids in white. I like it. It's not as gaudy as the super krewes."

A tall, willowy blonde was being introduced. *"Representing Corn is Miss Gina Annemarie Darcy."* A cheer went up from the crowd, and many of the guests gave her a standing ovation. *"The daughter of the late George Darcy and the late Anne Fitzwilliam Darcy, she is a student at Auburn University, studying marketing and graphic arts. Miss Darcy is a member of Gamma Gamma Gamma Sorority and serves in student government."* Elizabeth noticed a few of the ladies in the crowd were openly crying.

Emma leaned over as she clapped. "The Darcys were *very* popular with the krewe. Everybody's been anticipating this night for over five years."

Ever since May of 1999, thought Elizabeth as she wiped away her sudden tears. She turned her attention to Gina Darcy's escort. Even taller than the coed, the masked man wore a yellow chef's costume with two large ears of corn attached to the back of his chef's hat like bunny ears.

Could that silly person be William?

After the remaining maids had been introduced, two members wheeled in a large, papier-mâché king cake, purple ribbons hanging from its side. The maids were arranged around it, and at the

Grande Chef's command, the young ladies pulled at their ribbons. The maid representing Salt waved her ribbon about, a silver bean attached to the end. Her fellow maids rushed to congratulate her as it was announced she was the Queen of the Ball.

"It's all pre-selected," whispered Emma. "The queen's family has to pay for the post-ball breakfast, you know. This is all for show."

Elizabeth nodded and watched as the brunette had a tiara placed upon her head and a fur-lined cape draped about her shoulders. The new queen was presented by the Grande Chef to her sovereign, who rose from his throne and escorted her about the room to applause. They continued to the dais and took their seats upon their thrones while the maids sat in chairs arranged to either side.

"And now, to begin the ball, Epicurean XIX shall dance with his queen!"

The king and queen proceeded to the center of the dance floor. The band started again with "If Ever I Cease to Love," but at a more romantic tempo. To general applause, the two did a dignified waltz about the floor. At the end of the short song, they bowed and curtsied to each other before acknowledging the crowd.

The second dance was for the king and his wife, and the queen and her father. Elizabeth noticed the man dancing with the queen was her original escort.

So, it must be William in that corn outfit.

The king and queen returned to their thrones before the third dance began, this one for the maids. There was a whirl of colors as the young ladies took to the floor with their escorts, some waltzing better than others. Elizabeth couldn't take her eyes off Miss Darcy as her partner guided her expertly. They were some distance away, but Elizabeth could see the joy on the young lady's face.

Everyone cleared the floor for the fourth dance, reserved for the Grande Chef and his wife alone. The krewe once again rose to its feet to cheer their true leader.

"I'm just glad this first one for him has gone so well," said Emma.

"Who is it?" asked Charlotte.

Emma smiled. "I'll never tell, except to say it isn't George."

It's not hard to figure out, if you know the woman he's dancing with, Elizabeth thought.

The MC spoke again. "And now, the first call-out. First call-out if you please."

Elizabeth's mid-section started doing flip-flops as Chuck got to his feet and escorted Jane to the floor. Richard and Olivia remained seated as they were guests and not members of the krewe. Chuck was approached by the figure in yellow, with ears of corn on his hat. Chuck nodded and moved directly to Elizabeth.

"Your card, Lizzy?" he asked with a smile.

She fumbled about her clutch and withdrew the engraved card. Chuck barely glanced at it before holding out his hand for hers. Elizabeth managed to climb down from her seat without falling on her face and walked with tolerable grace to the tall man in yellow.

"Sir," said Chuck, hiding a laugh, "Miss Boudreaux." The masked man bowed deeply and held out his hand. Elizabeth managed to curtsy before allowing him to escort her to the edge of the dance floor. Before she knew it, she was in the position to dance as the music of Strauss filled the air.

Elizabeth was glad her partner knew the steps and was able to lead her so well. For her part, she was ready to collapse on the floor from nervousness. Yet, the man in yellow was gentle and strong and eased Elizabeth's feelings quickly. She could not hold her tongue any longer.

"William? William Darcy, is that you?"

"*Excusez-moi?* Who is *dis* William D'Arcy?" the gentleman said in an excruciatingly awful French accent.

She stared at him but could only make out the dark eyes from behind his mask. She decided to play his game. "Might I be informed as to whom I am dancing with?"

"*Ma* name?" He pronounced it *nams*. "*Mademoiselle*, on a night as *dis*, do names matter? Such an enchanting *jeune femme* should have other interests besides the pedestrian subject of names."

Elizabeth giggled at the cheesy accent. The Monty Python line, "Your mother was a hamster, and your father smelt of elderberries," came to mind. "Very well. What shall we talk about?"

"Do *vous* talk while dancing as a rule?"

Elizabeth glanced at the other couples. Jane and Chuck were awkwardly moving across the floor, laughing at their own ineptitude. Meanwhile, Emma and George were locked in an embrace so close Elizabeth that could feel the heat they generated.

"Yes. You, for example, might remark upon the music, and then I might observe how fine the dresses are."

The man in yellow grunted. "I notice but one dress tonight, *mademoiselle.*"

Elizabeth blushed. "And do you like it, sir?"

"Je l'aime beaucoup. Je l'aimerai encore mieux si elle vous était arrachée, ma chère."[1]

Before another word could be spoken, the music ended. "Ah, such a pity. Our time, it is so short!" He bowed and escorted Elizabeth back to her seat. He then dug into a pocket and presented her with a small box. "Thank you for the dance, *mademoiselle. Merci beaucoup.* A small token of *ma* appreciation." He turned to Charlotte as the MC called for the second call-out. *"Mademoiselle?"* He held out his hand.

Charlotte giggled as he walked with her to the dance floor, joining Emma and George. Elizabeth watched until the music started, then opened the box. Inside was a silver doubloon, the crest of the krewe showing.

"Oh!" cried Jane, who was sitting out the dance. "Usually the members give out the bronze doubloons as gifts. The silver ones are special!"

Elizabeth closed the box without a sound, a small smile about her lips. She gazed at Charlotte dancing with the man in yellow.

How is it I always seem to be dancing with you, Will Darcy?

AFTER THE SECOND CALL-OUT, GENERAL DANCING WAS ALLOWED. The band played five songs, and Elizabeth had dances with Chuck

---

1 I like it very much. I would like it better torn off you, my dear.

and George. Meanwhile, William danced with Jane and Emma before returning to his sister and aunt. Gina shared dances with her uncle, the king, and her cousin, the policeman. Finally, the court took another bow, the curtain was closed, and the ball was over.

It was time for the krewe to retire to the Queen's Breakfast, an event open only to members and their companions. But William had something he needed to do first.

"Hey, Gina," he said to his sister as he removed his mask. "Come with me. I want you to meet someone." Gina gave him a dubious look but went along with him across the dance floor.

On the far end, Elizabeth was gathering her belongings. She didn't see him, but Charlotte did and tapped Elizabeth's shoulder to get her attention. She stared at him as he and Gina arrived.

William offered his most welcoming smile. "Hi, everybody, I hope you enjoyed yourselves. We've got to get to the Queen's Breakfast, but before we go, I wanted to introduce my sister, Gina. Gina, you know George and Emma. Have you met Chuck's wife, Jane?"

"Yes," she said as she shook her hand. "She was my nurse, remember?"

William slapped his head. "Of course! I'm sorry, Jane."

"It was a long time ago. You look lovely tonight, Gina."

"Thank you, Mrs. Bingley."

"Oh, please—Jane is fine."

William introduced Charlotte and then turned to Elizabeth. "This is Elizabeth Boudreaux."

Elizabeth bit her lip, but shook her hand. "I am very pleased to meet you, Gina. Congratulations."

Gina gave Elizabeth a strange look but then broke out into a wide smile. "Thank you, Elizabeth. Or, is it Lizzy?"

"My friends call me Lizzy." She was clearly surprised by the question.

Gina gave William an impish look. "All right, Lizzy. I hope you had fun."

"I did, but I would like to thank the person who sent me the tickets." She turned to William. "Would you know who that is, Will?"

He ran his hand though his hair. "That would be me. I hope you liked the surprise."

"I did. Thank you very much."

"I did too!" injected Charlotte.

"Will," said Richard, one arm around Olivia's waist, "the breakfast starts in a few minutes."

"Yeah." William cursed his caution. He had played it safe, sending the invitation to Elizabeth and allowing her to decide whether to come. Now, it was apparent to anybody with eyes that Elizabeth would have accepted a personal invitation as his date. But he had not the courage to ask earlier, so instead of escorting both Gina and Elizabeth to the breakfast, he would take his sister alone.

"Ladies, please excuse us. Have a safe drive home." He hoped he hid his regret. They said good-bye in the southern fashion of kissing each other's cheek. Now was the moment to ask Elizabeth for a date.

But before he could form the words, Elizabeth leaned and whispered in his ear.

"*Bonne nuit, mon cher ami. Passez une bonne soirée.*"[2]

William started as she pecked his cheek, stunned at her words. Elizabeth pulled back with mischief in her eyes.

"Three years of French, Will. Good night!" She waved her fingers as she turned and walked away. Meanwhile, William had yet to pick his chin off the floor.

"What was that all about?" asked Gina, as Richard and Olivia walked backstage. George and Emma tarried a bit to wait for William and Gina.

"Nothing important," answered a mortified William. *Oh, good lord! She understood me!* He was so dumbfounded he forgot his intention to ask her out to dinner the next week.

But, he considered, was she swinging her hips a little more than those high heels warranted? *Maybe this night wasn't a washout after all.*

He felt a slight slap on his back. "You rat! You told me you were

2 Good night, my good friend. Have a lovely evening.

inviting someone from work instead of some babe!"

He grinned at his sister. "Lizzy and Charlotte work at EDNO, and I'm on the board there, so technically I told you the truth."

Gina grunted. "She looks awfully babelicious to me." She grew thoughtful. "So she's *the* Lizzy Boudreaux."

"Yes. Gina, are you upset? I told you she retracted—"

Gina put her hand on his arm to cut him off. "Will, it's okay. That was a long time ago. She seems very nice, and I would like to get to know her better." Her face darkened. "Anyhow, who am I to judge someone after what *I* pulled?"

William wrapped one arm around her shoulders and hugged. "*Almost* pulled, squirt. Stop beating yourself up over it." He stopped and looked at his sister. "I've got to stop doing that now."

"Stop doing what?"

"Stop calling you 'squirt.' You're a beautiful, confident young lady."

"Oh, Will!" She hugged him close. "I'll always be your little sister."

"Yes, you will. But times change, and we've got to change with them."

"Does that mean I have to stop calling you 'rat'?"

He chuckled. "Well, no, not if I deserve it."

George and Emma had given them some space, but his friend walked back to them. "Will, they're waving everybody in to the breakfast."

"Thanks, George. We'll walk in with you and Emma."

As they followed the Katzes, Gina leaned in. "So, are you going to see your babelicious colleague again?"

"That's the plan, Gina." *I'll have to call her next week. Not too soon, though. I don't want to sound like a stalker.*

"All right, Will!"

ELIZABETH'S CAR PULLED AWAY FROM THE HOTEL PARKING LOT. *William teased me at the ball. That's a good thing, right? So, maybe he's still interested in me.*

"Okay, Boudreaux—talk!" demanded Charlotte, breaking her dreamlike recollections of the evening.

"About what?"

"About Will Darcy! I was right about him sending you the invitation. Now, fess up! Did you know about it?"

"No." Elizabeth grinned. "I *suspected*, but I didn't know."

"And you didn't tell me?"

"Char, I…" Her voice trailed off. She didn't want to go into her reasons for keeping her suspicions to herself. "I didn't, okay? Can we drop it?"

"Only if you tell me what you said to him as we left. It sounded like French."

Elizabeth blushed. "Private joke."

Charlotte narrowed her eyes. *"Well?"*

"Well, what?"

"Are you going to see him? And don't tell me you don't know or you're fine with the way things are. Even *you* could see he was interested in you."

Elizabeth bit her lip. "Maybe."

"He should have taken you to the breakfast."

"Maybe he wanted to spend time with his sister." Elizabeth realized Gina must have remembered her from Tulane. She certainly looked surprised when she learned her name. *Does she resent me? Is that why Will didn't ask me to the breakfast?*

"Maybe," conceded Charlotte. "So, the question still stands. Are you going to see Mr. Dreamboat?"

"Does he have to wear the ears?"

"Lizzy…" Charlotte said dangerously.

"If he calls, I'll be very happy to see him again."

Charlotte gave a whoop. "All right! I bet he'll call by Monday! Maybe even tomorrow!"

Elizabeth wasn't so sure. William was nothing if not deliberate. He might think it over for some time before he made his next move. She might understand him, but she was tired of waiting.

You threw down the gauntlet, Mr. Darcy. Now the ball's in my court. Let's see how you handle my return.

Chapter 19

In the last twenty-five years of the twentieth century, it became apparent that the wetlands of southern Louisiana were receding. Saltwater was intruding closer and closer to the inhabited areas near the coast. It was killing the marsh. Not only were they the incubators of the state's all-important fishing industry, they were also the first wall of protection from hurricanes.

Scientists and environmentalists sounded the alarm and searched for the cause. Most pointed the finger at the canals dug by the oil and gas industry to serve the drilling rigs and to lay pipelines. Others claimed global warming was causing the seas to rise. Projects were demanded, and lawsuits were prepared.

Just as the century ended, the scientific community was taken aback when studies showed the real cause. It *was* man, but not in the way they first believed.

Southern Louisiana was built from silt carried from half of the United States and dumped via floodwaters by the Mississippi River over eons. Man used his engineering genius to tame the raging river with his levees. What man forgot was that geologic forces did not stop.

Beneath the water, mud, and soil of this part of the state, the billions of tons of deposited silt was compressed into sandstone and shale. Geologists knew this, but they had somehow forgotten it was still going on. Just because flooding had ceased, didn't mean gravity stopped doing its job. Marshes were not washing away; they were subsiding—sinking—as sandstone and shale continued to be made by compression.

The problem was that the replacement silt was now channeled to pour into the deep off the continental shelf of the Gulf of Mexico, rather than replenish the marshes of Louisiana.

How could so many learned minds overlook this simple cause of the problem? Scientists didn't stop to consider human nature. All people, even scientists, believed the world was perfect as they found it during their lifetime. It was easy to pretend that the forces that created the world—be they evolution, continental drift, geologic forces, or solar activity—had magically ended.

Now that the cause was discovered, the solution was obvious: silt would have to flow again onto the marshes. But how much and for how long? Studies were commissioned, and it was soon discovered that, while the situation was dire, it was not hopeless. A river diversion project on the east bank in southern Plaquemine Parish proved non-stop flooding over a year could make up for decades of mismanagement. The predicament was solvable.

But it would be very expensive. Diversion gates and pipelines would have to be built. Towns such as Lafitte would have to be protected. Lastly and most costly of all was the fate of the landowners in the vast Barataria Bay estuary. Some land would have to be sacrificed to save the whole marsh, and property would have to be purchased. Billions would be needed from Congress, and Congress wasn't convinced this was a national priority despite the efforts of the Louisiana delegation.

Meanwhile, a more immediate crisis in New Orleans surfaced. A check of the lakefront levees using the latest GPS technology showed they weren't uniformly fifteen feet high. Some portions had sunk as much as two feet. Obviously, the same forces that had damaged the marshes had endangered the city. Money was diverted from other Corps projects to restore those levees. The new southern levees in Jefferson Parish would just have to wait.

The same technology showed the city as a whole had subsided. Between the lack of new silt and the lower water table caused by the closure and filling in of old canals through what was now the central part of the city, the average overall elevation of New Orleans had dropped from above sea level to about one to two feet below.

No worries, said the Corps of Engineers. The beefed-up levee system will protect the city.

Monday, January 10: Warehouse District
On the Monday morning following the Epicureans Ball, William Darcy had just sat down at his desk to review the maintenance reports when his intercom buzzed.

"Yes, Barbara?" he asked his assistant.

"Elizabeth Boudreaux on line one."

William looked at the phone in surprise. Over the weekend, he had replayed details of their dance over and over in his head. He was sure Elizabeth had enjoyed herself. Her playful admonition at the end of the ball gave him hope that she also enjoyed his company. He had wrestled with himself as to when, not *if*, to call her. Sunday was too soon, he reasoned, while later in the week was too long. Tuesday seemed right. He would call her to ask if she had enjoyed herself and then ask if she would have dinner with him.

But now *she* was calling *him*. Was he wrong? Was she upset? There was only one way to find out.

"Thanks, Barbara." William punched the button for line one. "Hello, Lizzy."

"Hi, Will. I hope I'm not bothering you. I'm calling for a couple of reasons. First, I want to thank you so much for inviting me to the Epicureans Ball. I had a wonderful time. Oh, and before I forget, Charlotte thanks you too."

William could tell from her voice that she was smiling—smiling that same bewitching smile he had admired so many years ago. "It was my pleasure, Lizzy. I enjoyed myself too." He decided to let the French incident lie—no sense bringing it up again.

"I'm glad you did because I want to repay you by asking you to have lunch with me."

Would this woman ever cease to amaze him? "I'd like that very much. When would you want to do this?"

"How about Wednesday?"

Darcy checked his schedule. "No, I'm afraid Wednesday's booked. How about Thursday?"

"Oh, later in the week's not good for me."

"Well, darn." He frowned deeply as he returned to his calendar. This was not working out the way he wanted. "When are you free next week?"

There was a pause. "Umm, I know this is last minute, but are you free today?"

William started. *Today?* He looked at the schedule. "It's your lucky day. I'm completely at your disposal."

"Oh, good!"

"Shall I meet you in the lobby of your building?"

"That would be just fine. Say a quarter of twelve?"

"I'll see you then."

"Bye, Will."

William hung up his phone and sat back with an amazed look on his face.

Well, I'll be damned.

Downtown

IT WAS SELDOM COLD IN LOUISIANA, BUT WHEN IT WAS, THE HIGH humidity made it unbearable. William decided to drive the ten blocks to Elizabeth's office building rather than freeze in the breezy, damp mid-thirties weather. He parked in the garage and was in the lobby five minutes early. He took a seat in one of the upholstered chairs, preparing himself for his lunch date.

Remember, you have a hard time reading Elizabeth. Let her take the lead. Don't push, but be open. See what happens. And whatever you do, don't screw it up this time!

Elizabeth walked out of the elevator and approached him with a cheerful smile. William leapt to his feet.

"Hi, have you been waiting long?"

"No, I just got here." He smiled at her for a moment. "Well, where shall we go?"

Elizabeth gazed at the rain outside with disappointment. "Would it be all right if we had lunch here? The cafeteria upstairs isn't too bad."

"I'll take your word for it. Lead the way." The two walked to the elevators, William removing his overcoat as he walked. They had the car to themselves, and as they rode to the upper floor, Elizabeth explained that, while the cafeteria was provided by the insurance company that took up most of the building, it was open to all.

"We're really lucky to have it, especially on days like this."

"Do you eat there often?"

"Maybe once a week. I meet Mari there a lot. She works here, you know. Sometimes Char joins us."

"But not today."

Elizabeth smiled. "No, not today."

The door opened, and they joined the lunchtime crowd. William got a plate of the traditional Monday special of red beans and rice, while Elizabeth helped herself to the salad bar. Grabbing a couple of iced teas, they were soon at the checkout line.

"My treat, remember?" Elizabeth said as she pulled out her wallet.

"Okay," William responded. *This time.*

THEY ATE AT A TABLE NEXT TO A BANK OF WINDOWS THAT OVER-looked Poydras Street. "What a lovely view of the rain." Elizabeth laughed. "Ugh. Glad we decided to stay here. How are the red beans?"

William tasted the concoction of creamy beans, smoky sausage, and white rice. "Not bad, but it needs a bit of hot sauce."

"We have a lot of visitors here from out of town, so the food's a little on the bland side."

"No big deal, as long as we have this." He liberally sprinkled his plate with the hot sauce bottle on the table. "Ah, that hits the spot."

They talked of their favorite restaurants for a couple of minutes while they ate. Nothing unusual about that—in New Orleans, it was perfectly suitable luncheon conversation to talk about where one ate the day before and to discuss where one would have dinner later. In most parts of the world, people ate to live, but in the Big Easy, the residents truly lived to eat.

After exhausting the subject, William asked, "So, did you have a good time at the ball?"

"Oh, yes. It was very nice of you to invite us, especially on such a night." At his quizzical look, she added, "It was a big night for your family with your sister on the court and your uncle as king."

"Oh, that. Well, yes, I'm glad you got to share in that. It *was* a big night for Gina."

"She seems to be a very nice girl. You must be proud of her."

"Yes, I am. Except for the Fitzwilliams, she's the only family I have. We're very close."

"Thank you for introducing us."

William smiled. "You're welcome, but I was glad to have Gina meet my friends."

Friends. The word was like a happy bubble in Elizabeth's throat. "Was she disappointed she wasn't picked to be queen?"

His eyebrows went up a fraction. "Oh, no. In fact, if you want to know the truth, she let Uncle Ed, Ed Fitzwilliam, know she wasn't interested in being queen."

"Really? Isn't that the reason people join krewes? So their daughters can be on the court or crowned queen?"

"Yeah. Dad always wanted Gina to be a part of the krewe if it's what she wanted. But Gina didn't need to be queen, you know what I mean? Several of the girls on the court went to school with Gina, and she knew a couple of them wanted to be queen badly. Their folks were in the krewe as long as we were, and they had just as much right as Gina did. So, Gina let it be known she wasn't interested."

"Do you think she might have decided differently if your dad— Oh! I'm sorry!"

His expression never changed. "It's okay. I can talk about him." He thought for a second. "She might have done it for Dad."

"You were really close to your father."

"Yeah. I don't think a day goes by that I don't miss him. I see something and wish he were there so we could talk about it. Take the last Sugar Bowl. He would have loved watching Gina go all War Eagle-nuts over Auburn as they played Virginia Tech. I could just hear him chuckling in that kind, loving way of his."

Elizabeth's heart was in her mouth. She reached over to William, her fingers just brushing his. He glanced up in surprise, his dark eyes filled with wonder. She tried to form the words.

"William—"

"Hi, Lizzy! Mind if I join you?—*Whoa*! Will!"

The two turned to see Marianne, a tray in her hands, standing not five feet away.

"Hello, Mari," said William.

"You guys are having lunch together?" Marianne's eyes were as big as saucers.

Elizabeth was annoyed that the perfect time to have a very uncomfortable talk with William was ruined, but a friend was a friend. "Why don't you join us?"

"Thanks, but I don't want to disturb you." A nervous grin threatened to break out.

"It's okay," William assured her. "Grab a seat."

"All right." Marianne took a seat next to Elizabeth across from William. "So, what's the occasion?"

William grinned, showing his dimples. "Lizzy invited me to lunch."

"It's to say 'thank you' for the invitations to the Epicureans Ball last week." Elizabeth was trying hard not to notice those dimples. The darn things seemed to have the same effect on her now as they did in college.

"Oh, boy. Do I feel like a third wheel!" Marianne complained. "I should get another table."

"Nonsense. We're just friends having lunch. We're happy to have you. Right, Will?" Elizabeth couldn't help but bite her lip.

"Of course." William wore a rueful smile. That made Elizabeth very happy.

"Well, if you guys are all right about this. So tell me all about the ball!"

The next fifteen minutes were spent in rehashing the events of Saturday night. As Elizabeth went into great detail over William's costume and terrible accent, Marianne laughed so hard that other patrons looked at them.

Elizabeth smothered her giggles. "And I got to meet Will's sister, Gina."

"Wow. Sounds like a wonderful night. I wish I'd seen tall, dark, and handsome here with corn for ears."

"I can be hired," William said dryly. "I'm available for weddings, birthdays, and bar mitzvahs."

"I'll remember that for the wedding."

Elizabeth jumped on that subject. "By the way, since you've got two of the wedding party here, how's the planning going?"

"Fine. We've booked Chris's family's church in Lafayette for Saturday, August 27. We'll have a rehearsal late on Friday the twenty-sixth. I haven't found my dress yet, and that's a pain. And, of course, there's the pre-marriage class." She frowned. "You Catholics are sure making it hard for a body to get married."

"Suck it up," advised William good-naturedly. "No jumping-over-the-broom for us."

Elizabeth asked, "Do you have to take the classes in Lafayette?"

"No, that's one relief. We got permission to take 'em here in New Orleans. We start next week."

Elizabeth faked a pout. "Let's get to the important stuff. What about the bridesmaid dresses?"

Marianne smiled. "When I pick my dress, then we'll pick yours."

"But what about the color?"

"Don't worry. You'll like it. I'm thinking orange."

"*Orange*! Mari!"

"Chartreuse?"

William glanced at his watch. "As much as I would love to watch the catfight about to break out, I've got a conference call in about a half-hour. Mari, it was great to see you." He got to his feet, his eyes on Elizabeth. "Lizzy, thanks for lunch. I owe you."

"No, it was my pleasure." She joined him.

"Nevertheless"—he took a breath—"will you have dinner with me?"

Elizabeth blinked. *Breathe, Lizzy!* "I'd love to. When?"

"Saturday night?"

Elizabeth's face fell. "I can't! I'm leaving in a couple of days for Washington, DC, to help with the Mardi Gras Ball."

"I thought the Washington Mardi Gras Ball was next week."

"It is, but we thought we'd go early and get in a little lobbying for Government Quarter and our other pet projects while we're up there. Are you going?"

"I can't. I've got too much on my plate."

"How about after I get back?"

The two techno-nerds dug out their BlackBerrys. "No good," said William as he managed the little screen. "I've got to fly to Asia on a sales trip. Then as soon as I get back, Gina and I go to Vail for Carnival."

Elizabeth's disappointment was almost physical. "Then I'll have to take a rain check until after Mardi Gras."

"I'm sorry, Lizzy. Look, I'll make it up to you."

A small smile broke out on Elizabeth's face. "Really?"

"Yeah. How about Emeril's after I get back? I'll get a nice table."

She raised an eyebrow. "All right—as long as it's a *nice* table."

William smiled at her teasing. "I gotta go. Can I send you an email?"

"Sure." She lifted her cheek to be kissed. As soon as it was done, she wished she had been bolder and offered her lips instead. "I'll walk you out. Mari, I'll be right back."

"Go, go! Don't mind me!" Marianne cried.

William insisted on carrying both trays to the drop-off station, and Elizabeth escorted him to the elevators. The crowded waiting area prevented any serious conversation.

"Will, thank you for joining me on such short notice."

"Any time. I'm looking forward to dinner"—his smile faded—"even though it's a month away."

Impulsively, Elizabeth offered, "You can call me." Almost immediately, she regretted her rashness.

William's happy smile changed her mind. "I'll do that."

The down arrow lit up and the doors opened. Elizabeth kissed him on his left dimple. William's eyes were wide open as she pulled back. "Bye," she said.

William touched his cheek, a smile dancing on his surprised face. "Bye," he answered as he boarded the elevator. They locked eyes as the doors shut.

A very happy Elizabeth returned to Marianne. "Oh, Lizzy, I'm *so* sorry about butting in on your date! But"—she smiled—"I think it turned out okay. Forgive me?"

Elizabeth grinned. "Of course."

ELIZABETH CHECKED HER EMAIL ACCOUNT UPON HER RETURN TO her desk.

```
To: eboudreaux@edno.org
From: wgd@deltaglobalshipping.com

Lizzy,

Just a note to let you know how much I enjoyed
lunch and being with you. Good luck in DC, and I'll
see you after I get back from CO. I'll call soon.

Will

PS—My personal email is willtulane@cajunnet.net

PPS—I owe you something.
```

Her coworkers were surprised to hear a whoop of joy from Elizabeth's office.

Chapter 20

Rabbi Tuckmann's office was large enough for a sofa on the far side from his desk. Although his secretary accused him of using the sofa for an occasional afternoon nap, it was intended for the people who came to him for counseling. George Katz, however, preferred to use one of the armchairs next to it.

Tuckmann quickly glanced at his notes. This was George's second visit and the first without his wife.

"So, how are things?" he asked.

"Good. Everything's fine." He sat upright, his hands clenched in his lap.

"Good." Tuckmann made a note. "And everyone at home?"

"Much better. Emma's happier. We're talking more, like we haven't done in years."

"And how does that make you feel?"

"Me? Good. I mean, Emma's happy; I'm happy. Isn't that the way it's supposed to be?"

"Do you think so?"

George hated these therapist games. "Yes, that's what I want out of my marriage."

Tuckmann wrote again, and George resisted the temptation to reach over and grab the notebook out of his hands. "And Abe?"

George blinked. "Abe is…Abe. The same."

"I see."

George thought. "No, that's not quite true. He's been very involved in the renovations. Drawing up the plans, working with the contractors. It's like…"

"Yes?"

"It's like how he was before he got sick: engaged, enthusiastic. He's been pretty good during this whole thing with all the workers in the house tearing things up. He hasn't complained a bit."

The rabbi checked his notes. "Are you getting out of the house more?"

"Yeah. Last Saturday we—Emma, Abe, and I—went to an RV show." He chuckled. "Never in a million years would I have thought I'd go to something like that. Emma's idea of roughing it is to drive a subcompact to the Ritz. But we had a blast." George grew relaxed as he recounted their small adventure. "Abe was all over those things. He couldn't get over how much the designers could cram into a motor home. You know, we saw one fifth-wheel that had a real, operating fireplace. Can you believe that?"

"Sounds like you had a good time."

"We did. Of course, we'll never buy one of those things, but"—he looked out the window—"it's good to expand your horizons. You know what I mean?"

"Yes, I do."

"Next week, Emma and I are going to do something just by ourselves this time. We've both lived around here all our lives, yet we've never visited the plantation houses up the river. So, we're going on a road trip, playing tourist. We're going to spend the night at Nottoway Plantation over in White Castle."

"That's a beautiful place. Any issues over leaving Abe alone?"

"No. Things went well over Christmas. Mrs. Taylor stopped by every day to make something for him to eat. She'll do the same thing this time."

"Have you resolved your worries over money?"

"Trying to. The trip to St. Martin and the renovations cost plenty, and I don't like our savings depleted to that extent, but having Emma back the way she was when we got engaged…" He smiled.

"I've got the rest of my life to make money, right?"

Rabbi Tuckmann nodded. "I believe that's all for today. Shall we make it the same time next week?"

NEW ORLEANS IS BLESSED WITH A TREASURE TROVE of architectural styles. Especially beloved is a version of the foursquare from the Arts & Craft movement. The houses appear to be two-and-a-half stories, with large front steps leading to a front door on the *second* floor. Actually, the houses are traditional bungalows that have been raised. The family lives in the upper floors and the ground floor could be used for storage or as a bonus area.

This is done because New Orleans floods. Louisiana, one of the wettest places in the United States, receives almost sixty inches of rain each year. It took generations to build the world's largest and most efficient drainage pumping system. Huge pumps draw the water from drains all over the city and deposit it into numerous canals that empty into Lake Pontchartrain.

Hurricane Betsy proved the city could be flooded from storm surge coming from Lake Pontchartrain into the canals, and the levees along Mississippi River Gulf Outlet were inadequate. As part of the 1965 mandate, the Corps of Engineers needed to find a solution.

At first, they wanted to build storm gates at the mouth of the lake and the Mississippi River Gulf Outlet (MRGO or "Mister-Go"), modeled after the constructs the Dutch built to protect the Netherlands. However, environmental groups cried foul, claimed that gates would ruin the ecology of the lake, and filed suit. The Corps found compromise impossible. The environmentalists stood firm. They and the local opponents of the

MRGO didn't want a safer Mister-Go; they wanted it gone. The politicians from Orleans and Jefferson didn't want gates at the canals. They said with the canals closed, the pumps would be useless during a hurricane.

It was interesting that no engineer asked one of those bright elected officials to explain in public how one could pump more water into a Lake Pontchartrain already swollen to near flood level by a hurricane storm surge.

The last thing the bureaucrats of the Corps wanted was a public spat in court. Instead, they offered to build up the levees along the canals to withstand a Category 3 storm. This plan set off a new firestorm. The neighborhoods were adamantly opposed to traditional fifteen-foot tall levees, which would require tearing down blocks upon blocks of houses. Such a radical change to the middle- and upper-class areas would hurt property values, white residents claimed. The poor blacks in the upper and lower Ninth wards accused the government of racism by proposing to destroy their homes. The preservationists went nuts.

The Corps, faced with this intense resistance, came up with a technological solution: a hybrid, short, narrow earthen levee topped with a concrete storm wall. Steel pilings would be driven into the ground to reinforce it. Presto—the cities of New Orleans, Metairie, and Kenner were safe.

The people took the Corps at their word and stopped building expensive raised homes. New construction followed the usual southern method of slab houses, which saved tens of thousands of dollars.

Some streets flooded during thunderstorms, but it was considered part of living in the Crescent City. Few bought the federal flood insurance. "Why waste the money?" people said. "It's never flooded on my street."

January: Washington, DC

ELIZABETH WORKED THE CROWD IN THE MAIN BALLROOM OF THE Washington Hilton Hotel. This was the 48th Annual Washington Mardi Gras, one of the social events of the season, hosted by the Louisiana Congressional Delegation: three jam-packed days of luncheons, conferences, meetings, parties, ceremonies, and networking with almost three thousand people attending.

Members of the congressional delegation took turns chairing the ball, but the event was actually run by staffers and volunteers. This year, the representative from New Orleans had the honors. Louisiana music and seafood were furnished by lobbyists and corporate donors. The Washington Mardi Gras enjoyed a special exemption in the ethics code.

Elizabeth felt uncomfortable about wearing the same strapless royal blue sequined gown she bought for Epicureans. That outfit she now considered *William's* dress, but she couldn't afford dropping another five hundred dollars for a bit of fabric that would get one night's use. She kept the wrap on, though. She had no plans to dance that night.

What's the use of going to a dance without William?

Their interrupted lunch date was far from the disaster it could have been. The only way it could have been better—she had admitted to herself late that night—was if William had gathered her up for a serious kiss.

He likes me. That's why he wants to take me to dinner. But before I lose myself in romantic fantasies, William and I need to put Tulane behind us once and for all. I need to back up the words in my letter with words from my lips. I'm sure he's read the letter—I'm certain of it—and he deserves an apology face to face.

"Lizzy? Hey, Lizzy!" A tuxedoed man worked his way through the crowd.

"Tony?"

Anthony "Tony" Riviere's tie and vest were in purple, gold, and green, and a strand of oversized Mardi Gras beads hung from his neck. "Hey there, Lizzy. I heard you were in town." He gave her a kiss on the cheek. "Wow, that's a nice dress."

"Thanks. How've you been?"

"Great. DC's a blast. The hours suck, but it's where the action's at. *This* is the place where stuff happens. I heard y'all met with the senator about Government Quarter."

"The senator's been very helpful."

"It's about the only thing she and the other guy agree on." Riviere referred to the state's junior senator.

"As long as we get it done, I don't care who gets the credit."

Riviere laughed. "*Here*, it's all about taking credit. It's the mother's milk of politics." He took a sip of his drink. "So, you seeing anybody?"

Elizabeth hid a smirk. Sometimes Tony could be so transparent. "As a matter of fact, I am."

Tony couldn't quite hide his disappointment. "Anybody I know?"

"No, I don't think so." Elizabeth felt very protective and selfish about her burgeoning relationship with William. It was *hers*, and she didn't want to share it with anybody. If it went where she hoped, then she would be happy to shout it from the rooftops. Until then, she would keep it to herself.

"Well, I'm glad you're happy."

"I am, thanks. How about you?" Elizabeth wasn't really interested, but it was the polite thing to ask.

"Really, really busy. I've met some people. We go out for drinks, but nothing serious. It'll come, I guess."

"It will, Tony. There's more to life than work."

He looked at her. "That coming from you? This guy's really special, huh?"

Elizabeth was honest enough not to deny she was more interested in work than in Tony while they were dating. "Yes, he is."

With far more sincerity than before, he said, "I'm happy for you." The two stood in silence for a moment. "Well, it was good seeing you."

"You too, Tony."

"Maybe we can grab some lunch before you leave, introduce you to some more of the folks in the office," he offered.

"Maybe so," Elizabeth returned, knowing he didn't expect her to take him up on it, and she had little interest in doing so. "Take care." She waved as he left her.

She stood by herself, surrounded by the madding crowd, suddenly lonely for William's presence. A moment later, Eddie Masters and his wife were at her shoulder.

"Hey, Lizzy, wanna get something to eat? They've opened the buffet line. Carl's got a table."

"Sounds good. Let's go."

```
To: wgd@deltaglobalshipping.com
From: eboudreaux@edno.org

Will,

The DC Mardi Gras is finally over and done. We
fly back tomorrow. We think the meetings went as
well as could be hoped. Our lobbyists in DC will
continue to sell Government Quarter to the Navy.

Saw most of the delegation at the dance. I ran into
Tony R., and we talked for a little bit before
dinner. Still the same old Tony. Did I mention I
wish you were here?

I'm glad to be going home. I'm only sorry I'll have
to wait for that dinner. You did promise a good
table, right?

Lizzy
```

```
To: eboudreaux@edno.org
From: wgd@deltaglobalshipping.com

Lizzy,

Have I told you how much I hate international
```

travel? Even in business class, flying to China
sucks big time.

The PRC is a real example of contrasts. Some of the
most modern buildings in the world can be found in
Shanghai, yet they still have people in uniforms
along the train tracks, holding flags to let us
know if the tracks are clear ahead. I'm a lot more
comfortable in Japan. China's a beautiful place,
but I'm looking forward to leaving.

Sounds like you had a good time in DC. Do any
dancing?

And as for the table--yes, I promised you a good
one. And I keep my promises.

Will

To: willtulane@cajunnet.net
From: lizzy313@cajunnet.net

China sounds like an interesting place. I've never
been there, but I've heard a lot about it from
those who have seen it.

I didn't do any dancing in DC, but maybe I should
have. You always seem to be around when I do. Would
you have shown up magically if I did? Sorry--I'm
being silly.

You're going to Vail right after you get back,
right? Your sister must be excited about the trip.
Have you done much skiing in the past? I've gone
once. It was fun, but I really need lessons if I'm
ever to get off the bunny hill. I suppose you're a
master of the double-diamond runs. Oh, well, I can
après-ski like an expert. LOL!

Lizzy

PS I'm glad to hear you keep your promises.☺

Wednesday, February 2: Lakeview

Abe sat in what was going to be his new media room/bedroom. The contractors were doing the renovations in stages, and stage one was improving the interior insulation in the house. Abe wondered why they didn't do the rewiring first, but the contractor showed him the work order. They had finished that part of the job a week ago and had also put in solid wood doors. Abe had to admit they looked better than the hollow-core doors they replaced. They sure cost enough.

Abe loved his new 32-inch LCD television. He had his bed moved to one side so his beloved La-Z-Boy could fit. The cable had been run that morning, and Abe was a happy camper. There were some kitchen renovations to do before the painters moved in, but as long as Abe had his ESPN in HD, he wasn't worried about anything.

Except he was thirsty.

Abe left his room but hesitated in the dark den. It was about ten o'clock, but the night light in the kitchen was disconnected. Abe couldn't remember whether he had already finished the can of OJ in the fridge. He decided to ask Emma. He walked to the far end of the house and knocked on her door.

A moment later, the door was opened by a very irate Emma Katz. She was holding a thin robe closed at her throat with one hand. Her hair disheveled, her face flushed, and her eyes shot daggers at Abe.

"What is it, Papa?" she spat.

Abe gaped like a fish. It was obvious even to him that he had interrupted something. "Umm, sorry, princess, I'm sorry—"

"What is it, Papa?"

"Juice. Do we have any juice in the house?"

"Check the fridge," she said between clenched teeth.

"I, uh, thought we may have run out." Embarrassed, he could think of nothing else to say.

"There's a can of OJ in the pantry."

"Oh. Nothing cold?" he said weakly.

"That's why we have an *ice maker!* Good night, Papa!" She slammed the door. To his increased mortification, he heard her lock it.

Tap water will do fine, he thought as he scampered back to his room. He made sure he turned up the sound on the TV.

Emma walked back to the bed where George lay naked on his back, one arm over his eyes.

"Is he gone?" he groaned.

"Yes," Emma assured him as she shucked off her robe. Except for her Star of David, she was as nude as he was. "He won't be bothering us again."

"What makes you so sure?"

"If he didn't get the message tonight, I'll have *you* answer the door next time. That ought to take care of it."

He lifted his arm. "With or without a towel?" He gazed at his darling wife standing next to the bed with her fists on her hips, still fuming, her hard breathing causing her generous breasts to move in an enticing manner. The moonlight from the window danced across her skin, and her golden pendant glittered. "Mmm, nice."

Emma smirked. "I'm glad you think so, *Doctor*. You've got to finish your biweekly examination"—she glanced at him—"and I believe your *equipment* is ready."

George rolled over on his side as Emma climbed on the bed. "I'll say it is."

Emma smiled as she stroked him. "Good."

Friday, February 4: Vail Village, Colorado

```
To: lizzy313@cajunnet.net
From: willtulane@cajunnet.net

Made it safely into Vail. The flight into Eagle/Vail
airport took Gina's breath away. All this cold and
snow is very different from home.

The condo has a great view of the mountain. If you
stand on the balcony and look to the side, you can
see the gondola.

We hit the slopes first thing tomorrow. Gina's
```

```
breaking out the snowboard she got for Christmas.
I hope she doesn't tear up her knee with that
thing. There's a reason there's a ton of orthopedic
surgeons around here. Me, I'm sticking with my
tried and true skis.

As for me being the next Bode Miller, I don't know
what Darcy you're talking about, but it isn't me.
Sure, I like falling down a good mountain as much
as the next guy, but I'm no expert. I've never
pushed myself to see how well I could ski because,
if I ruin my knees, there goes my golf game. We all
have priorities.

Good lord, it's pretty here. I wish you could see
it. A picture just won't do it justice.

See you soon,

Will
```

Saturday, February 5

A FINE, CRISP EVENING FOUND WILLIAM AND GINA SITTING ON the patio of an inn near the Covered Bridge in Vail Village. They had finished a fourth run on the mountain and, after storing their equipment for the next day, stopped by to enjoy the afternoon with a warm toddy before their dinner reservation. It was a good time for a brother and sister who liked and loved each other to kick back, relax, and reconnect.

It had been a good day. William had not skied in a couple of years, but he was able to work out the rust and make all his runs without falling. Gina loved her new snowboard and showed some ability with it.

The sound of music caught their attention. A large number of people in costumes over their ski clothes were making their way down Bridge Street, throwing beads and doubloons to onlookers.

Gina looked at her brother. "What's that?"

William grinned. "For years, people from Louisiana have been coming up to Colorado to ski during Mardi Gras. They'd hold a pub-crawl or two to celebrate Carnival. Vail now makes it an official event. There'll be a parade on Mardi Gras, and a lot of the restaurants will be serving Cajun specials. The pub-crawl is tonight."

The two watched as the masked throng made its way up the snow-covered street. The onlookers were puzzled at first at the activity, but within moments, they were diving into the snow bank after doubloons.

William laughed. "They probably think those things are drink coupons." He raised his hands to cup his mouth. "Hey! Throw me sumthin', mister!" The pair was deluged with throws.

"Wanna join them?" William asked his sister as she was picking a strand of beads out of her parka.

"Nah. Let's just grab some dinner and call it a night. I'm pooped. If I want Mardi Gras, I'll go to the real thing."

The two gathered up their belongings and headed in the opposite direction from the revelers.

Chapter 21

IN 1975, THE LOUISIANA SUPERDOME OPENED FOR
business. At one time the largest domed stadium in the
world, it was built primarily for the NFL New Orleans
Saints. Tulane also played there, and it was the host of
the annual Sugar Bowl.

The Superdome revolutionized sports tourism in
the Crescent City. The Super Bowl was played there
six times and the NCAA college basketball championship five times. Muhammad Ali defeated Leon Spinks
there in 1978. Two years later, Roberto Durán cried
"No más!" at Sugar Ray Leonard.

The Dome, as the locals call it, hosted more than
sports. Eighty-seven thousand screaming fans saw the
Rolling Stones in 1981. Pope John Paul II held a youth
rally for eighty thousand in 1987. The Republicans used
it for their convention the next year.

It was also the catalyst of one of the greatest trans-
formations in the history of New Orleans.

Technically, the Dome is not in the downtown
Central Business District, but in the adjacent Warehouse District. This depressed area, comprised mostly
of brick warehouses and industrial buildings along

narrow streets, was nearly useless in the age of large eighteen-wheel tractor-trailer trucks. With the opening of the Dome, a renaissance occurred. Hotels and office buildings grew along Poydras Avenue. Without the Dome, the 1984 Louisiana World Exposition never would have happened. Without the World's Fair, the Ernest N. Morial Convention Center would not have been built. Thanks to the Convention Center, the revitalization of the Warehouse District went into high gear.

Thirty years after the opening of the Dome, the Warehouse District was filled with new boutique hotels and fashionable stores. Museums, condominiums, and apartments occupied buildings that once housed cotton bales and tool shops.

Friday, February 25: Warehouse District

IN 1990, THE WAREHOUSE DISTRICT BECAME A FOOD DESTINATION when Emeril Lagasse defied the naysayers and opened what would be his flagship restaurant in the heart of that neighborhood on the corner of Julia and Tchoupitoulas. Like all great New Orleans restaurants, Emeril's appeals to visitors and locals alike. It is very easy to tell the difference between them—just walk up and ask if they can pronounce Tchoupitoulas.

Two people—who could—at near the front window, enjoying Whole Truffle Fried Chicken for Two. Elizabeth and William had lunch a few times since his return from Colorado, but their busy work schedules had put off a true dinner date until now. It was a Friday evening after work because William was flying to Houston the next day.

He drove to Elizabeth's office, and with the weather unseasonably warm, Elizabeth suggested they walk the dozen blocks to the restaurant. Conversation started out with the usual suspects: work, friends and family, food, and the weather. They had moved on to movies by the time they were seated, playfully arguing whether *Sideways* or *The Aviator* would win the Oscar on Sunday.

A very nervous Elizabeth enjoyed the light banter during dinner. Her mistakes in college had left their mark, but she knew she was a better person for it. Never again would she go flying off without all the facts. She worked on being less judgmental, giving others a second and even a third chance.

Things were getting serious between William and her, and she knew a long-delayed and very painful conversation had become inevitable. Every time she saw him or talked to him over the phone, she lost a little more of her heart to him.

He had always been devastatingly handsome and a perfect gentleman, but since college, William was less domineering. At Tulane, he had a habit of interrupting her and summarizing her statements before weighing in with his opinion. That he was always respectful of her views didn't make the practice any less irritating. Now, he tended to listen more, sitting quietly and giving his opinion only when asked. He was more relaxed and open.

Elizabeth was excited and frightened by his gaze. It was the same earnest look from college. Back then, she fought her attraction to William, never knowing it had been mutual. Now she knew better. He was still interested in her, though heaven knew why.

"Elizabeth? Are you all right?"

Elizabeth started at William's worried voice. "Oh, sorry. I zoned out a bit. What was it?"

He held up the desert menu. "Do you want some banana pie?"

Elizabeth politely refused, and William called for the bill. A few minutes later, they were again on Tchoupitoulas Street, walking back towards Poydras.

Elizabeth, preoccupied with her thoughts, gave only one-word responses to William's comments as they walked. The modern skyscrapers of the Central Business District towered over the brick buildings in the Warehouse District. The uneven sidewalk was lit dimly by the streetlights.

Finally, William asked, "Is there something wrong, Lizzy?"

"No, nothing," she automatically returned.

"You just seem quiet."

"Is that so unusual for me?"

"Yes, it is." William's serious voice unnerved her.

She didn't want to start the talk now while they were walking. She remembered Lafayette Square Park was a half-block away. She took William's arm and guided him towards the little green oasis in the midst of a forest of tall, gray buildings. The Federal Courthouse was on one side, the NORD Theatre and Gallier Hall on the other, and a huge hotel with a chaotic checkerboard of lighted windows loomed over the park. The second oldest park in town was named for the Revolutionary War hero but was dominated by a statute of American statesman Henry Clay.

Ever the country girl, Elizabeth felt more comfortable with grass under her feet and trees over her head, even at night. She saw William's curious, expectant look. She took a breath and began.

"William, I've wanted to tell you for a long time how sorry I am for what happened back at school."

"Excuse me?"

She couldn't look at him, and she plunged ahead, knowing that, if she stopped now, she'd never finish. "What I did, what I wrote, what I said to you—that was so wrong. You were right. I should have tried to interview the frat before I wrote my piece. You had been nothing but honest with me. You never lied, even to save my feelings. But I took the word of a criminal like Greg Wickham—"

"Lizzy, stop!" cried William.

His hand lightly grasped her shoulder, and she was surprised he would touch her. The haphazard light from the streetlamp had his face half in shadow.

"You have nothing to apologize for. I can't believe you're even bringing this up. You were just doing your job. It was my fault. I'm the one who screwed up everything. I should have been more concerned about Waguespack getting what he deserved than the reputation of the chapter."

Elizabeth was confused. This conversation wasn't developing as she had anticipated. "But Marianne's reputation? George and Chuck said—"

"Of course, I was trying to protect Marianne. That was the most important thing. But that doesn't excuse what I said to you." She could just make out the self-disgust on his face. "You did nothing wrong; Wickham and Waguespack did. Sure, Wickham lied to you, but he lies to everybody. He's good at it! I should have been more mature. If I had talked to you as you deserved, then maybe—" He turned away from her, his hands now in his pockets.

Elizabeth listened to him in shock. She could never forget their confrontation, his declaration of love for her, and the hurt he had felt when she questioned his motives over what had happened to Marianne.

"Because of me, you lost your scholarship and your career," William said to the trees. "I can never forgive myself for that."

"What are you talking about?"

"You left Loyola and journalism. If I truly loved you, I would have supported you—"

"Will, no!" Elizabeth cried, shaking her head. She couldn't believe he was blaming himself for what happened! "That's not your fault. I gave up the scholarship to go to Nicholls and get a fresh start. Besides, the whole episode opened my eyes. I found out what the news business was really like, and I didn't like it. I allowed myself to be bullied, and that hurt innocent people."

Instinctively she reached over, took his arm, and forced him to look at her. "I really like what I'm doing now. Working in economic development, I'm building something up not tearing people down. I'm happy—really, I am."

William studied her face. "You're sure?"

Elizabeth knew she would have to explain everything. "William, what happened back at college was *my* fault, not yours. No, no—let me finish. I was blind to the kind of man you were—smart, honorable and loyal—the man you *are*. My troubles were all due to *my* immaturity, *my* insecurity. You challenged me by treating me as an equal, but I didn't see myself as your equal. Instead of facing my fears and changing my preconceived ideas, I took refuge in them.

"Because of that, I was a bad reporter. I was so angry at what happened to Marianne that I had to make somebody responsible. I should have trusted you would talk to me after I calmed down, after I confronted you, but I didn't. All I could think of was revenge. I listened to the first plausible story I heard. I let my prejudice about wealth, status, and even fraternities color my writing. And when Justin Middleton added that stuff about your family and changed the focus of the piece, I said *nothing*. I was a coward, I was immature, and I was irresponsible—all the things you weren't and never have been. I let down you, Marianne, the guys in the chapter, and everybody else. Too late, I realized how terrible I had been.

"To this day, I don't know why anybody has forgiven me. By rights, Marianne should never speak to me again, much less the rest of the gang—or you. That all of you have is a blessing I thank God for every day.

"And I will never forget how bad, how *wrong* I was. A person like me should never be a reporter. I'm very thankful I've found a profession I enjoy, and I feel I'm doing good things for the community. That's all I ever really wanted to do."

Elizabeth asked the question that had plagued her for five years. "I explained that all in my letter. Didn't Charles give it to you?"

"I got it," he admitted. William was silent for a time. "I couldn't answer it, Elizabeth."

"That's okay. I understand," she said automatically, her heart sinking as she began to draw away.

"If I did, I couldn't stay mad at you."

She stood frozen at William's words.

Again, he looked away. "I needed to be mad at someone. My dad had died, my sister was without a father, and I'd lost you." He huffed. "Hell, I never *had* you in the first place. But I couldn't sit around and mourn. I had a sister to raise. I had to help protect the company, save what my family had built. There were people who wanted to break DGS apart. I felt the whole world had come crashing down on me.

"So I used you to light a fire under me. I figured if I stayed mad at you, I could concentrate on what needed to get done, and I wouldn't hurt so much. It was months before I read your letter."

He gave a dry chuckle. "None of it worked, though. I never could stay mad at you."

"Why?" she asked in a soft voice.

His eyes caught hers. "Because you're the best person I've ever known, Elizabeth. Your passion, your loyalty, your courage. I've always admired it. I still do. You've always had my admiration. It took a lot of guts to write that retraction.

"So, no, I don't blame you. Mari was hurt, and you wanted to find out who did it. You were lied to by Wickham, and your editor blindsided you. That article hurt—I won't lie—but if I had talked to you that night, you wouldn't have written it, would you?"

"No," a stunned Elizabeth admitted.

William shrugged his shoulders. "So, you see? The author of all that crap is me."

She took a step closer to him. "I'm afraid we'll have to agree to disagree about that. I know what I did wrong, and I'll own it, thank you very much."

William stared at her. Elizabeth wondered whether he knew how intimidating he could be when he did that. He probably did. But she was growing immune to it.

"You're a stubborn woman, Miss Boudreaux."

"And you're not so tough, Mr. Darcy." She offered a tentative smile.

He face softened. "Not around you."

He reached out and caressed her cheek. She couldn't help but to tilt her face into his hand. She didn't know what he wanted from her.

"Elizabeth." His voice was deep and hesitant.

A gamut of emotions showed across his face. She waited, hopeful and scared.

"Elizabeth, please give me another chance." His thumb touched her lips.

"Yes," she answered immediately.

He blinked. Her quick answer must have startled him, but he stepped right up to her, hand still on her face. Elizabeth's body tingled from the attraction she felt for him. She couldn't move except to tilt her head upwards in invitation.

William accepted the offer. It seemed to take forever before his lips captured hers. The kiss was soft, warm, and searching—perfect.

"Told you I owed you something," he said softly.

She touched her lips. "You mean this?"

"The elevator." He grinned at her dawning remembrance of the daring kiss she had bestowed on his cheek. "I told you I keep my promises."

"You've already done that with dinner, or don't you remember?"

"That? Nah. You'll learn I don't get even. I get *ahead*."

Oh," was all Elizabeth could manage before he kissed her again.

Getting ahead was a good thing, she considered.

ELIZABETH AND WILLIAM COULDN'T SPEND THE REST OF THE evening necking like a couple of teenagers in the middle of Lafayette Square, so hand-in-hand, they left the park, crossed Poydras Street, and made their way into the parking garage. He insisted on walking Elizabeth to her car. She denied it was necessary, but she was pleased he did it all the same.

Next to her CR-V they made their good-nights, which included more unhurried kisses. By now, it was Elizabeth's considered opinion that William Darcy was the best kisser in the world. But all good things must end.

"Good night, Will. Have a safe flight."

"Call you when I get back?"

"Please." She gave him another smile as she unlocked the door. Suddenly, she recalled something he had mentioned earlier. "Will, you said something about people wanting to break up DGS. That's not happening, is it?"

He grimaced. "Not if I can help it. It's the reason I'm flying out tomorrow."

"Can you tell me what's going on?"

"You'd have to keep this to yourself, Lizzy."

"You have my word."

"Okay. Right after Dad died, an investment group bought a five percent stake in DGS. It's not a lot but enough for them to get a seat on the board. Phil Osborne is a real hatchet man, a break-up specialist. He sees the value of our ships and contracts. What he doesn't see is that we're primarily bulk carriers. We are expanding into containers, but they're a small portion of our business. We can't compete with the big Asian firms, so we carve out our niche and maximize market share. We're doing well, but we aren't generating the kind of profits these venture capital firms want."

"Don't VCs look for thirty percent on their investment?"

"Yeah, at a minimum. We've heard on the street that Osborne's been saying we could get double the value for our stock if we sold out to an international outfit. Ed Fitzwilliam, Leon Anderson, and I are flying out to put an end to that kind of talk. We're not selling, now or ever."

Elizabeth smiled. "Thanks for telling me, Will. Good luck." They shared one last kiss before she stepped into her car and started the engine. She waved as she pulled out, and in her rear-view mirror saw William watching her as she drove to the down ramp.

Well, that went a lot better than I thought, she reflected. She had been so scared his deep feelings for her had died in college. But tonight proved she was wrong!

But kissing is not love, she reminded herself. She had made that mistake once, back in high school. *Never again,* she vowed. *We'll take our time.*

However, she was already thinking about what she would wear when she saw William again. She had several ideas that had nothing to do with business suits.

Monday, February 28: Downtown

ELIZABETH WAS A VERY HAPPY GIRL AS SHE WALKED INTO THE EDNO offices on Monday morning. She and William spent a half-hour talking on the phone the night before, and she was convinced more than ever that he had feelings for her.

He was flying back from Houston tomorrow, and they set a dinner date for Saturday night. Elizabeth only wished it was Friday.

Maybe we can grab lunch on Wednesday, she mused happily.

A mug of coffee on her desk, she was firing up her computer when her phone rang. "Hello—Elizabeth Boudreaux."

"Lizzy, it's Will."

Her face lit up. "Will! I was just thinking of you! What's up?"

"Uhh, Lizzy, I've got bad news. We just found out one of our ships collided with a fishing boat off the coast of France overnight."

Elizabeth gripped the phone tightly. "Oh, no! Was anyone hurt?"

"Our ship received minimal damage, and the crew is safe. As for the fishing boat—Lizzy, it's not good. She sank after the collision. We're assisting French and British naval units in looking for survivors, but we haven't found any yet."

Elizabeth's thoughts flew to the families of the fishing boat crew. "How horrible!"

"This is a major incident. I'm going to have to fly to the scene to handle this."

"Of course. When are you leaving?"

"We're preparing the corporate jet now. We leave at noon."

Elizabeth swallowed. "How long will you be gone?"

He paused. "I don't know. As long as it takes. I'm afraid we'll have to postpone our dinner date. I'm really sorry."

Elizabeth closed her eyes. As disappointed as she was, she could not, would not, let William become distracted. "Don't worry about that. You go do what you have to do. Go take care of your people. We can go to dinner anytime."

"Elizabeth, I'm really, really sorry." The pain in his voice was evident.

"I'm disappointed, but you need to handle this. I'll be praying for those poor people."

"Thank you for understanding. I promise we'll get together when I get back. And I'll try to call. All right?"

Elizabeth tried to keep the catch out of her voice. "You bet, buster. Fly safe."

"I will. I gotta go pack. I'll email when I can. Bye, Elizabeth."

"Goodbye, Will." *I love you.*

Chapter 22

William ran into a wall in Paris. He had thought the shipping accident could be handled with a couple of meetings and a news conference expressing the corporation's concerns for the families of the missing. But he and the DGS execs did not count on the response of the European press, especially the French newspapers, to the tragedy. Already anti-American due to the war in Iraq, the headlines screamed of murder on the high seas as if the *Edmund Fitzwilliam* deliberately ran down the fishing boat.

When he wasn't doing his regular day-to-day job, William's ten-hour days were spent in meetings with bankers, insurers, advisors, and US and foreign government officials. Thanks to the Internet, he was able to handle most of his domestic business via e-mails from a hastily arranged office in the London branch. Crisis management experts were flown in, and a game plan was meritoriously laid out.

The key to the success of the plan was William Darcy himself. Young, tall, and handsome, he was the perfect spokesman for the corporation. That his family came from English and Norman stock didn't hurt, and his fluency in French proved vital. He could talk directly to the French officials and, with interviews on TV, to the French people.

The defining moment came when he met publicly with the families of the fishermen. His sincere concern for them, and the establishment of a trust fund for the children's future, turned the tide of public opinion. Shipping and fishing companies from both sides of the Atlantic contributed to the fund.

But the forced separation hit the couple like a blow. The six-hour difference between Britain and Louisiana restricted communications to e-mails William sent while having dinner, which was Elizabeth's lunch hour back home. Otherwise, one of them was sleeping while the other was working. Most of the e-mails were an exchange of news or a recap of how that day's work had gone. Both felt they had fallen into limbo.

Finally, in mid-April, William announced that the preliminary findings of the Court of Inquiry acquitted the *Edmund Fitzwilliam* of any fault, placing the blame squarely upon the master of the fishing boat. By then, the press had reported the previous missteps and violations by the incompetent captain, and the families' ire turned to the French company that had hired and retained him.

Friday, April 15: Lakeview

GEORGE, ABE, AND EMMA SAT AROUND THE DINNER TABLE ENJOY-ing a meal of Miz Taylor's chicken gumbo, Caesar salad, and garlic French bread. What was once rare was now a familiar routine at the Katzes' house. Certainly, there were days when George worked late, but they could now be measured in times per month, rather than per week. Husband and wife had recaptured the bliss of their early days. Even Abe was happier. The renovations to the house had gotten the old man out of a five-year-long funk. Now he was apt to take a cab to the nearby Museum of Art to while away an afternoon when Emma was at NCJW.

"George," Emma remarked over her gumbo, "I've been think-ing. Would you like to have some company for Passover this year?"

"That would be nice. Who were you planning to invite?"

"We haven't had Chris and Mari over for dinner since their engagement."

"Mari?" Abe chipped in. "Isn't she Lizzy Boudreaux's friend?"

"Yes, she's engaged to Chris Breaux."

"I like that Lizzy girl. Why don't you invite her too?"

George shrugged with a grin. "The more the merrier."

Monday, April 18: Downtown

"I'VE NEVER BEEN TO A PASSOVER SEDER," ELIZABETH ADMITTED to Marianne while sharing lunch, one eye on her BlackBerry.

"Me, either. Emma says it's a festive meal celebrating freedom. It ought to be fun." She dug into her chef's salad.

Elizabeth's response died in her throat as the BlackBerry chimed that an email had arrived. Marianne smirked as Elizabeth unashamedly read the message on the little screen. "What does Will say today?"

A huge smile broke out on Elizabeth's face. "He's coming home! Will's coming home!"

"No way!" All other thoughts disappeared. "When?"

"Friday." Her face fell. "Late."

"How late?"

"Real late—almost midnight. It'll take all day Saturday for him to get over jet lag. And Sunday, I'll be at the Seder. Rats. Maybe I'll cancel."

Marianne was quiet for a minute. "Hey! Why don't you invite Will to the Seder?"

"What?" Elizabeth turned to her friend.

"Sure," Marianne warmed to her idea. "Will's gonna rest all day Saturday if he's coming in that late on Friday, right? So, since we're all going to be at the Katzes' on Sunday, a well-rested Will gets to see all of us, kick back, and relax. Talk about celebrating freedom! Who needs it more than Will after the month he's gone through? It's brilliant!" She pointed at the device. "Go ahead and ask him."

"Mari, I can't invite Will to the Katzes' Passover."

"Why not?"

"Because it's their Passover, not mine! That's up to Em and George."

"Oh, to heck with that." She reached over and took the BlackBerry out of her startled friend's hand. Over Elizabeth's protests, Marianne quickly composed a reply to Will's email and sent it.

"We're all friends, here. There! We'll see what he says."

Elizabeth reclaimed her BlackBerry, her look as dark as the device. "Mari, honestly, sometimes you go too far!" She began pressing the keys.

"What are you doing?"

"Sending him a message to disregard yours. You get me so mad, sometimes." She stopped as the device chimed again.

```
To: eboudreaux@edno.org
From: wgd@deltaglobalshipping.com

Mari,

I'd ask you how you got a hold of Lizzy's
BlackBerry without her killing you, but I figure
you're running too fast to answer.

As for your invite, I'd be happy to come and join
y'all, if it's OK w/Em & George.

Lizzy, if you're reading this, have mercy on the
girl.

See y'all on Sunday the 24th.

Will
```

"Still mad, Lizzy?" asked Marianne with a grin.

"You were born to hang, girl," she said, but the threat held no malice. Elizabeth was too happy. She was going to be with William again on Sunday.

Faubourg Marigny

Marianne was not through plotting. "Will's coming home on Friday," she announced to Chris that evening over dinner.

"He is? That's great!"

"That's not all. I invited him to George and Emma's on Sunday for Passover."

"Wonderful! I haven't seen him since—wait. *You* invited him?"

"*How* I'm getting him there isn't important," she pointed out. "What *is* important is for Will and Lizzy to have some quality time. Get those two crazy kids together."

"I think they've been doing that on their own."

"Aw, c'mon, sugar. It'll be fun. You know Will's nuts about Lizzy, and we both know Lizzy feels the same. This isn't matchmaking. It's…greasing the wheels."

Chris grumbled. "Greasing—humph. Probably going to slip and break my ass over this."

"You're gonna help?" Marianne squealed.

"You think I'm entrusting this to you? We're going to do this right. First, we've got to call Emma."

Chapter 23

Emma tried not to wring her hands as she waited with her husband for their Passover guests to arrive. She and Mrs. Taylor had spent the last few weeks cleaning the house of any *chametz*—anything leaven, anything made with wheat, rye, barley, oats and spelt—like the saltines and Abe's beer. Anything used in the making or cooking of *chametz* was cleaned or stored away too. After all her preparation, the table was finally set with the Passover china and linen, and two long tapers burned in silver candlesticks. Delicious smells of roast turkey wafted out of the kitchen and filled the house.

Emma arranged the special Seder plates and wine glasses as she ran through her mental checklist. Had they forgotten something? She jumped as the doorbell rang.

George noticed and took her hand. "It's all right, honey. Everything's perfect. Let's just enjoy ourselves."

She gave him a relieved smile as he opened the door.

First to arrive were Chris and Marianne, with Elizabeth only moments behind them. All were still gathered in the foyer, laughing at an awful old chestnut of Abe's about a priest, a rabbi, and a goat in a bar when the doorbell rang again. Emma only had a moment to note Elizabeth's excited mood before George welcomed William into the house. Except for Marianne's cry of hello, all was quiet while he and Elizabeth locked eyes. The next moment, the two embraced and kissed.

Over a cocktail in the den, William quickly recounted his adventures in Europe. Then the party moved into the dining room and found their seats. Abe sat at the head of the table, Emma opposite him. To her right was George, to her left, William. Elizabeth sat next to him, while Chris and Marianne took their seats on the other side of the table. A Hagaddah, a small booklet, was set at each place.

Abe, as the eldest, was given the honor of leading the Seder. He slipped on his *kittel*, the simple white robe he wore when he married and would someday be buried in.

"*Shalom!*" he began with stentorian cheer. "Welcome to our Passover Seder, or as the ancestors call it, *Pesach*." Abe looked at William, who was testing the word on his tongue. "That's right, Will, you may speak French like a native, but tonight you'll get a little ancient Hebrew!"

Emma wondered why William flushed and Elizabeth choked back a laugh.

"I speak for my daughter and son when I say we are blessed you have joined us tonight. As this is, for most of you, your first Seder, I'll explain a little as we go."

"Like we can keep you quiet, Abe," George ribbed him.

"Ah! You see what I have to put up with? One day, Son, you'll have a little Katz who will put you in your place!"

"You've already given me one of those."

"*George!*" Emma laughed.

The rest of the meal went perfectly, to Emma's delight. Abe was at his entertaining best, enchanting all with quips, stories, and his best Jackie Mason routine. Emma had not seen her father so animated since his illness. He was funny and kind with his own brand of *schmaltz*. He explained the significance of the foods on the Seder plate. There was a huge twinkle in his eye as he "hid" the *afikoman,* the bit of *matzah* put away for the end of the meal, under Marianne's plate.

"Keep it safe, now," he said with a smile and a conspiratorial wink. Marianne had a surprise in store when Abe asked her, as the youngest in attendance, to recite the Four Questions from the *Hagaddah.* Emma clapped her hands in joy as Marianne held a sheet of paper and sang "*Ma Nishtana.*" When she finished her song, the table roared in approval, none more than Emma. Not only was it a song from her own childhood, what really touched her was the fact that Marianne had taken the trouble of learning the Hebrew words. She wiped tears from her eyes.

A scrumptious meal of gefilte fish, matzah ball soup, Turducken, and ratatouille was relished by all. George perhaps enjoyed too much for he got seconds of everything. Emma knew she would have to get on her hubby about watching his waistline.

Once the chocolate mousse was served and the *afikoman* was recovered and consumed, Emma's tears returned while Abe sat back and recalled how Irene and Emma would dash about the house, hunting high and low for the *afikoman* when they were little. She well remembered how much effort Papa put into hiding the piece of *matzah,* and how her mother used to scold him for his silliness while secretly charmed all the same by the uproar. Emma missed her mother and sister deeply.

Finally, the fourth and last cup of wine was poured. This was the *Nirtzah,* the final blessing of the Seder. Abe raised his cup, and with a voice of emotion that had been carried by his people for uncounted generations, declared, "Next year in Jerusalem!"

The crowd broke out in spontaneous applause. All took a hand clearing the table, and when they were done, they filed into the den.

ELIZABETH AND WILLIAM SAT ON THE COUCH, SHE TO HIS RIGHT, next to the armrest. For proprietary's sake, she left a little room between them, their hips separated by a hand's-width. William's arm was over the back, possessively encircling her. Elizabeth wasn't certain whether she would be delighted or mortified if he dropped it down and embraced her shoulders. Probably both.

Emma and George shared the other couch, Chris and Marianne were in adjoining armchairs, and Abe was holding court from his chair. During the older man's endless amusing stories,

Elizabeth would catch either Emma or Marianne smirking at her. She knew she was being obvious with William and tried not to be self-conscious about it.

The night before, they had spent an hour on the phone, William doing most of the talking, recounting the difficulties and obstructions inherent in an international incident. Elizabeth let him vent, understanding he needed to do it. It was a data dump of all his frustrations of the last six weeks. She couldn't blame him. She often did the same with Jane or Charlotte.

During that phone call, she realized William had no one to confide in. He didn't have a Jane or Charlotte. He couldn't talk about these matters with Gina. He only had her. The notion made her warm inside.

At times, Elizabeth wondered what she was getting into. When it was just the two of them, on the phone or sharing a meal, it was wonderful. Two young adults, dear friends who shared a sexual attraction. His kisses were heaven. She would dream about a life together.

Then worries intruded. Her boyfriend was William Darcy, a tycoon, a very important business figure in the city. There were incredible demands on his time, and not just from DGS. Politicians called him at all hours. Every charity and business group in the state wanted his time, his prestige, and his money. Did he have the time to be the kind of partner she needed?

Elizabeth was not made to be a trophy wife. She wanted no separate existence from her husband. At her core, she was old-fashioned. A family lived together, ate together, did things together, raised children together. As much as she loved William, was he truly the right man for her? Was she the right woman for him? The fears were always there.

And yet, when she talked to him or was with him, like now, those concerns vanished. He was not Mr. Darcy, wunderkind of the shipping world. He was just her Will.

During yet another tale from Abe, William failed to suppress a yawn.

"You must be exhausted," Elizabeth observed with a mixture of concern and disappointment.

"Haven't quite shaken off the jet lag, I guess," he admitted. There were bags under his eyes.

"So, get some rest," advised Chris. "What's the upcoming week like?"

"Awful. Bunch of lunch meetings early in the week." He gave Elizabeth an apologetic glance. She appreciated the unspoken message that he would be unavailable for lunch. "I'm playing catch-up, looking at ten-hour days. It lightens up by Thursday, but I've got to fly to New York next Sunday to meet with some Wall Street types first thing next Monday morning. Got to keep the investors happy—let 'em know DGS is going to survive after this near debacle."

"You know, Jazz Fest's next weekend," Marianne observed. "We never miss the opening. Chris and I are going on Friday. Lizzy's coming too." She turned to the Katzes. "How 'bout you guys?"

George shook his head. "I'm on call this weekend. If we go at all, it'll be the second week."

Chris leaned over. "Will, why don't you join us on Friday?"

"I don't know."

"C'mon!" Chris insisted. "You need a break. It's just what the doctor ordered!"

Marianne chimed in. "And he's a doctor; he should know!"

"You just said it's going to be light at the end of the week. Reschedule some stuff, and get your dancing shoes on!"

Elizabeth gripped William's hand in silent encouragement.

It was enough. "I've got a conference call early Friday morning, but after that—okay, but I'll have to meet you there."

"Yay, Will!" cried Marianne.

William nodded as he yawned again. As much as she didn't want the evening to end, Elizabeth knew he was dead on his feet.

"I think you ought to go home and get some rest before you fall asleep on George's sofa."

"As long as he keeps his *tuchus* off my La-Z-Boy," Abe interjected, "he can stay put."

"Thanks, Abe. But you're right, Elizabeth." He stood up, and everybody followed, Elizabeth stating her intention to walk him to his car.

"Need a ride, partner?" asked Chris.

"Nah, I hardly drank any wine. I'll be fine. I'll call you in a day or two. Good night, Mari," William gave Emma a big hug. "Thanks, Em. Everything was wonderful."

"Let's have dinner again soon, stranger," she told him.

"You got it." He hugged George next. "Thanks, buddy. And take it easy."

"Been talking to my wife, huh? Besides, look who's talking!"

William laughed. "Okay, let's both take it easy, all right?"

He took his leave of Abe and left the house with Elizabeth holding his hand. The couple walked quietly to his BMW. At the car, Elizabeth fiddled with William's collar.

"You get some rest, hear?"

"Yes, Mommy," he teased. "It was great seeing you. I'm glad I came."

"Me too. I'm looking forward to Friday."

His fingers moved on their own to caress her face. "I don't know. I might just pass out on you."

"Oh, I don't think so."

His lips were on hers, sweet and light, his hands on her shoulders as hers rested on the warmth of his chest. She never wanted the moment to end.

William pulled back, their faces in shadow. Time hung heavily between them.

"Good night, Elizabeth," he whispered.

Her tongue tasted her lips before she answered. "Good night, William."

"See you Friday." He climbed into the BMW and drove down the street.

She watched until he was out of sight, taking in the warm evening. Her heart pumped a mile a minute.

Maybe we're just horny. But it felt so good, so right. We fit together— Listen to me! I sound like a teenager! I'm twenty-six years old! I'm way beyond hearts and rainbows and unicorns. I want something rich and real, something that will last. I want to be with someone I want to make happy, and who makes me happy.

She made a promise to herself. From now on, she would follow her heart. If what she felt was real, Elizabeth would know it soon enough.

Perhaps Friday?

Meanwhile, in the car, William was a frustrated mess. Good lord, he wanted to kiss every last inch of Elizabeth's delicious body! But the last thing he wanted was to scare her off by pushing too hard, too fast.

Take it easy, man! You're just tired. We've got Friday. Let her take the lead, and let things work themselves out.

"I just hope I don't explode first!"

"Wow. You're slick, sugar," Marianne purred.

"Impressed?" Chris grinned as he drove Marianne home.

"I bow to the master. 'Just what the doctor ordered.' I thought I would break up laughing. I still don't know how I held it together."

"You did pretty good yourself, babe."

"You think either one of them suspects?"

"Nah. They're both so focused on one another, they have no clue."

"So, what's the game plan?"

"Hey, who needs one? We're going to Jazz Fest—good music, better food, and less clothing. We'll play it by ear. But let's make sure Lizzy and Will have plenty of time by themselves."

She stroked his hand as she looked at him though her lashes. "Really? Is that just for their benefit?"

He looked at her, his desire evident. "Nope."

"Good."

Chapter 24

Friday, April 29: New Orleans Fairgrounds

Elizabeth, Marianne, and Chris descended from the shuttle bus from the Superdome parking lot after picking up Elizabeth at her apartment. Parking around the Fairgrounds was thin. Elizabeth, wearing a teal sleeveless top and tan shorts, scanned the area around the front gate for William. But it was Marianne who spotted him first.

"Hey, Will!"

Elizabeth turned. Sure enough, William leaned against a power pole near the street, arms crossed over his chest, perfectly relaxed in his casual clothes and shades like he had just stepped off an exclusive desert golf course. Elizabeth was melting, and it was only ten in the morning.

"Hi ya, Will," said Chris. "Where'd you park?"

"A couple of blocks away. I know someone who lets me park in his driveway. Hi, Marianne. Hi, Elizabeth." His smile brightened.

Elizabeth had to say something. "So you didn't have to park downtown like the rest of us? It's good to be the king."

"Sometimes."

"C'mon, you two," said Marianne, "let's get in before the rest of the city does!" Her black hair tucked behind her visor and breasts bouncing in her shelf-bra red tube-top, she pulled Chris towards the gate.

William waved for Elizabeth to precede him. They moved towards the ticket takers, the crowd getting heavier as they continued. Elizabeth felt his hand on her lower back, his pinky touching the skin that peeked out between her shirt and shorts. She shivered in pleasure.

"You okay?"

"Yeah, fine. It's just a little crowded."

A few moments later and they were all in. "Meet y'all at the flagpole!" cried Chris.

New Orleans is celebrated for great festivals and parties. The most famous is Mardi Gras, but almost as well known is the annual New Orleans Jazz and Heritage Festival: two weekends of music, crafts, and food held on the last weekend in April and first weekend in May.

The Jazz Fest is different from the other great music festivals. It tries to concentrate on the music of New Orleans and the South. Organizers do bring in such artists as James Taylor, Steve Winwood, and the Black Crows, but they are the exceptions to draw in the tourists. Performing every year are local icons like Irma Thomas, the Neville Brothers, Olympia Brass Band, and Steve Riley & the Mamou Playboys. The Gospel Tent has choirs from all over. There are performances by Mardi Gras Indians and Native Americans. Rock, Dixieland, Jazz, Modern Jazz, Bluegrass, R&B, Zydeco, Soul, Blues, and Latin—the roots of music and its future. Held for most of its thirty-six years in the infield of the New Orleans Fair Grounds horse track on Gentilly Boulevard, the music starts at eleven in the morning and plays until sundown.

The Jazz Fest is also known for the food. It is quite simply one of the best food fairs in the country. Crawfish Monica. Alligator sauce piquante. Cochon de lait po'boys. Oyster loaves. Spicy Natchitoches meat pies. Abita beer. White chocolate bread pudding. Café au lait. Food is the soul of a town, and not many cities in the world can boast more soul than New Orleans.

The big crowds usually show up on Saturdays and Sundays. Fridays are more intimate. Hippies in their tie-dyes bump shoulders with yuppies playing hooky from work in their button-down shirts and loosened ties. Groups often carry large poles, festooned with flags, to let their friends know where on the vast grounds to meet. The weather is unpredictable. Sometimes it's chilly, sometimes it's broiling hot, and sometimes it's muddy and wet. No matter the conditions, the vibe is always hopping.

The NOPD is out in force to watch out for drunks and pickpockets. As they are the best crowd control police in the world, they are unobtrusive and welcome. The same cannot be said of the legion of meter maids who descend upon the neighborhood, marking for towing any vehicle left questionably parked. Not a few happy visitors have their day ruined by finding their rented car is now in the custody of the City of New Orleans. At least the city takes plastic.

THE TWO COUPLES QUICKLY MADE THEIR WAY TO THE CRAFTS AREA. Strolling through the stalls and tents, they browsed through sculptures, paintings, masks, clothing, jewelry, and souvenirs. Tourists bought the ubiquitous Jazz Fest Poster as though it were a priceless work of art.

Eschewing the large corporate stages and the headliners, the couples made their way to the Economy Hall tent to take in the Dukes of Dixieland. From there, they drifted to the Fais Do-Do Stage. A couple of Abita Ambers later, they were swaying with the music. During a set by Buckwheat Zydeco, hunger reared its ugly head.

"I'm gonna get something to eat, Will," said Chris. "You and Lizzy want something?"

"I'll go with you."

"No, y'all stay here," advised Marianne. "We'll take care of it. What'cha want? Crawfish Monica or cochon de lait po'boys?"

Elizabeth and William looked at each other. "Can't we get both?" asked Elizabeth.

"Yeah," agreed William. "One of each."

"You got it," said Chris. "Give us about fifteen minutes."

"Oh, and some mandarin orange iced tea?"

"Okay, Lizzy." Marianne and Chris moved towards the food booths. When they got there, Marianne grabbed her fiancé's arm.

"What's up?"

"You think it's working?"

Chris grinned. "Heh, Will hasn't moved from Lizzy's side since we got here. The boy's got it bad."

"Good! Lizzy needs someone in her life, and Will would be just right." Her arms snaked around Chris's neck. "Just like you are for me." She gave him a light kiss.

"What do you want, Mari?"

Even though she had on sunglasses, Chris could tell she was giving him a serious look. In a low voice she said, "I *want* you to take me home and take me to bed, Chris. But what we're *gonna* do is get the food."

They were kissing when the vender broke in.

"Okay, what can I get'cha?"

Marianne and Chris looked at each other and laughed.

MEANWHILE BACK AT THE STAGE. BUCKWHEAT WAS TEARING INTO "Hard to Stop." William and Elizabeth were being gently pushed from all sides. It seemed natural for William to stand behind Elizabeth and put his hands on her shoulders.

Elizabeth was determined to go with the flow, to follow her heart, and not to overthink things again. It felt so good, so right, to be in William's arms. She let herself lean back into his embrace, moving with the music, and allowed herself to get lost in the moment.

The music, the sun, the man. She could feel William's strong warmth against her back. She could smell his masculine scent mixed with his aftershave. She felt hot, chilled, nervous, and relaxed at the same time. William started humming along with Buckwheat, his hands sliding down to her trim waist.

Elizabeth turned and looked up at his face. She almost lost her breath, he was so handsome. She knew behind his sunglasses he was peering down at her breasts, and the knowledge aroused her.

Time seemed to stop. Her hand came up to caress his face. His lips descended. Her head tilted and lips parted.

The kiss seemed so natural that it took her a moment to remember they were in public. She then dismissed it. If William wasn't embarrassed, then neither was she. Elizabeth turned in his arms and deepened the kiss. She felt complete, as though something she never knew was lacking had finally fallen into place. Her body tried to communicate her desire for him.

They drew back one last time. Elizabeth watched as a devastating grin spread over William's features, those damn dimples making their presence known again. She didn't want to break the spell, so she slipped her arms around his neck, demanding his lips again. Like the gentleman he was, he complied.

It was in this manner that they were discovered by their friends.

"Woo-hoo! Get a room!" cried Marianne.

The couple broke apart, embarrassed.

"Here, partner," Chris smiled as he handed him their order. "It looks like you were hungry there."

William looked so adorably self-conscious that Elizabeth couldn't help but to slip an arm possessively around his back.

"Well, you guys took so long, we had to find something to do," Elizabeth teased.

William said nothing, but he returned the hug.

"Well, before he devours anybody, let's go find a place to eat," teased Marianne.

The two couples, now both arm in arm, went in search of an

open spot. It took some time before there was enough room for Chris to withdraw a blanket from his knapsack and spread it on the ground. Elizabeth and William reclined next to each other, nearly touching, while Marianne sat leaning back against Chris's chest.

"What do you want first, Elizabeth?" asked William, holding up the food.

Elizabeth glanced over the see Marianne feed some of her crawfish Monica to Chris. *When in Rome…* She took the crawfish, scooped up a spoonful, and held it out towards him. "Here, have some," she said with a sexy smile.

There was only a slight hesitation before he accepted her offering. She took a bite herself, making a bit of a show licking the spoon, and continued to share the crawfish between them. She delighted in driving him crazy.

After a sip of the tea, William unwrapped the po'boy and handed it to Elizabeth. "Watch it, it's pretty sloppy."

"Is there any other kind?" she boldly asked as she bit down.

The juicy roasted pork, garlicky gravy, and crunchy French bread was heaven on earth. Between the two of them, they made short work of the po'boy.

"Do you want anything else?" William asked as he collected the trash.

Elizabeth fought the temptation to answer with a cheeky remark. Instead, she laid her head down in William's lap.

"Maybe later, but right now I want to just take it all in."

He stared at her. "Don't go to sleep." His voice was slightly uneven.

She grinned at him. "And what if I do?"

"Then I'm stuck." He laughed. "But you'll get sunburned if you're not careful."

"I brought some suntan lotion. Don't worry."

"Need any help putting it on?" Now, he grinned.

"Perhaps, if you play your cards right."

A SHORT TIME LATER, THE BLANKET WAS STOWED AND THEY RE-joined the crowds. A New Orleans All-Star music tribute with Irma

Thomas, Allen Toussaint, Deacon John, Ivan Neville, and others was rocking the audience. Marianne was enraptured.

"Maybe one day, babe," said Chris as he slipped his hand around her waist. "One day," he pointed, "you'll be up there with them."

"I wish," Marianne whispered, bopping with the beat.

Meanwhile, William had other things on his mind. "Hey," he whispered in Elizabeth's ear, "what about that suntan lotion?"

Elizabeth smiled as she dug the bottle out of her purse. "Here, Mr. Sunburn Police." She turned around and held up her hair so he could apply it to her shoulders. "Now, don't miss a spot."

In the early evening, the group made their way to the shuttle bus stop to await the ride back to Chris's car. Chris noticed Marianne wore a very self-satisfied smirk, and he knew the cause. William had his arm around Elizabeth's shoulders, and she held on to his fingers with her free hand, her other arm around his waist, her head against his shoulder.

Mission accomplished. Mari's gonna be insufferable about this.

Outside the gates, William said, "Hey, Chris, y'all go on ahead. I'm taking Elizabeth home."

"You sure, Lizzy?" Chris asked. "What about your car?"

Elizabeth blushed, and Marianne punched Chris in the shoulder. "Y'all go on. Have a nice evening."

Marianne led Chris away, and they joined the crowd at the bus loading zone.

"Jezze, Chris, do you have to make a fool out of yourself? Lizzy's not thinking about her car! Don't ruin things for them!"

Chris shrugged. "Sorry. I guess I had a brain fart."

"Men!" She pouted. "What would you do if I weren't around?"

Shrivel up and die, probably. "Have a more peaceful life."

"Ha! Peace is overrated. You need excitement," Marianne drawled.

Chris leaned close. "And you're just the girl to provide it?"

"You better believe it, sugar," she said as she kissed his cheek.

Chapter 25

The buttery leather seats of William's BMW caressed Elizabeth's thighs like a lover. William smoothly navigated the pockmarked side streets of Mid-City towards the Lake and took the 17th Street Bridge from New Orleans into Metairie.

"Did you have a good time, Elizabeth?" he asked after getting directions to her apartment.

"I always have fun at Jazz Fest—turn here—but this one was special."

William glanced at her, but before he said anything, they had arrived at Elizabeth's apartment building.

"Well," she said, "here we are." She came to a decision. "Umm... would you like to come up for a coffee?"

William's expression was intense. She was sure he knew she wasn't just talking about coffee.

"Sure, that would be great." He opened his car door and got out, moving across the front of the BMW just as Elizabeth was swinging her legs out of it. He held out his hand. She blushed as he helped her up and walked her to her door.

Elizabeth fumbled getting the keys out of her handbag. *Why am I so nervous? It's not like he's the first guy I've invited in. No, not the first—only, he's William. Get a hold of yourself. You love the guy, for heaven's sake!*

The two walked into the apartment. "This is the place. It's not big, but it's home," Elizabeth babbled.

"Nice. Very neat and clean."

"Ha! You should have seen it last Sunday!" *Oh, God! Why did I say that? Now he thinks I'm a slob!* "Two bedrooms in case one of my sisters comes by for a visit."

"You've got four, I remember."

"Yes," she answered, pleased at his memory. "Mary's on her own, but Kit and Lydia are still at home." *At least Lydia is supposed to be.* "And Jane is in Covington, as you know."

He walked up to a picture on the wall of Chuck, Jane, and their kids. "Lucky guy. Beautiful kids and a wife who loves him. What more could a guy want?"

Elizabeth felt her stomach do somersaults. "Coffee!" she cried, remembering. She dashed into the kitchen. "Regular or decaf?"

"Full leaded, please."

"Good man." She busied herself readying the coffeemaker while William walked about the apartment. When done, Elizabeth glanced at him. *I hope I don't sound like an idiot.* She took a breath and committed herself.

"William, the coffee's going to take a minute, so I'm going to change out of these sweaty clothes."

He turned his head. "Sure. I'll be right here."

Elizabeth almost laughed. *Where else would you be?* Then she thought about where she expected they'd be in a little while. She almost ran into her bedroom, hoping he didn't notice how red her face was.

WILLIAM SAT ON THE COUCH AND WAITED. HE MADE NO ASSUMPtions about Elizabeth's motives for inviting him in. He had hopes, perhaps, but no expectations.

He leaned back, closed his eyes, and thought back on their history. Now, five years later, despite all they'd gone through, she had given him a second chance.

I've got to be careful. I can read most people, but I can't read Elizabeth. Is it because we're too dissimilar or because we're too much alike? I have no idea why. I've got to let her set the pace. I don't want to blow this again.

"Oh, William," came Elizabeth's voice from the kitchen. "Coffee's almost done. Do you want to wash up?"

William looked at himself. "Yeah. Where's the washroom?"

"Just through my bedroom there."

William looked over at the door. *I didn't see her come out. I must be more out of it than I thought.*

He walked into the darkened room and saw the light from the open bathroom door. He went to the sink and splashed water on his face, washing off the sweat. As he used a towel, he noticed her bra on the floor near a hamper. Seeing it sent a charge through his body. He replaced the towel on the bar and returned to the front of the apartment.

He found Elizabeth curled up on the couch with a cup of coffee in her hands, another on the coffee table. "You take it black, right?" she asked.

"Yeah." He couldn't remember how she would know that. He might have been able to recall, but he couldn't concentrate. Elizabeth had done more than change her bra. She was wearing a short crop-top white tank and blue yoga pants. She was sitting with her bare feet on the couch, and he could see her creamy skin peak out from the gap between her top and pants. Her hair was loose and flowing, and her face was freshly scrubbed. She was lovely, and William sat down next to her quickly before his arousal became apparent.

"Good coffee," he was able to murmur. "You have a nice place here."

Elizabeth nodded. She seemed edgy. "Thank you."

Her gaze was full upon him, and he was lost in her lovely dark eyes. He had always loved her eyes, he remembered. He leaned very close to her, and she didn't move either towards him or away. It was as though she were waiting for something. He noticed the scent of something other than coffee. Flowers—she had dabbed on some perfume. Her look, her smell—he found them intoxicating.

William took a chance. He pulled away to set down his coffee cup, then he reached for hers. Wordlessly, Elizabeth handed him the cup. Once it joined the other, he returned to her. Her eyes were nervous and expectant and...hopeful? She wet her lips with her tongue, and he was undone.

"I'm going to kiss you now, Elizabeth." His arm slid along the top of the couch.

She closed her eyes.

It started out sweet and warm, but as the kiss went on, it grew in intensity. Soon, he pulled her into his strong arms, and her hands touched his cheeks. They broke apart, gasped for air, and the kiss resumed. This time his tongue licked the corner of her mouth, and she opened hers to him. Her arms were around his neck, playing with his hair, while his hands began to wander, caressing her back through her top. Through a lust-filled haze, he discovered Elizabeth had neglected to replace her bra. His hands couldn't stop searching for skin. Her only response was to explore his mouth even deeper.

The next thing he knew, Elizabeth lay on her back beneath him. She gasped as his hands came from around her back to glide up and cup her breasts. In the instant of choice between acceptance and rejection, she arched her back in response. William pushed up her top and his hands began a teasing assault on her nipples. His lips left hers to trail kisses along her throat and neck. She moaned with pleasure, moans that turned into cries of delight as he took a nipple between his lips. He suckled her as his free hand caressed her bare stomach and fabric-covered hip. It was then he realized that she was missing more than her bra.

William regained control and returned to Elizabeth's neck. "Lizzy...oh my God, Elizabeth! We've gotta stop."

Elizabeth craned her head to look at him.

"I don't have any protection," he gasped in frustration.

"It's all right. I'm on the pill."

He shook his head. "It's not just that." He struggled to keep his voice calm. "It's not you! Look, it's not like I sleep around, but that's a lot of trust on your part."

"Will, I do trust you." She raised an eyebrow. "You never slept with Carrie Bingley, right?"

"Carrie Bingley? Hell, no!" He was pleased to see the return of Elizabeth's enchanting sauciness. "Besides, she's Carrie Buford, now."

"Is there a difference?"

"No. Okay, I've never slept with Carrie Bingley, or Carrie Buford, or any other girl named Carrie."

"Have you been a regular in Storyville?"

"Lizzy, Storyville hasn't existed for a hundred years! But, no, I don't patronize professionals."

She reached for his shirt. "Then come on, lover," she purred as she unbuttoned it.

Kisses and caresses resumed for untold minutes. Finally, as Elizabeth's hands slipped into his pants and traced the outline of his arousal, it was too much. He broke their deep kiss and gazed down on her. It was better than a wet dream: Elizabeth, below him, top pulled up, breasts exposed and nipples erect, her face flushed with desire and excitement, her bewitching half-closed eyes locked on his, her hair in complete disarray. He could feel her heat through her yoga pants.

I am not going to have her here on the couch like some coed! She deserves better than that.

He swooped in, gave her a brief, deep kiss, and got to his feet. Before Elizabeth could protest, he picked her up in his arms. She wrapped her arms around his neck and giggled as he made his way into her bedroom.

Gently, he deposited her on the queen-sized bed. The room was a mixture of shadow and light, lit by the open doors to the bathroom and living room. Almost immediately, Elizabeth tugged down her yoga pants, confirming his guess. He shucked his shirt off and began undoing his pants as she threw the covers toward the foot of her bed. As he kicked off his Topsiders, she started sniggering.

William joined his laughing love on the bed. "What's so funny?"

"You bob."

"Sorry, but they haven't invented a way for a man to remove his shoes gracefully." He took her into his arms.

"That's okay, I'll be good." Her hands encircled him. "You *are* a big boy, aren't you?"

"Oh God, Elizabeth…" He kissed her hard as they fell backwards on the bed, and they began to explore each other's bodies. They lost themselves in pleasure, hands and lips driving them insane.

"Please, Will. I'm so ready for you. I need you—*now*."

William wasted no time sinking his length deep inside her. She gasped and wrapped her legs around his waist. He was lightheaded. Finally, he was with the love of his life after so many years, so many sleepless nights.

"Oh, Lizzy, it's too much! So good… I'm trying to hold out."

"It's for you, William," she whispered. "All my love for you. Don't hold back."

Elizabeth's words ran down in a direct line from his ears to his core. His entire body shook, and he lost himself to a pleasure so great it was painful. A small part of him understood why some cultures called it *le petit morte*. He felt as though some part of his very life force was transferring to her. It seemed to go on forever.

They lay together for long moments, entangled, exhausted, and content. Finally, worried his weight was too much for her, William rose up on his shaky elbows and sweetly kissed her eyes and nose.

"Oh, Elizabeth… God, I love you."

"Y-You do?" Elizabeth's voice was uneven, broken, surprised.

His eyes flew open. "Honey, what's wrong?"

She was staring at him. "You said you love me."

"Yes, I love you. I guess I always have."

She frowned. "Always have? What about college?"

Reaching up, he drew a finger across her velvety cheek. "Even then. I was just too stupid to admit it."

To his horror, her eyes began to fill.

"Elizabeth, don't cry!"

"I can't help it." With that, she drew him into a tight embrace. "I love you too."

He pulled away just enough to look into her eyes. "This isn't the hormones talking, I promise. I'm in love with you."

"And I'm in love with you, Will Darcy." She kissed him, her lips full and demanding.

Finally, William allowed himself to fall on his back by her side, his forearm over his eyes. Elizabeth smiled, reached over to kiss him, and scampered out of bed. He assumed she was headed for the bathroom, so he just lay there, taking in all that had happened. For so many years, he had dreamed of this night. Now that it was here, he couldn't believe it. Elizabeth loved him. She was his, and he was hers.

His thoughts were cut short by the movement of a hip on the bed as a warm, damp washcloth encased him. He began to protest.

"Hush! Lie back, I want to do this."

He noticed a bath towel beside her. Knowing instantly what that was for, he reached over and took it into his hands. Flipping it open, he draped the towel where it was intended. He then rolled over on top of it.

"What are you doing?"

"What any true man would do in my situation, Miss Boudreaux! Don't you know a gentleman always sleeps on the wet spot?"

Elizabeth laughed as she crawled in bed to join him. She pulled the covers over them as she snuggled close. "Since when were you a gentleman?"

"Lizzy! You wound me!" He pulled her close. "I may have been a jerk and an asshole, but I've always been a gentleman."

"Don't say that," she said seriously.

"Why not? It's true."

"Will, stop. Let's not argue about who was most at fault. I'm too happy right now."

"Anything you say, sweetheart."

AN HOUR LATER, ELIZABETH SIGHED. NEVER HAD SHE FELT SO AT peace as she did in William's strong arms. They had made love again, but this time, he was determined she reach her pleasure first. She tried to tell him it wasn't necessary, but he wouldn't listen. Soon after his fingers and mouth began pleasuring her, her protests stopped. Her climax took her breath away, and when William achieved his again, aftershocks buzzed and raced through her body.

They lay together now, the light from the other rooms still illuminating the bedroom. She could not believe she could have loved him more than she did before, but this felt so right. They fit so right. So, as was her wont when things seemed perfect, Elizabeth began to worry.

She wanted nothing more than to awake in his arms tomorrow, but she had no idea whether he wanted to stay the night. Would he stay, or would he go? Did he love her as much as she loved him? Was she ready to be his girlfriend, his lover, his—? She couldn't even *think* the word wife.

While she wrestled with uncertainties, William moved to get out of bed. It was only ten thirty. They hadn't even eaten dinner.

"Will, where are you going?" she blurted out.

"I'm sorry. I didn't mean to wake you."

Elizabeth decided she was going to be mature about this. "Come here and give me a kiss me goodbye," she whispered.

"Huh? Goodbye? I'm not leaving. I'm just going to the bathroom."

Elizabeth was at once delighted and mortified. "Oh."

"Unless—" Now, William sounded unsure. "If you want some privacy, that's okay. I'll do whatever you want."

"No! Stay! Don't pay attention to me! I'm being silly."

"There is nowhere else I want to be but in your arms." He lightly touched his thumb to her lips. "I'll be right back."

She kissed it. "Good."

A few minutes later, William returned and climbed in bed. Instead of lying down, he propped up on one elbow and took her face in his hands. Elizabeth could only make out shadows. She couldn't see his eyes clearly, but she knew his gaze was intense.

"Elizabeth, this is important. I love you. You say you love me, and I believe you. But—and this is the important part—Elizabeth, do you trust me? I mean, not just trust that I'll be truthful but trust me with your heart?"

So this was it. The Big One. The Trust Question. If William wasn't worth it, who was? She closed her eyes and jumped off the cliff.

"Yes. I trust you." She opened her eyes, surprised at her relief in surrendering. "I trust you with my life."

He kissed her. "And I trust you. I will never let you down. If I ever disappoint you, if there is anything I do or say that you don't understand, if I ever do anything that bugs you, promise me you will tell me."

"I promise." She smiled. "You know me—opening my mouth is not my problem!"

"Oh, I know a good way to shut it."

Chapter 26

William groaned as the morning sunlight filtered through the window, drawing him awake. Squinting, he could make out details in Elizabeth's bedroom that had escaped him the night before: the soft pastel color of the walls and her dresser, various bits of jewelry lying about, and a Beanie Baby of Riptide keeping guard over it all. He wondered whether it was the same one he bought for her in Memphis so many years ago. He could hear the soft clanking of the ceiling fan, and he smelled coffee brewing.

That caused him to roll over and look at the other side of the bed. Sure enough, Elizabeth was already gone. Listening closely, he could hear her in the kitchen. He got out of bed, recovered his clothes, and made his way into the bathroom. He washed his face and brushed his teeth with his finger.

Leaving the bedroom, the first sight he beheld was the two place settings at the table, napkins and all, with the morning's newspaper between them. He looked in the kitchen, and the domestic scene was complete: Elizabeth was cooking bacon in a flowery robe of blue and pink, bunny slippers on her feet, humming softly to herself. He quietly stole into the kitchen and embraced her from behind.

"Guess who?"

"Hmm, Harry Connick, Jr.?"

William turned her around. "Bad guess." They shared a kiss.

"Good morning, my darling."

"Oh, don't you go start talking all lovey to me. You'll make me burn the bacon."

He released her. "Whoa! Burn the bacon? I'll behave, Mommy, I promise!"

She smirked. "Pour me some coffee, smart guy." The coffee machine had two Saints mugs, a sugar bowl, and a carton of half-and-half next to it

"Sugar and cream in yours, right?"

"You remembered?"

"You'd be surprised what I remember about you." He handed her a mug before taking a sip from his. "Mmm, just what I needed."

A bawdy grin spread over Elizabeth's face. She grew closer to him. "I wear you out, lover?"

"Now look who's trying to burn the bacon. Need any help?"

She playfully slapped his arm. "Go read the paper. Breakfast will be ready in a minute. How do you like your eggs?"

"Any way's fine." He retreated to the table but didn't pick up the newspaper. He was enchanted watching Elizabeth putter about the kitchen. *Is this my future? Man, I hope so.*

Less than ten minutes later, she placed two plates of scrambled eggs, bacon, and grits on the table. The two enjoyed their breakfast, Elizabeth playfully fending off his numerous compliments to her kitchen skills. During their second cup of coffee, he cleared his throat.

"Elizabeth, I've got to fly out of town tomorrow. I've got a meeting in New York first thing Monday morning."

Elizabeth nodded. Her smile slipped off her face.

"So, I was wondering. I know this is last minute, but do you think we can spend some time together today? Nothing big, we could just walk around the Quarter. The weather's so nice—"

"Yes!" Elizabeth almost squealed. "I mean, that would be lovely, Will." She looked down at herself. "I'd like to clean up, first. When do you want to go?"

"As soon as you're ready. We'll need to stop by my place, so I can grab a shower."

Elizabeth smiled as she gathered the plates and carried them to the sink, and then she retreated to her bedroom.

William had some time to burn, so he figured he'd give her a surprise.

FORTY-FIVE MINUTES LATER, A STILL DAMP-HAIRED ELIZABETH walked out of her bedroom fastening an earring, wearing a sleeveless blouse with a skirt and open-toed heels. She noticed William sitting on the couch with the paper in his hands, hiding a smug expression. Glancing at the sink, she got her surprise.

"You cleaned the kitchen?"

He grinned as he stood up, dropping the paper on the couch. "Yeah, it's no big deal. I've been a bachelor for too many years."

"Mr. Darcy, if you're trying to get on my good side, it's working!"

There were those darn dimples again. "Good. Ready to roll?"

Elizabeth swallowed nervously as she voiced the resolution that had come to her in the shower. "Umm, would it be okay if we ran over to my office so I can get my car and follow you?"

William was clearly puzzled. "If you want. Why?"

She could not look him in the eye. "Well, I thought I could drop you off at the airport tomorrow. You won't have to leave your car there." An extra-large handbag was slung over her shoulder. It was big enough to hold a change of clothes. The implications of her offer were obvious, and she blushed bright red.

Thankfully, William didn't laugh, gasp, or say anything stupid. He crossed to her and put his arms around her.

"I would like that very much," he began, his voice soft, "but you know what this means, don't you?"

Elizabeth's throat went dry. "No, what?"

Without changing the timber of his voice, he said, "You'll have to pick me up Tuesday evening."

Elizabeth grinned at his teasing. "You haven't ridden with me yet. You may regret that."

"I doubt it," he said before he kissed her breathless.

Warehouse District

THE TRAFFIC WAS LIGHT THAT MORNING, AND AFTER RETRIEVING Elizabeth's Honda, they were soon deep in the Warehouse District. She followed William's BMW to the garage of an old six-story brick building. He rolled down his window and waved for her to follow him as the automatic door opened. Elizabeth piloted her CR-V through the garage that took up most of the ground floor and pulled into an empty parking space next to William. Only after she had gotten out of her Honda did she notice that both spots were marked with the number "301."

"Each unit has two parking spaces reserved," he explained. "Extra parking is outside."

"Good, I didn't want your neighbors mad at me for taking their spot."

"Elevator's this way." As they got in, he added, "There's a pin code for the garage door. I'll write it down for you when we get upstairs."

Elizabeth was taken aback at his casual comment. She was trying to decide whether she should decline his offer when the doors opened to a tastefully appointed hallway. "My place is this way—down the hall at the end." He directed her with a hand on her back.

William's condo was a corner unit. It was an open-plan, modern industrial design, softened with a bit of New Orleans funk thrown in.

"Will, it's beautiful!" Elizabeth fell in love with it at once.

"Thanks."

"Is that a Michalopoulos?" she asked as she walked over to a large painting placed in a prominent location.

"Yeah, I got it a few years ago. You like it?"

"Oh, yes." Acclaimed by many as the premier New Orleans artist, James Michalopoulos's studies of the architecture and people who make the city unique were remarkable for their technical prowess and emotional verity. The slabs of paint, the curved lines, the mix of bright and dark—few people captured New Orleans like Michalopoulos.

"If you want, we can go by his gallery. It's on Bienville."

She nodded as she studied the painting. Then with a smile to him, Elizabeth continued her exploration, William silently watching her. Two other paintings caused her to laugh. A George Rodrigue Blue Dog was set opposite a Jim Tweedy Red Cat.

She looked over her shoulder at him. "You're bad!"

He grinned in appreciation. "You'd be surprised how many people don't get the joke."

She moved to the glass door to the outside balcony and looked out. "Will, it's great, but all you can see is the building across the street." She turned to him. "I'm surprised."

"How so?"

"Well, I figured you for a penthouse kind of guy."

He shrugged. "Nah. I mean, it's fine for now, but it's really just a place to sleep and eat. Home's Dansereau Plantation."

"If that's home, how come you have this place?"

"It's closer to work. St. Charles Parish is a forty-minute commute on a good day. And with Gina at Auburn, I'd just rattle around that big old place. If I had a family, it would be different. I'd live at Dansereau, and I'd have DGS buy this place to use for visiting customers. We don't need an expensive penthouse for that. So, until I settle down, I'll hang out here. Oh, that reminds me."

He turned and walked into the kitchen area. Rummaging through a drawer, he said, "Let me write down that pin number."

Elizabeth watched silently as he pulled out a pen and one of his business cards. "Just punch in the numbers, then the pound sign," he said as he gave her the card with the number written on the back.

"Will, you don't have—"

"But, I want you to have it. Look, I also gave you my private cell number. That way you can call me and leave dirty messages."

"Will!"

He kissed her cheek. "I'll get a key made for you. Just make yourself at home. I won't be long." He smiled as he left the room.

Elizabeth stood there in an agitated mood. He was still the controlling, domineering guy he was in college. She hated when he did that.

She began pacing. *Oh, why does everything have to be so compli-cated? One moment he's sweet and thoughtful, the next he's arrang-ing my life!*

She stopped as comprehension flowed over her. She remembered the last time she saw him in college—or wanted to see him, rather. She had hurried to his graduation to apologize only to find out his father had died in an auto accident the day before.

I'm such an idiot. He's been running things by himself for five years. No dad, no mom, raising Gina, running a billion dollar international shipping firm fresh out of MBA school. He's not controlling; he's self-reliant. He's not used to checking with anyone—something needs to be done, he does it.

She looked at the card. *He asked me to trust him! This is his way of saying he trusts me! He's opening his whole life to me. Have I been that open to him?*

And he loves me! I'll have to ask him to ask me first if I want some-thing done before he does it for me. Why am I afraid to do that? Am I afraid he's going to fall out of love with me?

There, I said it. Now, think about it. He said he's loved me since Tu-lane. Why is that so hard to believe? Haven't I loved him the whole time?

Okay, so we're nuts about each other. If we are truly meant to have a life together, I shouldn't be afraid of talking with him. Is our love so weak it can't stand up to a disagreement? What's the worst that can happen? We might get into an argument?

Like that won't happen if we get married—

The dreaded "M" word stopped her short.

Married. Do I want to marry him?

Yes.

She smiled. She enjoyed being with Will, and she knew she was going to hate it when he left. She didn't want to waste a minute.

She moved quickly into his bedroom and removed her clothes. Quietly opening the bathroom door, she saw William soaping himself in his oversized shower, totally oblivious that she had en-tered. After taking a moment to appreciate the view, she opened the shower door and embraced him.

"Wha—Elizabeth!"

"Need any help scrubbing your back, Mr. Darcy?"

DOWNRIVER OF THE WAREHOUSE DISTRICT LIES THE pie-shaped Central Business District, the heart of commercial enterprise in Louisiana. Tall skyscrapers and enormous hotels sit shoulder to shoulder. The grand boulevards of Canal Street and Poydras Street help define the area. Here, oil and gas companies, financial concerns, and transportation firms help build the economic strength of the nation. Hard against Interstate 10 is a medical complex comprised of Charity Hospital, the VA, and the medical schools for both LSU and Tulane. At the other end, the narrow end near the river, is the land-based casino and the iconic World Trade Center building.

One block downriver is the true heart of New Orleans: the *Vieux Carré*, the Old Square, the French Quarter. Stretching twelve blocks from Canal Street downriver to Esplanade Avenue, and seven to nine blocks inland to Rampart Street, it is one of the most famous areas of real estate in the country.

The tourists who turn down the numerous carriage tours don't know about any of that. They only want to visit one of the most infamous streets in the nation: Bourbon Street, the legendary home to jazz clubs, strip joints, T-shirt shops, discotheques, tattoo parlors, high-class hotels, white table cloth restaurants, and fast food stands. Some claim Bourbon Street has more bars per square foot than anywhere in the world.

The salesmen from Cleveland and teachers from Tacoma are both attracted and repulsed by the noise, sights, smells, and sounds. Barkers outside of questionable establishments entice people to view dancers of disputed gender remove most of their clothing. Street performers on every corner. The ubiquitous go-cups, containing Hurricanes or Hand Grenades or Sex on the Beach. The home of Girls Gone Wild and daiquiris-to-go. Where college guys from Harvard and oil workers from Texas City get the chance to learn firsthand that, contrary to popular belief, public urination is not legal in the City of New Orleans.

It may come as no surprise to learn that locals tend to avoid Bourbon Street. They can't stand the tourists. To them, the Quarter is more like Royal Street. It, too, has hotels, restaurants, and lounges. But it also has art galleries, fine furniture and antiques, and jewelry and dress shops.

Bourbon Street is for the nighttime; Royal Street is for the day.

French Quarter

WILLIAM AND ELIZABETH WANDERED SLOWLY DOWN ROYAL Street—she, with a wide-brimmed hat to keep out the sun, and he, with a sport coat over one arm. They entered almost every shop and gallery, simply enjoying the day, the city, and each other's company. More often than not, they held hands.

After about an hour, they found themselves in Jackson Square, the heart of the Quarter. They took in the artists and street performers for a bit before Elizabeth turned to St. Louis Cathedral.

"Will, can we go in for a minute?"

He nodded, and they entered the symbol of New Orleans together. Unconsciously, the two Catholics dipped their hands in the holy water before making the sign of the cross while facing the altar. William was looking at the various flags of Louisiana that hung from the pillars when he noticed Elizabeth had walked over to the shrine to the Blessed Mother. She lit a candle then knelt on the kneeler, saying a silent prayer. He watched her quietly, enchanted by this different side to her. With her dark hair, she resembled the Madonna. He felt a new stirring within himself, not passion or desire but a need to connect with such goodness, to be worthy of her.

His thoughts dissipated as she crossed herself again and returned to his side. "Okay," she said softy, "all done now."

He knew better than to ask what her prayer intention was, so he limited his response to a light kiss in her hair before escorting her outside. As they were leaving, a team of florists was bringing in a batch of flowers and garlands for the first of several weddings to be held that day. Elizabeth gave them a long look before giving one to William.

He shook his head. "You want to grab something to eat?"

AFTER A LUNCH AT THE GUMBO SHOP (ELIZABETH GOT THE SEA-food and okra while William ordered duck and andouille), the two of them toured the Louisiana State Museum in the Cabildo. They then grabbed a table at Café du Monde to enjoy an afternoon snack of beignet and coffee.

Elizabeth was thankful for the diversion. Thoughts kept intruding—uncomfortable thoughts, things she didn't want to face right now. Her only goal today was to enjoy her new intimacy with William. Problem was, that intimacy was one of her issues! Oh, why could she not turn off her head for a day? There was all day Sunday to worry about these things.

"Honey, are you all right?"

William's innocent question set off her emotions. Her eyes watered as she grasped his hand, almost upsetting the plate of beignets.

"William, I want you to know I love you."

He kissed her hand and assured her he loved her too. "What's bothering you?"

"Nothing," she lied. She didn't want to ruin their lovely day by dumping all her fears and worries on him.

"Are you regretting last night?"

Elizabeth just learned that loving an intelligent, intuitive man had its pitfalls. "Oh, no!"

William said nothing; he simply tightened his hold on her hand. Studying his penetrating expression, she knew he wasn't going to let this go. *Trust me*, he had said last night. She decided to do just that.

"I just don't want you to think I'm the kind of person to just—you know."

He pulled her hand up and kissed her knuckles. "Shush, love. I don't think anything like that. I only feel incredibly blessed that you're in my life." He lowered his voice. "Last night was magical, but I don't have any expectations regarding that. The only hope I have is to love you for the rest of my days. My only wish is to make you happy. How can I do that?"

She smiled at him, her eyes watering. He had the uncanny ability to say the right thing at the right time. "I don't deserve you."

"You deserve way better than me."

"You're all I want."

"Then you're easy." He blanched at his *faux pas*. "Oh, hell, I didn't mean it that way! Elizabeth, I'm sorry!"

"You're cute when you grovel."

"I've gotten good at it." He moaned. "What a stupid thing to say!"

"That's okay. I know what you meant."

"So, do you feel better?"

"A little." She looked around, still holding his hand. *Might as well tell him the rest.* "Will, there was a reason I asked to go into the church. Have I ever told you about my family?"

"Not really. I know you're from Chackbay, and you have four sisters—Jane and three others."

She nodded. "Mary is a school teacher in Thibodaux. She has her own place. Kit lives at home. She's studying to be a beautician." She paused. "It's my youngest sister, Lydia. She ran away from home."

He grew very grave. "When did this happen?"

"Over a year ago."

"Have the police been able to find her?"

She shook her head. "No. You see, Lydia's eighteen now, and she's not really missing." *Time to drop the bomb.* "She left to move in with...with Greg Wickham."

"The hell you say!"

Elizabeth had to hold his hand firmly to prevent William from leaping to his feet. As it was, they were attracting the notice of the other patrons.

William fought to gain control of himself and lowered his voice. "How did that happen?"

"I don't know. They met at some party, Kit says. She didn't know who he was or what he was."

He ran a hand through his hair. "Crap! We've got to get her out of there."

Elizabeth was touched by his concern more than she could ever express. "It's okay. She left him. She called and told us she found out what Greg did for money." She looked away, not wanting him to see her shame. "I'm sure she *participated* a bit, but she told Kit the really heavy stuff scared her. That's why she moved out."

"So where is she now?"

Elizabeth shrugged. "That's the problem. We don't know. She didn't tell us what her plans were. She told Kit she couldn't go home again."

"Oh, Elizabeth, I'm so sorry." His concern turned to anger. "The idea of Wickham taking advantage of another young girl—it just burns me up." He paused a moment. "Do you want me to make some calls?"

"That's not the reason I told you, Will. I just wanted you to know. We shouldn't have any secrets." William, as usual, was trying to fix someone else's problem, and she needed to break him of that. "We're worried sick about Lydia, but she's got to make up her own mind when to come home."

His temper turned to understanding. "You were saying a prayer for Lydia."

She nodded. "Are you okay?"

"Me? You're asking about me?"

Elizabeth laid her greatest fear on the table. "I just wanted you to know what you were getting yourself into. With all my baggage—"

"Hah!"

Elizabeth was startled he had interrupted her.

"Baggage," William mumbled. "You're not the only one with baggage." He looked around the restaurant. "Can we go for a walk?"

Scared and concerned, she agreed, and they left the cafe. They ended up strolling on a somewhat empty Moonwalk. He took her hand and stared out at the ships moving up and down the Mississippi River.

"Wickham keeps turning up like a bad penny," he began. "Three years ago, he was stalking my sister, Gina."

"Oh, no!" cried Elizabeth. This was worse than she imagined.

"She was a senior at Sacred Heart. One day, about a month after I came back from London, I went by to pick her up instead of letting her ride the streetcar to the condo. When I got there, she was waving at this guy in a Camaro across the street. When I looked over, instead of some boy from De La Salle or Jesuit, I see that drug-dealing scumbag, Greg Wickham. That SOB's driving the same car as before." He grunted. "He saw me and peeled out of there like he was in NASCAR. When we got home, I had my cousin Richard come over. Did you ever meet him?"

She shook her head.

"He's in the NOPD, a captain at the Third District. We explained to Gina who Wickham was. That scared her, and she told us how she knew him." He sighed. "She kept it a secret from me. They met at a football game. I guess he was scouting around for some fresh meat or delivering to a customer—who knows? Anyhow, once Gina was introduced to him, he pours on the charm. Really gets to her. She swears it was all innocent. God, I hope that's true. She admitted he had been putting some pressure on her to—you know."

Elizabeth whimpered.

"We got her a bodyguard, the same guy who watched over me after the last time. The school didn't like it, but a donation helped change their mind. Richard got the police to keep an eye out for Wickham, but he never turned up again. I guess we spooked him. Either he went to ground somewhere or he left town for a while. God, Lizzy! I almost lost my sister to that creep."

"But you didn't. You saved her."

"But if I had spent more time with her like she wanted, this never would have happened! But no, I was too busy. The whole scare hurt her, Lizzy. The rest of her senior year was hell. She never went to her prom—never met a boy. It was awful for her.

"And now you tell me Wickham ended up in Thibodaux and charmed your sister. It's like my fate is to be haunted by that bastard. Payback, I guess—after all, it's my fault."

"Will—"

"If I had done the right thing, turned in that bastard back in college, then maybe Gina or Lydia—"

"William Darcy, shut up!" Elizabeth cried.

He looked in shock at her.

"I am so sick of this! Will you ever understand not everything is your fault?"

William stared at her with no expression on his face. Elizabeth recognized it for what it was—he had retreated into his mask of inscrutability as was his wont when he was agitated.

All right, this will be either very good or very bad, but maybe this is what he needs me for.

"William, please, you must see that sometimes things just happen." She took a breath. "Like what happened to your father. It was terrible. I felt so bad for you. But, darling, you survived. The company your father built—it survived. Gina is still here—she survived. And it's all because of *you*. You've done so much. There is so much you *will* do in the future. Good things. Darling"—she touched his face—"I want to see you do those wonderful things. But you can't—you won't—if you keep beating yourself up over things you have no control over."

"But Wickham, your sister—"

"William, do we have to go over this? All right. We *both* screwed up in college, right? *Marianne* decided not to press charges back then, not you. *Gina* decided to meet an older man behind your back, not you. *Lydia* decided to run away from home, not you. Yes, love, you tried to help Mari, and you did save your sister, but there is only so much one person can do." She chanced a smile. "Even you."

William stared a hole in his shoes. The moment dragged on. Elizabeth could hear the horn of the Canal Street Ferry pulling into Algiers Point. Finally, he sighed.

"Even me, huh?"

Elizabeth did not realize right away that he was teasing her. "Oh, baby, you know you're my Superman." She hugged him tight.

"You just keep me straight, Lizzy, and maybe I can leap tall buildings with a single bound."

"Okay." She kissed his cheek. "How is Gina now?"

"Better. Going away to college was good for her. Nobody at Auburn knows who she is. She's found a place there and made some good friends. We're in touch all the time, and she comes home as often as she can. It's all good if I can keep the Wickhams of the world away from her."

She patted his face. "I know you want to, but she's got to learn to fend for herself. That's what college is for. Besides, she knows you're there for her if she needs you."

"You're right, but it's hard."

She squeezed his hands. "You can do it."

"If you're with me."

Elizabeth put her head on his broad chest. "Will, I don't know where this is going, but I want to be there with you."

"I love you." He kissed the top of her head.

"And you keep saying that, buster." In return, she kissed him. "Well, c'mon, you said we would stop by the Michalopoulos gallery."

THE FOOD IN NEW ORLEANS IS LIKE NOWHERE ELSE. Millions of visitors want to find out first-hand what this Cajun/Creole craze is all about. After a few days, they learn that everything they thought they knew was wrong.

Thanks to the success of Paul Prudhomme, Emeril

Lagasse, John Folse, and countless others, eateries across America have been adding "Cajun" dishes to their menus. Unfortunately, most of these joints think all they have to do is add lots of hot sauce or pepper jack cheese to something and—*voila*—you've got Cajun.

What you really have is very bad Cajun.

Ten minutes in Louisiana tells you that Cajun and Creole are two very different things. Cajun is the cooking of the county, the one-pot dishes the people made out of the ingredients close at hand. Jambalaya, sauce piquante, boudin, étouffée, and gumbos. Hundreds of styles of gumbos. If you ate in fifty restaurants and had gumbo in each one, each would be different and each would be delightful.

Creole is city cooking. Basing it on the intricate French sauces, trained chiefs and black cooks invented dishes like Shrimp Creole, Red Beans and Rice, Chicken Bonne Femme, Eggs Sardou, Bananas Foster, and Grillades and Grits.

Both styles were influenced by immigrants. Slaves from the Caribbean brought spices and okra. The Germans brought sausages. The Spanish, their rice. The English, their sandwiches. The Italians, tomatoes and pasta. The Asians, stir-frying. Cajun and Creole dishes are not set in stone; they continue to evolve and grow, incorporating the best of the ingredients and techniques and blending it like a gumbo, creating the great American Cuisine.

Some tourists, following the truism of most places, eat mainly in their hotel's restaurant. Others flock to the tourist traps. The fearful will tragically stick to the familiar national chains. But the adventurous will try the best the city offers: Mother's Poor Boys, Commander's Palace, Acme Oyster House, Broussard's, Emeril's, Pascal's Manale, August, Jacques-Imo's,

K-Paul's, Bayona's, and others too numerous to list.

But to truly understand New Orleans cooking, one should forgo for at least one meal these magnificent purveyors of neo-Creole and patronize one of the remaining standard bearers of the style—a place where you can eat exactly what your grandparents could have eaten fifty years before. Their mighty names: *Antoine's. Tujague's. Arnaud's. Brennan's. Galatoire's.*

THE REASON WILLIAM CARRIED A SPORTS COAT WITH HIM ON THIS warm April afternoon was that Galatoire's required gentlemen to wear a jacket after six. Many locals would never walk into the place without one, no matter the time the time of day, and William was one of them, so he was prepared at four thirty. Stationed near the door was a coat rack of several waiters' jackets of varying sizes for those unaware of this throwback to a more civilized time.

Galatoire's did not take reservations for the main room downstairs, but by going early, William knew there would be no line for a table. Besides, this was when all the regulars ate, and they ate downstairs.

"Good afternoon, Mr. Darcy," said the waiter, a man renowned for remembering the names of his regular customers even if they only came in four times a year.

"Hello, Pierre. A Sazerac, please. What do you want, Elizabeth?"

"I think a white wine."

"We have an excellent Pinot Gris just in, ma'am," Pierre said as he indicated the wine list, "and a superb Pouilly-Fuissé."

"The Pinot Gris."

"Why don't you get us a bottle of the Pinot Gris?" said William.

"Very good, sir. Sazerac and a bottle of Pinot Gris." Pierre left to get the drinks; he had not taken a single note.

Elizabeth and William perused their menus in companionable silence until Pierre returned with their drinks. Elizabeth ordered Oysters en Brochette and Crabmeat Mason.

William looked up at Pierre. "How's the Pompano?"

Pierre screwed up his face in thought. "Get the trout," he advised.

"Okay." William grinned. "Trout Amandine. I'll have the Shrimp Remoulade too." Pierre nodded and left. Once he was safely out of range, Elizabeth let go of the giggle she had suppressed.

"Will, that look on his face! That was so funny!"

"Yeah, it pays to be a regular or a local. He's been working here for twenty years and his dad before that." He picked up his drink. "Here's to you."

"No," she said, her eyes sparkling, "to *us.*"

William felt a wonderful lurch in his gut. *I could get used to that look.* "To us."

William dug into his Shrimp Remoulade almost as soon as it hit the table. Cold boiled shrimp nestled on a bed of lettuce, the shrimp were coated with Galatoire's spicy version of remoulade sauce. William's eyes watered in delight. Elizabeth delicately consumed her skewers of fried oysters laced with bacon, drizzled with New Orleans-style meuniere sauce. It was hard to decide who was happier.

Trout Amandine was two flash-fried filets of salt-water fish, in this case speckled trout, covered in the same just-on-this-side-of-being-burnt meuniere sauce with toasted almonds. Crabmeat Mason was a large ramekin of blue crab folded in a cream sauce, served with toast points. Each took pity on the other and shared, having fun feeding each other. Strong chicory coffee and Crepes Mason finished the meal.

By the time they sipped their coffee, the six o'clock rush had started, and William watched with amusement as a conventioneer struggled to put on one of the jackets by the door. Elizabeth's sigh caught his attention. She gestured with her head to an elderly couple just completing their dinner. The seersucker-suited man—in his seventies, he figured—rose to help his wife out of her chair. They walked out of the restaurant, the gentleman holding her hand with his right and a Panama straw hat in his left.

Elizabeth glanced at him with a gleam in her eye.

"What are you thinking?" he asked.

"That couple. Will that be us in forty years?"

"Nah. You'll be a lot cuter."

She rolled her eyes. "You're impossible."

"Ready to go?"

She nodded and got her things, the bill having been placed on Darcy's tab, a courtesy reserved for the regulars. They stepped into the Bourbon Street warmth as it ramped up to full nighttime glory. People filled the street and barkers cried their familiar cries. Behind them, a line of customers had formed at Galatoire's front door.

"What do you want to do?" asked William into Elizabeth's ear as he pulled off his jacket.

"Maybe a little jazz before we call it a night?"

"Okay. There ought to be something playing up the street."

Hand-in-hand, the lovers set off to enjoy what the city had to offer.

Warehouse District

THAT NIGHT ELIZABETH LAY IN WILLIAM'S ARMS, REVELING IN HIS quiet strength. It had been an emotionally draining day but a good one, and Elizabeth knew it was the beginning of their life together. Their coupling after returning to the condo was a reaffirmation and celebration of their commitment.

Elizabeth considered their discussions. William was kind, generous, and loved to be of use to people, especially her. It was reassuring that he felt he could fix all her problems, but it was foolish. He needed to be reminded he was not a knight in shining armor, adults should take care of themselves, and he could not save everyone from their foolish choices. She assumed that would be her chief job from now on.

She absently stroked his chest as she lay between sleep and wakefulness, astonished by how quickly she became comfortable with this intimacy. She had slept so well last night, knowing he was beside her, and she looked forward to seeing him first in the morning. That was the only good thing about the day. She would not see him again until Tuesday.

"What's wrong, beautiful?"

"I didn't know you were awake. I'm sorry."

"Don't be. I wasn't sleeping. What's the matter?"

"Just thinking about…things."

"That sounds serious."

"Nothing bad, really."

He rolled on his side closest to her. "If it's nothing bad, then you should be able to tell me."

"Can't you take no for an answer?" she teased him.

He rolled away. "I'm sorry. I don't mean to pry." His voice was low and unemotional. Elizabeth realized he was hurt.

"Oh, Will! Thank God you don't take no for an answer!" She firmly embraced him. "I'm so, so, *so* stupid!"

William stroked the back of her head as she continued. "What I was thinking—it's silly, really." She snuggled closer. "I feel so comfortable with you."

"So, are you trying to say you're going to miss me while I'm gone?"

"Yes," she admitted in a low voice.

"I'm sorry, hon. I wish I didn't need to go."

"I understand you need to. It's your job, jetting off to faraway places for high-end meetings and stuff like that. I—if we are going to continue on—" Embarrassed, she buried her face in his chest. "Don't look at me in that way!"

"What way?"

"That what-the-hell-is-she-talking-about way!"

"I'm not looking at you in that way." His laughing tone said he was.

"*Sure* you're not!" She sighed and pulled away from his chest. "Will, this is for real, right?"

"*I* think so," he said with fervor.

She squeezed him hard. "Me too. So…I'll just have to get used to you having to travel a lot."

"Maybe sometimes you can come with me."

She snorted. "Yeah, right. I gotta work, buster." It was just like him to kid around about something like that. She suddenly realized he *wouldn't*. She looked up. "What are you suggesting?"

He kissed her forehead. "I'm suggesting nothing. Just know the offer is there, okay? No private trips, no *you'll get bored, so just stay home.* I promise. You want to come with me, anytime, just say the word."

He didn't really answer her question, but what he did say warmed her heart. Still, she asked, "What about my job?"

"You get vacation time, right?"

"It's not like I can leave at the drop of a hat."

"Not every time, but I can't believe they're that big a stickler about taking time off."

Elizabeth was forced to agree. If there wasn't any board meeting or big event, it was not unusual to announce taking some private days with only a week's notice, as long as it didn't become a habit. "Maybe next time, okay?"

"Sure." He kissed the top of her head. "I'll make it up to you. Zoo-To-Do is coming up. Do you want to go? DGS has a table."

"I thought that was for your corporate clients."

"It is. I want you to be there."

Elizabeth blinked. "You want me to help entertain the customers?"

"Not really—it's a social event. Spouses are invited."

"I don't think I qualify for that!"

"You're my girlfriend. That'll work."

William Darcy's girlfriend! Unfortunately, the song "My Boy-friend's Back" started going through her head. *Stop it!*

Elizabeth's thoughts turned to her mother. Now that she had a name for their relationship, she knew she had to move to the next step. Frances Boudreaux would never forgive her if she kept something like a boyfriend secret from her. She loved her mom, but she could be so pushy! How would William react to that?

"Will, umm, my family in Chackbay. We have this tradition of a family crawfish boil on Memorial Day weekend." She was nervous. "It's on May 28. I would love it if you would come with me."

"Meet the folks? Sure," he easily agreed.

Elizabeth let go of the breath she did not realize she had been holding. *You haven't met my folks, yet.*

Sunday, May 1: Kenner

THE NEXT MORNING, ELIZABETH PULLED UP TO THE CURB NEXT to the Jet Blue terminal. By the time William yanked his suitcase and laptop briefcase out of the back of the car, Elizabeth was standing beside him.

"Fly safe," she murmured into his shoulder as they embraced.

"I'll be back before you know it."

"I hate this! I'm missing you already."

William pulled back and looked into her face. "I guess this is what love's all about, sweetie." He gave her a kiss. "I'll call your cell after I'm settled in the hotel."

"Okay. I love you."

"I love you too. See you Tuesday."

Elizabeth, eyes watering, stood beside her car as William entered the terminal to a chorus of honking horns. With an "All right, already!" she climbed into her Honda and sped off for her Metairie apartment.

Chapter 27

NEW ORLEANS' AUDUBON NATURE INSTITUTE HAS two of the finest urban zoological facilities in the nation. The Aquarium of the Americas sits on the Mississippi River between the Central Business District and the French Quarter. The older Audubon Zoo is also hard against the river levee but up the river across from Audubon Park and Tulane University. Two thousand animals make their home in the zoo's fifty-eight acres.

A fortune is needed to support all these creatures. The annual evening fund-raiser, called the Zoo-To-Do Gala, is one of *the* black-tie events on the social calendar. Guests, who are expected to shell out big bucks for tickets and spend much more at the silent auction and raffle, want to be pampered and they are. Big-name performers and small musical combos entertain the crowds as they wander through the exhibits. Scores of the city's finest restaurants provide marvelous hors d'oeuvres on which to nibble. Copious amounts of alcohol flows. The gala brings in millions every year.

What the animals think about Zoo-To-Do, no one knows.

Friday, May 6: Uptown

Because Zoo-To-Do was on a Friday night, Elizabeth changed out of her work clothes at William's condo. She bought a royal blue cocktail dress with matching pumps. Her justification for the expense was that William's girlfriend needed to look the part. Fastening the pearl necklace she got for her twenty-first birthday, she admitted the dress's neckline was a bit deep for her, but she assumed William would like it. His delighted expression when she came out of the guest room was all she could have asked for.

The cream of society filled the walkways between the exhibits on that lovely, warm evening. The zoo was a different place at night. The low lights gave it an exotic feel. The ladies' dresses spanned the colors of the rainbow; a few were of a shade only a mad scientist could imagine. The hemlines ranged from floor-length to up-to-*there*. Most of the men were conservative in tuxedos or business suits, but few looked as handsome as William.

That boy was born to wear black, Elizabeth thought happily. His dreamy good looks and his hand constantly on her lower back made her feel beautiful and desirable. Wine glasses in hand, they made the rounds, meeting William's business associates.

Tonight wasn't just social. Her boss, Carl Eden, was there, and he was happy that Elizabeth was attending too, especially on someone else's dime. So Elizabeth made sure to get people's cards and put in a good word about EDNO.

Marianne Dashwood and her combo was one of the minor acts scattered around the zoo. They caught her in the middle of a set, so the two chatted with Chris Breaux for a while, promising to return later.

DGS, as a mid-level sponsor, had a table set back from the main dance floor. Elizabeth and William were early for the main act, Big Bad Voodoo Daddy, and had the table to themselves. William took the opportunity to refresh their drinks. Elizabeth gazed around the space and waited for the rest of the DGS party to arrive, enjoying the decorations and regretting she hadn't done something different with her hair, when a man in a business suit sat next to her.

"Hi, there," he held out his hand. "I'm Phil Osborne. And you are—?"

"Elizabeth Boudreaux." The stranger was slim, middle-aged, and balding. His accent was East Coast—New York, perhaps. Why was he at the DGS table? The name was familiar.

"Ah," said Osborne, "you're Will Darcy's girlfriend. I've heard a lot about you."

The name clicked into place. "And I've heard a lot about you too, Mr. Osborne." He was a DGS board member, a venture capitalist, and a thorn in William's side.

Osborne grinned. "Nothing good, I'll bet." He took a drink from his glass. It appeared to be scotch. "Will abandoned you?"

"He'll be right back. Is your family here?"

"No. I was in town taking in some meetings, interviewing new investment opportunities, and Will said he had an extra ticket. I couldn't pass up free food and booze."

She didn't remind him this was supposed to be a fund-raiser. "Are you enjoying yourself?"

"It's okay." He sat back and studied her closely. His eyes gave nothing away. "So, how long have you known Will?"

Elizabeth couldn't tell whether Osborne was checking her out or playing intimidation games. She had met both kinds in the business world. She was irritated in any case. The last thing she wanted to do was recap with this guy her complicated history with William.

"Years, but we started dating seriously in January." Her voice was flat and dismissive.

Osborne laughed. "Oh, you're Will's girl, all right. You don't like me, do you?"

She struggled to keep her face neutral. "I don't know you well enough to decide."

He took another drink. "Look, I don't know what he told you, but we aren't the bad guys. We're like the bank of last resort for dreamers. Guy comes to us with an idea we like: we back him. Not just with money. We get in there and give him the benefit of our expertise and experience. Get him going in the right direction. In a few years, things work out, we sell out, spilt the money, and everybody's happy. Things don't work out…" He shrugged and sipped again. "You know how many times we make money? Seven deals out of ten, we don't make squat. Two deals, we make five to ten percent. But the tenth deal, we might triple our money. It makes up for the losers. This is a numbers game, Elizabeth."

"I'm aware of that, *Mr. Osborne*." Elizabeth put a slight emphasis on his name because she didn't like his casual familiarity. "I work for the local economic development group. We've actively reaching out to venture capital firms like yours to participate here. But we assumed you were looking for entrepreneurs. Isn't it unusual for VCs to invest in established companies?"

"Not our outfit," he admitted. "Like I said, we look for opportunities wherever they are. DGS looked like one six years ago."

"And today?" She had a hard time keeping the disgust out of her voice. Osborne resemblance to a vulture increased every second.

"Remains to be seen." He threw back the last of his drink. "I've enjoyed talking to you, Elizabeth, but I've got to get out of here. I'm flying out first thing in the morning. I coach my son's Little League team, and we've got a game tomorrow afternoon." He stood and Elizabeth did too.

"Good night and have a good flight. I hope your son's team wins."

"Thanks, Elizabeth." He paused. "You work for the local economic development group, you said? Tell them to get some more non-stop flights in here. You ain't going to grow if business people have to make connections to get here. The only non-stop I could schedule was at dawn. That sucks, I'm telling you. Oh, hey there, Will."

Elizabeth turned to see William approaching with two wine glasses in his hands. "Phil, I see you've met Elizabeth." His face was impassive as he handed Elizabeth her wine.

"Yeah, she's been keeping me company. Got to run—thanks for the ticket." The men shook hands and Osborne left.

William sat and took a sip from his glass. "So you met Phil Osborne."

"Yes." Elizabeth wouldn't look at him. "William, I broke

a promise."

William frowned. "How's that?"

She played with her bracelet. "I promised myself I would stop judging people until I got all the facts. I had written Mr. Osborne off as a jerk, and then he said something nice. Do you know he coaches his son's baseball team?"

"Oh, yeah. Phil brags about them all the time. He thinks his boy will play in the majors someday." He leaned over and kissed her forehead. "But you were right the first time. Osborne *is* a jerk."

The mood lightened as Leon Anderson, his wife, and the rest of DGS's guests arrived.

Big Bad Voodoo Daddy put on a great show. Elizabeth succeeded in getting William to dance most of the set before he retired from the field. The band took a break, a DJ took over, and William and Leon retreated to the bar. They sipped drinks, watching their ladies line dance to "The Macarena."

"What'cha laughing about, Will?" asked Leon.

William stopped chuckling and gestured with his glass at the dance floor. "Look at that. Some of those folks are pushing seventy, but they know all the moves."

"Yeah, funny. My wife—you can't get her off the dance floor. Lizzy, either, it looks like. She's a nice girl, that Lizzy."

"Yes, she is." William smiled.

"You two getting serious?" At William's inquisitive glance, he explained. "Ed and I were talking 'bout it yesterday."

William grew irritated. "I didn't know my love life was so interesting."

"Back down, Will. It's because we care, that's all. We're not trying to butt in."

"I know."

Leon set his drink down and gave the younger man a mock glare. "Your daddy was the best man I ever knew. He hired me, you know, at a time when a lot of outfits wouldn't give a black man the time of day. He believed in me. I'll never forget what a great boss and great friend he was. So, if I'm interested in my friend's son, well, that's just the way it goes."

William sighed. "Yeah, it's serious. We're waiting until the time is right before making it official."

Leon snorted. "You sound like my daughter. 'We'll know when it's time, Daddy,' she tells me. Shoot, you wait too long, it'll be too late. I've been married twenty-five years, an' I don't regret a moment."

William studied the older man. His round, light-brown face sported few lines, but his short hair was graying. William couldn't remember a time when Leon Anderson didn't work for DGS.

"Leon," William began carefully, "I've always been meaning to ask. Are you okay with me being president?"

"Of course, I am." He stared at the younger man. "Why are you asking?"

"Well, you've been with DGS for so long. You've been an invaluable part of the team. I just wondered, if… You know—"

"Are you asking if *I* wanted to be president?" Leon asked incredulously. "Are you kidding me? Hell, no! William, I know marketing and promotion. I'm good at investor relations. And I know just enough about operations so I don't embarrass myself. Now, your daddy and Ed? They knew the shipping business inside and out." He poked William in the chest. "And you're just like them."

"I don't know a fraction of what Uncle Ed knows."

"You will. Give it time. Meanwhile, you're doing a great job. Take the incident in France. You proved yourself. Nobody could have handled it better than you did. You know your stuff, and you can communicate it to people. And if you don't know the answer, you admit it and go find out. You don't bullshit. The investors and customers *love* that.

"The next few years are gonna be tough with industry consolidation. You, William Darcy, are our best chance at staying independent."

"Thanks, Leon. I'm going to need you to help me."

"I ain't going anywhere. My wife's dreading my retirement. Says on weekends I hang around the house doing nothing but bothering her."

"What does she want you to do?"

"Some sort of couple's thing," Leon moaned, "like bridge or running or ballroom dancing. Shoot, this ol' boy is too old to be doing no foxtrot."

William looked over to the dance floor. "Well, we'll be doing something. Here come the girls."

Leon threw back the last of his drink. "I got my second wind. Let's show 'em how it's done, Will."

Tuesday, May 10: Baton Rouge

John Buford returned home to find his wife, son, and dog awaiting him in the kitchen. John picked up the squealing and wiggling three-year-old Trey and kissed him while Max sat and whined. The dog got his cropped ears rubbed after Trey was set down again. John then turned to his wife, who was cooking dinner at the stove.

"Hello, baby," he crooned into her ear as he embraced her from behind.

"*Now* you say hello," Carrie grumbled as she stirred a pot. She had changed out of her work clothes into sweat pants and one of John's Army T-shirts, slippers on her feet.

John chuckled as his hands caressed her pregnant belly. "Saved the best for last. Have I told you how sexy you look?"

"Sexy—yeah, right. I'm fat."

"You're not fat, Carrie. Heck, you're only three months along."

"Says you." She sighed. "I've got to pull out the maternity clothes already."

"So what? It's still *your* incredible body." His hands moved up. "Besides, there are advantages to your condition. *These* are definitely larger, that's for sure."

"Stop it, those aren't for you." She pretended to be offended. "They're for the baby."

"He won't be using them for a while."

"Isn't that how I got into this condition in the first place? You sweet-talkin' me?"

He nibbled her neck. "You didn't complain at the time."

"Enough, Johnny." She hid the smile on her face. Her blasted husband could always get her out of a foul mood anytime he wanted. "Chop up some parsley for me?"

"Sure." Buford got some parsley out of the fridge and retrieved his favorite chef's knife. After placing it down on the chopping board, he picked up Trey and sat him on one of the stools by the kitchen island. "Now, watch a master at work, Son," he advised the boy.

Carrie glanced over. "He should be in his booster seat."

"It's only for a minute," he said. "You stay still, all right?" he asked Trey.

"Yes, Daddy," his son assured him.

With practiced stokes, Buford expertly minced the parsley, scooped up the herb and dropped it into Carrie's mushroom-and-meat spaghetti sauce. Carrie had learned to be an adequate cook, but she couldn't match her husband's knife skills. She put the sauce on low, placed the pasta into the large pot of boiling water, and then gave her Johnny the welcome home kiss he wanted.

Fifteen minutes later, the little family was seated at the table, Carrie and Buford eating spaghetti. Trey, properly in his booster seat, was having Spaghetti-Os. "Next year, Trey," Buford said, "you'll be big enough for Mommy's special sauce."

Carrie blushed. *Special sauce, ha! Jarred spaghetti sauce, hamburger meat, and sliced mushrooms—real gourmet.* She chewed her food. "Mom called."

Buford looked up from petting Max. "Oh, boy. What happened now?"

Carrie glanced at Trey. She couldn't speak openly in front of him. "*C.B.*," she said, instead of Mother or Grandmother, "was full of advice."

Buford caught on. "Nothing new about that. What did she say this time?"

"I'm spending so much time at work that…umm…"—her eyes shifted notably towards Trey—"someone is spending too much time with others instead of at home where he belongs."

Buford's eyes darkened at his mother-in-law's hypocrisy. "I'm glad C.B. has become such an expert in child-rearing. When does her book come out?"

"The twelfth of never."

"Is that right after hell freezes over?"

"Johnny!"

"Oops, sorry. Don't pay attention to that, Son."

"Daddy, you're silly." Trey giggled.

"That's me," he replied with a grin and a wink to his wife. As expected, Carrie relaxed as the tension dissipated.

Later, Buford was sprawled on the couch, trying to review a brief, while Carrie sat on the floor and played with Trey, Max curled up next to her. The boxer knew the difference between his toys and Trey's, so he just watched the boy with affection. Buford couldn't concentrate, so he watched the interaction between mother and child, his fingers idly playing with Carrie's hair. He could not imagine anything more peaceful. Of course, looking down his wife's top at the bounty contained within didn't hurt.

Soon, the two of them put Trey to bed, and then Buford took Max out into the fenced back yard for a romp while Carrie cleaned the kitchen. Another hour later found Max comfortably in his dog crate in the laundry room and the couple preparing for bed. Buford took Carrie in his arms as they snuggled together.

"What the hell is wrong with Catherine?" Buford's question was rhetorical. A popular topic of conversation in their household was Catherine's interference in their lives.

"She's always been this way."

"She's getting worse," he complained. "She was a working mother before your dad passed and she got all that insurance money. She should remember what you're going through. I believe she's really mad at me, not you. She thinks I can't support you."

"I've tried to tell her I enjoy my work, but she won't listen."

"Damn that mean bitch, anyway! You feel guilty enough with Trey in day care without her laying that crap on you. If she's so concerned, why doesn't she volunteer to take him, if only for a couple days of the week? Want me to talk to her?"

"John, we don't want Mom watching Trey! Besides, your relationship with her is bad as it is. Making it worse won't make me feel better."

"I know, I know. Look, I'm here this time. Use me, lean on me, vent to me. Don't let Catherine get to you."

"I try not to, but she's my mother. She can really push my buttons."

The first time Carrie was pregnant was right after 9/11. Buford had been sent with his National Guard unit to Afghanistan. Her fears for her husband's safety were multiplied by the discovery, two weeks after he shipped out, that she was carrying their first child. For the next nine months, Carrie had to deal with the joys, fears, and anxieties of a first-time mother and fend off Catherine's unreasonable demands alone. She insisted Carrie move in with her for the duration and dismissed as irresponsible her daughter's determination to remain in the home she and John had made.

Carrie's overseas calls and e-mails to her husband did little to console her. Thankfully, Jane was with her during the last couple of weeks and was able to drive her to the hospital when her time came. The babe was healthy, but it meant little to Catherine. She never forgave Carrie for her willfulness.

Four months later, John's unit returned from Afghanistan. Carrie thought her heart would burst when she saw her husband hold his son for the first time. The last two-and-a-half years were the happiest Carrie had ever known. Knowing John would be there for his second child just added to her bliss.

If only her mother wasn't like her mother.

Buford nibbled on her lips as his free hand caressed her growing bulge.

"Mother's not the only one who can push my buttons." She giggled.

"It's all about knowing which buttons to push."

"I'm so glad you're here this time." She placed her hands atop his. "Have I told you you're sexy?"

"Yes, you have, and I don't believe you. I'm a whale!"

"You are so far from a whale, Carrie. You're way too critical of yourself. You're gorgeous." He looked her in the eye. "I see you with that certain glow, knowing my child is inside you—Lord above, I just want to worship you, to let you know just a little of how I'm feeling right now. How proud I am. How thankful I am. How much I love and need and want you."

His heartfelt admission caused Carrie's eyes to water, but she couldn't resist one last tease. "You're just turned on 'cause my tits are so big."

He smiled. "That they are. But you doubt me? Mrs. Buford, you'll have to excuse me. I've got work to do."

And so he did. By the time he completed his labors, Mrs. Buford felt very worshiped indeed.

Chapter 28

May

Elizabeth and William were hardly out of each other's sight for the rest of the month. They would have dinner almost every night, either at his place or hers, and lunch at least twice a week. They engaged in the physical aspects of courtship new lovers enjoy, of course, but what they did most often was talk. They had five years of catching up to do, and they both felt now was the time to do it.

They talked for hours about everything: their families, their childhoods, their dreams, and their disappointments. They spent a lot of time discussing what had happened in the last five years. Elizabeth told him about the men she had dated and found William had a slight jealous streak. She was amused that a man with so much going for him could be envious of anybody, but she swore to herself never to tease him about it. She had her own jealousy issues to deal with.

She had playfully demanded he fess up to what he had been doing since college, and to her surprise, she disliked the answer. She did not like hearing about all the women who had thrown themselves at him, no matter how humorously he told the tales. It was unfair, she knew, but in her mind, all those bimbos resembled Carrie Bingley. She knew Carrie was married to John Buford, and happily too if Jane's reports were accurate. Still, Elizabeth found it hard to forget the woman's dogged pursuit of William back in college, and her darker side wondered whether Carrie hadn't, if only a little, regretted her choice.

Who wouldn't? This is William Darcy, after all! Her mind sometimes reeled with the knowledge that she had won his affection.

It was hard for her to believe, but apparently, he had been pining for her almost as long as she had for him. He told her that, once he got over his resentment, his feelings were full of regret over lost opportunities. If he was slightly smothering in his affections for her, Elizabeth would deal with it. Why he thought she was such a great catch baffled her, but she was pleased all the same. She understood that only time and experience would prove theirs was a relationship built for the ages. So Elizabeth reassured William, believing he would learn to trust in their love and commitment in the months that followed.

Saturday, May 28: Chackbay

SHRIMPS 4 SALE
LIVE CRAB
SWEET CORN

Elizabeth had to giggle at the familiar sign, selling seafood and vegetables from the back of a pick-up, as they passed by the roadside vender on Highway 1 along Bayou Lafourche. The intentional misspelling was always an attention getter. It was a sure sign she was getting close to home.

Home, she thought. *I'm bringing Will home to meet the parents. I guess the movies are right for once. I'm so nervous I can barely sit straight. Lord, I hope this goes okay.*

"You're awfully quiet, honey. You feeling okay?"

"I'm fine—fine."

He glanced at her. "Don't worry. I'm sure everything will go great."

It was William's first trip to the Boudreaux homestead, and they were headed to their annual Memorial weekend crawfish boil. All of Elizabeth's immediate family would be there.

"I'm not worried," Elizabeth claimed. "I just want everything to go well today."

"It will."

"You haven't met my folks."

They spent the next fifteen minutes in comfortable silence, the bayou on one side of the road and the vast sugarcane fields behind the houses on the other. Once they reached Thibodaux, they turned onto Highway 20 and drove into the cane fields and swamps. For a couple of miles, the highway was bordered by magnificent cypress trees in water, before opening up to a hamlet hugging the winding road.

"Well, here we are," Elizabeth announced. "Welcome to downtown Chackbay."

Chackbay was an unincorporated ribbon of houses and shops, hard against the highway. Dominating the scene was Our Lady of Prompt Succor Catholic Church at the intersection of two roads, the center of the community. As they drove past the church, both of them unconsciously crossed themselves. A half-mile down the road, Elizabeth pointed to a house on the left.

"There it is: the famous Boudreaux estate."

The Boudreaux house was one-and-a-half stories in the classic A. Hays Town style: hip roof, "old-style" red brick, pale yellow plaster entrance to cypress French doors, and fully operational Creole shutters in dark green. It looked like it *belonged* on the lot, the timelessness of the design shining through.

"Nice," William commented as he turned into the driveway, threading his way between the Bingleys' van and a large pickup truck.

"I see Mary and Bubba are here," Elizabeth mentioned as she left the car. The couple had taken only a few steps towards the house when the front door was thrown open and three women hurried out.

"*Lizzy!*" cried a middle-aged lady. "You're here at last! Oh, give me a hug!"

She disappeared as the woman engulfed her in a bear hug. Two young ladies stood behind her with smiles dancing on their faces. The woman, a bit shorter than Elizabeth, had short, dyed blonde hair. She had on a flower-print, scooped neck sleeveless blouse over white Capri pants. Numerous bracelets dangled from her wrists and a crucifix hung from a necklace.

The woman released Elizabeth and eyed William with undisguised excitement. "And, who is this handsome man? As if I didn't know!"

"Mom," Elizabeth managed, vacillating between amusement and mortification, "this is Will Darcy, my boyfriend. Will, this is—"

Before Elizabeth could finish, William was affectionately attacked. "Oh, I'm so glad to meet you at last!" Mrs. Boudreaux cried as she embraced him. "Lizzy," she said as she released him, "he's a strong one, isn't he? And so good looking! You've done well for yourself!"

Elizabeth turned beet red, but William seemed unfazed. "Mrs. Boudreaux, I'd say I'm the lucky one. I'm glad to meet you too."

"Oh, none of this 'Mrs. Boudreaux' stuff." She waved her hand. "Call me Frances."

"All right, Miz Frances."

Elizabeth turned to the other two. "And these are my sisters Mary and Kit."

Mary had black hair and wore an intelligent but slightly sardonic expression behind her black-rimmed cat-eye glasses. She was dressed in a T-shirt that proclaimed, "Teachers know how to do it," over shorts. A small diamond ring adorned her left hand.

Kit was as blonde as Jane and looked young for her age with her tight tank-top and low-rider jeans. She resembled her mother. "Wow, is that your car?" she cried, pointing at the BMW. "That's so bitchin'!"

"Kit, watch your language!" Frances exclaimed. "Children these days! Come in, come in!"

The group walked into the foyer, which opened into a living room filled with unremarkable antique reproduction furniture over a pale Oriental rug and hardwood floor. The dark room was lit by the lamps and brass chandeliers because the curtains were closed.

"We spend most of our time in the den in back," said Kit.

"Yes," said Frances, "it's so warm in here. I told T.B. we need to get a bigger air conditioning unit."

"Mom, William doesn't need to know that," said Elizabeth. Besides, it wasn't the truth. People kept the curtains drawn in South Louisiana not just to keep out the sun but also to hide from the prying eyes of their neighbors. Folks knew people were always trying to see into the house to find out your business, for it was the common sport of Cajun country. Cajuns were notoriously nosy, and Mrs. Boudreaux was nosier than most. And like most snoops, she was slightly paranoid.

Family photos and graduation portraits dominated the walls. Frances guided William to a particular grouping. "I think you'd be interested in this one, Will," she said slyly.

Elizabeth groaned softly and tugged at his arm, but he leaned forward to inspect the center picture. It was Elizabeth's high school senior portrait, in the traditional off-the-shoulder stole with pearls.

"I hated that hair style," Elizabeth grumbled before she gasped. "Mom! What is *that* doing here?"

She pointed at another photo: Elizabeth in a prom dress next to a long-haired boy. He was the boyfriend from high school who had cheated on her during her first year at Loyola. *Why is that still here? We broke up years ago!*

Frances blanched, mumbled her apologies, and removed the picture. "Oh, just an old photo. No need to have that here!"

William looked at an angry and embarrassed Elizabeth and squeezed her hand in understanding. Elizabeth turned and gave him a thankful smile.

The rest of the wall had three other similar groupings, representing Jane, Mary, and Kit. Frances sighed. "Oh, yes, I've been blessed with such beautiful girls."

Elizabeth thought the tour was over as they began walking to the kitchen. Too late, she forgot what was awaiting them.

Along the hallway was a new grouping of pictures, one far more extensive than the others. There were framed notes and drawings, portraits, snapshots, and other photos—those of cheerleaders and swim parties and vacations to Disney World. All featured a pretty, short brunette with laughing eyes.

Below it was a small table with a prayer candle lit and a single pink silk rose in a crystal vase. Behind the candle were photos of the same girl, much younger, in her First Communion dress and the same girl as a teen receiving her Confirmation. The collection was flanked by a teddy bear with a rosary draped upon it. The setup appeared to be an altar.

Elizabeth's fingers bit heavily into Will's, but his only response was to turn to her in astonishment. *Oh, no!* She cringed.

Mary stopped behind them while Kit continued on to the kitchen with a groan.

"My…my baby," Frances sobbed, her eyes filling with tears. "My dear, dear Lydia. She disappeared, you see, over a year ago. Right after she graduated. Such a beautiful child—only Jane was lovelier."

Elizabeth thought the ground was going to open up and swallow her.

William remarked, "She's very pretty. I expect it's been very painful for you."

"She prays before it," mumbled Mary.

There was a pillow half-hidden beneath the table. "Oh, yes," Frances confirmed. "Every day I pray to our Blessed Mother to keep my girl safe and return her to me. See?" She pulled the pillow out and demonstrated. On her knees, her eyes glued to the photos, she said, "It's very peaceful here. I feel very close to my darling child."

"Mother!"

William helped Frances to her feet. "I'm sure she'll come home soon, Miz Frances. Just have faith."

"Oh, I do. Thank you, Will." She turned to her daughter. "He's very nice, Lizzy."

Elizabeth rolled her eyes before she noticed William studying the center photo carefully.

"Her father's eyes and my looks—just like Lizzy," Frances claimed.

Elizabeth didn't think so. Sure, they both had Daddy's blue eyes, but Lydia's hair was mousy brown, rather than her rich chocolate.

And Lydia's smile always seemed a little vacant.

"Yes," William said with a smile as he took Elizabeth's hand again. "I'm a very lucky guy."

Frances dabbed her eyes and grinned. "Well, you know what they say about the mother and the daughter. I'm not a vain woman, Will, but you have to be happy to know what Lizzy's going to look like in twenty-five years!"

"Mother!" Elizabeth and Mary cried.

"Oh, stop it," she scolded her girls. "I'm sure Will isn't offended in the least. Will, can I get you something cool to drink?"

The party continued to the kitchen, William glancing one last time at the bizarre memorial.

A COLD BUD IN HAND—THE ONLY BEER TO BE HAD WAS EITHER Budweiser or Coors Light—William and Elizabeth left the house to meet Mr. Boudreaux. Upon entering the backyard, they waved to Chuck and Jane, playing with their children on an enormous homemade swing set. After kisses and handshakes, the four walked over to two men working beside a table next to a large, tall, steaming pot on a portable propane burner.

The larger of the two, in an oversized bowling shirt, had to be six and a half feet tall. The older man was wearing a type of light blue coverall, common in the oil service industry, with white shrimp boots on his feet. Both wore ball caps and watched the newcomers approach with interest.

"Daddy!" cried Elizabeth. "I want you to meet somebody special. Daddy, this is Will Darcy."

"How do you do, sir?" William stuck out his hand.

Mr. Boudreaux stripped off a plastic glove and took Will's hand. "I ain't no 'sir.' You can call me T.B., Will. Welcome to my house."

He was half a head shorter than William. His crew-cut hair was steely gray under his B&B Oilfield Services cap with sideburns down to his earlobes. His face was tanned and wrinkled from years in the unforgiving Louisiana sun, but he did have the same expressive eyes as Elizabeth: blue and open, teasing and searching. His grip was firm and confidant. He then kissed his daughter with affection.

"And this is Bubba Teresina, Mary's fiancé," said Elizabeth.

"Pleased to meet you, Will." The gentle giant's voice gave away the intelligence behind the bulk.

William noticed the NSU cap. "You played ball for Nicholls State, right?"

"Yes, sir," he answered, pleased.

"I remember watching you play. You were a good lineman."

"Thanks. I remember you throwing the ball for Destrehan."

William laughed. "That was a long time ago!"

Bubba grinned. "My daddy was a big Thibodaux High fan. We had to watch you take us apart too many times."

"I understand you're coaching for E.D. White. How's your daddy taking that?"

"He's the biggest Cardinal fan you ever met now!"

William could not help but notice T.B. was eying him with interest.

"Did ya play any in college, Will?" he asked.

"Just golf, but I like to stay in shape. As for football, I wasn't good enough to start, and I had better things to do than sweat like a pig just to sit on the bench."

Jane glanced back at the swing set. "I've got to get back to the kids, Daddy. Coming, Lizzy?"

"You go on," said T.B. to Elizabeth's glance at her boyfriend. "We'll entertain Will here." Elizabeth kissed William on the cheek and left with Jane.

"I used to watch you guys train in the summer," said Chuck. "That was brutal."

T.B. didn't look at Chuck. "You didn't play ball, did ya, Chuck?"

"No, I was in the marching band."

"Yeah, dat's right."

William was surprised at the thinly disguised sarcasm in the older man's voice.

Bubba piped in. "Shoot, if marching band practices at your school were anything like ours, I wonder who's got it tougher! Those kids work hard! Every time one of my players starts dogging it, I just point out the band, sweating up a storm on the practice field, and threaten to send them over there."

Chuck laughed. "We weren't the best around, but we did our share of sweating."

William, standing close to T.B., thought he heard him mumble, "Thought so."

William was puzzled by T.B.'s hostility towards Chuck, but he figured this was not the time to ask about it.

Chuck glanced back at the swing set. "I'd better go back and help out with the kids. Unless you need me, T.B.?"

"Nah, we've got dat covered." His head was down as he sliced some sausage.

Chuck smiled weakly and walked back to his children. Bubba glanced at William and raised his eyebrows in sympathy. *So, Bubba sees it too.* William liked the big man more for it.

"Yeah," T.B. said, "I played a little baseball in my day. Thought 'bout goin' semi-pro, but I had to pay the bills, ya know? You do any fishing, Will?"

William had noticed the boat and pickup in the large building behind the house and now saw the point of this interrogation. "Yes, we have a cabin cruiser down at Venice. We do some deep-sea fishing when we get the chance."

T.B. nodded. "Me, I like dat coastal fishing. Go after specks and redfish. But I chase da big ones every now and then."

"I noticed your rig," William said. He also noticed that T.B. was pushing his accent. "Nice setup."

T.B. looked up with a proud look on his face. "Yeah, it'll do da job. Real stable and fast, but it don't draw any water at all. I use it for duck huntin' too. Bubba's come out with me."

"T.B.'s quite the sportsman," observed Bubba.

William nodded, the pieces of the puzzle coming together.

"Come on, Bubba," said T.B. "Time to put da crawfish in." They moved towards a large perforated basket filled with live crawfish and covered with wet burlap.

William knew he was being tested again. "Hang on. Let me do

it, T.B." Without waiting for an answer, he took the other end of a sturdy wooden pole Bubba had inserted between the basket and its handle. The two of them lifted the basket and the forty pounds of crawfish inside before slowly lowering it into the large pot of boiling water and spices, careful not to allow the liquid to spill over the side.

The change in temperature brought the liquid below the boiling point. T.B. said nothing but dumped a large bowl filled with red potatoes, corn on the cob, and sausage into the pot. He tossed in a few trimmed heads of garlic for good measure and stood back, waiting for the liquid to start boiling again.

"How long do you boil it?" William asked T.B.

"Seven minutes, and then I cover it, shut off the fire, and let it soak for twenty."

"Ever throw in any artichokes? It comes out nice."

"Have to try dat next time." The three men stood, sipping their beers, and watching the pot return to a boil. T.B. then shut off the propane, slapped on the cover, set a timer, and finished his beer.

"Want me to grab you another one?" asked Bubba.

"Yeah, if you don't mind. You ready for another, Will?"

This is as bad as any fraternity. "Sure. Thanks, Bubba." The large man left to retrieve the brews, leaving William alone with his girlfriend's father.

"So," T.B. began, "what do ya do?"

"I'm in the shipping business—DGS." William decided he was going to play this game at his speed.

"Dat's Delta Global? I can't remember all dem letters."

Yeah, right. William had dealt with Boudreaux's type before—a self-made Cajun who appeared to be a good ol' boy, but was crafty and closed mouthed. They appeared simple just to see if anyone underestimated them.

Having grown up along the river, William knew the signs. The house wasn't over-the-top, but there were two new Cadillacs in the garage. That boat had twin 200-horsepower sea drives and couldn't be but a couple of years old. The truck that pulled it was a Ford 250 and probably had leather seats. T.B. might wear an oilfield coverall, but the watch on his wrist was a gold Rolex.

Yet, the swing set and crawfish cooker were homemade and, by looking at T.B.'s hands, William figured he was the man who cut, pieced, and welded them together.

William was being judged, and T.B. was the type of man who judged men by his own standards, by what they had in common. Darcy had known this type of Cajun his entire life: men who demanded people meet them at their level instead of accepting people for who *they* were. They found it hard to feel comfortable with people who were different or had different pastimes.

Thus, the strained relationship with Chuck Bingley. It didn't matter that Chuck was as good a man and as good a husband and father as could be found anywhere. It was hard for T.B. Boudreaux to warm up to someone with whom he had nothing in common other than his grandchildren.

"Yes," William answered. "I'm president."

"Young," T.B. observed. "You ever been aboard ship?"

"That was the plan after I got out of college. But, with my father's death, the company put me on an accelerated management training schedule."

"Well, you didn't miss nothin'. I was in the Navy during 'Nam. Dat was enough of dat."

"My dad was a few years in the Air Force, but my grandfather served in the Atlantic during WWII. Destroyer—convoy duty."

"How many people you got working for you, Will?"

"Worldwide—just under a thousand." William hid a smile at T.B. easing up on the accent.

The older man raised his eyebrows. "Pretty big outfit."

"There're bigger ones. How about you? You own B&B Oilfield Services, right?"

"You heard of us?"

"Sure, I've lived 'round here all my life." Plus, he had read up on them the week before.

"Where you say you're from?"

"Dansereau Plantation, St. Charles Parish."

He nodded. "Still raising sugarcane?"

"It's leased out, but yeah."

"Lots of cane 'round here." The two men looked at the fields.

"So, how are things?" William asked.

"Not bad. Hurricanes are awful for most, but good for the oil service companies. After all the storms last season, we got a lot of work fixin' up the rigs that got tore up."

"Are you finding workers?" William asked as Bubba returned, carrying three beers.

"Hell, no. They're rarer than hen's teeth. Thanks, Bubba."

William accepted his beer. "Know what you mean. We're okay internationally. The problem's in the States."

The two men bonded over workforce woes as the football coach looked on.

WHEN THE SOAK WAS DONE, WILLIAM AND BUBBA CARRIED THE pot over to a series of tables covered in newspapers and dumped the crawfish before the gathered throng. The smell was a delightful mixture of pepper and spices. The sea of steaming, bright red crustaceans was pockmarked with rust-brown potatoes and yellow ears of corn. Rolls of paper towels were strategically placed about the table, and Mrs. Boudreaux brought out small cups of seafood sauce dip.

Experts in the art of sucking heads and pinching tails, everyone dived right in. Some used the sauce, while others did without. Beer, colas, and iced tea quenched the spice. Piles of discarded shells grew like trophies to a conquering horde, as the diners, particularly the men, seemed to be in competition to determine the shellfish-eating champion. It was a close, hard-fought race, but in the end, the man called Bubba proved he had earned his nickname.

The remaining crawfish were reserved for Mrs. Boudreaux and the stews she would make in the future. Papers filled with peels were rolled up and discarded in the trash cans, and then the satisfied Cajuns lounged about, enjoying full bellies and fellowship. Elizabeth was relieved and pleased to see William had struck up a friendship with her father as the two engaged in an earnest, whispered conversation.

Dessert and coffee were accepted or declined, and as the sun began to disappear below the horizon, setting the South Louisiana sky ablaze in red and orange, Elizabeth and William made their farewells. T.B. and Frances walked their daughter and her boyfriend to his car, T.B. getting in one last conversation.

"Chuck's really your banker?" he asked. The doubt was clear in his tone.

"One of them," answered William. "Last year, we ran over fifty million in loans and working capital through him."

T.B. shook his head. "Damn." He peered unbelievingly at the young CEO.

"T.B.," William said, "do you think I would risk my family's money with someone who didn't know his business? Chuck's *real* good at what he does."

He nodded. "That makes sense. I'll think about that." He shook William's hand. "You come back anytime, eh, Will?"

"Be pleased to, sir," he said to Elizabeth's joy.

T.B.'s comment to her was whispered in her ear: "That's a keeper, *chère*."

Elizabeth's eyes danced. "I know, Daddy."

Frances's farewell was more vocal. "Now, you drive carefully, and keep my girl safe! Goodbye! Goodbye!" The BMW turned around in the lawn and drove down the highway.

"Where are you going?" asked Elizabeth since William was going in the opposite direction from town.

"I thought I'd take the River Road to the Gramercy Bridge going home."

Elizabeth settled back, dreamily happy. "I'm glad you and Daddy got along. He can be a bear, sometimes, but his heart is good."

William grunted. "I've dealt with guys like him for years. Find something in common with him, and he's your friend for life." He paused. "Poor Chuck."

"You caught that."

"It was kinda hard to miss."

"I don't understand why Daddy doesn't like Chuck."

"He doesn't respect him. He can't, because he can't understand Chuck. Chuck never played sports, doesn't fish or hunt, and would rather hang out with his wife and kids than the guys. Plus, he's a banker. Your dad really doesn't like bankers, does he?"

"They gave him and Uncle Bernard a hard time when they started B&B. He claimed they were trying to steal the business from them. He hasn't forgotten." She looked at him. "But you said something about Chuck before we left. What was that about?"

"I was trying to get T.B. to see that Chuck is a very good loan officer. I'm trying to get him to give Chuck a piece of his business. So, I put in a good word."

A beautiful smile broke out on her face as she grasped his forearm. "You are too good. Thank you so much."

"No thanks necessary, love. It was the truth. I hope he takes me up on it. Why don't you sit back and rest? It'll be another ninety minutes before we get home."

She snuggled back. "You'll be okay if I take a nap?"

Assured he had only two full beers, Elizabeth relaxed and closed her eyes. She had been concerned over William meeting her folks, and to her disappointment, they had both been in rare form. Yet, William disarmed her demanding father and captivated her excitable mother—all without losing the adorable smile on his face. Even Kit had been awestruck.

"Damn, Lizzy, he's so hot!" Kit admitted to her privately. "Are there any more like him?"

She didn't know how long she had been napping, but when the car slowed down and stopped on the side of the road, Elizabeth somehow knew that not enough time had passed for them to be back in New Orleans.

William said softy, "Lizzy, wake up. I want you to see this."

She cracked open her eyes. They were just off the River Road. Night had fallen, and the headlights illuminated the gate to a driveway. William pressed a button on the overhead console.

"What's going on?"

"It's a surprise."

The gates opened, and the car moved forward onto a curving blacktopped driveway flanked by immense live oak trees and azalea bushes.

"Are we going to a plantation house?"

"You'll see." There was a childish enthusiasm in his tone.

As the car made its way down the driveway, the headlights revealed a large, white, two-story house. Elizabeth started to get excited. "What *is* this place?"

There was laughter in Will's voice. "Can't you guess?"

The beams from the BMW revealed a mansion done in the Greek Revival style, with enormous pillars framing a full porch across the front of the house. Plantation green shutters framed every darkened window. Azaleas, camellias, and crepe myrtles bordered the exterior of the manor. The scale of the place indicated the interior ceilings had to be over twelve feet high.

Elizabeth had visited Oak Ally, San Francisco, Rosedown, and the other the great plantation homes, but she had never seen this one before. Therefore, it could only be—

"D-Dansereau?"

"Right the first time!" William lifted her hand for a kiss. "Welcome, my love, to Dansereau Plantation."

Chapter 29

William parked in front of a closed, detached garage, and they walked quietly through the dark towards Dansereau House.

"Are you sure this is okay?"

"Elizabeth, this is *my* house. Of course, it's okay."

William opened a covered keypad installed shoulder-high next to an exterior door, punched in a combination, and then unlocked the door with a key. "Turned off the alarm," he explained, before he stepped aside and gestured. "After you."

"Thanks. Have me go inside a dark, scary house first," she teased. "What a gentleman *you* are!" Elizabeth entered the darkened house and walked in a dozen steps.

"Stand still," William advised. A second later, the ceiling light came on.

It took a moment for Elizabeth's eyes to adjust, but when they did, she beheld a modern kitchen with gleaming stainless steel appliances, stained cypress cabinets, and a black granite countertop island. The floor was oak with throw rugs under the sink and a six-burner gas cooktop. On one wall was a Rodriguez Blue Dog painting. On another was a flat-screen TV.

"Oh—my—*God*! Will! It's so beautiful!"

"It was the last renovation Dad had done to the place. He loved to cook, and he always said if you spend so of your time in the kitchen, why not make it the most comfortable room in the house?"

Elizabeth walked about the room speechless. The state-of-the-art appliances were warmed by the natural color of the woodwork. "This is the most perfect kitchen I've ever seen."

"Want to see the rest of the place?"

"Of course!"

Elizabeth was given a tour of the manor. The front part of the house was very formal with dark mahogany Chippendale furniture and Oriental rugs. The pieces were large, but with twelve-foot ceilings, they did not overpower the rooms. The walls were painted in strong colors of blues, greens, and yellows with gleaming white woodwork. Beautiful artwork in golden frames adorned the walls.

The centerpiece of the living room was a large portrait of a beautiful, blonde matron. The blue of her gown matched the deep color of her eyes. A small smile played across the lips as if the subject was amused by the whole production of having her likeness captured on canvas. She was regal yet likeable at the same time.

"My mother," William said simply. "It was my dad's favorite painting."

Elizabeth could feel a lump in her throat as she gazed at the portrait, hearing the emotion in William's voice. In any other house, the huge, nearly life-sized painting would be too much. But here, it fit. It *belonged* on that wall.

The rear of the house was more relaxed. The carpets were no longer formal, and the sofas and chairs, while still of the highest quality, were built for comfort. The walls were painted in darker hues, and while the trim remained white, the cabinets and bookshelves were made of stained cypress, the same color as the kitchen. It was a little masculine for Elizabeth's taste. A few *objets d'art*, a couple of throw pillows, and some flowers in vases would soften the place, she considered.

She blinked back tears as William showed her the study. The room gave her a glance into who George Darcy was, and she knew she would have liked him very much, just as the portrait in the living room made her long to have met Mrs. Darcy. She felt that, like the kitchen, this room was perfect the way it was. It was supposed to be Mr. Darcy's study, yet to her eyes, it was William's—from the oxblood leather chairs to the vast collection of books. *His* taste—*his* character. Truly, she considered, the son was much like the father.

He opened the French doors and led her outside again. Live oaks outlined the backyard, a small swimming pool just off the brick patio. There was a covered outside kitchen and a bar with stools. The light from the house made tracks on the bricks.

William and Elizabeth sat on patio chairs, looking out into the yard, and holding hands. She could see the stars above the trees. A light, warm breeze carried the scent of unknown flowers.

"Well? What do you think?" he asked.

"Will, this is lovely. I had no idea what kind of place Dansereau was. This is a paradise!"

"So, you like it here."

"Of course, I like it."

He paused, and she could hear him take a breath. "Like it enough to live here?"

Elizabeth couldn't answer at first, the implications of his question rattling around her mind. "Will," she managed, "what do you mean?"

"I just want you to know what you're getting yourself into."

"William, are you asking me to— to *marry* you?"

The light from behind lit half his face. The smile on it was very slight. "Not yet—officially."

Confusion racked her brain. "What do you mean *officially*?"

William laced his fingers through hers. "Elizabeth, you have to know I love you more than anything else in this world. I want us to be together forever. I brought you here to show you what I hope—what I pray—will one day be your home. *Our* home. The place I hope we raise our children. I want you to know I fully intend to propose to you. Just—not right now."

Although a proposal was the last thing she expected, she unconsciously blurted out, "Why not?"

"Because I'm selfish. I'm sorry, honey, forgive me. But after all these years, I finally have you again, and I don't want to share you with anybody else. Elizabeth, for a private guy, I'm a very public man. As a non-engaged couple, we still have some privacy, but once I propose, we'll be at the mercy of others: friends, co-workers, investors, customers, venders. Oh, they'll mean well. They'll want to share in our happiness through parties, events, dinners, and a dozen other public ways. Our lives won't be our own until well after the wedding."

"You mean they'll take over the wedding?"

"I've got *a lot* of acquaintances and business contacts." He let go of her hand and sat up, his elbows on his knees. "Let me ask you: How many people do you see at your wedding?"

"I haven't really thought about that. I guess as many as were at Jane's."

"Maybe a hundred?"

She nodded.

"Sweetie, I can't get married without inviting at least eight hundred people."

Elizabeth was astonished. "You want eight hundred people there?"

He shook his head. "No, I don't, but I may have no choice. At my level, weddings are corporate affairs. If I don't invite my entire board, the senior staff, political contacts, business associates, and major customers, feelings will get hurt. And that doesn't include your family, my family, and all of our real friends. And what about your dad's business contacts? The EDNO people? If we can keep the guest list under a thousand, we'll be lucky."

"A thousand people? My family can't afford that!"

He brushed the remark aside. "Oh, DGS will pick up the tab, of course. It can write off most of it as a business expense."

"Of course," she repeated shakily.

"Not everybody will show, but we'll still get a boatload. And those who can't make it will feel obligated to host a party for us. We won't have a weekend alone for six months." He took her hand again. "I just don't want to go through that circus right now."

Elizabeth tried to pull away as the impact of his words sank in, but William tightened his grip.

"Please don't doubt my love for you, my devotion to you. We will get married, *if* you'll have me, I promise. We could just elope, run away to Las Vegas, but that wouldn't be fair to our families." He kissed her hand. "I just want to have you to myself for a little while before we start the insanity. But if you want to hear the words now, then I'm willing to say them."

It was too much. Elizabeth's head was spinning. She loved him, but she didn't want a spectacle. If marrying William Darcy was going to be like that, she certainly wasn't ready for it.

Looking at his adoring gaze made her feel better. He centered her. She lifted his hand and returned his kiss.

"I trust you, Will. I trust in our love. I can wait for the words. I want this special time to be just between us too."

"You know that those words are in my heart, for you own it."

"And you own mine." They reached over and shared a kiss, which grew deep and passionate. When they broke apart, he pulled her up out of her chair.

"Come on. We haven't finished the tour."

Elizabeth had no doubt about where the tour was headed. A non-sensical thought occurred to her. "But, I haven't anything with me."

He grinned. "Yes, you do. I packed a bag. It's in the trunk."

She stood open-mouthed at him.

He shrugged. "What can I say? I'm a Boy Scout. You know: be prepared."

She laughed. "You devil. Lead the way."

Sunday, May 29

THE MORNING SUN AWOKE ELIZABETH, AND SHE CAREFULLY stretched once she extracted herself from William's arms. They were in his old room, not the master bedroom. He had not moved into his parents' room. The bed was only full size, but they made it work.

She turned over to watch her lover sleep. Elizabeth enjoyed this moment of the mornings she shared with William. He looked so peaceful while he rested. The years slid off his face, and he was again the handsome graduate student she had fallen in love with so many years ago.

Last night William had fulfilled her need for love and affection—several times, in fact. Now, she wanted to fulfill a need for coffee.

She thought for a moment. William may have packed a bag of clothes, but it was still in the trunk of the car. It never occurred to her to wake him and request he retrieve it. Instead, she decided to surprise him with coffee in bed. Smiling, she carefully slipped out of bed, went into the attached bathroom, and wrapped his large robe about her nude body. She looked in again on William before quietly letting herself out of the bedroom.

Walking barefoot down the grand Dansereau staircase, wrapped in William's bathrobe on a Sunday morning, gave her a chill. She wondered whether his parents' spirits were watching. She was glad she didn't have to go through the living room. Passing Mrs. Darcy's portrait practically nude was not something she wanted to do.

Dansereau's formal rooms looked different, a little otherworldly, in the morning. The strong Louisiana sun streamed through sheer, gauzy panels covering the windows, throwing off a warm glow. Once she reached the kitchen, she felt more comfortable.

She eyed the coffeemaker by the sink. Taking a guess, she opened the cabinet below it, and sure enough, there was a container of ground coffee. She opened a drawer and found the filters. She grinned. As much as William loved to surprise her, he was so predictable about certain things. He had set up his coffee station in the condo exactly as it was at Dansereau.

Within minutes, the machine was doing its thing. Elizabeth then took the time to think over the events of the night before.

William as much as proposed last night. Part of me wishes he had, but I can understand why he didn't. Everyone would demand our attention. We wouldn't have a secret engagement. What's the use of being engaged and not telling anybody? It wouldn't feel like a real one.

A thousand people at a Darcy wedding! Do I want that many people? But, Will's right. Daddy would want all his business contacts there too.

Well, we'll worry about it when the time comes.

She realized with the casual acceptance of her future that one day she would be Elizabeth Darcy, and a chill ran through her.

As the coffee dripped, Elizabeth sat on one of the stools before the island, idly thinking how it would be to wake up in this house every day. Surely, it would feel more inviting once she got used to it. She expected she could make this place her own. A part of her longed to walk around, digging into every nook and cranny, discovering all of Dansereau's delights.

Lost in her daydreaming, she belatedly realized the scratching noise behind her was not the hissing of the coffeemaker but the sound of a key in the dead bolt of the kitchen door. She whirled around just in time to see a middle-aged African American woman in a dress and heels enter the kitchen.

Elizabeth screamed. "Who are you?"

"Ahhhh!" the woman shrieked.

"Will!" Elizabeth jumped off the stool and dashed around the island, putting it between her and the stranger.

"Who am *I*? Who are *you*? What are you doing in here?" the newcomer demanded.

Holding the top of the robe closed with one hand, Elizabeth answered, "I asked you first! *Will!*"

"I work for the people who own this house! How did you get in?"

"My boyfriend let me in! *Will! Will!*"

"Your boyfriend?" the black woman said in a lower volume. "Mr. Will? Mr. Will is here?"

Elizabeth realized what the woman said. "Wait! You said you work for him? You work for the Darcys?"

She sniffed. "I've worked for the Darcys for twenty years, and I keep an eye on this place. Now, what's your name?" she demanded.

Before Elizabeth could answer, there was the thundering sound of running feet. A moment later, the disheveled master of Dansereau Plantation burst into the kitchen, wearing only his silk boxer shorts and brandishing a golf club, ready to do battle to protect his woman.

"Mrs. Reynolds?" he sputtered.

The two women stared at the sight before them before dissolving into laughter. Mrs. Reynolds leaned against the countertop, while Elizabeth collapsed over the island.

William slowly lowered the club. "Umm...well, I guess I ought to—" He jerked a thumb over his shoulder. "I'll just get dressed now, all right?" He backed out of the room and fled upstairs, igniting additional giggles from the ladies.

The older woman approached the younger, hand extended. "I'm Betsy Reynolds, the housekeeper."

Elizabeth shook hands. "I'm Lizzy Boudreaux."

"I take it you're here with Mr. Will. I'm sorry I disturbed you, but when I saw a strange car in the driveway, I had to check it out. I live right next door."

"No, it's all right. I'm just so embarrassed!"

She smiled kindly. "Well, why don't you go up and change, and I'll fix you a nice breakfast. Eggs and toast all right?"

Elizabeth nodded and returned upstairs. William sheepishly dashed to the car to retrieve the overnight bag so she could dress. Twenty minutes later, the two of them sat at the kitchen island, enjoying scrambled eggs and toast with their coffee. Mrs. Reynolds declined to eat. She had already had breakfast, she claimed. While the housekeeper had nothing but smiles for Elizabeth, her employer earned a glare.

"I was just finishing dressing for Mass," she said, "when I looked out my window and saw this strange car close by the garage. At first I was going to call over, but I thought if it had turned out to be Mr. Will, I didn't want to bother you. So, I let myself in. Scared me to death—no offense, Miss Lizzy."

"None taken. I was as frightened as you."

"I bought the car a couple of weeks ago," William admitted. "You should have called. What if we had been thieves?"

"I had my cell phone," she said. "If I saw any evidence of a break-in, I would have called the sheriff. Why didn't you just park the car in the garage?"

"I only had the remote for the gate. The one for the garage is still sitting on the kitchen counter in New Orleans."

Mrs. Reynolds rolled her eyes. "Well, everything turned out all right." She turned to Elizabeth. "Mr. Will means well, but sometimes he doesn't think things all the way through, bless his heart. Hmm, it's time for me to go to Mass. It was nice meeting you, Miss Lizzy."

"I look forward to seeing you again, Mrs. Reynolds," she said as they shook hands again. The older woman turned to William, the question on her face.

"You *will* see her again—bank on it," he promised with a grin.

The housekeeper's face was spilt by a wide smile. "Well, that *is* good news! Y'all take care now! Just leave the plates. I'll see to them later." With that, she let herself out of the house.

As soon as the door closed, William picked up the plates and carried them to the dishwasher. At Elizabeth's amused smile, he admitted, "It's a game we play. She tells me not to do something, and I do it anyway. Will you hand me the pans from the stove?"

As she did, Elizabeth stated, "Will, I'd like to go to Mass this morning."

He glanced at his watch. "We've got about thirty minutes to make it to St. Charles Borromeo. We can make it if one of us finishes up here while the other packs the bag."

Elizabeth pushed him away. "I've got this covered. Go get our stuff."

Two hours later, William was motoring down the I-10 towards Kenner. Elizabeth sighed.

"Honey, what's wrong?"

"This morning."

"Oh."

"I'm sorry, I shouldn't have brought it up. It's just I'm mortified about how Mrs. Reynolds found us. I like her, don't get me wrong. But I can tell she wasn't comfortable with...us."

He groaned. "I know. She's known me since I was nine years old. She helped raise me after Mom died. She's like a second mother to Gina. She's very traditional. As far as she's concerned, we've jumped the gun."

"That's another thing—Gina. You said she's coming home this week?"

"Yeah."

"How do we handle that?"

William glanced at her. "You're right. Gina's coming home, and we're setting a bad example. So…" his voice trailed off.

"So, what?"

"So, do you want us to stop sleeping together for the time being?"

"Well, definitely no more of that at the condo. And no more overnighters, either."

William grunted. "I feel like a parent already."

"Will, you *are* a parent."

"Yeah." He sighed. "All right, we'll be good for the duration."

Elizabeth bowed her head and crossed her arms. "Don't think this is going to be easy for me, buster. I've gotten used to you. It's hard for me to sleep now without your big, noisy self parked right next to me."

"Good." He chuckled. "Might be best in the long run. Probably will make this courtship a lot shorter!"

She smirked at him. "So, what are you saying? You'll miss me? Am I that irresistible?"

"Yes, you are. Now, stop that!"

"Yes, sir." She smiled.

"So, where do you want to eat?"

"How about passing by Popeyes?"

"Sounds good."

"So, what do you like—breasts or thighs?"

"Lizzy! Cut it out!"

She laughed all the way into Kenner.

Part Three

If New Orleans is not fully in the mainstream of culture, neither is it fully in the mainstream of time. Lacking a well-defined present, it lives somewhere between its past and its future, as if uncertain whether to advance or to retreat. Perhaps it is its perpetual ambivalence that is its secret charm. Somewhere between Preservation Hall and the Superdome, between voodoo and cybernetics, New Orleans listens eagerly to the seductive promises of the future but keeps at least one foot firmly planted in its history, and in the end, conforms, like an artist, not to the world but to its own inner being—ever mindful of its personal style.

—Tom Robbins, *Jitterbug Perfume*, 1984

Chapter 30

The 2005 Hurricane Season started fast on June 8 with Tropical Storm Arlene off the coast of Honduras. The storm ran northwards right by the tip of Cuba and made landfall on the Florida Panhandle late on the 11th, right where Ivan had hit the year before. With maximum winds of around fifty miles per hour, Arlene wasn't worse than most thunderstorms, but it was worse than a pain to those who still had blue tarps on their roofs.

Tuesday, June 14: Gentilly

IT WAS NIGHTTIME, AND G-DADDY WAS OUT CRUISING, LOOKING to sell his rocks. Since fleeing to the Ninth Ward, Wickham found it impossible to reestablish his Uptown territory. Other gangs had closed the door. So he was left pushing crack in nickel and dime bags in Gentilly, and he was barely getting by.

Wickham parked his car along a shadowy street, keeping a lookout for customers and police. Every now and then, Wickham fingered his trusty Glock, secured under the car seat. He rubbed his nose. God, he could use a hit of powder right now! But blow was for after work. Wickham needed all his senses fully functioning.

He was just finishing a transaction with a gap-toothed, bling-covered, crack-head white kid when he noticed a van with its lights off slowing down right in front of him. Once again, his instincts took over, and he ducked, just as the side door of the van slid open and guns started blazing. Amazingly, the gangbangers caused only minimum damage to his dear black Camaro, several rounds going right through the open side windows while three other bullets slammed into the rear panel. The crack-head customer shrieked and ran off.

The van gunned the engine and pulled away. Wickham, sure that they'd circle back to inspect the carnage, threw the car into gear and burned rubber in the opposite direction. A glance in the rearview mirror showed the van turning around to pursue.

Wickham made for the I-610, hitting the on-ramp at eighty. The van must have been modified, because it was right behind him and gaining. The two recklessly dashed westward at almost a hundred miles an hour, Wickham swerving as he could see one guy leaning out of the van with a Uzi, trying to get a bead on him.

Out of the corner of his eye, Wickham saw he was gaining fast on a slow-moving tractor-trailer truck. Desperately, he swerved, missing the truck's rear bumper by inches. The van wasn't so lucky. The impact flipped the vehicle on its side, right on top of the gangbanger hanging out. The damaged eighteen-wheeler remained upright, its tires smoking as the driver locked his brakes.

Wickham didn't wait around to gloat and sped towards the I-10 interchange, barely making the ramp. He only slowed down to seventy-five once he got past the railroad underpass. Ten minutes later, he took the Elysian Fields Avenue exit and made his way to his hidey-hole.

G-Daddy's current crib was a raised two-bedroom bungalow on a quiet lane in the Upper Ninth Ward. He triggered the electric garage door and drove directly off the street. He made sure the door closed before getting out of the Camaro. Only then did Wickham allow himself to react to what almost happened. He was breathing hard, and his legs were unsteady. He thought he might get sick. Collecting his Glock, money, and product, Wickham shakily made his way up the stairs to the main floor. He dumped his stuff onto the coffee table and collapsed on the sofa for a few minutes.

Forcing himself to his feet, he walked to his tiny kitchen. Opening a fridge that contained a couple of soft drinks, some half-eaten pizza, and a case of beer, he grabbed a brew and returned to the sofa. Besides the three chairs at the table, it was the only place to sit in the house. His bed was in one bedroom, and the meth lab was in the other. Wickham drank his beer, but it didn't help; he was too agitated. He needed to take the edge off. He needed some blow.

He crossed over to a locked closet, and undoing the dead bolt, he opened the door and removed a black case. He sat down at the dining table and extracted from the case a mirror, a razor blade, and a small glass vial filled with white powder. He ran the razor expertly through the small amount of cocaine he poured onto the surface of the mirror lying on the table. Once he had the drug cut and shaped into a proper line, he pulled his key chain from his pocket. Attached to it was a small tube.

Wickham held his head back after snorting the blow, allowing the last grams of the drug to seep into his nasal passages. He quickly returned the paraphernalia to the case and closed the box. He then stumbled over to the sofa and threw himself down upon it, allowing the euphoria to kick in.

For the next twenty minutes, G-Daddy was the King of New Orleans.

Wednesday, June 15: Third District Headquarters

FITZWILLIAM HEARD ABOUT THE RUNNING GUN BATTLE ON THE I-610 as soon as he got to work. It had ended with a fatal collision that tied up the Interstate for hours: one person dead, one injured. The uninjured driver of the truck claimed he saw a third man, African American like the other two, climb out of the burning overturned van and escape down an exit ramp. An all-points bulletin was out for a black two-door that fled at a high rate of speed. Unfortunately, the make and model of the car was undetermined, as was the description of the driver.

Fitzwilliam suspected drug dealers fighting over turf. There had been a rash of incidents like this over the last six months, but this was the first fatality. The only way to get control over it was to increase patrols on the interstate. But that would put a great strain on the NOPD.

Fitzwilliam was in a tough spot. To beef up patrols on the 610, he would have to pull people off the streets. There were only so many officers to go around. The NOPD was undermanned, and Fitzwilliam knew the Third District could use dozens more people.

Of course, it would be easier to recruit if the city would drop the residency rule, he thought irritably. Forcing NOPD officers to live in the city might sound like a good idea, but in reality, it was a disaster. It was no secret that New Orleans Public Schools was the worst system in the state, and police officers liked to send their kids to good schools like everybody else. So all the best candidates lived in Jefferson and St. Tammany. Meanwhile, the washout rate at the police academy was high.

Fitzwilliam needed more people. The police chief was trying to get the residency rule changed, but the mayor took a hands-off position on the issue, and City Council refused to reconsider it.

Sighing, Lt. Fitzwilliam pulled out the duty roster and began making patrol changes to propose to the precinct captain.

Saturday, June 25: Metairie

FOR WOMEN, THE BONDING RITUAL IS SUBTLE. SHARED EXPERI-ences and shared thoughts are essential. And there is something buried deep in their DNA: by nature, women are gatherers. Modern American society has created a place that invites women to indulge in this need. It is called a shopping mall.

What better place for women to bond?

A couple of weeks after Gina Darcy's return from college for the summer, Elizabeth suggested an afternoon of power shopping at Metairie's Lakeside Shopping Center. Gina readily agreed, and the two amused themselves in the region's most popular mall. After hours of hitting big stores and small, Gina and Elizabeth gave their sore feet a break at the Lakeside Café du Monde.

When most people think of New Orleans coffee, especially the dark, sweetly bitter and rich coffee-and-chicory, they think of the famous Café du Monde, a coffee and doughnut stand at the foot of

Jackson Square in the heart of the French Quarter. It was almost a requirement for tourists who visit New Orleans to wait in line for the opportunity to drink a streaming cup of *cafe au lait* and wolf down a beignet, a square French doughnut covered in powdered sugar, in a large, covered sidewalk café, served by Vietnamese waiters. And it should be. There was nothing more New Orleans than sitting with a special person at a table late at night, having coffee and beignets while the lonely sound of a jazz saxophone drifts over the Square like fog over the river.

The popularity of the place convinced the owners to expand. The experiment of a Café du Monde in Lakeside was a rousing success.

Gina and Elizabeth relaxed as their coffee and beignets arrived. There was only one way to order coffee at Café du Monde: *cafe au lait*—half chicory coffee cut with an equal amount of steamed milk. The coffee without milk is undrinkable. The beignets were served with powdered sugar covering them, three to an order. The girls grinned as they bit into the fried pastries, as there is a technique to eat the thing without choking on the sugar or getting it all over their blouses. Lifelong residents of the area, the two women were experts on eating beignets and enjoyed their treats without incident.

"I'm glad we could do this," offered Gina as she set down her coffee. "I've been dying to get to know you since the ball. I don't want to embarrass you, but I have to tell you I've never seen Will so happy. I think you've been really good for him."

Elizabeth laughed nervously. "Well, I'm afraid you have succeeded in embarrassing me, but thank you. Your brother is a special person. I think you're giving me more credit than I deserve." She was still a little anxious over the outing.

"I don't think so. He's been so...*not Will* since Daddy died. You've brought him back to life. That means everything to me."

"He's told me how close you two are."

"All I've been hearing about for the last three months is 'Lizzy this' and 'Lizzy that.'" She waved her hands around for emphasis.

"You're kidding."

"Nope." She laughed. "Will's got it bad!" At Elizabeth's blush, she added, "I feel I can tell you this because I've seen you with him. You're so good together. I'm so happy Will found someone as nice as you are."

What is it with Darcys being so open all of a sudden? William certainly wasn't like this at college. Elizabeth felt unworthy of the girl's praise and decided to confess. "Gina, you know I knew Will back in college—"

"I know. Oh! You mean the newspaper thing."

Elizabeth's mouth dropped open. "You know about that?"

"I remember the article and the brouhaha. I have to admit I didn't like you too much then. But Daddy showed me the retraction in the paper. He told me that, when somebody does something wrong, they shouldn't cover it up, but own up, make it right, and take the consequences. Like you did."

Elizabeth was stunned. "Your father forgave me."

"That's the way Daddy was: tough as nails but always willing to give somebody a second chance."

Elizabeth wiped away a tear in her eye. "I wish I'd gotten to know him."

Gina's bright smile returned. "But you do! Will's so much like him in so many ways."

"And you forgave me without even knowing me."

"That's because I learned I can screw up too. It taught me a hard lesson." She lost her smile. "Lizzy, since I know about that article, what you did, you ought to know what *I* did. That's only fair."

Elizabeth had an inkling of what she was talking about. "Gina, you don't have to—"

"But I want to tell you! It was my senior year in high school, and Will was in London at the time, so I was living in the condo with Mrs. Annesley, a governess he hired for me. I thought I was like so grown up and didn't need to listen to anybody. So, I met this guy at a football game—an older guy—and he was telling me like how beautiful and sophisticated I was. Really feeding me a line, you know? I was *so* stupid!

"He started hanging around, showing up when I got out of

school, stuff like that. We fooled around a little but nothing serious. Don't know how long it would have stayed that way, though, 'cause he started getting a little forceful—you know what I mean?"

Elizabeth's stomach clenched.

Gina continued. "Lucky for me, Will came home from England early and surprised me at school. The guy—Greg was his name—beat it out of there. That night, my cousin Richard—he's in the police department—came over to the condo, and he and Will told me everything about Greg. Turns out he was like this real bad man. He had threatened Will back in college, and that's why he had a bodyguard."

She sighed. "Will was so worried and hurt. He had to get a bodyguard for me, just like him. I felt so bad about that and letting him down and all that stuff. He tried to tell me it wasn't my fault—that it was Greg's—but I still took it out on myself. That's when he showed me your letter."

Elizabeth's hands went involuntarily to her mouth. "Oh, my God. He showed you *that*?"

Gina grew alarmed. "I'm sorry. I didn't think you'd be upset."

"No, I'm not upset. I'm just surprised Will would do that." She was shocked William hadn't burned it.

"He wanted to prove to me what kind of guy Greg was—how he deceives and hurts people." She looked Elizabeth full in the face. "That was the day I forgave you. We were both Greg's victims.

"I think I even started liking you then. I admired how you took responsibility. It taught me a lot." Her tone became bitter. "Besides, who am I to cast aspersions on anybody when I was as bad?"

Elizabeth knew this was no time for secrets. "Gina, I have to tell you a few things, and I hope I don't upset you. Will already told me a little about what happened—about Wickham." Elizabeth spoke quickly. "The reason he told me is my little sister, Lydia, ran off with Wickham last year."

"Oh, my God!"

"She left him, thankfully, but she vanished after that. We don't know where she is now."

"Do you think something happened to her?"

"We hope not. The last time she called, she said she couldn't come home again. She felt she didn't deserve to. We're afraid she's left the state. Gina, I don't want you ever to feel in any way responsible for what Wickham tried to do. The man's a menace, and we're well rid of him."

Gina giggled. "Richard is looking for him, and I wouldn't want to be in Greg's shoes when he catches up with him!"

"From what Will's told me of him, I can believe that." She patted Gina's hand. "Both you and I have made mistakes, but we've both made amends. The past is the past. It does no good to dwell on it."

Gina grinned. "How about dwelling on shoes?"

Elizabeth laughed. "Now you're talking! Dillard's awaits. Let's go!"

Warehouse District

In the evening, the ladies had successfully "gathered" and returned to William's Warehouse District condo, finding him preparing a dinner of grilled streaks, asparagus, and baked potatoes. Within a half-hour, the three were enjoying the meal with a sassy little Shiraz he had found at Martin Wine Cellar. The ladies volunteered to clear the table as William set up the DVD selection of the night, *Bridget Jones's Diary*.

It was not the first time they had seen the comedy, and after Bridget's adventure on the fire pole, Gina excused herself to retire to her bedroom and chat online. In her absence, William and Elizabeth got comfortable, he lying on his back with her draped over him, her shoes on the floor.

It was a mistake. Both were committed to remain chaste in the condo while Gina was in residence, but Elizabeth's lush form was having the expected effect on William's body. That she took to nibbling his ear made things harder, one might say.

"Lizzy…stop that." William moaned.

"What if I don't want to?"

The fine dinner of protein and wine, on top of the emotional conversation with Gina, broke down her resolve. Elizabeth was feeling a need that only her sweet William could fill. Her tongue lightly licked his neck.

That did it. A moment later found her beneath her lover as he assaulted her lips, his arms holding her tight. She arched into him, feeling the strength of his desire, the blood rushing through her, when he stopped.

"Damn, Lizzy, you make it hard to keep a promise," he said, panting. "But, promise you I did, so we're gonna behave ourselves."

As the haze of passion began to fade, Elizabeth was torn between thankfulness for his iron-hard control and regret that her gnawing need was unfulfilled. Her better side won out, and she rewarded her man with a light kiss. "Thank goodness one of us can keep us in line. I don't want to shock Gina."

"That makes two of us. Don't worry. It won't be forever. C'mon, upsy-daisy." He pulled her into a sitting position beside him.

"I was comfortable," she grumbled.

"Maybe, but too damn tempting," he said before lightly blowing in her ear.

"Will! You know what that does to me!"

"So, now we're even." He laughed. "But I promise you one day we will enjoy this couch *thoroughly*."

"I'm going to hold you to that, mister."

His eyes were very dark. "And you know I keep my promises."

"Yes, Will, I know you do." Every time he did that—proving his character and his devotion—her love for him grew stronger. *How is that possible? And yet, I can't help it.*

They settled down to watch the rest of the movie. Before the final credits rolled, Elizabeth was sound asleep, leaning on William's arm. He didn't have the heart to wake her up so she could go home, so he carefully picked her up in his arms and gently carried her into his bedroom. He placed her onto his bed and pulled the comforter over her.

He took a moment to drink in the lovely vision before him: Elizabeth, sweetly sleeping, her thick hair spread over his pillows. Good Lord, he wanted her! But he made a promise.

He grabbed his favorite pillow and returned to the den to sack out on the couch.

William slept soundly, knowing he had provided for and protected those he loved for another day.

Sunday, June 26

GINA WOKE UP AT DAWN AS USUAL. SHE THREW ON A ROBE AND made her way to the kitchen for a cup of coffee to fortify her while dressing for Mass. She was halfway there before she realized her brother was sleeping on the couch—again. She smiled to herself, knowing Elizabeth had to be in William's bedroom, just like last week.

She padded to the kitchen to fire up the coffeemaker.

THE UNITED STATES IS A LUCKY ACCIDENT CAUSED BY a huge body of water to its south. The Gulf of Mexico, an enormous, relatively shallow sea, is the reason America earned the title of Bread Basket to the World. Weather systems moving in from the Pacific, which lose their rain climbing over the mountains of the west, are replenished with moisture from the Gulf. The resulting rains onto the vast, rolling land of the Great Plains and Midwest nourish the farms feeding the planet. Without the Gulf of Mexico, the central part of America would be a dry wasteland.

There is a cost to this bounty. The same characteristics that make the Gulf so valuable to America's Heartland make it ideal for the development of tropical weather systems. The air currents pull those systems into the coastal areas. That is why the Caribbean Islands, Mexico, and the United States suffer more tropical storms than anywhere else. Residents of Florida, Texas, Louisiana, Mississippi, Alabama, Georgia, and the Carolinas know it is never a matter of *whether* a hurricane comes but *when*. The average time between storms is about three years.

Fortunately, the vast majority of them are fairly benign. But sometimes, given the right conditions, monsters are born.

Chapter 31

The Fourth of July was disrupted by the approach of Hurricane Cindy. The weak Category 1 storm came ashore July 5 near Grande Isle, causing no damage.

Friday, July 8: Metairie

WILLIAM RELUCTANTLY GOT OUT OF HIS CAR IN THE PARKING LOT of Aphrodite's Dreams in Metairie. He was not a fan of strip joints. If he wanted to see a naked woman, Elizabeth would happily fulfill that desire anytime he wanted.

But he didn't want to be a wet blanket. Some men thought it was a required life passage for men to celebrate the impending marriage of a buddy by spending a great deal of money drinking too much and ogling strippers. Chris Breaux's brother, Mike, certainly believed it. So, on a hot July night, William joined Mike, Chuck Bingley, John Buford, and George Katz to mark the end of Chris Breaux's bachelorhood.

"So, why did we pick a place in the boonies instead of one in the Quarter?" George asked Chuck as they made themselves comfortable in a private room.

"A co-worker suggested it," Chuck replied. "He was here for his cousin and said it was great. Cheaper too. Mike liked that."

"Wonderful," Buford chimed in sarcastically. "A bargain strip joint? A good time will be had by all."

At that moment, the manager of the club, a heavy-set, middle-aged man with a goatee, came in with a scantily dressed waitress. "We all set, gentlemen?"

"Yeah," answered Mike. "We got two dancers, right?"

"Yep. Got a real nice act for you. They've been workin' together for the last couple of months. Very hot. We'll have the waitress take care of your drink order, an' the girls'll be here in about ten minutes. Y'all enjoy yourselves, gentlemen, and thank you for patronizing Aphrodite's Dreams."

The club was pushing champagne, but this was a beer crowd. After the drinks were served, a couple of lights came up in the low-lit room, and from the speakers, a voice said, *"And for your pleasure, Aphrodite's Dreams presents Sugar and Spice!"*

The door opened, and two young women came in, both masked. One was a petite and voluptuous blonde, wearing bright pink lacy lingerie with white thigh-high stockings, boa, and high heels. Her partner was a tall and slim brunette in black leather and garters. The blonde's mask was silver and the brunette's was red. They struck a pose, the brunette behind the blonde.

"Good evening," said the brunette in a low voice, "I'm Spice."

"And I'm Sugar!" cried her partner in a higher tone.

"And we're here to entertain you!" they said in unison.

An up-tempo, techno dance song came on, and the two began gyrating together. Their hands moved sensuously over each other as their hips moved in time to the music.

William did not find the writhing women enticing in any way. The whole thing seemed silly. Chris's disinterested expression indicated he agreed with him, and the others showed various levels of interest, from boredom to amusement. Only Mike was truly enjoying himself, shouting encouragement to the dancers along with rather lewd suggestions as to how to improve the performance.

The song ended as the two ripped off each other's masks. Sugar's long hair partially obscured her face while Spice's sharp features were in full view. Another song started, and Spice began dancing solo, unfastening her bra. She pranced before the assembled men flashing her small breasts. She twirled on her heels, holding her bra high above her head, and finished in Buford's lap.

"Are you the guest of honor?" she murmured, low and sexy, her breasts heaving.

"Umm, no, ma'am. That would be *that* gentleman." He pointed out Chris.

Spice got to her feet. "Too bad." She walked over to Chris and leaned over, giving him a very good view of her trim body and perky breasts. "Don't worry, baby," she crooned, "you're gonna have a *good* time tonight!"

With that, she stepped to Sugar. It was now time for her partner's solo striptease. It was quickly apparent that Sugar had less experience; her moves were forced and jerky. She made up for it with her curvier body and wide smile. Unlike Spice, William could believe she was enjoying herself. When her top came off, there was applause from more than one of the audience. She strutted her stuff, taking time to shake her goods for each and every one of them.

William was experiencing a sense of *déjà vu* as he watched her dance when the girl did something strange. She froze before Chuck for a moment and then quickly turned her back to him, wiggling her ass in his face. William could see her face was slightly panicked.

She ended her dance and quickly returned to Spice's side. She whispered something in the other girl's ear, and Spice nodded. Sugar rearranged her hair to fall over her face as Spice spoke to the group.

"I understand someone's getting married." The men gestured to Chris. Spice whispered something to Sugar, to which she nodded, and the brunette turned back with a grin on her face. "The rules are simple, boys. No touching or the party's over. No hands, arms, or lips, okay? Just relax and enjoy the show."

She moved to Chris. "Hmm, I don't know if you can handle me," she said as she grasped his chin. "I'll let Sugar do ya." She looked at Darcy and then Chuck. "Now, you," she moved to Bingley, "you wanna lap dance, baby?"

Before he could answer, the music started again. Spice turned away from Chuck and began moving her hips in a seductive way. She stuck her thong-covered ass in Chuck's face before slowly sitting down on his lap, facing away from him. She leaned back against his chest and undulated in his lap. Chuck's face was red, delighting almost everyone.

Meanwhile, Sugar performed a lap dace on Chris. Her moves were similar to Spice's, but instead of gazing into the face of the guest of honor, she turned towards William, away from the others. For his part, Chris stared straight at the ceiling, trying to ignore the topless girl in his lap and the crude outbursts from his brother.

William was detached and bored, so to pass the time, he analyzed the two girls' techniques. Spice was definitely the more seasoned of the two; her movements were relaxed and unforced. As for Sugar—

Just as he studied the buxom blonde, he noticed her eyes looking into his. Dancing blue eyes. Familiar eyes. Eyes he had seen before. He started. *She has Elizabeth's eyes.*

Sugar noticed the shock of recognition and broke eye contact. Her moves became even more jerky and nervous.

William began examining her face and body in earnest, trying to remember where he had seen her before. The girl looked like his Elizabeth—just shorter and duskier with a dye job. Her dark eyebrows proved she wasn't a true blonde. Elizabeth had gorgeous, chocolate brown tresses. No, this young woman's eyebrows were more a mousy brunette, about the color of—

William started again. He remembered a group of photos lovingly displayed on a wall by a grieving mother. He knew who she was.

Immediately, William put on his most placid and disinterested face. The last thing he wanted to do was to let Sugar know he was on to her. He idly watched the two performers complete their dances and joined in the applause.

"Hey, how 'bout some action here?" Mike pointed at his lap.

The girls performed on Mike and Buford after William declined Spice's offer. At the end of the set, Spice collected the tips as Sugar gathered their discarded clothing. Bras back on, the two exited the room.

The group wandered into the main room to share a last beer. The guys swapped stories of wild stag parties in the past while

William kept a lookout for either Spice or Sugar, a plan forming in his mind. Finally, the beers were done, the tab was settled, and Chris and Chuck announced they were taking off.

Mike complained that the group had turned into a bunch of pussy-whipped wusses for calling it a night. "Me and Will ain't gotta worry 'bout no wife," he declared as he dropped an arm around William's shoulder. "Let's close this sucker down, bro!"

William's plans were dependent upon being alone. He quickly thought about the best way to refuse when Chris came to his rescue. "Mike, you came with me, and your ride's leaving. Don't worry, there's a bar hosting ladies night just down the street from my apartment."

"Well, shit, why didn't you say so? I'm tired o' payin' ten bucks a beer anyhow. You comin', Will?"

He begged off and followed the crew to the parking lot. He purposely delayed, following the Breauxs to Chris's SUV to wish them a good night. By the time he got in his BMW, the others had pulled out of the parking lot. Still, he sat in his car and counted to one hundred before returning to the club.

THE DANCER KNOWN AS SUGAR WAS BACKSTAGE, FRESHENING UP her makeup, when the manager stuck his head into the dressing room.

"Hey, Sugar, got a customer for ya in room three. Solo. Asked for you particular."

"What's he look like?" she asked, "He don't got spiky blonde hair, does he?"

"Nah. Dark-haired white guy. Well-dressed. Got money."

She looked at Spice. This was her first solo act.

"Go on, honey, I'll be on stage," Spice reassured her.

Sugar adjusted her costume, gave Spice a kiss, and left to meet her customer. She walked through the club to room three, declining a couple of drink offers. She nodded at the bouncer, stationed near the private rooms for the dancers' protection, and walked in.

It was dark and sparse—only a couple of chairs lit by low, indirect light. The dance music from the main room filtered in through the walls. The customer was sitting back in one of the chairs, his legs crossed.

"Hey, honey," Sugar said as she crossed to the speaker control. "Want me to dance for ya?"

"No, thank you," said the man. "I just want to talk to you."

Sugar shrugged. She was told it wasn't an unusual request. Some of the customers were simply lonely. They wanted to feel desired and appreciated and only wanted a pretty, half-dressed girl to talk to them for a half-hour. It was one of the bigger surprises Sugar experienced when she entered the business. She thought guys would only be interested in her tits, not her time.

She walked over and took a seat next to him. "Did the bouncer explain the rules?"

"Yes, he did."

Sugar peered at him. "Weren't you part of the bachelor party earlier?"

"Yes. My name's Will."

She stuck out her hand. "I'm Sugar. Glad to meet ya, Will. What brings you to Aphrodite's Dreams?"

"Originally, to celebrate my friend's upcoming wedding. But now, I want to spend some time with you."

"Umm, you know we don't date the customers."

"Yes, I know. I've got a girlfriend."

"Okay. Ya want me to take off my top?"

"Whatever you're comfortable with."

Sugar pulled off her bra. "Ya want something to drink, Will?"

"I could use a beer. Get yourself something too."

Sugar got up and ordered a draft and a diet lemon-lime over the intercom. She had learned from Spice that it was a bad habit to drink while working. It was easier to stay in control if you were sober. She returned to Will and made small talk while waiting for the drinks.

He talked about his job—he was in shipping, he said—and his lack of experience in places like Aphrodite's Dreams. A soft knock on the door signaled the waitress. Sugar took the drinks, and by the time she got back, she saw the man had placed a hundred dollar bill on the table.

Sugar glanced at the money and then looked Will in the eye as she handed him his beer. "Uhh, honey, we can close out your tab later."

"This isn't for the tab. It's for you."

Sugar got nervous. "Will, I don't know what you're expecting, but—"

"Nothing but your time. It's a tip."

"Thanks. Just want there to be no misunderstanding."

Sometimes the new customers thought the dancers did a lot more than dance topless. Most of the girls didn't prostitute themselves because it was a surefire way of getting banned from the good clubs. It wasn't unheard of that a desperate girl might pull a trick every now and then or attach herself to a special friend if she was frantic for money for drink or drugs. Sugar had never been in that situation, and as long as Spice was there to help guide her, she never would be.

Will took a sip of his beer. "So tell me about yourself. How did you get into dancing?"

Sugar took a sip of her drink through the stirrer-straw. With a lime in it, the customers thought it was a gin and tonic. It certainly cost as much. "I was getting out of a bad relationship, y'know? I was looking for a place to crash, and I walked into this bar in the Quarter. Only, I didn't know what kinda bar it was, ya know what I mean?"

"No, not really."

She laughed. "It's not the kinda place you take the tourists unless they're from San Francisco, *comprende*?"

"Oh, I see."

"Well, anyway, I'm getting all these dirty looks from the regulars when I meet Spice. She really helped me out of a jam. She put me up and got me my audition. So, here I am."

"An exotic dancer."

"Yeah."

"How come you didn't just go home?"

"*This* is my home, Will."

"You have another home, Lydia."

Sugar almost dropped her drink. "What did you call me?"

He looked her full in the face. "Lydia Boudreaux, you have a home in Chackbay."

Lydia leaned back in her chair, fear gripping her. "W-Who are you?"

"My name's William Darcy." He placed his business card on the table. "I know who you're running from, Lydia."

"I'm not running from anybody."

"Yes, you are. You're running from a psychopath named Greg Wickham. My cousin's in the NOPD. I know all about Wickham."

"How do you know so much about me?"

"I'm dating your sister."

That bit of information calmed Lydia down. She thought about his claim. *Jane's married, and Mary's dating Bubba, last I heard.* "Lizzy? You're dating Lizzy?"

"That's right. I've been to your parents' house. Your family's very worried. There's a missing persons alert out for you."

Suddenly, Lydia felt exposed. She retrieved her bra and put it back on before she answered him. "I was right," she said to herself. "That was Chuck out there tonight."

"Yes, it was."

"Oh, God." She covered her face.

"I don't think he recognized you."

"Thank God for that. I almost did a lap dance on him—did ya know that? Shit, how would that have gone over?"

"Not too well."

She dropped her hands. "How'd you recognize me?"

"The blonde hair threw me off, but your eyes—they look like Elizabeth's."

"You were looking at my *eyes*? Crap, I gotta work on my routine."

He grinned. "Wouldn't have helped."

She stared at him. "Sounds like you've got it bad for my sister."

"I'm not here to talk about me but about you. Lydia, you should go home."

"No, I can't!" She grew agitated. "You don't understand—"

"Your mother has built a shrine to you in her living room. You can't let your family remain in that much pain any longer."

Lydia shook her head. "No...no, I can't. You better leave."

William raised his hands. "Okay, calm down. I'll leave, and I'll keep my mouth shut—under one condition."

"What's that?"

"You meet me in a public place where we can continue this discussion."

"Why would I wanna do that?"

"One—because Wickham is still out there. Whether you believe it or not, Lydia, you're in danger. Two"—he pulled out another hundred—"there'll be three more of these waiting for you." He placed the bill on the table next to the first. "Five hundred dollars—two now, three later."

"Just to meet with you. How do I know I can trust you?"

"You don't. Any more than I can trust you to show up. Fair?"

"Yeah, that's fair. Where and when?"

"Are you working tomorrow?" At her nod, he said, "Then we'll meet on Sunday. Do you know where the Morning Call is?"

"Behind Lakeside Mall? Yeah, I know it."

"Are you up by the afternoon? Can you meet me there at, say, three o'clock?"

The girl nodded again, and William got to his feet to leave. Just as he reached the door, he turned. "Don't be late, Miss Boudreaux. Because at five minutes after three on Sunday, I'm calling my cousin in the NOPD just before I call your family. Good night."

Without waiting for a response, William left the room, leaving Lydia staring at his business card and cash. She was desperate for Spice's advice.

Covington

IT WAS ALMOST MIDNIGHT WHEN CHUCK PULLED INTO HIS DRIVEway. He quietly let himself into the darkened house and tiptoed to his bedroom. He stopped when he saw a sliver of light from beneath the bedroom door.

Opening it, he saw Jane sitting up in bed, reading a book, the lamp lit on the bedside table. She glanced up at her husband's entrance.

"So, how'd it go?"

Chuck approached her side of the bed. "Fine. Chris' brother, Mike, got two dancers." He leaned down to give Jane a kiss. She lifted one hand to pull his head closer while placing the book away with the other.

"Mmm…were they pretty?"

"They were okay."

She grinned. "Did they get all nasty? Did they give lap dances like they do on that HBO show?"

"Yes, they did." Marriage was full of surprises for Chuck Bingley. For example, Jane's trust and confidence in him and their relationship was total. She was not jealous of other women.

"Did you get excited?" She groped him with her other hand. "Oh! I see you did!"

"It wasn't them, honey. I kept imaging it was you doing it."

"Really?" Her eyes sparkled. The sheet covering her upper chest slipped away, revealing her lack of a nightgown.

This was another pleasant surprise: his angel of a wife slept *au naturel*. Jane said she loved the feel of cool linen against her skin, and Chuck loved knowing he was sleeping with a naked woman every night. It made things easy when the urge was upon one of them, as it was tonight. He chuckled as he removed his shirt while Jane unfastened his trousers.

"My goodness, Charles! You drove all the way home in *this* state?" she asked seductively. "This appears to be a dangerously chronic condition! You need intense treatment right away." With a smile, the lovely nurse applied the treatment topically with her hands and mouth.

Within moments, Chuck joined his wife on the bed, giving as good as he got. Soon, the two were engaged in the eons-old dance of life, each striving to give pleasure to the other before collapsing in ecstasy.

Later, as the pair lay intertwined in the now-dark bedroom,

Jane asked her husband, "Did you really imagine it was me giving you a lap dance?"

"For a few minutes," Chuck admitted as he stroked her hair. "But it got too intense. I was afraid I was gonna make a mess in my pants."

"Well, I'm glad you didn't. That would have been so embarrassing!"

"You got that right, honey."

Jane giggled. "I was thinking about you being in that place all evening—how excited those girls were trying to make you. It was making me excited."

"Well, you told me you were going to wait up for me. You notice I didn't waste any time getting home."

"You didn't leave early on my account, did you?"

"Nope, the party was over when I left."

Jane smiled. "Would you like me to give you a lap dance?"

"Oh, honey, that would make my year!"

"I've never done anything like that. Maybe we would have to visit one of those places so I can learn."

Chuck turned to Jane. "You'd really want to go to a titty bar?"

"With you, it might be funny."

"Have to be someplace where they wouldn't know us."

"I should hope so! I would *die* if I ever met somebody I knew in one of those stripper places."

Chuck frowned. "We won't be going to Aphrodite's Dreams, I'll tell you that."

"Why? What happened?"

"I don't know. It was weird. You know, I only go to those places for bachelor parties. Anyhow, I got the strangest feeling this time about one of the dancers tonight. Like I had met her before outside of the club—with her clothes on, of course."

"Maybe she came into the bank for a loan?"

"Maybe. Aw, hell with it. I'll never see her again."

Jane was in a teasing mood. "Are you going to miss your little nudie-doll?"

"No way, Janie, not as long as you're here." He kissed her slowly and hungrily.

"Mmm…I thought you were tired."

"Give me fifteen minutes, and I'll show you who's tired."

Jane grinned in the shadows. "Now, that's the kind of talk I like to hear." She kissed him back.

Chuck got serious. "I love you, Janie. I don't know what I would do if I didn't have you and the kids."

Jane lovingly placed light kisses his face. "I love you too."

His hand stole between them to lightly caress her slightly swollen belly. "Think Junior here would mind if I loved his mother again tonight?"

Her laughter bubbled up in the darkness. "I'm sure *she* won't mind. I know her mother doesn't. After all, that's how she got there."

"I love it when you're pregnant. You're the most beautiful pregnant woman in the world."

"I love that you make me feel that way."

They continued to talk to each other in the deep of the night until words were no longer enough.

Chapter 32

Lydia is a *what?*"

William stood in the middle of Elizabeth's apartment, and she was not a happy camper. "It's true, Elizabeth. I saw her last night, and I spoke to her."

"Oh my God, oh my God!" Elizabeth almost fell onto her sofa. "She's all right! We were so worried—" She looked up at her boyfriend. "Where is this place? I've got to go see her!"

"Lizzy, wait. You can't—"

"What do you mean, I can't?"

"I promised her I wouldn't tell your family how to find her. I'm breaking that promise by telling you I saw her."

Elizabeth gasped. "How could you promise such a thing?"

"She demanded it. It was the only way I could get her to agree to meet with me."

"But we've been suffering for over a year—thinking terrible things!"

William tried to console her. "I know, I know. It's just for a few more days. Things are really dicey right now. She might rabbit, and then we'll never find her."

"At least I can call Mom!"

"No, don't!" He sat down next to her. "If Lydia gets wind the family knows what she does for a living, she'll take off." He took a breath. "It's really complicated. I'm going to meet with her—alone—to try to talk her into returning home. We've got to get her out of the city before Wickham decides he wants her back."

"How do you know Wickham will come after her?"

"I don't. But do you want to take that chance?" He took her hands. "Elizabeth, you've got to promise me you won't call anybody about your sister until you hear from me. That includes Jane." She started shaking her head. "Lizzy, you've got to! Promise me, love! Please!"

Elizabeth stared straight ahead. "All right, I promise."

"Thank you, sweetheart. It won't be long. A couple of days, at most."

Elizabeth's mouth was in a firm line. She had no control over events, and she hated it. "Where and when are you meeting her?"

"I can't tell you."

She whirled on him. "That's my sister! I have a right to know!"

"If we want to get her back, you're going to have to let me play this my way."

"Then, let me go with you."

"No, I've got to handle this alone." He interrupted her retort. "If she walks into our meeting place and sees you, she could bolt out of there, and we're right back to where we started. You've got trust me on this one, honey."

Elizabeth clenched her fists. "I *do* trust you, Will, but...but that's my sister! How can you ask me—" She caught herself before she could say any more. "Do you understand how frustrating this is? I'm sorry. I should be more grateful, but—oh, damn!" She dropped her face into her hands.

William sat next to her and gingerly placed a hand on her back. He felt some of Elizabeth's tension dissipate at his touch.

"What are your plans, Will?"

"Play it by ear. A combination of pleas and threats." He paused. "I do understand your frustration. I'm really sorry, but I just don't see any other way of doing this."

"It's not just that." She looked up. "I feel out of control, cut out. All of the decisions are being made for me without consulting me."

"I'm not trying to cut you out," he protested, "but we have to move fast. Don't you agree?"

"Yes, I do. I just want to be consulted!"

"I had to make a decision. I didn't have time. I'm sorry."

The two sat in silence for a moment.

"How is she?"

"She looks fine… I mean she's healthy. Not sick—she's in good shape…oh, hell."

Elizabeth put her hand to her forehead. "She danced for you, didn't she?"

"Yes."

Even though she knew the answer, she couldn't help but ask, "Naked?"

"She left her thong on."

She buried her face in her hands again. "Oh, God. Can this get any more mortifying?" The knowledge that William and her brother-in-law had seen her sister topless in just a G-string turned Elizabeth's stomach.

"At least she didn't give me or Chuck a lap dance."

"That doesn't make me feel better." Elizabeth looked up. "Do you think Chuck recognized her?"

"I don't think so. She's dyed her hair blonde." He paused. "Elizabeth, there's more."

She flinched at his cautious tone. "Tell me."

"There was another girl with Lydia. They were a team. From what she said later, I think they're more than just friends."

She took a moment to digest his words. "No, I can't believe it. Are you sure?"

"Pretty sure."

"How can she come home? Mom and Dad will *never* accept that!"

She didn't fight William when he took her into his arms, allowing herself to be held closely against his chest.

"Hang in there, honey, and it'll get better."

"Keep saying that, and I might believe it. It can't get much worse." She could do nothing about her rebellious sister at the moment, so she brought up the other troubling matter. "Will, can I ask you to promise me something? In the future, please talk to me *before* you make a decision for the two of us."

"I'll try, honey."

Elizabeth would not let him slide on this. "*Trying's* not good enough. I love you to death, but you have to let me in. I have to be your equal—your partner—or I don't see how we're going to make it."

"You're right, you're right. I will do better, I promise. We're a team."

Elizabeth said nothing, but she relaxed in his embrace, mollified by his vow.

He stroked her hair. "Look, just because I have to meet with Lydia by myself doesn't mean you can't help. You know her. I don't. Are you up to telling me about her? How you remember her? What she was like back in Chackbay?"

"I don't know what good that will do. My parents didn't raise us to be strippers." She instantly regretted her bitter words and closed her eyes. "Lydia was the youngest of all of us, the baby of the family, and we all probably spoiled her…"

THE CATEGORY 3 HURRICANE, DENNIS, WAS INDEED A MENACE AS it slammed into the Florida Panhandle near Pensacola on July 10, revisiting destruction to the area that was still reeling from Ivan the year before. The nation wondered whether 2005 was going to be another Summer of Storms for the Sunshine State.

Metairie

CAFÉ DU MONDE WAS SYNONYMOUS WITH COFFEE AND BEIGNETS and rightfully so. But many connoisseurs of chicory coffee preferred its 135-year-old Metairie competitor, the Morning Call Coffee Stand.

William took a back table and surveyed his surroundings. Things were slow this time of day, as he had expected. Only one other table was occupied. The decor was right out of the 1920's with a large carved wooden bar scarcely illuminated by bare light bulbs. The air conditioner was cranked up. The joint's atmosphere was cool and dark.

He ordered a *cafe au lait* from a waitress still tired from the morning rush and had just started sipping when the front door opened.

A tall, short-haired brunette walked in and peered over her sunglasses, obviously looking for someone. She wore a cropped T-shirt and hip-hugging jeans. She stopped when she saw him, stood still for a moment, and stepped back outside. Another moment passed before she returned with a short, buxom blonde in in pigtails, tank top, and shorts. Even with her Ray-Bans, William recognized Lydia.

"Well, we're here, and right on time," she announced. The two women stood by the table.

"And not alone," William said as he glanced at the brunette. "Sit down. I don't believe we've been introduced. I'm Will Darcy."

"Anne Betancourt, stage name Spice," she said in a hostile voice. Without makeup and wig, her sharp features were slightly mannish, unlike Lydia. The cool air in the restaurant revealed that Anne saw no need to wear a bra under her shirt.

William waved over the waitress. "Y'all order something first," he offered. Anne went for coffee, Lydia a Coke, and both ordered beignets.

Lydia glanced at Anne. "Mr. Darcy, I want you to pass over Lizzy's picture right now." Her girlish voice weakened her demand.

William extracted a photograph from his wallet. The two women examined the picture closely, turning it over to read the inscribed sentiment: *To William. All my love, Elizabeth.*

Lydia handed the photo back and smiled. "Sorry 'bout that, but I know my sister. There was no way you could've been her boyfriend and not have her picture."

William chuckled, impressed with Lydia's survival skills. Upon his return from his New York trip in April, the first thing Elizabeth did, after kissing him senseless, was hand him that photograph along with a key to her apartment. He glanced at it before returning it to his wallet, experiencing the same warmth he felt when his girl gave it to him.

Anne had not relaxed. "Just to let you know, I looked you up on the Internet. You own some big shipping company, huh?"

"That's right."

"So, what's this all about?" she demanded. "You promised us three hundred dollars."

"I promised it to Lydia." William removed an envelope from his sport coat pocket and put it on the table. "Don't bother opening that. There's only a hundred in it." At their looks of outrage, he continued, "You get the rest when our conversation is done."

Anne huffed. "Well, let's get it over with. What do you wanna talk about?"

William knew he had to maintain control of this interview, so he put to use strategies that proved successful in negotiations. He sat back, silent, and narrowed his eyes. He allowed the tension to build. He acted as though he was doing a favor for *them* rather than the other way around. If they had any inkling he needed their cooperation, he was doomed to failure.

When the time was ripe, he leaned forward. "I'm going to let you in on a little secret, Lydia. I'm going to marry your sister, though it's not official yet. We're just waiting for the right time. You're my future sister-in-law, and what I've got to say is family business." He turned to Anne. "*Private* family business. You're not welcome right now. Get lost."

Anne scowled at the insult. "If you think I'm leavin', you're cracked! You got something to say to Lyddie, you can say it in front of me, asshole."

William deliberately removed his cell phone from his coat and placed it on the table. He crossed his arms.

"Ms. Betancourt, I want to have a private conversation with Lydia. You will please move to that table next to the front window and give us some privacy. When I have something to say that concerns you, I will call you over." He glanced at the phone. "If you do not leave, not only will you forfeit two hundred dollars, I will immediately call Captain Richard Fitzwilliam of the NOPD and inform him that Lydia Boudreaux has been found. He, in turn, will have the JPSO pick her up for questioning as a material witness in a drug and murder investigation. They're looking very hard for her former friend, Greg Wickham. They think she knows where he is." He stared right into Anne's eyes. "How would your place of employment feel about that?"

Anne cursed, but Lydia restrained her with a touch of her arm. "It's okay, Annie, I'll be all right."

"But baby—" Anne complained.

"You're gonna be right there. If I need ya, I'll call."

Anne hesitated and then cursed again. She defiantly kissed Lydia hard on the lips, gave William an insolent look, and stormed over to the table indicated.

William relaxed. His bluff worked. He had chosen a table for Anne that was directly behind Lydia's back. He had her undivided attention.

"Sorry, she gets protective sometimes. So, are you really gonna marry Lizzy?"

He almost shook his head over Lydia's change of topics. "Umm… yes, I am, someday."

"Wow. I never thought Lizzy would ever get hitched. You must love her, huh?"

"Yes, I do. How about you, Lydia? What are your plans?"

"I don't know. I mean, I thought about gettin' married an' all that stuff, but… Hell, the only guys I meet are first class assholes." She shrugged. "Most of the guys at the club are cool, but as Annie says, ya don't date the customers. Breaks the illusion, she says. She's right. There was this one gal. She met a guy while she was dancing and fell in love and all that shit. Moved in with him. She kept dancing, though. He was cool with it at first, but after a while, it got too much for him. Got jealous, ya know? Last I heard, he put her in the hospital, an' he's in jail. Just sad."

They were interrupted by the waitress with their order. William pointed out where Anne was sitting and instructed her to get Anne anything she wanted. Meanwhile, Lydia was powdering her beignets. The Morning Call served theirs plain, allowing the patrons to decide how much sugar they wanted. It was no surprise to William that Lydia was heavy with the sugar.

"How long have you been with Anne?" he asked as she carefully bit into the hot doughnut.

"Since I got away from Greg. You were right about that. He's a real bad dude. Crazy, ya know? Annie took me in. She's the nicest person I've ever met and so smart! If it wasn't for her, I don't know what would've happened."

"Aren't you afraid of Wickham finding you?"

"Not really, living in St. Rose—Aw, shit! You tricked me!"

William gave her a small grin. "Maybe a little."

"It's okay. I can trust you. You got a good face. That's how you got Lizzy, huh? Those dimples?"

He flushed a little. "I don't know. You'll have to ask her." He reached for her hand. "I can take you to her apartment right now."

Lydia's face fell, and she pulled her hand away. "No. I can't do that. I can't see any of 'em. Not now."

"Why not? They love you."

Lydia barked a humorless laugh. "Yeah, I can just see *that* homecoming. Lydia, the stripper, with her *friend*, Annie. You wanna kill my momma? Shit, my daddy'll kill *me*!"

"Lydia, I've met your family. I don't think you're being fair to them. They love you."

Lydia sniffed back tears that had formed. "You think that'll make it easier? They might love me, but they'd never understand. They'd be ashamed of me. Better for them to think I'm dead."

William changed tactics. "Do you like what you're doing?"

"Yeah, I do," she claimed as she wiped her nose. "I'm good at it, and the money's great. Better than workin' at the Wal-Mart, that's for sure. The other girls are cool, and I get to work with Annie. You know, she's going to school, part-time, workin' on her degree. Like I said, she's real smart."

"You know you can't keep working anywhere near New Orleans. One day or another, Wickham will find you."

Lydia stared at the floor. "Maybe he's not lookin' for me."

"You willing to take that chance?" William glanced over her shoulder. "Willing to bet Anne's safety on that?"

Lydia looked up at him.

He lowered his voice. "You know what he'd do to her, don't you? To his competition?"

Her face flushed in fear and anger. "Damn you."

"Look, Lydia, if I'm scaring you, it's for a good reason. Wickham's a dangerous, vindictive bastard. I know it, and you know it. You've got to get out of town, whether or not you stay in this business." He let Lydia stew on that.

"I still won't go back to Chackbay. I won't give up Annie."

William was afraid of that. Time for Plan B. "If you could go somewhere else—anywhere—where would that be?"

"Vegas," she said immediately.

"Why Las Vegas?"

"I've always wanted to be a showgirl. You know, one of those beautiful women in those fancy costumes, walking and dancing on stage. I'd love to do that!" At his incredulous look, she added, "Oh, I saw that terrible movie about it. That was all make-believe—some director's wet dream of a story. Not the way it really is. Annie's done some research on it."

If she has, then you ought to know you're too short to be a Las Vegas showgirl. "How does Anne feel about that?"

"She thinks Vegas is cool, but we don't have enough money to make the move."

William needed to think for a minute. "You want another Coke?" She nodded, and he waved at the waitress. "I'll order you another one. Why don't you invite Anne to join us?"

By the time Lydia returned with the other dancer, William had placed her order and formulated a plan. He stood to meet the other woman. "Thank you for your patience, Ms. Betancourt. Please sit down."

Anne was still scowling. "So, we finished yet?"

"No. Let me be blunt with you," he said as he returned to his seat. "I share Lydia's family's concern for her well-being. I tried to talk her into returning home, but she insists she won't do it. Now, I could force the matter by calling my cousin on the NOPD, but

I'd rather not. It is not my intention to hurt Lydia or you. I only want her to be safe."

Anne grasped Lydia's hand. "Don't worry about that. I'll keep her safe. We're fine by ourselves."

"Doubtful," he said dryly.

"I've been takin' care of myself since I was fifteen, mister!"

"I'm sure you have, but this situation's a different matter entirely. I've had dealings with Wickham, so believe me when I say that, if he ever gets the idea in his head he wants Lydia back, he'll come for her, and nothing will stop him. You get in his way, he'll just kill you."

"You tryin' to scare me?" Anne spat as Lydia blanched.

"Yes." The waitress arrived just at that moment. "Ah, here's your Coke, Lydia. Care for anything, Ms. Betancourt? No?" William turned to the waitress. "Thanks, that'll be all for now."

Anne's face was red, a sure sign she was angry. William wondered whether she were angry because her judgment had been called into question or angry because he was right.

She capitulated. "So, we'll leave."

"I assume you plan to remain in your current career?"

"Yeah, the money's good. I'm goin' to college in my spare time, ya know."

"So Lydia tells me. Good for you. Lydia expressed a desire to go to Las Vegas. How do you feel about that?"

"It'd be great. There are good clubs there, and the money's better. Trouble is, we can't afford to get there, an' housing is out of our reach."

"But you're confident you could get work there if you were established?"

"Oh, yeah. Guys love girl-on-girl acts, an' it ain't bragging if I say we're one of the best—lots better than those fake porn stars."

"I'm sure." That was a subject William didn't want to explore. "All right, I have a proposition for you. I'll help you move to Las Vegas and arrange an apartment—first year paid up, utilities too. Lease will be in my name, and you'll sub-lease for free. That will give you the chance to get established in the Vegas clubs." He turned to Lydia, "You said you want to be a showgirl. I'm sure there are classes to teach you the right way to do that. I'll cover the tuition. And, I'll see you get an audition or two. How's that?"

Lydia was almost speechless in her surprise, but Anne was wary. "Yeah, this sounds nice, but what do you get out of it?"

"Lydia safe from Wickham." William sat back, knowing his offer was a winning one.

"Yeah, sure. And I guess you mind having a local stripper in the family, huh?"

"Believe what you like."

"What's the catch?"

William grinned. "Lydia calls her family before she leaves."

The two started at that.

"I'd prefer that Lydia actually visited her family, but I'm willing to settle for a long phone call to her parents and each of her sisters—that, and not telling anybody about our arrangement."

"But, what do I tell them?" cried Lydia. "I can't tell my family about what I do or about—" Her eyes flew to Anne for an instant.

"Anything you want," William replied. "Why not the truth? You've been hiding from Wickham, and now you're going to Las Vegas to be a dancer. Ms. Betancourt here is your roommate. Who would question that?" William winced at his small lie, knowing damn well Elizabeth would.

"What about my college credits?" asked Anne.

"Where are you going?"

"University of Phoenix."

"Oh, please. They have campuses everywhere. Any other objections?"

The girls looked at each other in wonder. "That's it?" asked Anne, her voice for the first time hopeful. "We get back in touch with Lydia's family, and you'll bankroll our move to Vegas?"

"Basically, yes. There will be a few other requirements. Both of you will take a drug test before you leave at a lab of my choice. There'll be a background check on you, Ms. Betancourt. I have the right to evict you if there is any illegal activity in the apartment.

And I would expect you to remain in contact with the Boudreaux family for the year of our agreement. There might be a few more specifications spelled out in the agreement I'll have my lawyer draw up, but nothing onerous. Do we have a deal?"

Anne and Lydia shared a quick, whispered conversation. "You've got a deal, Mr. Will!" cried Lydia. Both women shook hands with Darcy.

"All right. I'll need your contact information, including your Social Security numbers." He looked at Anne. "It's for the background check."

Anne shook her head. "No problem, Mr. Darcy. I'm as clean as they come. No drugs, no whoring. You knock yourself out." The girls wrote down the requested information on the back of one of William's business cards. After they handed it over, William gave them a second envelope with two hundred dollars in it.

"Your family's current phone numbers are in that envelope along with my contact information and the rest of the cash. We'll stay in touch as to the timing and logistics. I think we can get this done in less than a month, don't you?"

They nodded, and Lydia gazed at William wistfully. "You're doing this for Lizzy, aren't you?" she declared with surprising insight. "You must really love her."

William felt funny about admitting his deepest feelings to a couple of exotic dancers. "Yes, I do, Lydia."

She stuck out her hand. "Well, welcome to the family, Mr. Will!"

He took it and took the hand extended by Anne.

"Please call me Anne, Mr. Darcy."

"All right, *Annie*," he said with a small smile.

Chapter 33

E lizabeth rushed to answer the doorbell. She was expecting William and hoped he had more news of Lydia. Perhaps he had managed to bring her with him!

She was dying to see him. For the first time since Jazz Fest, they hadn't talked to each other on the phone at night before falling asleep. She had been too emotionally torn up. She now regretted it; she missed him terribly.

She opened the door to a subdued William. He was alone, his hands in his pockets. Fighting a stab of disappointment, Elizabeth greeted him with a kiss on the cheek.

They made their way into the den. "Did you see Lydia yet?"

"I just left her."

"And?"

"And, you should be receiving a phone call very soon." He wearily plopped on the couch.

A weight fell off her shoulders. "Good! Is she coning home?"

He shook his head. "I'm sorry, but no. At least she'll be safe."

Elizabeth's good feelings turned to ashes. "What do you mean? I thought you were going to get her to come home."

"Elizabeth, I'm sorry, but she's won't. Let me explain…"

In the next fifteen minutes, he talked of his meeting with Lydia and her girlfriend, Anne Betancourt—how he had laid out the reasons for her to return to Chackbay and Lydia's absolute refusal to change her mind. He reported her sister's reasons, including her relationship with Anne. He explained his Plan B: his bankrolling of Lydia and Anne's relocation to Las Vegas.

His brow was furrowed as he concluded. "Elizabeth, I know it's not perfect, and it's not what you wanted. But honey, at least she's safe from Wickham. That's got to count for something, right?"

Elizabeth's face was white with astonishment. "Are you saying that, instead of getting her to go back to Chackbay, you're sending her to *Las Vegas*?"

"Honey, I know it's a shock—"

"'Shock' is an understatement! How is Las Vegas better than what we have now?" Her voice was rising as her shock turned to anger. Before she could accuse him of getting rid of an embarrassing problem, the phone rang.

The two glanced at each other as Elizabeth reached for the receiver. "Hello?"

"Lizzy? Lizzy, it's Lydia."

Elizabeth stared at William as she managed, "Lydia! Oh, Lyddie, I'm so glad to hear from you! Where are you?"

"Callin' from home—uh, my home. I live in St. Rose. Is Mr. Will there?"

She looked at William again, who was following her side of the conversation solemnly. "You mean Will Darcy? Yes, he is."

There was a laugh on the other end. "Thought so. Tell him thanks for me?"

She put her hand over the receiver. "Lydia says thanks."

He gravely nodded. "She's welcome."

Elizabeth returned to the phone. "He says you're welcome. Oh my God, Lydia! We've all been worried sick. Where have you been?"

"Oh, wow. I guess I better tell you everything, seeing as you're dating Mr. Will. He's nice. Don't tell Mom or Dad about me, though, please?"

Elizabeth promised as she retreated to her bedroom for the remainder of the call, leaving William on the couch.

A HALF-HOUR PASSED BEFORE ELIZABETH EMERGED FROM HER bedroom, the cordless phone still in her hand. William had lain down on the couch, and he quickly sat up. He was concerned when she said nothing. She avoided his eyes while she returned the receiver to the cradle.

"Elizabeth, how did it go?" His voice was filled with concern. "What did she say?"

Wordlessly, she sat on the far end of the couch. Finally, she managed, "Lydia's…fine. She's going to call Jane next, then Mom and Dad. She's…" It was obvious she was wrestling with her emotions. He waited patiently.

"She's the same." Elizabeth seemed to be talking to herself. "She hasn't changed a bit. She's still the thoughtless, self-centered, immature girl she was back home. It took everything I had not to scream at her for her stupidity, for what she put Mom and Dad and all of us through in the last year."

She turned to William. "Did she tell you what she wants to do in Vegas?"

He nodded.

"A showgirl. She wants to be a showgirl! Short, curvy little Lydia wants to be a six-foot tall Vegas showgirl!" She waved her hands in the air in frustration. "I have no words."

William tried desperately to think of something comforting to say, but nothing came to mind.

Elizabeth dropped her face in her hands. "What must you think of me?"

"Think of *you*? What are you talking about? I love you, sweetheart."

"I don't know why. I really don't," Her hands muffled her words. "My stupid, *stupid* little sister runs off with a drug dealer, and then leaves him to shack up with a stripping lesbian. She doesn't call her family and lets them live in this terrible limbo because *she's* embarrassed. The police have been looking for her for a year with no results, and it's up to my boyfriend, a guy who runs a shipping company, to find her and get her to call home!" She turned to him. "She told me what you're doing for her. How much is this going to cost?"

"Honey, that doesn't—"

His dismissal fueled her ire. "Yes. It. Does. Tell me, William, how much you're shelling out."

He had already done the numbers in his head. "The apartment—nothing fancy—will run at least $1,000 a month before utilities. With moving expenses, deposits, and dancing lessons, something like thirty to thirty-five thousand, tops."

At Elizabeth's horrified expression he added, "Sweetheart, I spend more than that on a car. I can handle it."

"You're going to spend almost half my yearly salary so my slutty little sister and her lover can move to Sin City, and you say it's no big deal."

"It's worth it if it keeps her out of Wickham's hands."

"I know, I know." She covered her face again. "I'm nothing but trouble for you. After *everything* we've been through… After you've taken me back after all those awful things I said and wrote…You've been so sweet and loving… Now this comes up, and you have to go out and assume all the cost and mortification of cleaning up my family's mess!" She broke down. "You should just leave. I'm no good for you."

Elizabeth's despair frightened William. He reached out and took her by the arms. "No, goddammit! I'm never leaving!" He made her look at him. "Don't you understand by now? I'm nothing without you. I'd spend every last nickel I have and send every crazy woman in town on a world cruise if it meant we could be together." His heart broke at the sight of her tears. "I love you, Elizabeth, and you're never getting rid of me."

The lovers found themselves in a passionate embrace, Elizabeth crying in his shoulder while William gasped for air, so great was his anger and fear. He began to kiss her tears away, the salt on his lips reaffirming the love he had for this woman. With a shudder, Elizabeth returned his soothing kisses with her desperate ones. Each kiss was a healing balm on their wounded souls, murmured apologies met with whispered endearments.

Finally, they broke apart. Elizabeth looked into his eyes. "Will,

God help me, but I do love you so."

He grasped her face in his two hands. "You're my life, Elizabeth. Never forget that."

"I won't, I won't. I never will again."

JULY REMAINED BUSY AS HURRICANE EMILY, THE MOST POWERFUL storm yet of the young season, tore through the Caribbean Sea. Contrary to the normal occurrence that hurricanes leave a cold wake behind, Hurricane Dennis had instead made the waters warmer, fueling the storm that followed. At one time, Emily reached Category 5. It was a Cat 4 by the time it hit Cozumel on July 18. The storm crossed over the Yucatan Peninsula into the Gulf and made final landfall in Mexico as a Cat 3 on July 20 just south of Brownsville, Texas.

It was exceedingly rare to have two major storms so early in the season and so close together. People living on the Gulf Coast wondered whether these two monsters had dissipated all the stored energy in the waters or this was a harbinger of things to come.

Saturday, July 23: Metairie

IT WAS MID-MORNING, PARTLY CLOUDY, AND STEAMING WHEN TWO vehicles pulled into the mostly empty Lafreniere Park parking lot. Elizabeth and William got out of the BMW while the Bingleys' van came to a rest beside them. Nearby was a beat-up Saturn sedan in need of a paint job, the back seat packed to the roof with belongings. There were several picnic tables with benches next to the lot. Seated at one were two young women, both in T-shirt and jeans.

A silent and anxious Elizabeth grasped William's hand tightly as she waited for her sister and brother-in-law only steps from the car. Her expressive eyes where hidden behind sunglasses, but her apprehension and anger were evident by the strength of her grip and the thin line of her lips.

"Is that Lydia?" Jane asked as she and Chuck joined them.

Lydia hesitantly moved towards them. A moment later, Jane broke towards her, Elizabeth just behind, and the three sisters tearfully embraced for the first time in over a year. After hugs and kisses, Lydia introduced her companion, an exercise she repeated when the men joined them. The six stood around for a moment before, by unspoken agreement, the three Boudreaux sisters walked away together to talk among themselves several tables away.

Anne Betancourt perched herself on top of the nearest picnic table and gazed at the men. Everyone wore sunglasses and it was hard to read each other's expressions.

She spoke first. "Mr. Darcy, it's nice to see you again."

"Annie," he returned. "Thanks for agreeing to this. It means a lot to Elizabeth and Jane."

She looked out at the three women. "I'm sure. My family? Shit, I haven't seen them in ten years. No loss." She changed the subject. "We go to visit Chackbay after this. It's all arranged. We're going to spend the night after we have dinner with Lyddie's parents and her sisters."

"I'm glad you changed your mind. Have you worked out your story for Lydia's family?"

She looked down. "We're staying with what we told 'em already. We're roommates, an' we're getting outta town so Lydia can be a showgirl. We start out for Vegas in the morning."

"How far do you think you'll get the first day?"

"We're going to take it easy. Lyddie doesn't drive so good. We'll take I-49 and stop at Shreveport. We should make Amarillo on the second day. Then, a little place called Hollbrook in Arizona before pushing onto Vegas. Four days."

"You have your reservations made?"

"Nah, we'll just stop at the first cheap place with a vacancy. Truck stops, probably. Worse comes to worst, we'll just sack out in the car at a rest stop."

William extracted a credit card from his jeans pocket. "Here. It works like a gift card. There's a limited amount on it. It should cover your rooms, food, and fuel for the trip."

Anne initially refused to take the debit card, claiming he had already laid out too much for the girls' move. As they both knew she would, Anne eventually accepted the additional help and tucked the card into her wallet. "You're too good to us, Mr. Darcy."

William ignored her comment. "When does the moving van arrive in Vegas?"

"Next week. Good thing I've got a sleeping bag, huh?" She turned to Chuck. "I don't know if you remember me, Mr. Bingley."

Chuck flushed. "Umm, I do. You do look a little different without the wig, but…yeah, I remember." He swallowed, embarrassed. "You're going to dance in Las Vegas?"

"Sure am. Already have a line on a couple of clubs. Look, about the other night, I hope I didn't—"

"No, no. You're very good at what you do. I'm sure you'll do fine in Vegas."

William almost laughed at his friend's mortified expression.

Having nothing else to say, the three sat in the sun, the day getting warmer, watching the women they loved talk and cry and hug each other. After another ten minutes, the discussion broke up, and the Boudreaux sisters returned to the parking lot.

"Well," Lydia exclaimed as she wiped her eyes with the heel of her hands, smearing her mascara, "I guess we oughta get going. Bye, Mr. Will!" She cried as she hugged him. In his ear, she whispered, "Take care of Lizzy, huh?"

"I will."

Lydia and Anne took their leave of the others, congratulating Jane once again on her pregnancy, and climbed into the Saturn, Anne behind the wheel. Windows rolled down, the two women waved as they backed out of the parking spot and drove off. Elizabeth and Jane hugged their men as they waved back.

William looked at the others. "Want to grab an early lunch?"

Jane and Chuck exchanged glances. "No," she said. "We've had one of our neighbors watching the kids, and we don't want to take advantage of them."

"Besides," added Chuck, "payback is hell!"

Jane embraced them. "We'll get together soon. Maybe dinner next week?" The other couple agreed, and the sisters nodded to each other. Elizabeth and William stood arm in arm as the Bingleys left.

"What was that look you and Jane shared?"

"She's going to call Mary and clue her in." Elizabeth took William by the hand and led him to a table in the shade. "That cockamamie story of Lyddie's won't fool her for a second. Jane will tell her what's really going on, so Mary won't challenge Lydia in front of my parents." She noticed William's worried expression. "She won't tell her about your financing of the relocation."

"It's not that I'm embarrassed," William protested. "It just saves a lot of awkward questions."

"I know." Elizabeth sat down at the table.

"What about the rest of your family?"

"Momma will buy it. She'll be so happy to see Lyddie again that she'll believe anything. And Kit is just like Momma. They'll never know unless we tell them. And as for Anne... Well, *that* kind of relationship would never occur to them, so unless Anne and Lydia forget themselves—"

William sat down and put his arm around her. "Honey? Are you all right?"

"I'm mortified, Will. Completely and utterly mortified. The whole time Jane and I were talking to her, Lydia was going on and on about how she's going to be this big star in Las Vegas. She invited us to come stay at her mansion once she and Anne hit it big. She's completely delusional. You say Anne has a head on her shoulders?"

"Seems to. She's attending college in her spare time, and she's been putting away money." He didn't have to say both girls had come back clean from both the drug and background checks. If they hadn't, they wouldn't be on their way to Vegas on his dime.

"Does she really care for Lydia, or is she just using her?"

William reminded Elizabeth of Anne's behavior at the Morning Call before his offer. "I think she's genuine, honey. Only time will tell for sure."

"Lydia will never be a showgirl."

"Anne knows."

"She'll protect her?"

"Oh, yeah. Remember, she tried to protect her from me until I proved myself." He paused. "What about your father? He's pretty bright. Won't he catch on?"

"Not necessarily." She looked down again. "Will, in the last couple of weeks, I've done some thinking, and I've come to realize something. Daddy's not the man I thought he was. Lydia will come home and Momma will be so happy, and Daddy will be happy for *them*. He'll buy Lydia's story because it'll be convenient. Daddy only sees what he wants to see.

"Don't get me wrong, Daddy loves us. It's just that he loves his peace of mind more. He works hard, so he doesn't want any drama at home. If he allowed himself to question Lydia's story, he'd be forced to challenge her *and* her relationship with Anne. It would break his heart and Momma's too. Daddy would either drive Lyddie away—or worse, convince her to stay in Chackbay without Anne. There's no way he could allow that kind of goings-on under his roof.

"So, he'll just rest easy in a state of denial, and he'll hope Lydia's a success in her dancing career." She shuddered. "I just pray to God nobody he knows ever catches Lydia's act in Vegas and reports what she *really* does for a living.

"You were right, Will, about getting her out of town. The chances of her career and lifestyle getting back to Momma and Daddy are a lot greater if she stayed around here."

William felt he didn't deserve her praise. "I was more worried about Wickham. I still could've done better. I should have forced Lydia to allow you to come to the meeting at the Morning—"

Elizabeth cut him off with a touch of his arm. "I'm not sure that would have been good. I've been doing a lot of thinking, remember? I don't think I was ready to talk sense into Lydia when I didn't have much myself."

"What do you mean? You're one of the most sensible people I know."

"Not all the time. I'm my father's daughter." She looked away. "I always thought Daddy was the smartest, most clever man in the world. I adored him. But what I thought was cleverness, I see now was a kind of smallness—meanness. Daddy's not clever; he's sly and sarcastic. Look how he treats Chuck. Just because he can't value him and his choices, Daddy has to put him down.

"Daddy trusts too much in his own judgment, and it's cost him. He's hard working and loyal and loves his family, but he's stubborn. Do you know he almost lost the business during the 90s? If it weren't for Uncle Bernard, he would have. But Daddy doesn't learn from his mistakes. To this day, he blames the bankers who demanded greater cost controls and better profitably from the company instead of his own errors and bad business decisions.

"And I'm just like Daddy. Shoot first and ask questions later. I can't have my own judgment called into question. I lash out. That's why Tulane happened. I'm so in love with my own mind I fail to see that sometimes there might be somebody who knows more than me."

William wanted to say something, to tell her she was wrong, but instinct told him to just hug her first. It was the right decision. It took a couple of minutes for Elizabeth to calm down.

"I don't know why you love me, darling, but thank you," she said in a small voice.

He kissed her hair. "I love you because you are my life. And I need you. I need to learn from you. To learn how to share. You were right before when you reamed me out."

"When?"

"Back in April on the Moonwalk, remember? You were right; I do take too much into my hands. Lydia's your sister. I had no business trying to fix her problems, without your input. I should have talked with you before I made my plans."

"But everything worked out. You were *right*. I couldn't have come up with anything better."

"Maybe. Maybe I just got lucky. But, honey, you're right too. If we're going to have a life together, I've got to learn to open up with you. While I may have been right this time, it was the wrong way of coming up with a good solution."

He took a breath. "I've been a hypocrite. If one of my managers had gone all Rambo over some crisis at DGS and fixed it himself instead of going through channels, he would have been fired. Period. No matter how good the solution was. Clean out your desk, and we'll mail you your two weeks' pay. I want teamwork out of my employees, not heroes. If I expect that from my people, how can I expect less from myself?"

Elizabeth shook her head. "You're too hard on yourself."

William shrugged. "Maybe—maybe not."

"So, I guess we're a mess together," she said.

He chuckled. "We'd be a bigger mess apart, love."

Her only answer was to squeeze him. They sat in silence for some time.

Finally, William took a breath. "That brings up something else. I decided *I* would choose when we get married. That was wrong of me too."

"But all those reasons you gave. They were true, weren't they?"

"Yes, they were. But since when have I allowed anyone to control my life unless I wanted them to? If people ask more than you want to give, the proper thing is to say no. Kindly, politely, but firmly. I guess I didn't want to be bothered."

"So…what are you thinking now?"

"I'm thinking I made a bad decision, and I want to rectify it. The last few weeks have shown me that life can change in an instant. This time, it was your missing sister. Earlier this year, it was the *Edmund Fitzwilliam*. Who knows what will happen next?

"Our wedding is our business and nobody else's. If we like the idea of a big production, fine. Let 'er rip. If we want just family and close friends there, then that's what we'll do, and that's the end of it. The decision is up to us. If we know what we want, why shouldn't we move forward, and the hell with everyone else?"

With that, William pulled his arm away from her shoulders. He gently grasped her forearms and had her face him. He smiled, removed first his sunglasses, and then hers.

"I want to see your eyes when I say this," he said in a low voice. "Elizabeth, my one love, the only woman I've ever dreamed of spending the rest of my life with, do you want to marry me?"

So many words occurred to her, but the only ones she was able to voice were, "Yes, I do."

"Then we will, and whenever you want." They shared a tender kiss.

"I'm sorry I came unprepared," he whispered against her lips. "Can you take a long lunch hour next week to pick out a ring?"

A cheeky smile grew on her lips. "You mean I have to pick out my own ring? What am I going to do with you?"

"It will be unique, just like you are."

"I'll accept that as a compliment, I think. I'll have to check my schedule, though."

He kissed her soundly. "When?"

She pursed her lips. "Hmm, Wednesday?"

"Not soon enough," he growled as he assaulted her neck, an area he knew from experience was very vulnerable.

"M-Monday," she gasped.

"Much better."

"Well, I have to say you were very persuasive, darling."

"Now you know how it feels."

"Really? I can do that to you?" Her smile turned positively wicked. "I'll have to remember that." They kissed again until a noise caught their attention.

"I guess I'm hungry," a sheepish William admitted, holding his stomach. "Sorry."

"Well, come on, we can't let you starve," Elizabeth laughed as she took him by the hand to walk back to the car. "Let's go get a bite."

"Where do you want to go?" William asked as he backed out.

"I've got some stuff in the fridge. Let's go back to my place."

"You don't want to go celebrate somewhere?"

She caressed his face. "We *are* going to celebrate, lover. Just not with so many people around."

"Uhh, Lizzy—"

"Will, if you say *one more word*, I'll scream. Now hush! I've got to call Jane."

Chapter 34

The responses of family and friends to the announcement were all that could be expected. The congratulations from Jane and Chuck were heartfelt and sincere. Frances Boudreaux was ecstatic! On the same day she would see her long lost youngest again, she learned her second daughter was engaged to the most eligible bachelor in New Orleans. Her father's reaction was more muted but also genuinely happy for her, for he respected William Darcy. Mary was as happy as a sister who was already preoccupied with her own engagement could be. Kit wondered what color the bridesmaid dress would be. Gina Darcy laughed and cried at the same time.

Richard Fitzwilliam shook his head as he hung up the phone. "Well, I'll be damned: Will's getting married."

"To Elizabeth?" asked Olivia from the kitchen as she was preparing lunch.

"Yeah."

"Well, I'm glad they've put Tulane behind them."

"It sure seems that way."

"Richard," Olivia asked, changing the subject, "have you thought any more about the opportunity at DGS? Managing the security department there?"

"Still thinkin' it over."

"Uncle Edward said the money's real good."

"I said I'm thinkin' about it, okay?" Fitzwilliam groused. "I don't know anything about international shipping."

"You know enough to protect the ships, and what you don't know, you can learn." She threw down her towel. "An opportunity like this doesn't come every day."

"It'll mean a lot more travel—"

"At least you'll be safe!" she yelled. "At least people won't be trying to kill you!" She caught herself and gripped the kitchen counter as she fought her agitation. Fitzwilliam came in from the den and tried to comfort her, but she shrugged him off.

"Look, baby," he tried to explain, "I mainly ride a desk at the Third District. Nobody's takin' a shot at me. I'm as safe there as anywhere."

"Until something happens—a riot or…whatever. I know you love your work, but I am so tired of worrying about you. Worrying you won't come home after the next hostage situation. Can't you understand?" She finally allowed her husband to embrace her.

"Shush, shush. I told you I'll think it over, right? I don't have to make a decision until September. Don't worry, baby, please?"

"I've been worrying for ten years." She sighed. "I'm sorry. I shouldn't have said that. Let me finish lunch. Can you call Megan?"

"Sure. She's in her room?" Fitzwilliam walked down the hall to retrieve his daughter, already putting his wife's arguments out of his mind.

Baton Rouge

AT THE BUFORD HOUSEHOLD, JOHN GLANCED OVER AT A BEMUSED Carrie as she hung up the phone. "What did Jane want?"

"Oh, she wanted to tell me Lizzy finally got engaged to Will Darcy."

"Humph. Took 'em long enough," he commented as he returned to his sports page.

LSU Medical Center

CHRIS BREAUX WAS WALKING A SUNDAY ROUND ON THE WARD

when he got a call on his cell. Glancing at the caller ID and knowing Marianne would not disturb him for anything unimportant, he flipped it open. "Hey, babe," he answered as he slipped into an empty consulting room, "what's up?"

"He did it! He did it!"

"What? Who did what? What are you talking about?"

"Will! He asked Lizzy to marry him!"

"Oh, that's great. What did she say?"

"She said yes, of course, you big doofus!"

Chris laughed. "Looks like all our hard work has finally paid off."

"I told you we could do it. Oh, this is the best news ever!"

"Better than our own wedding?"

"Now, you know I don't mean that! Oh, I'm so happy! I don't know what to do with myself!"

Chris glanced at his watch. "I ought to be wrapping up here in another hour or so. You can gloat some more then. I'll see you soon."

Lakeview

AT THE KATZES', ELIZABETH'S PHONE INTERRUPTED EMMA AND George as they were engaged in an exotic physical activity. Their reaction was hearty and happy, and Emma's eyes were still shining as she hung up the phone. "What's with the waterworks, Em?" asked George.

"Six years, George. It took them six years to get there. They've been so right for each other for so long. How can I not cry a little at a time like this?"

"Does that mean we should stop what we're doing?"

Her voice turned firm. "No, it does not! George, you need to exercise! You don't walk or jog or ride or anything. You don't even play golf! I'm going to fix that and in a way we can do together, privately."

"But, honey, I've been keeping my weight under control. I'm just too busy to use the gym at the hospital."

"You might be in decent shape now, but it's my duty to keep you that way. Now, hush up and assume the position."

"I still feel funny doing this for exercise."

"We can do it together, and that makes it fun. Besides, you promised."

"I'm with George," said Abe as he walked from the kitchen. "You look weird."

Emma glared at her father. "Papa! You stay out of this, or I'll have you on a mat!"

"Not me," he said as he returned to his room.

"Now," Emma resumed, "we'll start nice and easy. On our knees like this is called the Child's Pose. Center yourself by breathing deeply, George." Emma closed her eyes and took a deep breath. She heard George make a funny sound. Without opening her eyes, she said, "George, please, yoga is serious exercise. Try to take it seriously."

George knelt beside his wife in a T-shirt and shorts. "I *am* trying, but if you knew what you wearing that leotard does to me—"

A small smile crept onto her face. "That's for later, dear. Besides, yoga gives a person both flexibility and endurance. Is that enough of an incentive for you?"

"You've sold me."

"Good. Now, close your eyes and breathe. The next pose we'll attempt is the Downward Facing Dog."

PRIOR TO THE GREAT MISSISSIPPI RIVER FLOOD OF 1927, local communities were responsible for flood control. The citizens were willing to pay taxes to build levees as long as the funds were used for that purpose and not to line politicians' pockets. Unfortunately, that's exactly what happened again and again.

In the late 1800s, the legislature established a series of levee district boards responsible for "the operation and maintenance of levees, embankments, seawalls, jetties, breakwaters, water basins, and other hurricane and flood protection improvements," and they were given taxing power.

Cooperation is an alien concept in Louisiana. The good people in Plaquemines and St. Bernard could not trust Orleans officials to safeguard *their* homes. In Jefferson Parish, the East Bank mistrusted the West Bank and vice versa. Individual levee districts were set up. The politicos used the new positions as patronage for supporters, so the calls for reform were muted.

In the aftermath of the 1927 Flood, Congress gave the Army Corps of Engineers control of the design and construction of flood control throughout the Mississippi Valley. Local levee boards remained in charge of day-to-day inspection and maintenance of the levee systems in their areas. They also were responsible for raising the matching funds the government required for projects.

With the Corps of Engineers designing all projects and choosing all contractors, the levees were consistent. There was also little for the levee districts to do. Inspections involved driving to see whether there were any leaks in the levees. The Corps handled all but the most minor dredging of the canals and waterways.

So, the legislature gave the districts additional powers. They were put in charge of operating "public parks, beaches, marinas, aviation fields, and other like facilities." The Orleans Levee District ran two marinas, a casino, and the Lakefront Airport. It even had its own police department. East Jefferson had its own law enforcement too. Corruption on these boards was rampant, and not a few commissioners would end up in jail.

The people were, by degrees, unhappy about the dishonesty, but since protection was mainly in the hands of the federal government, no one got really upset over it.

There was one outcome of the Corps dealing with

separate levee districts. Projects were based on need (population) and funding (money). Orleans and East Jefferson had the most of both, so they got the lion's share of the projects. That was why the Lake Pontchartrain levee was fifteen feet high, while the 40 Arpent levee protecting St. Bernard from the MRGO was between seven and nine. As for the West Bank of Jefferson, its projects were always on the back burner.

Chapter 35

Two tropical storms appeared in the latter part of July. Franklin developed in the Atlantic Ocean near the Bahamas and tracked northeast along the Gulf current, between the US mainland and Bermuda. Gert popped up in the Bay of Campeche and came ashore in Mexico.

In early August, Tropical Storm Harvey remained in the middle of the Atlantic, as did Hurricane Irene, bothering only shipping and fishing interests.

Friday, August 5: Downtown

WILLIAM, STANDING IN SHIRT AND TIE, WAITED IN LINE FOR HIS turn to pay for two dressed roast beef and debris po'boys, with drinks and chips, wondering again at his fiancée's choice of restaurant for lunch. This was a special day, and she wanted to go to *Mother's* to celebrate? Sure, it was the standard when it came to roast beef po'boys, but it wasn't every day a girl got her engagement ring. Accepting his receipt, he carried the tray of food through the crowded joint to where Elizabeth had claimed two seats at a table.

"Here you go," he said as he slid in next to her. She smiled and handed him the extra napkins they would need, a glittering treasure in platinum and blue adorning her left ring finger. They unwrapped their sandwiches and munched happily.

"Hey, you're getting gravy all over your ring."

Elizabeth looked at her engagement ring. A week ago, they had selected a two-carat diamond set in platinum, with a sapphire on each side. They had just picked up the ring from the jeweler before lunch.

"You think it will hurt it?" With a sultry look, she slowly licked the garlicky thin gravy off her finger. She smiled and smacked her lips.

"Don't do that in front of me in a crowded restaurant," William pleaded.

Elizabeth gave him a flirtatious look. Pitching her voice low, she said, "Wouldn't you just love to lick this gravy off my body? Just slather me with it and take your time removing it from every nook and cranny?"

"Elizabeth, you're driving me insane!"

"Just want to make sure I've still got it."

"You're enjoying yourself, aren't you?"

She grinned. "Mmm-hmm."

"You're gonna make us go to confession again."

She gave him a peck on the cheek. "I'll behave. Call it a preview of coming attractions."

"You're going to drive me nuts 'til I make an honest woman out of you."

"I'm driving myself nuts too, sweetie. At least you won't have to quit the EDNO board anytime soon."

While the management of EDNO was overjoyed at Elizabeth's news, it did raise a potential conflict of interest problem. It would be extremely awkward for Elizabeth's boss to answer to a board that counted among its members Elizabeth's husband. William had foreseen the issue, and it was agreed that, until the wedding, he would remain on the board but would recuse himself from any personnel matters. Once Elizabeth became Elizabeth Darcy, William Darcy would formally resign. He pledged that DGS would remain an investor in EDNO, and he would be happy to volunteer for committees.

The two were interrupted by a middle-aged couple. "Do you mind if we take these seats?" the man asked.

"No, go ahead," William assured them.

The two, tourists from their garb, made themselves comfortable. The woman scowled at her roast beef sandwich. "Andy," she said to the man, "go get me a knife and fork. I can't eat this mess with my fingers."

He got up. "I told you to get the ham and cheese, Doreen," he mumbled as he retrieved the silverware.

Elizabeth and William watched the two newcomers as they finished their last bites. Wiping his hands, he asked, "Are you here on business or pleasure?"

"Both," Andy answered. "I'm a salesman working the Work Boat trade show that starts Monday. Me and the missus came in a little early to see Bourbon Street." His accent was straight from Philly.

"How do you like it?"

"It's so hot!" the wife cried as she ate her po'boy open-faced. "How can people stand it?"

"Well, it *is* August," answered Elizabeth. "Have you gone to the Aquarium or one of the museums? It's nice and cool there."

"Save the Quarter for the evenings," William suggested.

"Maybe it'll smell better," grumbled Andy. "Place stinks to hell. That trolley'll take us to the D-Day Museum?"

"Streetcar," William replied dryly. "It stops a block away."

"Streetcar—trolley! What's the diff?" Andy said as he bit into his po'boy. "Ain't a cheese steak, but it's pretty good."

"Those are messy too," complained Doreen.

"Aww, pipe down."

"*Be nice or go home*," Elizabeth muttered to herself. William almost laughed.

The pair stood up and William said, "I hope you have a good visit. Take care." As they left the restaurant and walked back to Elizabeth's building, he pulled out his BlackBerry and made a quick call. "Barbara? Please reschedule my Monday. I'm going to attend the Work Boat trade show after all."

Elizabeth looked at him. "What's that all about?"

He grinned evilly. "Oh, I wouldn't miss Monday for the world when ol' Andy back there steps up to the DGS booth."

Elizabeth laughed. "I wish I could be there."

"Andy sure won't," he promised.

The gleam in his eye told Elizabeth that perhaps William was more like T.B. Boudreaux than either thought.

Friday, August 12: Gulfport

THE GENERAL MANAGER OF THE JEAN LAFFITE RESORT & CASINO rose from behind his desk as his assistant manager in charge of entertainment walked in.

"Have a seat, John," he said as he waved at a chair.

John Waguespack sat nervously, wondering what the meeting was about. He didn't have to wait long.

"It's like this, John." His boss, Edward Denham, leaned back in his chair. "The head office in Vegas isn't happy with how things are going. They were disappointed in the last quarter's numbers."

"Sure, I can understand that. But it's the same for everybody. Beau Rivage is kicking everybody's ass," he said, referring to Biloxi's premiere casino.

"You know that, and I know that. Hell, *they* know that. The point is they don't care. They want to see some progress on improving market share and return per guest. I'm having this conversation with the whole team." He looked at the papers in front of him. "Some of the mainliners you signed up did okay, but that jazz combo you put in the nightclub has been a disaster."

"Jazz isn't selling any more."

"I don't know. The last time I was in New Orleans it was doing pretty good."

"That's New Orleans."

"Maybe. But we're close enough to New Orleans that our guests expect that kind of atmosphere." Denham looked at the spread-sheet. "Get rid of the combo. Get somebody new. Somebody with a female singer—real torchy and sexy. The conventioneers like the gals." He looked at the window. "I caught this one group at the Chat Noir. What was her name? Dingham? Davis? Dashwood! That's it—Marianne Dashwood! See if she's available."

Waguespack took notes, his stomach turning into acid. "She's got a bad rep, Den."

"Who cares? You've seen the noise on that Paris Hilton babe? The more bad news, the better."

"All right. I'll get a new group for the nightclub. Someone with a female lead."

"Start with that Dashwood group. She might have a following." He looked at the sheets again. "We've got to get the handle up, or we'll both be looking for new jobs, understand?"

"Yeah."

"Meanwhile, we can improve the margins. We're going to have to cut some fat. Take a look at who you can do without in your department."

"Yes, sir."

Denham picked up a sheet. "Lucy Steele's had a lot of absences. What's up with that?"

"Been sick, I guess."

"Look into it. If you can cut her loose, do it."

"I don't wanna get us sued, Den."

"I'll leave it to you. If not her, somebody else. In any case, see what's happening with Lucy. If she has been sick, find out what's going on—what's her prognosis. She might have to go on disability. Otherwise, she's going to have to be here, or she's going to have to go. Okay?"

"Okay, Den."

"Look, John, I like you. You've got a future. But we've got to turn this place around, or Vegas will find somebody else. Everybody's expendable, including me. It's not personal."

"Don't worry. I've got it covered." Waguespack stood and shook his boss's hand before returning to his own office. As soon as he got there, he pulled out his bottle of Johnny Walker. He needed a scotch bad.

Denham could not have been clearer. The entertainment department was not performing to expectations. Waguespack was aware of it, but he was surprised at the level of Vegas's concern. He now knew his whole career with the company was on the line.

Waguespack had several problems. One was that Denham wanted Marianne Dashwood at the Jean Laffite. Otherwise, he wouldn't have mentioned her three times. If he hired her, she could cause trouble for him if she remembered anything from college. It was dangerous.

But it was also dangerous to disregard Denham. The man was a hard-ass. If he didn't hire Marianne, Denham might fire him.

Waguespack could look for another jazz combo—one with a front-woman—but they would have to be damn good. How many of them were around?

He set that aside for now. The second problem was Lucy Steele. Her cocaine habit had grown so bad that she was missing work. Of course, a lot of her usage was at his condo with him. Waguespack had known it was risky to dip in the company pool, but he had figured he had it beat. Besides, he was getting off on it.

Now, he was truly fucked. If he canned Lucy, she might rat him out, and then *he'd* be out. Was there any way of getting Lucy to dry out?

Waguespack cursed. The third and biggest problem was he might get screwed no matter what. If he did bring in Marianne, was able to get rid of Lucy, and survive both events, it still didn't guarantee things for the Jean Lafitte would turn around. Casinos needed bodies to pull the levers and throw the dice, and there simply weren't enough people coming into the place. They needed more customers, and with the Beau Rivage, Grand Casino, and others setting new records every month, there might not be any new people to bring in. The company would look for scapegoats, which put a big, red target on Waguespack's back.

He looked out his window at the large structure floating in the placid Gulf waters by the Gulfport shore. Like all the casinos in Mississippi, the Jean Lafitte was a "riverboat" facility. Translated, the gambling hall had to float. It didn't have to sail under its own power, but it had to be capable of being moved. Therefore, the casino was a huge barge dressed up to resemble a pirate's castle.

True, the real Jean Lafitte didn't actually have a castle, but some other casino had already built a pirate ship. Besides, the slot zombies didn't care. They were there to gamble.

As he watched small waves lap at the sides of the structure, Waguespack realized he was in a trap. There was very little chance of success by doing things the expected way. His future was in the hands of others. He could leave, but that would mean starting over again with another organization, working and scraping for years to pull himself up to his current level.

Or, he could think outside the box and do something extraordinary—something that would impress the boys in Vegas and be his ticket out of Gulfport.

But what?

Waguespack threw back the rest of his drink. He would think of something. Meanwhile, he had to start looking for a new jazz combo. One that, hopefully, didn't include a girl named Marianne.

Saturday, August 13: Uptown

"Oh, hon, it's beautiful," gushed Mrs. Dashwood. Mrs. Breaux nodded in agreement.

Marianne twirled in the mirror as the seamstress checked her alterations to the wedding dress, an off-white, scoop neck, short sleeve gown with beaded Alençon lace on the fitted bodice. Satisfied with her work, she assured the bride she never looked lovelier. Marianne smiled and returned to the dressing room of the St. Charles Avenue boutique as her two bridesmaids tried on their dresses.

Her sister, Margaret, and Elizabeth were happy with the choice of a tea-length modified halter dress in pleated periwinkle organza with a shirred midriff and double tier hemline. Margaret was actually of the opinion she might wear the dress again.

The girls collected their dresses and carried them to their cars. The group, along with Emma Katz and Gina Darcy, then strolled across the avenue, dodging the Saturday traffic, to grab a light lunch.

Margaret sat next to Gina. "This is so much fun, isn't it?" she gushed. "I haven't spent this much time in New Orleans ever!" She and her mother were staying at Marianne's house.

"I'm glad I could come along and see the dresses," said Gina. "I won't be able to make the wedding. School, you know."

"I won't have to worry about that until next year. They're not so picky about it in high school."

"You graduate this year?" At Margaret's nod, Gina asked, "Do you plan to go to college?"

"Sure, but I don't know what my major's going to be. What are you studying?"

"Marketing and graphic arts. I'll probably go for my MBA like Will."

"Wow," breathed Margaret, "that's, like, so organized. I'll bet you're smart." Their lunches of shrimp salad were delivered. Margaret got a sweet tea while Gina stayed with water.

Gina shrugged. "I don't know about that. I study hard. My suggestion for college? Just take your freshman classes and worry about declaring a major later." She decided to change the subject. "Do you like your dress?"

"You bet! It's so pretty. I'm sorry you can't come to Marianne's wedding. How about Lizzy's? Does she have a date set?"

Gina laughed. "They just got engaged!"

"But you're gonna be in the wedding, huh?"

Gina smiled. "Lizzy and Will have already informed me my presence is not only desired but *required!*"

Margaret looked over at Elizabeth, sharing a laugh with Marianne and Emma. "I like her. Emma too. Marianne's got good friends."

Gina followed Margaret's gaze. "Yes, she does."

Yes, I like Lizzy too—and her friends. Gina tried to take in the trio objectively. At first glance, the only thing they had in common was that they were brunettes. Marianne was boisterous, Elizabeth was sparkling, and Emma was quiet. They complemented each other, sure, but was that all?

No, it wasn't, she determined. Gina Darcy was a very intuitive person. Having gotten to know Elizabeth over the summer, she knew her future sister-in-law didn't suffer fools gladly. She spent her time with people of worth—not of money but character—an attribute she shared with William.

During the summer, Gina had learned that Marianne and Emma were both kind and loyal. They were open, intelligent, and responsible. They were strong like Elizabeth. Their only difference from her was in their strength—not hidden, exactly but kept deep inside. Marianne and Emma could be easily underestimated. Elizabeth? Only a blind idiot would challenge her.

Gina knew herself. As much as she admired Elizabeth, she knew her own personality was more like those secretly strong women, Marianne and Emma.

"Yes, Marianne's got good friends," she said.

Chapter 36

Man has an insatiable need to name everything. For eons, names were given to everything on the planet—multiple names if the languages were dissimilar. For example, New Orleans is *La Nouvelle-Orléans* in French and Новый Орлеан in Russian.

Second only to the need to name is the desire to know where one is. This is particularly important to mariners. A system of latitude was easy enough to establish: the center of the Earth at its widest part would be the Equator, which was called 0.00.00 degrees. The poles, North and South, would be 90 degrees, as if they formed a triangle from the center.

But to accurately determine longitude would be one of the great challenges facing mariners. Only after the invention of an accurate mechanical clock would it be possible. Since the seagoing nation of Great Britain came up with the method, it divided the world to its own conceit. They chose to run the Prime Meridian through the Royal Greenwich Observatory in London, placing its opposite, the 180-degree meridian now called the International Date Line, on the other side of the planet. The French, unsurprisingly, refused to acknowledge what the rest of the world agreed to in 1884. It would be another thirty years before they bowed to the inevitable.

It is by simple accident that New Orleans falls almost exactly at 30 degrees North by 90 degrees West.

In the vastness of the oceans, it is extremely important to be able to locate oneself. Therefore, thanks to hundreds of artificial satellites orbiting in space, a true global positioning system is available.

By this, the forecasters at the National Hurricane Center in Miami knew at 23.2 N by 75.5 W in the Atlantic Ocean near the islands of the Bahamas a tropical depression, the twelfth of the year, formed at 2000 hours Central Daylight Time on the twenty-third of August, 2005.

Wednesday, August 24: Downtown

IT WAS JUST ANOTHER MORNING IN THE OFFICES OF EDNO, THE staff working on their PCs and talking on the telephone, when a shout came out of Eddie Masters' office.

"We did it! It's just been announced the BRAC commission has given final approval for Government Quarter!"

Pandemonium broke out. Staff members were literally standing and screaming at their desks. Economic development is a profession cursed with long lead times for projects, most of which fade to an unremembered death. To get a win, especially a very public win, was something to celebrate. This was one for the ages—the most important project in the area in a generation.

Carl Eden leaned on the door frame of his office, laughing and watching Eddie Masters dance with Sarah Hunt in the middle of the bullpen while Bonita Carasso and Charlotte Lucas tried to start a second line, using James Williams's umbrella. Jan Hill and Kaywanda Johnson were high-fiving each other. It was all good.

The only person missing was Elizabeth Boudreaux. As communications director, her partying would have to wait. She had press releases to send and reporters to call. But her first call was not to the *Times-Picayune* but to the executive offices of DGS.

BY 1000 CDT, THE WARM WATERS OFF FLORIDA HAD PROVIDED the energy needed to help the tropical depression intensify rapidly, its sustained winds over forty miles per hour.

It had earned itself a name: Katrina.

Downtown

THE EXCITEMENT FINALLY CALMED DOWN, AND THE WORKERS AT EDNO actually completed some tasks before five o'clock rolled around. Elizabeth was shutting down her computer as Carl Eden stuck his head through the door.

"Good work, Lizzy. The AP's picked up our press release. The investors will be happy."

"Great! Well, I'm off for the next two days. If you need me, I'll have my BlackBerry handy."

"Enjoy yourself in Lafayette. Don't eat too much crawfish."

"Carl, honey, you can't eat too much crawfish!"

He laughed. "Say hi to Will Darcy for me."

Elizabeth smiled that special smile that graced her face each time her fiancé's name was mentioned. "I will. See you Monday, Carl." She had a celebratory dinner date to keep with William, and Gina had left for Auburn the previous Sunday.

THE NHC'S MODELS WERE GRIM. THEY FORECASTED A VERY RAPID strengthening of Tropical Storm Katrina. FEMA was alerted, and by daylight, its National Response Coordination Center Red Team was activated. The call went out to warn southeast Florida a hurricane was coming.

Thursday, August 25: Lafayette

CHRIS SAW MARIANNE, HIS MOTHER, AND THE OTHER WOMEN OFF to do God knows what women do two days before a wedding. As he returned to his parents' living room, he noticed Mike sitting at the kitchen table.

"Hey, Chris, can I tell you something?"

Chris ambled into the kitchen. "What's up?"

"I should have said it before. It's good you and Mari are gettin' married. She's a good gal, and I think y'all will be real happy." He stuck out his hand.

"Thanks. That means a lot."

The handshake became a bear hug. "I'm proud of you, y'know?

You're not gonna screw things up like me."

"Things can get better, Mike."

His brother grinned. "They already are. I got me a new job. Mechanic on a rig, working offshore. I start next month after I pass my physical and drug tests and take some training courses."

"That's great! Do Mom and Dad know?"

"Told 'em last week, but I asked them to keep it quiet 'til I could tell you myself."

"Why's that?"

"Because you're the reason I got the job. I've been watching how successful you are. I finally realized I gotta get off my ass and make somethin' of myself. I've been cuttin' down on the beer and making some calls. This ol' boy who works at the outfit that hired me got me an interview."

Chris was uncomfortable with Mike's praise. "You did it yourself, Mike."

"It's fourteen-and-fourteen, but that don't bother me. Hell, two weeks without beer'll do me good. I'll get my own place in a couple months. Start livin' on my own again. Be a man."

"You are a man."

"Hell, no." Mike's gaze was unflinching. "But I might be one someday. Be a man like you."

There was nothing to do except share another hug.

At 2000 CDT, the NHC upgraded Katrina to a hurricane. Ninety minutes later, almost fifty hours after it was born, the Category 1 storm made landfall near Hallandale Beach on the Miami-Dade/Broward county line. But instead of moving inland, the storm jogged hard left and ran south, almost parallel to the coastline of densely-populated metropolitan Miami.

Lafayette

Elizabeth was snug in bed in her hotel room by 10:00 p.m. when her BlackBerry rang. She answered it with, "I love you."

"Is that how you answer your phone? What if I had been

Eddie Masters?"

"Will, I have caller ID."

"Still, you never know. He might have stolen my cell phone."

"You're silly. I miss you. I wish today was Friday. I wish you were here."

"How can you miss me? You just saw me last night."

She lowered her voice to a seductive growl. "That's why I miss you, baby."

"That's not helping, you vixen." She laughed. "How did it go today?"

"Oh, fine." After leaving William's condo in the morning, she had packed and left for Lafayette. "No trouble driving over. Mari, Mrs. Dashwood, and Mrs. Breaux kept me busy doing stuff."

"What kind of stuff?"

"Getting married stuff. Mari had to show me all the wedding gifts that came in. Do you know they got two barbeque pits? And they've got enough place settings in their china to feed half of Lafayette."

"What are they going to do with all that?"

"Return it for credit, of course! Oh, we also checked on the flowers and the caterer. Wait until you see how they're going to decorate the reception hall—it's lovely. Then we had a bridal shower with some of Mrs. Breaux's friends."

"Sounds like you had fun. What did Chris do?"

"Kept a low profile."

"Smart man. What's on tap for tomorrow?"

"Margaret and I are taking Mari shopping, and then we'll prepare for the rehearsal. What time are you getting here?"

"I'm leaving at five, so I should be rolling up to the church right around seven. I'll call before I leave."

"All right. Darling, did I tell you I miss you?"

"Yes, you did."

She snuggled down into the sheets. "And, do you miss me too?"

"You know I do. Shall I tell you how much?"

"Mmm-hmm. I'm all ears."

And so he did. It was safe to say Elizabeth didn't get to sleep right away, but when she did, it was a very satisfying rest.

KATRINA CONTINUED ITS PATH THROUGH CORAL GABLES AND southwest Miami, and then traveled southwest through the unpopulated Everglades National Park. It entered the Gulf of Mexico near the southern tip of Florida. By midnight, the storm was downgraded to Tropical Storm status.

At 0400 CDT on Friday, Katrina had recovered sufficiently over the warm waters of the Gulf to regain its standing as a hurricane. The scientists' models showed the highest strike possibility was for the Florida panhandle. But it was early in the game, and the warnings were sent out as far west as Louisiana.

Friday, August 26: Lafayette

ELIZABETH DELIVERED THE WEDDING GIFT SHE AND WILLIAM HAD bought, a lovely hand-blown glass sculpture, but she and Margaret decided Marianne needed something special just from the two of them. Right after the Mall of Acadiana opened, Elizabeth and Margaret took Marianne to Victoria's Secret, spent an hour picking over the sexiest lingerie available, and embarrassing the hell out of the bride. A sheer leopard-print baby-doll set, guaranteed to light a fire under Chris, was finally selected, and the ladies had lunch in the food court.

The girls returned to the hotel to nap before dressing for the rehearsal and dinner.

THERE IS ONLY ONE WAY TO ACCURATELY GAGE THE POWER OF A tropical storm. One has to fly through it.

Two groups in the United States are assigned to this unique mission. The National Oceanic and Atmospheric Administration has two Lockheed WP-3D Orion aircraft based at MacDill Air Force Base in Tampa, Florida. The US Air Force Reserve 53rd Weather Reconnaissance Squadron, the famous "Hurricane Hunters," fly ten WC-130H Hercules turboprops out of Keesler Air Force Base in Biloxi, Mississippi.

The mission of the two teams is the same. Their aircraft fly any-where between 1,000 and 10,000 feet above the ocean. The planes, with special weather related equipment, penetrate the storm's eye wall twice during what are known as an "alpha pattern," resembling a huge X. The ride is turbulent as the aircraft near the eye wall.

Winds and pressure are measured by onboard equipment. GPS dropsondes, a small tube with instruments, radio transmitter, and parachute, are ejected into the maelstrom. The "sondes" transmit data twice a second to the aircraft during its decent to the sea—temperature, humidity, barometric pressure, wind speed, and wind direction.

The flights average over eleven hours, six of them inside the storm. Depending on the storm, there can be as many as five missions a day.

The planes are not reinforced and do not carry parachutes for their crews.

On August 26, aircraft reported that Katrina was intensifying rapidly. It was a very strong Category 2, and it was expected soon to reach Category 3 because of unusually warm waters and a lack of high-level shearing winds. By 1300 CDT, the storm was at 24.9 N by 82.6 W, with sustained winds of ninety-eight miles per hour.

The models still called for landfall somewhere in the Flori-da Panhandle

Atchafalaya Swamp

CHRIS AND HIS FATHER SPENT THE LAST AFTERNOON OF HIS BACH-elorhood in a fifteen-foot bass boat, poking around underwater stumps in the never-ending, often futile, quest to land the biggest largemouth bass ever seen. Mr. Breaux kept his boat under the shade of a tall, overhanging cypress tree. The day was still and hot, the air thick with the smells of the swamp. The only sounds were the buzzing insects, the whirl of the fishing reels, and the occasional hum of the trolling motor.

To the two Breaux men, this was paradise.

Non-fishers never understand why someone who didn't catch any fish would proclaim a fishing trip successful. The attraction wasn't the number of fish landed. The beauty of the sport to true fishermen was the actual process of *fishing*. The time spent with only the water, the wind, and your thoughts. Sometimes by yourself, sometimes with a friend—and if that friend was your father, the time was priceless.

Mr. Breaux checked his watch. "Ought to be gettin' back soon," he said as he made a cast.

"Yeah," agreed Chris as he continued to fish.

Mr. Breaux kept a steady retrieve, the rod tip low, feeling for the bass with his plastic worm. "This time tomorrow, it'll be all over but the shouting. How you doin'?"

Chris tossed his line expertly next to an overhanging limb. "Good, except I wish this was over with. A whole lot of bother. But it means a lot to Mari, so I guess I ought to suck it up."

"Yep. Chris, your momma and I are real proud of you. Mari's a good girl. You'll do fine."

"Thanks, Dad."

He made another cast. "Just remember to never go to sleep mad. That's the secret of a good marriage. That and treating her like a queen." He smiled. "Thirty years, Chris. Your momma and I been married thirty years, an' each one's been better than the year before.

"Not like we didn't have hard times—we did. But love an' trust an' faith—in yourselves an' in God—well, it can get you through anything. A lot of work and a lot of tears, but it's all worth it if you do your workin' and cryin' together."

Suddenly, Mr. Breaux jerked back on his line. Rod tip high, he reeled in as fast as he could, trying to set the hook. Chris watched the battle intently, his hand ready to grab the fishing net. A swirl of water, a large tail slashed the surface of the green-tinted water, and his father's line sagged.

"Lost 'im! Damn, but that was a big one." He quickly reeled the bait in.

"Heck of a fish, Dad."

"It's all right. He'll be here when we come back." Mr. Breaux put away his rod and fired up the outboard. "Raise up the trolling motor, will you? We better get home, or your momma and Mari will rip us each a new one."

TRYING TO FORECAST THE STRENGTH AND EXPECTED PATH OF A hurricane is as much an art as a science. So many factors come into play that the NHC uses supercomputers to calculate all the variables. Each year and each storm provide data to refine the models, increasing the accuracy of predictions. However, surprise is more the norm than civilians realize.

During the afternoon of August 26, the calculations coming out of the mechanical brain stunned the Miami-based scientists. They ran and re-ran the numbers, but it came out the same. A massive shift in the forecast track was becoming evident, as well as other predictions.

They had another monster on their hands, and it wasn't going where they had thought.

Lafayette

AFTER NAPPING FOR A COUPLE OF HOURS, THE GIRLS SAT IN MARIanne's room, reminiscing. It was Elizabeth who noticed time was getting away from them; it was already past four o'clock. Marianne shooed the two out, Margaret went to the suite she shared with her mother, and Elizabeth returned to her room to take a shower.

The process of becoming beautiful began in earnest after she donned her lingerie. Elizabeth tried one hairstyle and another before settling for keeping her hair down. Just before five o'clock, while she was applying mascara, her cell phone rang.

That's Will—right on time, she thought happily. "Hey, baby! Are you on the road, yet? We're all getting dressed around here—"

"Elizabeth, I'm still here in New Orleans. Do you have the TV on?" William's voice was urgent.

Elizabeth was taken aback. Her surprise that William hadn't yet left the city was overcome by her concern over his tone. "No, we're getting dressed. The TV? Is something going on?"

"Get the TV on—now!"

"Why? What's happening?"

"Honey, listen to me. This is damned serious. Our private weather service just sent us an advance of the 5:00 p.m. National Hurricane Center advisory, and it's bad. The expected track of Katrina just shifted three hundred miles to the west. It's headed for New Orleans."

END OF VOLUME TWO

To be continued in

Ruin and Renewal

Volume Three of
CRESCENT CITY

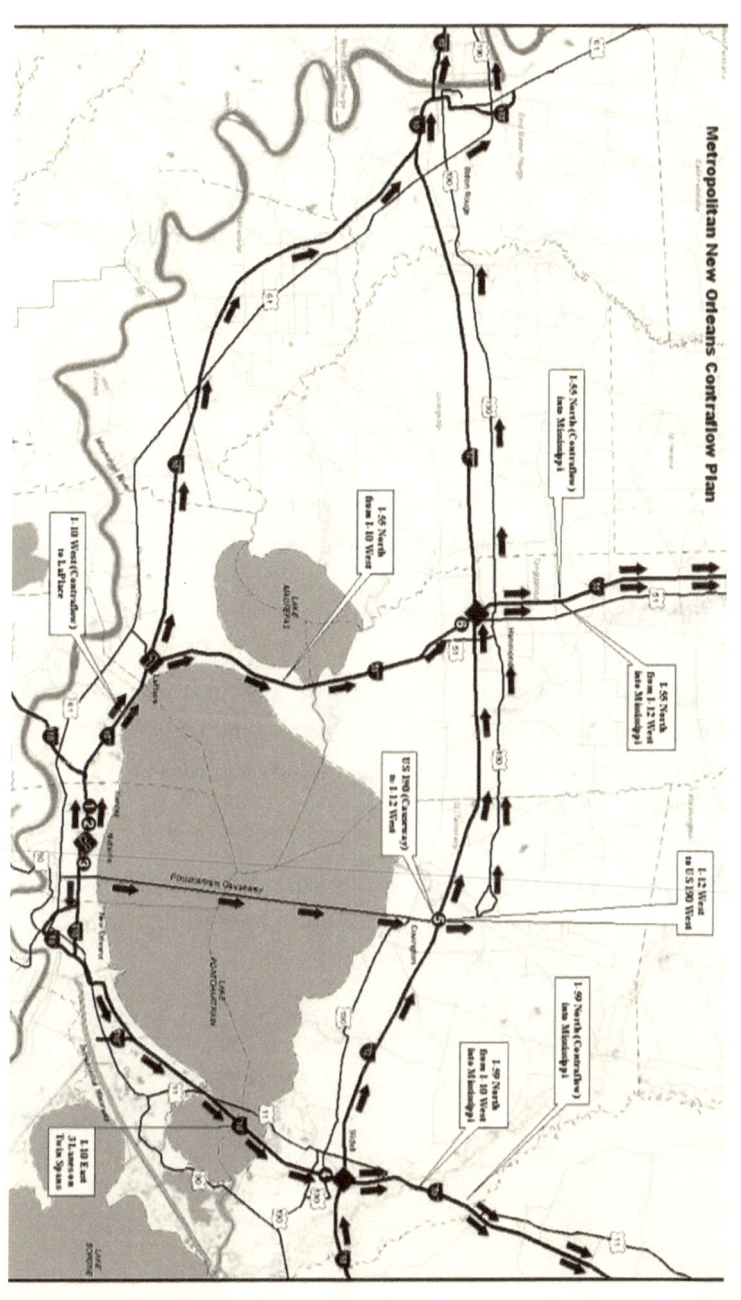

Metropolitan New Orleans Contraflow Plan

Appreciation

When taking on a project of this scope, an author cannot do it alone. I am fortunate to have a number of wonderful ladies who serve as my **Beta Babes**, reading and correcting my gross errors. If the story you have just read speaks at all to you, it is because of these ladies' dedication to this thankless task.

Debbie Styne and **Ellen Pickels,** along with my wife, are the major editors of this work.

Sarah Hunt, Bonnie Carasso, Amy Robinson, Nicole Newchurch, and Mary Anne Mushatt helped make the original manuscript sing.

Ladies, thank you so much.

Thanks go to my fellow members of "The Six-Pack"—**Linnea Eileen, June, Susan, Shelby,** and **Meg**—who whined for me to write a modern. If it weren't for you ladies, *CRESCENT CITY* wouldn't have happened.

And to my #1 Beta Babe, **my lovely wife, Barbara**, who encouraged me to write this story and supported me while I relived the agony. I love you, my dear.

Bibliography, Sources, and Suggested Readings

Austen, Jane. *Emma.*
—. *Pride and Prejudice.*
—. *Sense and Sensibility.*

Caldwell, Jack. *The Plains of Chalmette: a Story of Crescent City.*
Venice: White Soup Press, 2015.
—. *Bourbon Street Nights: Volume One of Crescent City.* Venice:
White Soup Press, 2015.
—. *Ruin and Renewal: Volume Three of Crescent City.* Venice:
White Soup Press, 2015.

Dufour, Charles M. *Ten Flags in the Wind: The Story of Louisiana.*
New York: Harper & Row, 1967 (out of print).

The National Hurricane Center website archives.

The New Orleans Times-Picayune archives.

Remini, Robert V. *The Battle of New Orleans: Andrew Jackson and
America's First Military Victory.* New York: Viking, 1999.

Rose, Chris. *1 Dead in Attic.* New Orleans: Chris Rose Books,
2005.

Definitions

It should be noted that New Orleans and Southern Louisiana are not part of what is commonly called the American South. They have a different culture and do not have the southern drawl common to Northern Louisiana and the rest of the Southern United States.

BANQUETTE: The sidewalk.

BAYOU: A slow moving stream or river. The term, used primarily in the Southern US, is thought to be derived from the Choctaw word "bayuk."

CAJUNS: The Acadians, the original French settlers in the maritime provinces of Canada. After the British expelled the Acadians from their homes (*Le Grand Dérangement, 1755-1764*), most ended up in Louisiana. The name *Acadian* became corrupted over time to *Cajun*, which is used to describe the country folk of Southern Louisiana, their culture, language, and style of cooking.

CHER or CHERE: Sweet, sweetheart, a Cajun term of endearment to a loved one.

COKE: A cola, a soft drink. Really, any soft drink.

COONASS: A controversial term in the Cajun lexicon. The word originated in Southern Louisiana and is derived from the belief that Cajuns frequently ate raccoons. To some Cajuns, it is regarded as the supreme ethnic slur, meaning "ignorant, backwards Cajun." To others, the term is a badge of pride. In Southern Louisiana, for example, one can often see bumper stickers reading "RCA: Registered Coonass American."

CRAWFISH: Sometimes spelled "crayfish," they resemble lobsters but are much smaller. Locally, they are known as "mudbugs" because they live and grow in the mud of freshwater bayous. They can be served many ways: in étouffée, jambalaya, gumbos, or simply boiled.

CREOLE: The term "Creole" has long generated confusion and controversy. The word invites debate because it possesses several meanings, some of which concern the innately sensitive subjects of race and ethnicity. In its broadest sense, Creole means "native" or, in the context of Louisiana history, "native to Louisiana." In a narrower sense, however, it has historically referred to black, white, and mixed-raced persons who are native to Louisiana. In short, the word means different things to different people, and more than one ethnic group arguably has a claim to the term. The term has expanded and now embraces a type of cuisine and a style of architecture.

DIRTY RICE: Pan-fried leftover cooked rice sautéed with green peppers, onion, celery, stock, liver, giblets and many other ingredients.

DRESSED: Adding mayonnaise, lettuce, tomatoes, and pickles to a sandwich.

FAUBOURG: A French term for a neighborhood.

GALLERIES: An outdoor balcony, supported by posts or columns anchored to the ground. Technically, the "balconies" in the French Quarter are really galleries.

Laissez les bon temps rouler: "Let the good times roll."

LAGNIAPPE: Pronounced "LAN-yap". A little something extra.

MAKING GROCERIES: To go grocery shopping, visiting the market.

NEUTRAL GROUND: The grassy or cement strip (medians) in the middle of a divided street and boulevards. In the early 1800's, a grassy strip along Canal Street between the *Faubourg St. Marie* (where the Americans lived) and the *Vieux Carré* (home of the Creole aristocracy) was designated as a place where merchants and politicians could meet in peace. It was called the Neutral Ground, and the name stuck. The terms "median" and/or "island" are never used in New Orleans.

NEW ORLEANS: How the name of the major city of Louisiana is pronounced has caused great consternation among the locals. New Orleans may be pronounced "nu or-le-ons," "nu or-lens," or "NAW-lens." It is never pronounced "nu or-leeens." Yet, the parish where the city is located is pronounced like its French namesake, "or-leeens." Confusing, isn't it?

PARISH: A county, a political subdivision of the state.

PASS BY YOUR MAMA'S: Go to your mother's house.

PECAN: Pronounced "pa-KAWN," not "PEE-can."

PO'BOY or POOR BOY: A sandwich made with French bread, stuffed with almost anything.

PODNA: "Partner." A form of address for men, usually for ones with whom one is not acquainted.

PRALINE: A sugary Creole candy, invented in New Orleans (not the same as the French culinary/confectionery term "praline" or "praliné"). The classic version is made with sugar, brown sugar, butter, vanilla and pecans, and is a flat sugary pecan-filled disk. Pronounced "PRAH-leen," not "pray-LEEN."

SHOTGUN: Usually part of a "double"—a single row house in which all rooms on one side are connected by a long single hallway. Supposedly, one can open the front door and shoot a gun straight through the back door, without hitting a single wall.

SNOWBALL or SNO-BALL: A snow cone—shaved ice covered with favored syrup. It's something you eat, not something you throw.

STOOP: The front steps of a house.

SHOW: The movie theater.

UPTOWN SIDE, DOWNTOWN SIDE, LAKESIDE, RIVERSIDE: The four cardinal points of the New Orleanian compass. "North, south, east, west" do not work in New Orleans.

VIEUX CARRÉ: French for Old Square. It refers to the original settlement of *La Nouvelle-Orléans* (New Orleans). The district is now known as the French Quarter.

WHERE Y'AT!: The traditional working class New Orleanian greeting, and the source for the term "Yat", often used (primarily by non-New Orleanians, it is said) to describe New Orleanians with the telltale accent. The proper response is, "Awrite."

Y'ALL: The plural form of the second person verb, "you all." It's not pronounced as they would in the south, though—no twang, no drawl. Just "y'all."

YAMS: Sweet potatoes. They are not real yams.

YAT: A New Orleanian of working class roots.

YEAH, YOU RITE: An emphatic statement of agreement and affirmation, sometimes used as a general exclamation of happiness. The accent is on the first word, and it's spoken as one word.

About the Author

Jack Caldwell is an author, amateur historian, professional economic developer, playwright, and like many Cajuns, a darn good cook. Born and raised in the Bayou County of Louisiana, Jack and his wife, Barbara, are Hurricane Katrina victims who now make the Suncoast of Florida their home.

Jack is the author of four Jane Austen-themed books. PEMBERLEY RANCH is a retelling of *Pride & Prejudice* set in Reconstruction Texas. THE THREE COLONELS: JANE AUSTEN'S FIGHTING MEN is a sequel to *Pride & Prejudice* and *Sense & Sensibility*. MR. DARCY CAME TO DINNER and THE COMPANION OF HIS FUTURE LIFE are *Pride & Prejudice*-flavored farces.

In 2015, he released the first four of a series of historical novels about New Orleans, titled THE CRESCENT CITY SERIES. THE PLAINS OF CHALMETTE begins the series, commemorating the Bicentennial of the Battle of New Orleans. He marked the tenth anniversary of Hurricane Katrina with three modern novels: BOURBON STREET NIGHTS, ELYSIAN DREAMS, and RUIN AND RENEWAL.

When not writing or traveling with Barbara, Jack attempts to play golf. A devout convert to Roman Catholicism, Jack is married with three grown sons. Jack's blog postings — **The Cajun Cheesehead Chronicles** — appear regularly at **Austen Variations**.

Web site: **Rambling of a Cajun in Exile**:
　　　　　https://cajuncheesehead.com
　　　　　Austen Variations: http://austenvariations.com/

Facebook: https://www.facebook.com/pages/Jack-Caldwell-author/132047236805555

Twitter: @JCaldwell25

The Crescent City Series:

Other Novels by Jack Caldwell: